𝔍𝕮𝕾
119 Terrace Drive
Lake Geneva, WI 53147

Love Song

(Instrumental)

JCS
119 Terrace Drive
Lake Geneva, WI 53147

Love Song

(Instrumental)

For Jan,
May you always have
music in your life.
Lisa McLuckie

LiSA McLUCKiE

Love Song (Instrumental)
A Hidden Springs Novel

Please direct all inquiries to:

The Betty Press LLC
PO Box 4120-30758
Portland, OR 97208-4120
www.thebettypress.com
(503) 482-9399

Betty Press

ISBN-13: 978-1-941744-00-0
ISBN-10: 1941744001

For Grandma Mary,
who always knew I would finish the story.
I'll make the Bahama Mamas.
You bring the fancy hats.

PROLOGUE

Eighteen years ago

"It's time."

The loud whisper dragged Callie out of a deep sleep.

"Go 'way," she muttered, rolling over and snuggling deeper under the covers. Waking up at midnight, even on their birthday, didn't seem like such a good idea anymore.

She heard Mel whisper, "I'll get her," and tensed instinctively. Sure enough, Mel poked her hard in the back and said, "Happy birthday, dork."

When Callie still didn't respond, Mel simply yanked the covers off. Callie tried to hang on, but tumbled out of bed instead and landed on the wood floor with a thud. She crossed her arms and glared up at her sisters.

"I'm not going," she declared. "You can't make me."

"Shut up," hissed Mel. "You're going to wake up Mom and Dad."

Mel made a move, probably to drag her out the door, but Tessa blocked her and crouched down next to Callie.

"We need you to come, Cal," she whispered. "It has to be all three of us, and it has to be tonight. Three times three, remember? We only turn nine once, and the magic will only work if all three of us are there."

Callie pressed her lips together. If she spoke, Tessa would talk her into it, and she didn't want to be talked into it.

"There won't be another full moon on our birthday for eighteen years," Tessa pleaded. "I looked it up at the library. Do you want to wait that long?"

Callie looked away. She really didn't want to wait that long.

"Besides," whispered Tessa. "You promised."

Callie felt the guilt slip past her anger and banged her head back against the side of the bed. She hated it when Tessa did the guilt trick.

"Fine. I'll go," she grumbled. "But only because I promised. Not," she bit the word out, turning her angry eyes on Mel, "because you said so."

Tessa gave a little squeak of delight. Mel rolled her eyes.

"Great," said Tessa. "Let's go."

The three crept slowly downstairs, skipping the squeaky spot on the landing. They huddled in the mudroom, pulling on snow pants and winter gear right over their pajamas. The lake had thawed, but spring had barely started and it was still freezing cold outside. Callie felt a shiver of excitement.

"Do you have the lighter?" Tessa asked Mel.

"In my pocket."

"Flashlight?" she asked Callie.

Callie nodded.

"And you've each got your wish lanterns?"

Both Callie and Mel nodded.

They followed as Tessa led the way out the back door. The full moon glowed so brightly that Callie didn't even need to turn on the flashlight. She could see their breath on the cold air and was really glad she had pulled on her boots instead of her sneakers. The flagstone steps leading down to the lake had frost on them, making them extra-slippery. Callie held on to Mel's arm, and Mel held on to Tessa's. If one went down, they would all go down together.

Once they reached the shore path, they turned right, heading toward the beach. Callie kept a firm grip on Mel's arm. She hadn't expected everything to look so . . . different. During the day, all the empty summer houses felt normal. Callie and her sisters were used to being among the few who stayed all year round. She knew exactly who lived in each of the twenty-two cottages circling the lakefront commons, even though she could see only five or six of them in the dark. The rest faded into the darkness behind the fat oak trees. But even the familiar houses looked wrong. Dark windows stared down at them like giant empty eyes. Callie could feel the hair on the back of her neck stand up, and she didn't like the prickly shiver that walked down her back.

Finally they made it to the little beach, which was really more rocks than sand. Tessa knelt and tugged off her mittens. She pulled her wish lantern out of her pocket and began to unfold it. Callie and Mel followed suit.

Callie had never seen anything as beautiful as the flying sky lanterns at Annabelle's birthday party. At the end of the party, each girl had been given a small package about the size of a pancake—not the little pancakes on the kids' menu at the diner, but the big grown-up pancakes that take up most of a plate. Inside each package they found what looked like tissue-paper and some sticks, but really it was two lanterns, one for now and one for later. Annabelle had showed them how to unfold the delicate paper and attach the tiny candle to the bamboo frame. Then they had all lined up here on the beach so that Annabelle's dad could light the candles. After Annabelle had closed her eyes and made a wish, her mom had given the signal for everyone to let go of their lanterns. The sight of those fifteen glowing wishes floating up into the sky had imprinted itself on Callie's heart forever.

Only later had Annabelle explained how the wishing worked. The more special the occasion, the more powerful the wish would be. Annabelle had even shared a secret spell that they could use for wishing by moonlight.

Assembling the lanterns in the dark, with freezing fingers, took a long time. The usual noises of the daytime—squirrels, ducks, people—were replaced by mysterious noises that Callie had never heard before. She began to wonder what kinds of animals came out on dark, not-quite-spring nights, and if any of them might be dangerous. A sudden movement from the commons made Callie's heart thump hard, until she realized it was just a family of deer. She held herself very still as they wandered through, watching them until they disappeared between Annabelle's house and the empty house next door. Mel and Tessa had their backs to the commons and they hadn't even noticed.

Callie began to wonder if the spell would work when it was this cold outside. She didn't feel special or magical—just cold.

Finally, when all three wish lanterns stood before them on the sand, Tessa pulled the crumpled spell from her pocket and smoothed it out, trying to look important.

"Do you really think it will work?" asked Callie. "I've never heard of a Moon Goddess from China."

"Of course it will," said Tessa. "I got the spell from Annabelle, and Annabelle's mom got her from China, and the magic is from China, so it *has* to work."

Callie still had her doubts, but she kept them to herself. Tessa wouldn't listen anyway. Mel winked at her, which made her feel a little better. She wasn't the only one who wasn't feeling the magic.

Callie would never forget this night, magic or no magic. This was the first time they had ever snuck out of the house, and the first time they had ever played with fire—not that they were playing, but that's what Mom and Dad would call it—and it was their birthday.

"Let's do this," said Mel, "or I won't be able to feel my fingers."

Tessa gave her an annoyed look, then cleared her throat and recited the spell:

O Goddess of the darkest night,
O Goddess of the brightest moon,
Hear us on our night of birth,
We will send our wishes soon.

Catch the fire that floats on air.
Learn our deepest secret wishes.
If they please you, keep them close.
If not, let them swim with fishes."

"Are we supposed to say Amen or something like that?" asked Mel. Callie stifled a giggle.

"Just light the lanterns," said Tessa, shaking her head.

Mel fumbled with the lighter, clicking it until the flame finally sparked and held. She lit Tessa's wish first, then Callie's, and finally her own. The girls picked up their lanterns and held them out, waiting for the candles to warm the air inside.

Callie thought about the words she had written so carefully on her lantern. On the first side, she had written her name, so the Moon Goddess would know whose wish was whose. On the second side, she had written 'music.' When she grew up, she was going to write songs and play music for her job. On the next side, she had written 'water.' Even if she was on the road all the time, she would need a place to come home to, and she wanted it to be here. She wouldn't be happy away from the lake.

On the last side, she had written the name of the person she wanted to marry. She would definitely need help from a goddess on this one. Adam Reese was already fifteen, and she wasn't sure he would wait for her to catch up with him. She had decided to marry him the summer after first grade, when she had skinned her knees so badly and he had patched her up. He hadn't yelled at her for crying or even when she had thrown up on his new gym shoes. He was the only big boy who could tell her apart from her sisters, and she loved him with her whole heart.

Tessa's lantern rose first, floating into the sky, charting a crooked path toward the full moon. Mel's rose next, then Callie's. They watched, silent, as the three wishes drifted apart, carried by competing breezes. Tessa's bobbled suddenly, jostled by an unseen hand, and then tumbled end-over-end into the frigid lake water. Callie heard her sister's choked cry of disappointment and put an arm around her. The two remaining wishes rose higher, tilting and bobbing on invisible waves of air. Mel's tilted so far to one side that the candle flame licked the paper of the lantern and the lantern itself burst into flame. It burned so quickly that only the bamboo frame landed in the water, followed by a few scraps of paper fluttering behind. Tessa reached over and put an arm around Mel.

"Shit," said Mel, showing off her newest swear word.

"I'm sorry," Tessa whispered.

"Who cares," said Mel. "I don't think Chinese magic can work for us, anyway. We're not from China."

The girls fell silent as they watched Callie's lantern continue to rise, the flame flickering but staying strong. The lantern rose so high and so far that Callie could barely see it against the backdrop of stars. Then it floated across the face of the full moon and disappeared.

The girls gasped in shock. Then they turned to each other.

"Did you see that?" Tessa squeaked. "It worked. The Goddess took it."

"It just disappeared," whispered Callie. "It was there, and then it wasn't."

"I don't know if that was magic," said Mel, "but it was pretty cool."

They watched the moon together in silence until a cloud covered it, then turned to head back up to the house. Callie smiled to herself. She knew for certain now that her wish would come true. She just needed to be patient.

CHAPTER ONE

Callie shut off the car at the top of the hill and looked out across the lake. The sun had yet to crest over the trees on the far shore, but she could see glimmers of it through the screen of bare trunks and branches. The landscape had that ragged, morning-after look of spring. No blanket of snow softened the harsh hangover of winter. Only a few brave buds and shoots dusted the view, hinting at a new beginning. The world was dark, wet, and cold, and Callie wondered if she had made a mistake in coming home.

The sudden silence woke Roscoe, who stretched on the passenger seat, hind leg twitching, then sat up to look around. He shook off his nap and drool splattered around the interior of her ancient Bronco. Callie wiped a few drops off her cheek.

"You're disgusting, hound dog," she said as she scratched behind his ears.

"Arrghuumfp?"

"Yes, you. Truly disgusting."

He didn't seem concerned. Roscoe had seen some hard times before Callie found him at the shelter, and he knew he had a good gig. He flopped back down, head in her lap, and Callie continued to rub his head while she stared out over the water.

"Well, Roscoe, we made it. Welcome to rock bottom, the place where dreams come to die."

She shifted the car into neutral, eased off the brake, and let the Bronco coast down the long gravel drive until it rolled to a stop in the shadow of the old house.

No curious face appeared at the window over the kitchen sink. Nobody opened the back door. Apparently the old high-school trick still worked: with the engine turned off, they hadn't heard her coming. She couldn't remember who had first thought of it—Mel, probably—but shook her head thinking of all the times it had saved their butts. Given the Bronco's current state of disrepair, she counted herself lucky once again and muscled the gearshift into park. She refused to think about how pathetic it was to be using that trick at the ripe old age of twenty-seven.

Roscoe pawed at the passenger-side door handle.

"Just a sec, Roscoe honey."

She leaned her head back against the headrest. After twelve hours on the road, her legs were stiff, her shoulders sore, and she wanted nothing more than a hot bath and a change of clothes. She looked down at the tabloid under Roscoe's feet, now featuring spatters of his drool, and sighed. She couldn't hide from her parents forever. After several swats in the face with an overactive tail, she gave in.

"Okay, okay. We'll get out. But you keep your voice down."

She shoved her door open and he bounded out, too distracted by all the new sights and smells to waste time barking.

As she climbed out after him, that first breath of icy air cleared her head. The gentle spring of Tennessee had faded into her rear-view mirror more than five hundred miles back. This far north, just into Wisconsin, winter still ruled. She wrapped her long sweater more tightly around her body and crossed her arms, wishing she had thought to pack more sweaters. Maybe some of her old ones were still in her bedroom, if her sisters hadn't appropriated them this past Christmas.

She gently closed the door of the Bronco and followed Roscoe around the side of the house, delaying the inevitable for a few minutes longer. The flagstones on the path were slick with frost, but Callie determinedly picked her way down the hill toward the lake. Roscoe had disappeared, but she didn't worry. He wouldn't venture far without her. When she reached the shore, she breathed deeply, closed her eyes, and listened to the waves breaking on the pebbled beach.

She had missed this. The stillness. The water flowing through her veins. Her roots sinking deep into the earth. Love it or leave it, this was home. And at this moment, the best thing about home was the distance separating it from Nashville. There were no lies here, no roles to play. No photographers or reporters. Best of all, there was no Brian—and no need to stand by her man.

There was only stillness—for the moment, anyway.

She opened her eyes to see her breath on the cold air, echoing the trails of mist rising off the water. She could hear the rhythm of the breaking waves and the branches creaking as the wind passed through them. All around her, the world began to wake up. Two squirrels chattered angrily above her in the trees. An odd assortment of gulls, ducks, and geese gathered in a sheltered inlet nearby, the ducks occasionally turning tail-up to dive beneath the surface of the water. Two chipmunks chased each other through the maze of disassembled docks that had been pulled from the water last fall and stacked on the shore for winter storage. Roscoe explored the beach, overjoyed to discover a dead fish.

She heard the scrape of a shoe on the shore path.

Callie tensed, her fragile peace broken. She turned her head to search for the intruder and found him immediately. Down the path to her left stood a young boy, staring out at the water. He seemed as unaware of her presence as she had been of his. This seemed odd at first, but then she realized he was deep in thought, muttering from time to time under his breath, and punctuating his monologue by kicking a mixture of dirt and gravel from the path into the water. He was awfully young to be down here by himself. Growing up, she and her sisters had known the mantra by heart: Nobody goes down to the water alone.

But where had the boy come from? Most of the cottages along this stretch of the shore belonged to summer people. The arrival of a new family, particularly a year-round family with children, would have been big news, worth at least a mention the last time her mother had called. Then again, maybe not. Callie had been ducking her mother's calls, or cutting them short, for more than a year. Who knew what other news she had missed?

She shot a sharp glance up toward the cottage next door. Had the Reese boys finally sold their grandmother's cottage? Or rented it? Surely her mother would have said something.

"Danny!" A man's voice called out from up the hill—from next door—the sound breaking the stillness of the morning. Roscoe snapped to attention, assessing the threat level. She stiffened as well, every sense on high alert as the implications echoed through her. Somebody was living next door. She had heard enough to sense the tension in the man's voice, the edge of panic, but not enough for her to be sure of his identity.

The boy froze like a startled deer, then darted up the path toward the cottage. Thankfully Roscoe did not give chase. A moment later Callie heard a screen door slam shut. Little Danny was in for a lecture. The question was, from whom?

As far as she knew, Adam was still in Singapore—not that she could be sure of anything anymore. She had cut ties with him years ago. He might as well be on the moon. But his little brother Evan had married Lainey and had a couple of kids. Maybe they had decided to live up here full time. Or maybe they had sold the cottage and nobody had bothered to tell her. Her stomach clenched and she fought a wave of despair. How had she allowed herself to drift so far away? It had been more than two years since she had last been home, and that had been for Christmas. She hadn't been home in the summer, when everyone would be here, since that summer after high school. She sighed, wishing—not for the first time—that life came with at least one do-over.

Callie took one last look across the water. The rising sun made a weak attempt to warm her nose and cheeks, but it didn't help much. She was cold, and like Danny next door, the time had come for her to go inside. There were no answers to be found out here.

She whistled for Roscoe, who scampered behind her as she climbed back up the hill, smelling everything along the way. She grabbed her purse and duffel bag from the car, along with a bag of food for Roscoe, but left the crumpled tabloid on the passenger seat. She would burn it later. The back door didn't open as she approached, and Callie hesitated for a moment, wondering if she should knock. But that seemed too strange, knocking at home, so she just walked in. Her parents sat at the kitchen table, finishing their tea as they shared the morning paper and listened to the news on the radio.

"Hi," said Callie weakly. Too late she realized that she must look a complete mess after driving all night. Her curls straggled down her back, tangled and limp, her clothes felt like she had slept in them, and she hadn't thought to hide the dark smudges under her eyes. This was not going to go well.

By the time she took two steps through the mudroom to the kitchen, they had both jumped up from the table, leaving mugs and newspapers behind. Mom got to her first.

"Callie, sweetie, what in the world are you doing here?" she demanded. Roscoe joined the fun, weaving in and out of all the legs until he found his way into the kitchen and disappeared, exploring again. "And since when do you have a dog?"

Her father neatly grabbed the duffel and set it aside. Her mother pulled her into a huge hug, talking all the while.

"Not that we don't want to see you because of course we do, anytime, you know that. But you didn't call! We had no idea you were coming." Callie found herself suddenly released and held at arms' length. "You didn't send me an e-mail, did you? You know I never check the computer. But your father does." She shot an accusing glance at Luke, keeping hold of Callie. "Luke, did you get an e-mail from Callie and not tell me about it? You know I count on you to tell me about all the e-mails."

He shook his head, smiling. He knew better than to interrupt before she had a chance to wind down on her own.

"Well then. No call. No e-mail. Oh my God, what's the matter?" her mother asked. "Tell me, quickly. Is it something with the band? What did Brian do this time?"

Her mother's fingers had tightened on her shoulders, so Callie gently pried herself loose while trying to reassure her mother. It was more difficult than usual because her voice was in particularly bad shape this morning. It came out as something between a whisper and a frog.

"I'm fine, Mom," she croaked. "Everything is fine." Callie kept the lie short and sweet, not wanting to trip the parental lie detectors.

At the same time, her father said, "Dora, relax, I'm sure everything is fine."

But then both her parents reacted to the sound of her voice.

Dora planted her hands on her hips. "Everything is certainly not fine, young lady. You have no voice. Running yourself ragged with that band and look what happens! Now you can't even talk. You're pale, you have dark circles under your eyes and your hair looks like it hasn't been brushed in weeks. And why do you need to dress like a hippie? There's a reason it all went out of fashion, you know. You're not even wearing a coat! Are you sick? You don't have throat cancer, do you? Oh my God. I'll call the doctor."

By this time Callie was laughing, hoarsely, which turned into a coughing fit. With her voice gone, she couldn't talk over her mother as she normally would. Luke looked concerned as well, but he put his arm around Dora and drew her back toward the kitchen table. "Now, Dora, let's give Callie a chance to explain why she's here. Sit down," he said more firmly as she tried to walk around him to get back to her daughter. "Callie, would you like some tea? Might help that throat, and the kettle's still hot."

She nodded, giving her father a quick hug. She took a seat across the table from her mother, who was muttering something under her breath about how she had always known that the band would be trouble even before they had chosen the name Deep Trouble. Callie didn't feel like arguing the point.

She waited until her father joined them with the hot tea and took a slow sip, easing the roughness in her throat while she thought about how much to say. Her father took a seat next to her mother, mostly so he could anchor her to her chair.

The seating arrangement gave Callie a disorienting sense of déjà vu. This was not a press interview. There were no TV cameras to capture every slip of the tongue or any telltale body language, but she couldn't help feeling the similarities. As if he could sense her unease, Roscoe chose that moment to return to the kitchen and curl up on her feet. Before her mother could freak out about the dog, Callie took a deep breath and began.

"You can hear that I have no voice," she whisper-croaked.

"Yes, but why?" asked Dora, as Luke simultaneously said, "Hush, let her finish." They both smiled at her in encouragement.

"It's not cancer," she said as firmly as she could. "It's not even a virus. I'm not sick, exactly."

Callie paused to clear her throat, even though the doctor had told her repeatedly that throat-clearing would only make the problem worse. She just couldn't help it.

"The doctor calls it vocal fatigue, and he said the only cure is to rest both myself and my voice for at least a month. Maybe longer."

It was the 'longer' that really scared her. Callie intended to follow the doctor's advice, but she needed to get back to Nashville by the end of May to prepare for the summer tour. No matter how bad things might be with the band right now, the tour was her only path forward—unless she abandoned her career completely. Hopefully four weeks of rest would be enough. It had to be enough.

Callie continued before her parents could ask more detailed questions.

"So of course I came home. Things are just too crazy in Nashville. Even if I'm not singing, there's so much work to do. . . . I needed to get away—really away. So I came here."

Callie stopped and took another sip of the tea, bracing herself for the follow-up questions. But they never came. Luke spoke first, while simultaneously giving Dora a warning squeeze.

"Of course you came home," said Luke. "This is the perfect place to get the rest you need, and we're so glad that you knew you would be welcome"—he gave Dora a pat on the shoulder—"no questions asked."

Dora shot him a dark look. Callie knew the questions were simply on hold, but she appreciated the reprieve.

"Did you drive all night?" her father asked.

Callie nodded.

"Are you hungry?"

Callie shook her head.

"Then it's off to bed with you. Don't show your face back downstairs until noon at the earliest. Got it?"

Callie nodded again and smiled with relief. Yes-no questions were easy.

"I have to go to work, but I'll see you ladies later today." He turned to Dora as he stood up. "And don't pester her with questions. You'll get your answers soon enough."

Dora crossed her arms like a petulant child, but she nodded curtly. Callie stifled a smile as she stood up, wiggling her feet out from under Roscoe. She grabbed her bags, then gave her dad a peck on the cheek and her mom a hug.

"Thanks," she whispered. "It's good to be home."

She turned quickly, blinking back tears, and headed for the stairs with Roscoe padding after her. She could hear her parents arguing in whispers as she turned the corner on the landing, but the bathtub was calling, and the bed after that. Everything else could wait.

Adam parked in front of the elementary school and paused for a moment with his forearms resting on the steering wheel. He stared into the woods across the street, forcing himself to relax, to be cool. He studied the pattern that the bare branches made against the pale gray sky, their outline starkly beautiful. If only the rest of his life could be as clearly defined.

This meeting was as much an evaluation of Adam and his amateur parenting skills as it was a discussion of Danny's progress. He needed to bury his frustration deep, along with the anger and intermittent panic. He would be a model of patience and understanding. He would demonstrate how he was giving Danny time and space to work through his grief. Never mind that it had been nearly ten months, and Danny still hadn't spoken a word. Never mind his own grief, or the ghosts of summer memories that lurked everywhere here at the lake. He needed to consider the fact that he would lose Danny if the boy's grandparents succeeded in challenging his guardianship.

Adam unclenched his fists and took three deep breaths. *Patience, understanding, acceptance,* he repeated to himself.

Sometimes he wondered if Evan and Lainey had made a mistake in choosing him. What the hell did he know about kids? He knew how to structure investments and how to make numbers tell a story, but people remained a mystery. Why Evan had asked him to do this, despite his obvious lack of qualifications, Adam would never understand, but he would find a way to do it. Danny was the only family he had left.

He silently chanted his new mantra as he slammed the door to the SUV and strode toward the main entrance. Patience. Understanding. Acceptance. He kept repeating it as he waited to be buzzed in, signed the visitor's log, and took the stairs two at a time to the school psychologist's office, which was tucked into the far back corner of the building. Before he could knock at the half-open door, a voice called out from inside.

"Come on in, Mr. Reese." Doc Archer had heard him coming.

"Good morning," Adam said calmly as he pushed the door open the rest of the way and entered the now-familiar office. It was cramped but neat, reminding him of the proverbial link between a clean desk and insanity. The pint-sized table and chairs in the corner always unsettled him. What were kids that small doing in a therapist's office? He focused instead on the kid behind the desk. Adam sat in his usual chair and reminded himself that this 'kid' was a trained and licensed psychologist. He had an entire bookshelf full of thick textbooks and reference books to prove it. Now that Lainey's parents had raised the stakes, it was important to make him an ally, not an adversary. For this reason, Adam didn't fidget during the small talk that followed, nor did he push the Doc to get to the point of the meeting. Adam could be patient when necessary, and he was damn well going to prove it.

After what seemed like hours, the Doc finally settled into the meat of the discussion.

"Mr. Reese, I asked for this meeting because I need to report on Danny's progress to the guardian *ad litem*. I thought you should have an opportunity to provide input."

Adam nodded calmly. "Thanks. I appreciate that. Danny's grandparents are worried about him—understandably so—and they think he might do better with them." He paused for emphasis. "I disagree."

"We're lucky that Kat Rodriguez, the same GAL who originally handled Danny's case, is available to handle this new development," said the Doc. "She's already familiar with Danny and his situation."

Adam fought the urge to rant about how the system was broken, how the overloaded case workers couldn't remember their own names—let alone the details of specific cases, but that wouldn't be fair to Kat. She had been incredibly professional last summer, despite her large caseload, and helped them through a difficult time. None of this was her fault. If anyone was to blame, it was him.

So he closed his mouth and simply nodded. "She and I have a meeting set up for Monday."

"Good," answered Doc Archer, leaning back in his chair. "I don't think anything in my report will surprise you. The good news is that Danny is stable, he's learning in school, and he doesn't cause any trouble." He took a deep breath and then sighed. "The bad news is that nothing has changed. It's been almost ten months since the accident—eight since school started—and he's still not talking. Not to his teachers, not to the other students, and not to me during our sessions. It's amazing that he's able to function as well as he does. He's worked out a system where he'll answer yes-no questions by nodding or shaking his head, and he'll provide written answers to more complex questions if needed." The Doc sighed. "It's not ideal, but it works. Have there been any changes at home?"

Adam shook his head. "No changes. We've settled into a comfortable pattern. . . ." He saw no need to clarify that by 'comfortable' he meant 'predictable.' Nothing about his relationship with Danny felt comfortable. The boy wouldn't even look him in the face. ". . . And we're getting by." That didn't sound particularly optimistic. "We're doing fine," he amended. "If we just give Danny the space he needs—"

"Mr. Reese," Doc Archer interrupted. "Let's be real, here."

The kid—the Doc—had never before dropped his therapist façade. Adam was so startled by this glimpse of the bleak and cynical man beneath that he shut up.

"More of the same is not going to help Danny. He's had plenty of time to come to terms with his new reality, but he won't live in it. You're letting him off easy. We all are. We're so understanding and patient that we're not pushing him to rejoin the world. Danny needs a push. Maybe that's a change in his custody arrangement—"

Adam leaned forward and opened his mouth to protest, but Doc Archer held up a hand to stop him.

"—or maybe it's something else. All I know is that something needs to change."

Adam clamped his mouth shut as he thought through the implications, his gut twisting painfully. If Doc Archer wanted to separate him from Danny, then he was in for a fight. But the Doc wasn't an adversary yet. Adam forced himself to respond to the Doc's ultimatum calmly and evenly.

"I thought you said that stability and predictability were the two most important things I could give Danny," Adam replied.

"They are," agreed the Doc, "but only if he responds to the stable, loving environment. If he doesn't respond, then a change is in order."

Adam did not like that answer.

"So what exactly are you going to recommend in your report?" He fought to keep his hands relaxed, when all they wanted was to clench into fists.

Doc Archer cocked his head to one side and studied Adam.

"I'm going to outline our plan of action. We'll attempt to draw Danny out by introducing a series of small changes, both at school and at home. If we are not successful in convincing Danny to rejoin the world, then a larger change is in order."

"So let's talk more about those small changes," said Adam. If Danny needed change, then Adam would give him change.

Not a problem. He would do whatever was necessary to keep Danny.

"Great," said the Doc, opening a folder on his desk. "I've come up with a few ideas."

Half an hour later, Adam climbed back into his SUV and sat staring out at the woods again. Somehow the gnarled branches looked darker and more menacing than they had earlier. Tangled. Complicated.

How in the hell was he supposed to connect with Danny if the boy wouldn't talk? Doc Archer's suggestions (they came across more like commands) were absurd. *Find an activity that you can do together at least once a week. Find an activity that Danny can do on his own at least once a week.* Adam tried to imagine himself coaching a kids' basketball team or taking Danny fishing. He tried to imagine Danny joining in any sort of activity that involved other kids. He let out a short laugh and thumped his head back against the headrest. What a joke. He had no idea what Danny would want to do. Wasn't that the whole problem? But he could easily imagine what would happen if he tried to make Danny to do something the boy didn't want to do. He closed his eyes, letting the scene play out in his mind. Danny's face would go from passive to stubborn, looking so much like his dad at that age that it hurt even to think about it. He would turn around and stomp off to his room, closing the door, and shutting Adam out. Sure, he could physically compel the boy to leave his room—pick him up, maybe, in a fireman's carry—but Danny was getting bigger every day. He might be on the small end for third grade, but Adam suspected that a struggle would still hurt both of them.

This left Adam with only one other choice: Do nothing. And if he did nothing, they would end up right back where they started.

He sat up straight. This kind of defeatist thinking was useless. The time had come to shake things up—to take action. He had made a promise, and he wasn't going to go down without a fight.

CHAPTER TWO

Eleven years ago

Callie watched from her sheltered perch inside the old treehouse. She couldn't quite bring herself to join the impromptu game of touch football that swirled below. Her sisters, her friends, and the guys—they all jostled and teased, eager to kick off another summer at the lake, but she stayed on the sidelines, watching. She had no patience for games today.

Adam had come back. She could think about nothing else.

In a way, she felt like she had been swimming underwater for the entire school year, everything muffled and dim—meaningless. Today, she had at last broken the surface and taken a deep breath of fresh air. She was awake. Alive. The entire world shimmered with a new clarity that centered around Adam. Her body thrummed with this painfully intense new energy. She held herself back, her senses so heightened that the idea of a simple conversation—let alone a game of football—overwhelmed her.

He stood to one side, catching up with his summer friends but always keeping an eye on his little brother. She smiled to herself. Evan could hardly be called "little" anymore. He had shot up to match Adam, and at eighteen, chances were good that he would beat out his older brother. Adam was twenty-two now. A man, not a boy.

She sucked in a breath when he looked up at her, hidden among the leaves, almost as if he could sense her thoughts. He grinned at her, then turned back to his friends. She froze, unable to release her breath for a full minute.

He was off-limits. Too old. She knew that. But still. . . .

Adam smiled as he turned back to his friends. That was little Callie James up in the treehouse. He would bet on it. Some kids couldn't tell the triplets apart, but Adam had never had much trouble. Callie was the quiet one, Mel was the troublemaker, and Tessa was always trying to boss the other two around. Problem was, they weren't quite so little anymore. They must be about fifteen, maybe sixteen now. There was a whole pack of girls around that age, and not enough boys to go around. Dangerous, the lot of them. They were looking for trouble, and his little brother was more than eager to help them find it. How was he going to watch out for Evan if he couldn't be here?

Adam's summer friends would be no help. They were all out of college and working now. What little time they could spend at the lake this summer would be spent exploring the local bar scene and getting laid. He would be in the same boat soon enough, minus the drinking and the girls. He would start his first "real" job on Tuesday—the kind that didn't involve mowing lawns or delivering pizza—and after that he wouldn't have time for getting drunk and getting laid. He would be working too hard. Gran had called in some serious favors to get him a foot in the door, and he didn't plan on screwing it up.

So how to keep an eye on Evan? That was the real problem. The kid completely lost his mind when he was around girls. Even now he was showing off, leaping to make a wildly improbable catch, and then taking the fall so that Lainey could make a touchdown. It would be funny if Adam weren't convinced it would land his brother in the hospital—or jail. Nearly all of these girls were underage, technically off-limits to Evan now that he had turned eighteen. If Dad were still alive, he would probably give Evan the same sage advice he had given Adam at eighteen: *Take whatever the girls are offering, kid, but you'd better be goddamn sure to use protection or you'll end up screwed like the old man.* Now that Adam was the one offering the advice, he planned to deliver a slightly different message, one involving respect, responsibility, and obligations that last a lifetime.

Evan took a turn at quarterback, and he threw a hopeless Hail Mary that got lost somewhere above the treehouse. There was much rustling of branches and shouting of insults as the players waited for the ball to fall back to earth. Adam caught Callie's eye again just before the ball collided with her head. She disappeared from view and yelped in pain. The ball dropped to the ground with a thunk. Amid general laughter, someone called up, "Hey Callie, you okay?"

It was a moment before her shaky voice responded.

"Yeah, sure, I'm—oh crap, I'm bleeding."

Adam's mouth tightened. They hadn't even been here half an hour and already Evan was in trouble. He strode over toward the base of the tree, where Callie descended the ladder into a throng of chattering girls. He waded through to meet her just as she put her feet on terra firma and turned around. Sure enough, there was a gash on her cheek that was dripping blood down her face and neck. One of the girls shrieked. Another gagged.

He sighed. It really wasn't that bad. He and his brother had patched each other up enough times to know. She wouldn't need stitches, but she would probably end up with a scar.

"What happened?" demanded her sister Tessa, elbowing Adam out of the way.

Callie blinked back tears and shrugged.

"The ball knocked me against the treehouse. I think I hit a nail or something."

The kids nodded. They had all helped build the treehouse, so everybody knew the construction work was shoddy.

Callie looked like she was about to faint.

"Let's get you patched up," he said, putting an arm around her for support.

Tessa and Callie whispered back and forth, but he couldn't hear what they said. Then Tessa stepped back and let him lead Callie gently through the crowd of useless gawkers.

"Evan," he barked.

Evan snapped to attention and jogged over, but he couldn't quite look at the bloody side of Callie's face. Adam didn't ask him to help with the cleanup. His baby brother didn't do so well with blood.

"Apologize to Callie for that ridiculous pass," he ordered his brother.

Evan's mouth tightened, but he wasn't stupid enough to argue. They could hash it out later, along with the new rules for dealing with girls.

"Oh man, I'm so sorry, Callie. I had no idea you were up there."

She smiled weakly.

"Don't worry about it. It was an accident."

He took a step back, clearly eager to return to the game. Adam nodded, and Evan disappeared.

Callie's was the second-to-last in a curved row of houses surrounding the commons and looking out on the lake beyond. Adam led her slowly through the trees toward the kitchen door. He didn't want to rush her. He had made that mistake the first time he had patched her up. She had been five or six at the time, and she had puked on his shoes.

"Let's get you home."

She nodded, but didn't speak. If anything, she looked paler now.

"You're not going to faint on me, are you?"

She shook her head.

"Puke?"

Her mouth tightened and she turned a little green. Adam didn't want to take any chances. She was a tiny thing, barely over five feet. He scooped her up and carried her the last few yards to the house, then up the stairs and onto the porch. He managed to pull open the screen door and get her inside without bumping her around too much. Just a few more steps into the kitchen, where he sat her on the counter right next to the sink.

"There. Now if you need to puke you can do it right into the sink."

"Thanks," she whispered, and held on tight to the edges of the counter.

"Is your Mom home?"

She nodded slowly. "But she's painting upstairs, so we shouldn't bug her. Dad's not back from his trip yet."

She swallowed hard, and he suddenly realized he might need to deal with tears as well as blood. He was going to kill Evan.

"Don't worry. It's not a bad cut. We'll get you cleaned up in no time."

She opened a drawer next to her leg and fished out a bottle of antibiotic spray. He found some paper towels and turned on the water, giving her time for her stomach to settle. Blood and tears he could handle, but not puke. He had thought about his father enough for one day.

Callie took a few deep breaths as her stomach settled down. Thank God. Nothing would be more humiliating than puking on Adam again.

He stood just inches away, waiting for the water to warm up. She couldn't believe that she was actually alone with him, close enough to feel his body heat and to smell his soap. Her palms began to tingle, and the throb in her cheek faded into the background.

The water temperature must have met with his approval, because he wet the first paper towel, wrung it out, and moved to clean her up. She sat still, barely breathing, waiting for him to touch her. With one hand, he cradled her head, tilting it to the side. Her eyes closed and she focused on the feeling of his palm against her cheek.

She wanted to remember every second of it.

The hot towel cooled as it moved across her skin. He stroked from the base of her neck up toward her jawline, his touch firm as he wiped away the blood. He wet a second towel and began to clean her cheek. Her breath caught in her chest, but she forced herself to continue breathing in and out, slowly and evenly, so that he wouldn't know how close she was to freaking out.

This was so much better than spin the bottle, and he wasn't even kissing her.

Adam needed to get this over with. This was little Callie James he was touching. Even in her brand new woman-body, she was and always would be totally off-limits. And yet his own stupid body crackled with energy. No matter how well his jeans masked his growing hard-on, he was painfully aware of it.

She should not be alone in her house with a grown man. She should not trust him enough to lay her cheek in the palm of his hand and close her eyes. She should be playing truth or dare, or spin the bottle, with younger guys like his brother. His stomach turned a little at the thought. Not his brother. Much younger boys.

Harmless boys.

He kept his attention on cleaning the cut, wincing along with her as she felt the sting of the antibiotic spray. Not once did she pull away.

"It's not bad at all," he murmured, examining the cut closely to make sure it was clean. His breath moved across her skin, and he could see goose bumps rise in its wake. A surge of lust swept through him, so strong that he almost lost it. Carefully, as if she were live explosives, he removed his hand from her head and stepped back. Her eyes blinked, then stayed open, and he almost groaned out loud. Her pupils had dilated so wide that her eyes looked black. She might not understand what was going on, but he knew desire when he saw it. The girl needed a warning label: Danger—Highly Combustible.

"Do I need a bandage?" she asked, her voice husky.

He nodded and cleared his throat, not quite able to talk. She searched the open drawer to the left of her bare thigh and fished out a box of bandages, then waited while he struggled to free one from its wrapper. He needed to stop thinking about things that came in small wrappers. When he finally smoothed the bandage across her skin, she sighed. His hand twitched, but he managed to finish without hurting her. He needed to get away, but before he could retreat, she caught one of his hands.

He froze. It took every ounce of self-control for Adam to simply hold still. This girl filled the room like water. He was drowning, and he didn't even have the sense to swim. He couldn't think. He could only feel the blood pounding in his ears and the fire of her hand on his wrist.

"Thank you," she whispered.

He yanked his hand away and turned the kitchen sink on full-force, using the icy cold water to splash his face. He dried his face with a paper towel, taking a moment to get a grip before turning back to Callie. He didn't care if she thought he was crazy. This was a matter of survival.

Callie's entire body was singing. She had always known that she and Adam were meant to be together, but she hadn't expected. . . . She hadn't even known that feelings like this existed. He didn't seem happy about it, though. In fact, as she watched him dry off his face, he seemed kind of pissed. She grinned. He could be as angry as he liked. He could even pretend that nothing had happened.

She knew better.

"Are you going to be okay?" he demanded.

She nodded.

"You're not dizzy or anything?"

She shook her head, keeping her expression innocent.

"Good." He started backing toward the door. "Make sure your parents take a look at that cut. They might want to take you to see a doctor."

"Yes, sir," she responded, sitting up straight and giving him a little salute.

His eyes narrowed.

"Stay out of trees, Callie," he cautioned, then turned on his heel and escaped.

She stretched, then hopped off the counter. She had an idea for a new song, and she wanted to write it down in her notebook immediately, before she could forget: "Touch of Fire."

Callie woke slowly, floating up layer by layer from the depths of sleep and memory. Her eyelids flickered, revealing soft greens and blues infused with late afternoon sunshine. The murmur of voices, music, rose from somewhere beneath her. The kitchen. Home.

It had been a long time since Adam had infiltrated her dreams. Centuries, maybe. Those memories belonged to another time—another Callie. She had long since grown up and moved on.

Something wet and cold snuffled her hand. She smiled to herself. Why in the world had she chosen a hound dog? The animal was a slobber fountain.

Now completely awake, she lay still, scratched Roscoe's head, and studied her room. It felt like a time capsule, a shrine to her teenage years. How odd that it remained unchanged after all this time. She had left for college nine years ago and only been back a handful of times. The gauzy, underwater theme that had felt so bohemian back then seemed naïve now and unsophisticated compared to the designer loft that she and Brian shared in Nashville. That thought brought her up short. *Used to share*, she corrected herself. She had left Brian and the loft behind. Despite her professional commitment to the band, she had no intention of living under the same roof with Brian ever again.

Callie threw aside her covers and rolled out of bed, rooting around in her duffel for clean clothes. Screw sophistication. She would choose her homemade bedroom over a fancy decorator showplace any day. She found her monster slippers in the closet, still parked in their old spot. Brian would hate these slippers. Smiling grimly, she jammed her feet inside them. She loved them.

On the way downstairs, she peeked into her sisters' rooms to see if they had the same frozen-in-time feeling as her own, but they didn't. Tessa's room felt spare and empty, as if she had packed up her entire childhood and put it in cold storage. Mel's room was a disaster area—as usual—making Callie wonder if she had just been up last weekend.

It occurred to her that, at some point, she would need to tell her sisters what was going on. They would see the tabloids or the Internet headlines and they would worry. But she couldn't quite wrap her head around what she would say, so she put the problem aside for later. More than anything, right now she needed food.

When Callie entered the kitchen, Roscoe padding along behind, her parents abruptly stopped talking. She smiled at the pair of them, looking like guilty children. Gosh, what could they possibly have been talking about?

"What's cookin', good lookin'?" she rasped, using one of her dad's favorite greetings.

"We were thinking omelets for dinner," said her mother, hopping to her feet and trying to look busy. "You know, that dog is smarter than he looks. I sent him to wake you up and he actually did it. You must be starving. You've slept the whole day away."

Soon Callie was chopping and toasting and setting the table, making sure Roscoe had his own food and water, and listening to her mother chatter about her day. She let the steady stream of words flow over her, finding comfort in the familiarity of it all. Growing up, she and her sisters had concluded that their mother's solitary days spent painting in the attic studio left her with a huge, pent-up need to talk. They didn't need to listen closely, just nod occasionally and let her get it all out. Callie put aside all the jumbled emotions of the past few days and her worries about the future, floating instead in the present—at least until they sat down to eat.

"So how long can you stay?" asked Luke.

So much for 'no questions asked.' Callie breathed deeply, trying to unwind the knot in her stomach. It was bad enough that, at twenty-seven, she was running home to Mommy and Daddy. She was an adult now. She had her own life, and her parents had theirs. She couldn't just assume that it was okay to stay. She needed to ask.

"I have until June first to get my voice back in shape. I'd love to stay for at least a few weeks," she paused, feeling awkward, "if that's okay."

"Of course it's okay!" Dora huffed. "Since when do you need to ask permission to come home?"

Callie grinned, the wave of relief stronger than she had expected.

"It's called good manners, Mom. I have no idea where I picked them up. Must have been that 'social graces' class in junior high."

Luke turned his laugh into a cough, hiding it in his napkin. Callie took a bite of her omelet, keeping her expression innocent. Dora frowned, then opened her mouth to give Callie a piece of her mind. The social graces class was still a sore subject in the household, more than fifteen years later.

Luke dove in before Dora could work up any momentum. "So the doctor really thinks it's overuse? It's not an infection or allergies?"

"Don't worry, Dad. I've been checked and scanned and poked and prodded. The guy is a specialist, and he says that all I need is a rest. We've been working our asses off—" She ignored her mother's raised eyebrow at her choice of words. "—and it's just been too much. Too many weeks of rehearsing, recording, songwriting, playing gigs, taking care of business. It's not sustainable."

"That's what worries me," said Luke. "What happens in a month if your voice isn't back?" He gestured broadly, nearly knocking over a glass in the process. "What happens if you need more time?"

Dora saved Callie from having to answer. She reached across the table and squeezed her daughter's hand. "Then she takes more time, Luke. It doesn't have to be complicated."

"When you're in a band, it's always complicated," he said.

Callie smiled. What he said was true, but she took his sage pronouncement with a grain of salt. Her dad's glory days in the band, lo those many years ago, had been brief. Sure, he had photos to prove it, and even an actual vinyl record, but he had been a grade school music teacher for nearly thirty years now. Any residual coolness had worn off long ago. That didn't stop him from telling stories, though. The older they got, the taller the tales. By the time they were teenagers, he claimed to be making buckets of money from his songwriting hobby, and that his best friend from the old days was a top music producer in Nashville. Suspiciously, though, there was no bucket of money to fund prom dresses or vacations. She sighed. There was no way she could tell him—either of them—about the vast gap between dream and reality.

The kitchen was quiet for a few minutes as all three focused on their food. Her father was right. When you're in a band, it's always complicated. Bands were like great big dysfunctional families that decide to go into business together. In Callie's particular band family, she wrote all the songs and played the role of peacemaker. She filled in the gaps, picked up the slack, and got things done. If they needed to compromise, she was the first to bend. She was the stretchy, sticky, flexible glue that held the band together, both onstage and off. At first she had relished the feeling of being necessary, but over the past few years, as the gigs got bigger and the money got serious, she had come to feel trapped by her own stretchy, sticky self.

As unexpected as her vocal troubles were, they also gave her a welcome reprieve from the day-to-day craziness of the band. This was a one-time chance to redefine her role, and she planned to make the most of it. Someone else would have to organize rehearsals, make the coffee, and act as referee. They could all keep those jobs when she returned.

"Speaking of complicated," said Dora, "how did you manage to arrange for a month away?"

Callie paused, fork halfway to her mouth. "A few weeks ago, when I realized that my voice was getting worse instead of better, I found some backup singers to cover for me."

"Plural?" asked her father.

"Three of them." She didn't mention the tabloid images of Brian's naked rehearsal with the new girls in the studio. "Brian thought it would be fun"—Callie fought to keep herself from gagging—"to be able to do some more complex harmonies."

"Can they carry their own weight?" probed Luke. "What else can they do besides sing?"

Callie knew what Luke was getting at, although Dora, crinkling her brow, seemed mystified. He was thinking about the financials, and the way the money can get thin if the band gets too big. You need utility players, he always said. People who can really contribute. Of course these girls had already proven that they could contribute—to Brian's satisfaction anyway.

"They have some range," she responded mildly. She sifted through her experiences with them, searching for information she could share with her parents. "One of them has a great voice and she does decent percussion. Another is a competent fiddle player. The third plays a little banjo. Nothing to write home about, but they're covering for me just fine."

Little overachievers, those three.

"And the harmonies?" he asked. "Can they deliver onstage?"

Callie ate the forkful of food that she had been holding in midair so she had time to consider her answer. It took some effort to calmly chew and swallow her food, given her overwhelming urge to vomit.

"They're young," she said, "and inexperienced. They're getting the hang of listening to each other onstage, and following Brian's lead"—perhaps they were too good at that—"but it takes time to get used to the monitors and the lights and the noise from the crowd. It's a big change from the studio, but they're getting it." She smiled, hoping that it looked real. "They'll do."

Dora chuckled at that. It had been one of Luke's favorite phrases when the girls were little, especially during their music lessons. When one of them finally mastered something, he would give her a big grin and say "You'll do."

Luke smiled, looking wistful, or at least Callie thought so. Maybe it was because she felt wistful herself. Being back at home made her want to go back in time as well, to start over instead of having to change course mid-journey.

"I guess you can't ask for more than that, can you?" he said.

Sure I can, thought Callie, as she looked down at her nearly empty plate and toyed with the last bits. *I can ask for Brian to keep his pants zipped and the new girls to keep their clothes on. But maybe I'm just old-fashioned that way.*

Of course she didn't say any of that out loud. There were some things that Dora and Luke would be happier not knowing.

"What I'd like to know," began Dora, "is why you drove all night to get here."

Callie couldn't help the guilty flicker of her eyes as she looked up in surprise at her mother and then immediately back down at her plate. There was no way her mother could read her mind, but she wasn't taking any chances. Roscoe chose that moment to finish his own breakfast and reclaim his favorite spot on top of her feet. Her mother didn't acknowledge the distraction.

"I know you're young and all-nighters mean nothing to you, but it makes me sick to imagine you dozing off at the wheel on a dark highway in the middle of nowhere. Or being run off the road by a sleepy truck driver. What were you thinking? It's certainly no way to begin a month of rest. Did something happen yesterday? Did you and Brian have a fight?"

Callie tried to pull off a lighthearted laugh, but completely failed. With her scratchy throat, it ended up sounding like a cry of distress.

"Don't be silly, Mom. Everything is fine. I was just itchy to get going, before some emergency came up and I would have to stay. So I packed up and left. Not a big deal. I had Roscoe to keep me awake."

Callie couldn't quite meet the eyes of either of her parents, but she did at least glance at each of them during her little speech, hoping it would be enough. She shut up after a few sentences. If she babbled for too long, they would know she was lying.

"Well I think it's great that you have a whole month off," said Dora, when it was clear that Callie wasn't going to say anything more. "You can rest and relax and maybe even play some music with your father." She gave Luke a meaningful look. "He's been missing you."

"Dora, there's no need to fuss," he said.

Dora rose and carried her plate to the sink, talking as she went.

"Luke, it's been months since you wrote anything, and it's making you crazy." She held up a hand to forestall comments.

"Trust me, it's making us both crazy. Retirement isn't a death sentence. Do me a favor and give your muse a kick in the rear, all right?"

Callie raised an eyebrow at her father, grateful for the new direction in the conversation. Luke shook his head briefly, letting Callie know that he wasn't going to talk about it now. She didn't plan to let it drop, though, and started plotting how she would corner him later. As she got up to clear her plate, she patted him on the shoulder.

"Don't sweat it, Dad," she said. "I haven't written anything good in months either."

Over at the sink, Callie whispered to Dora, "Is something bothering him?"

Dora glanced sideways at Callie, handing her the dishcloth so she could help with the clean-up. "If there is, I'll find out eventually," she said. "There are no secrets in this house." Then she turned her attention back to the dishes.

Callie knew that look. Her mother wasn't talking about Luke. She hadn't bought Callie's story. She would keep digging until she had unearthed all of her daughter's secrets. Without the distraction of the holidays or her sisters as backup, Callie was going to have a hard time keeping her private life private. She had better get her story straight—and maybe train Roscoe to eat her mother's shoes.

CHAPTER THREE

Callie slipped silently out the back door, Roscoe at her side. She had found herself awake at 5 a.m., her mind churning through the last three days over and over again. She didn't want to wake her parents. She didn't want to talk. Unable to escape back into sleep, she decided to try music instead. The spring weather had followed her up from Tennessee. With luck, the summer house would be warm enough to play without disturbing the peace.

The guitar case thumped against her back as she navigated the path down the hill. She carried her banjo case in one hand and the violin case in the other. The rising sun streaked fire across the calm surface of the water and cast long shadows up the hillside. Once the morning mist burned off, it would be a beautiful day.

The boathouse, nestled into the hillside, provided shore-level storage for the canoe and the sailboat, but Callie was more interested in the 'summer house' on top. Ancient storm windows protected the woodwork and the wicker furniture during the off season, and also captured the early morning sunshine.

The door creaked as she opened it and she paused, a wave of memories taking her by surprise. Rainy-day crafts on the Fourth of July weekend. She and her sisters painting stripes on their toenails. Her first taste of beer, courtesy of Annabelle's older sister. And then, of course, Adam. She flushed, remembering how he had pinned her against the wall and growled at her to slow down. Slowing down had been the last thing she wanted, from him or from the world. She had wanted to go fast, to get started, to get out of this small town and start her 'real life.'

Now she felt a thousand years old and she missed that girl—the girl she had been before 'real life' took over.

She shook off the past and stepped through the doorway. Talk about water under the bridge. She should know better than to waste time swimming upstream. She laid the instrument cases in a row on the floor and opened them one by one. Roscoe scouted out a comfortable chair and climbed up onto the seat to nap. Callie tuned the instruments, beginning with the guitar, using an old-fashioned tuning fork as her father had taught her. Brian had tried to talk her into selling her instruments once, when they were low on cash. Thankfully she had stood her ground. Her great-grandfather had invested in beautiful instruments and cared for them all his life. She would never insult his memory by selling them, no matter how valuable they might be.

When all the instruments were tuned and ready, Callie picked up the guitar again, took a breath, and cleared her mind. She absorbed the rhythm of the tiny waves breaking on the rocks below. She began to play, using the guitar to soothe the tension of the past few days, and the frustrations that had been building for much longer. She took out her aggression on the banjo, eased her hurts with the fiddle, and ended up back on the guitar, struggling with a partially finished song that had been giving her trouble. No matter how she reworked it, she couldn't get it right.

The sun continued to rise. Two squirrels chased each other along the outside of the window sill. Callie sank into the solitude, hungry for the deep flow that came from creating music.

After wrestling with a particularly tricky chord progression for a few minutes, she growled in frustration and thrashed out a few hard, satisfying chords to clear her head. One of the strings snapped, whipping back to bite her finger. She yelped and stuck her finger in her mouth. Then she heard a creak behind her. Someone was watching.

She twisted around, adrenaline surging through her veins, ready to fight. She stopped, confused, when she realized it was just a boy outside the storm door. The boy from yesterday morning. Danny.

Roscoe offered a lazy half bark.

"Some watchdog you are," she muttered, giving him a dirty look.

Turning back to Danny, she asked, "Do you want to come in?" He took a step back, poised to run. Maybe her harsh voice made him nervous. Either that or the dog.

Callie took a deep breath and softened her voice as best she could.

"I'm sorry. I didn't mean to scare you." She waved in the direction of the dog. "Don't worry about Roscoe. He's too lazy to bother you."

The boy couldn't be more than eight or nine, with big ears, freckles, and painfully short red hair. There was no longer any doubt in her mind that this was Evan and Lainey's child. Those ears came straight from Evan, and the red hair was all Lainey. Just looking at him was giving her flashbacks—and a disorienting glimpse of the road not taken. All her unspoken doubts and misgivings and regrets came wriggling to the surface like worms after a hard rain, forcing her to acknowledge the cost of chasing her dream. Part of that cost was giving up the daydream of a 'normal' life.

Danny's gaze shifted from her face to her guitar, reminding her of the first time her father had placed a guitar in her arms. It had been almost as big as she was, but she had been desperate to try it. How old had she been? Four? Five? Something about the way this boy looked at her guitar made her suspect he needed music as much as she did.

"Come on in," she offered. He still seemed uncertain, so she took her time hunting through the guitar case until she found a bandage. He hovered outside the door, wearing nothing but jeans and a T-shirt. He must be freezing. She watched him out of the corner of her eye while she tended to her finger. Then, fishing a new E-string out of her guitar case, she replaced the broken one. She could feel his eyes on her as she loosened the pegs, released the remnants of the broken string, coiled a new string around the pegs, and then tightened and tuned until the instrument was ready to play again. Callie held still, giving the boy time to make his decision.

Finally he pulled open the door and slipped inside. She smiled and motioned for him to sit beside her.

"Do you play?" she asked, already knowing the answer. He looked the way she felt—hungry for music.

He nodded. She lifted the strap over her head and passed the guitar to him. She said nothing else. She never had the right words, anyway.

The full-size guitar dwarfed Danny, but he didn't seem to mind. He rested it across his lap and tested a few chords, making sure he had them right, his small fingers straining to press down hard enough on the strings. She resisted the urge to show him the correct finger positions, and soon enough he found them on his own. He began to play. She recognized the Irish folk song "Danny Boy"—an appropriate choice, given his name. It seemed odd to sit there and do nothing, so she pulled her fiddle out of the open case on the floor and started to play the melody line.

He played it through two or three times, growing more confident each time. After he stopped, she played the melody one last time, the lonely sound floating out over the water. Then she rested her fiddle in her lap and waited to see what he would do next.

He sat staring at the lake, holding on tight to the guitar. Judging by his white fingertips, he was feeling something powerful. But none of it showed on his face, and he wasn't exactly inviting conversation. She herself had been accused—more than once— of shutting people out. Most times that was because she didn't want to talk about whatever she was feeling. Words weren't really her thing, unless they were part of a song. If he didn't want to talk about whatever he was feeling, she certainly wouldn't force the issue.

The raucous call of a gull startled them. They both jumped, then looked at each other and smiled. Callie relaxed. He was going to be okay.

"I'm Callie," she offered, trying to make her voice sound as normal as possible. "What's your name?" she asked, even though she knew the answer.

He hesitated a moment before answering.

"Danny."

Normally, Callie let other people carry the conversation so she couldn't screw it up, but Danny wasn't exactly jumping in to fill the void.

"So, Danny-boy, where are you from?"

"Next door." His voice sounded rusty, as though he didn't use it often. Kind of like hers.

She pretended that he was keeping up his side of the conversation, asking where she lived. "I used to live here, too, but now I live in Nashville."

Callie realized that further conversation about where she lived would only be confusing to a kid. *What kind of a house do you live in?* A loft, but I don't live there anymore. *What's a loft?* It's one big room with brick walls and trendy furniture. *Why don't you live there anymore?* Because my ex is an asshole. *So where do you live now?* Well, I'm not exactly sure. Here, I guess. For now.

She changed the subject.

"Who taught you how to play the guitar?" she asked.

Danny's face crumpled briefly before he got it under control again. "My dad." His voice cracked as he said it. She remembered Evan playing sometimes around the bonfire. She had always liked his voice.

"My dad taught me to play, too," said Callie. "He loves country and bluegrass music, and now it's my favorite music, too."

"My dad loved Irish songs," he said softly. "We used to play them for my mom and make her cry."

Callie felt her stomach lurch. This was why she avoided conversation. It was a minefield. In this case, Danny was talking in past tense. Had Evan and Lainey divorced? Maybe Evan didn't play music anymore, since the split. Callie couldn't help her irrational rush of anger at him for being an idiot. How could a father do that to his own child, just when Danny would need music the most? Evan should know better.

"Do you want to play another song?" she asked.

"Okay." He looked relieved.

"You choose," she said. He thought for a minute, then started to play. She listened, realized he had chosen "The Water Is Wide," and joined in. No wonder they made Lainey cry, with songs like these.

While they played, Callie kept her eyes on the lake and her mind on the music. Somehow the water made her feel lighter, and the music set her emotions free. Sharing music felt right. It felt good. Maybe this was exactly what the both of them needed.

"Danny!"

At the sound of the voice calling from up the hill, Roscoe roused himself and barked. Danny stopped playing and jumped up. He lifted the guitar strap over his head, placing the instrument back in its case. He paused, looking at Callie as if he wanted to say something, but instead he slipped silently out the door of the summer house, giving Callie a smile and a wave before running through the woods back home.

Callie stared after him, wondering about his story. Would he tell Evan about playing music with the lady next door? Would Even remember her after all these years? Would he pull his guitar out of the closet and play again, maybe for the first time since the divorce?

She let the story spin in her mind and sketched out a few ideas in her notebook. There might be something to this story, a sliver of truth she could weave into a new song. If nothing else, perhaps helping Danny would take her mind off her own troubles. Maybe it would help her stop thinking about Adam.

"Danny!" Adam called out the back door and then waited, his ears straining for some sign of the boy. He hated this. He hated waking up every morning, wondering if Danny would be in his bed or out wandering. He had nightmares about Danny slipping on the shore path and falling, hitting his head, tumbling into the icy water. Thinking about it made his gut hurt. He had lost everyone else. He was not going to lose Danny.

"Danny!" he called again, louder this time. Finally he heard the rustling of the bushes and Danny appeared at the gap in the fence. The boy picked his way through the garden, sidestepping the dormant plants, and slowed as he approached the house. Adam stood on the front porch, chilled in only a T-shirt and a pair of flannel pajama pants.

"Danny, goddamn it, where have you been?"

As soon as the words were out of his mouth, Adam wished he could pull them back in. Too loud. Too harsh. And he shouldn't be swearing. He took a deep breath, rubbed his forehead, and willed himself to relax. Danny studied his shoes and said nothing.

"Danny," he said, more calmly this time. "You need to remember the house rules. You can't leave without telling me." Adam paused, giving Danny a chance to respond, but the boy kept his eyes down and said nothing.

"If you don't want to tell me that you're going out, at least leave me a note, will you? And remember, you never, ever go down to the water alone. That's non-negotiable. Got it?"

He waited, longer this time, and at last Danny nodded. It wasn't much more than a twitch, but at least it was a response. He wondered if Doc Archer would consider this progress.

"I'm going to take a shower and make some breakfast. I'll call you when it's ready, okay?"

Danny nodded again, more quickly this time. Two responses in one morning. What the hell? Adam glanced curiously at the gap in the fence, wondering what had happened to make Danny so . . . interactive. But the bushes looked the same as they did every morning.

Feeling optimistic, Adam held the screen door open for Danny. But instead of coming inside, Danny turned his back on Adam. He sat on the wet, cold grass and looked out over the lake, shoulders hunched and chin on his knees. And as quickly as it had come, Adam's optimism faded. He closed his eyes briefly, took a breath, and gently closed the screen door.

Adam held on tight to his frustration until he reached the bedroom. He closed that door gently as well, then slammed his fist against the wall. It hurt. A lot. But it helped take the edge off the frustration and despair that threatened to overwhelm him. It gave him something else to be angry about, something tangible, instead of this impenetrable wall that Danny had built. The boy kept retreating, deeper and deeper inside himself, and Adam had begun to worry that he would never break through.

Hell, the kid wouldn't even look at him.

Adam stepped into the bathroom, turning on the hot water at the sink and pulling out his shaving gear. He let the water flow over his hands as it warmed, until the scalding sensation focused his mind on the here and now, not the past or the future.

Adam studied his face, watching it blur as steam rose from the sink and slowly fogged the reflective surface. The blur softened his face, making him look like a ghostly version of his little brother. His dead little brother. Adam fought the urge to smash the mirror, instead forcing himself to start shaving, calmly, carefully. He saw Evan's face often enough in his dreams. Daytime hallucinations were simply the next stop on the way to Crazytown. Sometimes, in the dreams, Adam found himself in the living room of Evan's old house. Lainey rested on the couch, pregnant and happy, laughing. Evan rolled on the floor, wrestling with Danny as his little sister climbed onto his back, 'helping.' Inevitably, a ghostly double of Evan would appear beside him, watching the tableau along with him and smiling in a nostalgic kind of way. Adam would try to speak. Something. Anything. To ask for help? To beg him to come back? But before Adam could ever say a word, Evan would clap him on the shoulder and say, *'Don't let me down, man.'* And then he would disappear. They would all disappear. And Adam would be left alone, wondering how the hell he was going to keep his promise.

Damn it! Adam had cut himself with the razor. Served him right for not paying attention. Danny needed him here. Now. Not in dreamland.

He kept his shower brief, threw on some clothes, and made a quick scrambled eggs and toast for breakfast. He could see the lawn and the lake from the kitchen window. Danny sat in the same spot on the grass, motionless, while Adam prepared the meal. Finally, Adam cranked open the window and called out.

"Danny. Breakfast."

Only then did Danny move, rising slowly and trudging toward the house. When he came into the kitchen, he continued to avoid Adam's eyes, although his gaze had moved from Adam's shoes up to his knees. At this rate, Adam would be lucky to make eye contact with Danny by the time the kid graduated high school.

They ate in silence for a few minutes. Adam didn't believe in talking for the sake of talking. But before they left the table, he tackled the subject of the custody challenge.

"There's something important we need to discuss," he began.

Danny stilled. It killed Adam to realize that, at eight, Danny had learned to recognize the warning signs of a critical conversation. For him, 'we need to talk' involved somebody dying. Adam didn't keep him in suspense.

"Your grandparents are worried that you don't talk, so they've asked the judge to review your situation. They would like you to try living with them."

Adam paused to let the words sink in. Danny didn't respond, so he continued.

"I want you to stay with me. I promised your parents that I would take care of you, and I'm not going to let them down. However—"

At that, Danny did look up, briefly. Then he returned to studying the bits of egg left on his plate.

"—your opinion matters. The judge will want to know what you want. If you want to stay here, with me, it would help a lot if you could say it out loud."

Adam clenched his jaw and waited for a response. A nod would have been nice. Even a head twitch. Something. But he got nothing. Just another chance to study the top of Danny's head.

Patience. Understanding. Acceptance.

Adam took a deep breath.

"Let me know if you have an opinion. I'll let you know if anything changes."

Danny took that as a cue to leave. At least he remembered to clear his plate before escaping from the kitchen.

Adam leaned forward on his elbows, resting his forehead in his hands. Nothing in all his years of corporate deal-making had prepared him for this. The business world may have been cutthroat, but the rules of the game had been very clear: Do the analysis. Make the deal. Make money. Move on.

Parenting was a completely different game. There were no deals to be made, no numbers to analyze. Only the painful knowledge that he was failing Danny, and he didn't know how to fix it.

Given tools and time, Adam could restore a boat that had suffered years of neglect, but with Danny, he lacked both. He hadn't found the right tool to break through Danny's barriers, and he was running out of time. What made it worse was the feeling that he was missing something. Danny looked so much like Evan at that age. Adam should just know, instinctively, how to get through to him. They were both suffering. Hell, Danny's pain had to be ten times worse than Adam's. But Adam would gladly take on all of Danny's grief if only he could reach him, even just to give him a hug.

One way or another, Adam would find a way, but Danny certainly wasn't making it easy.

Callie left her instruments in the living room and found her mother sitting at the kitchen table, a flowered box full of letters and photos on the table in front of her. Dora was reading one of the letters, and she looked slightly sick. Roscoe stayed behind in the mudroom, sniffing around his empty food bowl as if more food might be hiding nearby.

"You okay, Mom?" asked Callie, modulating her harsh voice so as not to startle her mother. Dora jumped anyway, put a hand to her heart, and stuffed the letter back into the box.

"Oh, sweetie, you scared me half to death." Dora quickly put the lid on the box and tucked it into the corner of the window seat. "What on earth are you doing up so early? I thought you were still sleeping."

"Woke up," she said. "Couldn't sleep, so I went down to the summer house to play. I didn't want to wake you." Callie discovered that the kettle was hot and poured herself a cup of tea, warming her hands on the mug. "What's all that in the box?"

"Oh nothing," said Dora, her hands fluttering nervously, waving away Callie's question. "Just some old letters. Nothing to worry about. Nothing important." She got up from the table, giving the box one last glance, as if she wished she could lock it, or burn it. Then she started fussing in the refrigerator and making random comments about breakfast.

Her mother was a terrible liar.

If Dora said that the letters were 'nothing to worry about' then she must be worried about them. Under normal circumstances, her mother would talk endlessly about whatever bothered her, until she had worked through it or talked herself out. Callie tried to imagine what her mother might want to keep a secret from the family, but couldn't come up with anything plausible, except maybe naked photos from her art school days. She suppressed a giggle at the thought. Her curiosity piqued, Callie promised herself that she would sneak a peek at the box later, while her mother was up in the studio.

Roscoe whined from the mudroom, clearly upset by the delay in his breakfast. Dora hurried to help him, suddenly very interested in the health and eating habits of her 'best boy.' Callie leaned against the doorway, watching her mother fuss over the dog, and watching Roscoe bask in all the attention.

"Who's living next door?" asked Callie, deliberately casual, as Dora returned to the kitchen. "I keep seeing a boy." She really wanted to ask about Adam, but she also wanted to know what had happened to Evan and Lainey, who had been so happy together, and to find out why their son needed music so badly. For some reason, though, she was reluctant to mention actually meeting Danny this morning.

Dora stopped short.

"Didn't I tell you?" she asked, surprised. "Adam Reese lives here full time now."

The world stopped spinning. Callie grabbed the edge of the kitchen counter to keep from falling down.

"The boy's name is Danny." Dora gave Callie a pointed look. "You haven't been home in a long time, sweetie. If you had visited last summer, or come home for Christmas. . . ."

Dora let her last remark hang in the air as she pulled several boxes of berries from the fridge. Callie ignored the guilt trip. She was still reeling.

"Adam has a son?" asked Callie, grateful for the camouflage her rough voice provided. She had been so sure that the boy belonged to Evan. It had never even occurred to her that he might be Adam's. She cleared her throat and forced herself to ask. "Who did he marry?"

"Oh, he didn't," answered Dora, and Callie sagged with relief. Not that she had any right to be upset or relieved or anything else. She had relinquished her claim on Adam long ago. She slid onto a counter stool and tried to settle the her swirling thoughts.

"The whole thing is a big, sad mess if you ask me," continued Dora. "It happened last summer. Adam was still living overseas. Evan and Lainey and the kids lived down near Chicago, but they spent a lot of time up here at the cottage in the summer. They were on their way up for the Fourth. All that traffic, you know, and the other driver had been drinking. . . . Lainey and the little girl were killed instantly. Evan made it to the hospital, but eventually died of his injuries. Poor little Danny was the only survivor, and he didn't have a scratch on him."

Dora paused to wipe her eyes and pull out a pot for oatmeal.

"Adam flew home the second he found out, and he never went back. He brought the boy here. Now it's just the two of them."

She scooped the oats into the pot and added water, putting it on the stove to heat.

"That's horrible." Callie fought back tears. Her stilted conversation with Danny made perfect sense now. Thank goodness she hadn't poked and prodded him with a bunch of stupid

questions. She couldn't imagine losing her family. Maybe she
didn't come home as often as she should, and maybe she didn't
keep in touch like she should, but she knew that her sisters and her
parents were alive and well somewhere in the world. Adam had
lost his brother and little Danny was adrift, with only his uncle to
anchor him.

"That's not all," said Dora, looking over her shoulder at Callie.

"How could it be worse?" asked Callie, not sure she wanted to
know. She grabbed a tissue and scrubbed her face.

"The boy hasn't spoken since the day of the accident," said
Dora. "Certainly not at school. Luke would know. The teachers
have gotten very creative in working around his silence. They say
he doesn't speak at home, either. Can you imagine? He seems
perfectly normal. Quiet, obviously, and shy. But he doesn't talk.
At all."

Callie was speechless. She wanted to protest, 'Of course he talks!'
He had spoken to her just that morning. But she couldn't do it. A
wave of emotion, part fierce protectiveness, part raw pain, swept
over her. If Danny had trusted her with his music and his words
when he had trusted no one else, then she would not betray him.

Dora set down the spoon, turning to face Callie.

"Are you going to be okay, sweetie?"

Callie reached for another tissue and blew her nose.

"I'll be fine, Mom," she said. "It's just a shock. Even though I
haven't seen Evan and Lainey in years, it's so strange to think that
they're gone." Callie considered how to phrase the next bit so that it
wasn't completely a lie. "I'm glad you told me, though, in case I run
into Adam or Danny. I'd hate to say something dumb and make
either of them feel uncomfortable."

Dora smiled. "The weather is getting warmer, and I bet Danny
will start spending more time outside. Maybe you'll get a chance to
meet him, and to catch up with Adam."

Callie nodded blankly, her mind spinning. Would Danny come back to play music with her again? Would she really see Adam? By the time she and her mother sat down to eat, Callie had all but forgotten about the letters. Then she caught her mother's guilty glance at the flowered box. Callie smiled, distracting her with questions about the rest of the summer neighbors.

But when she came back later, the box was gone, and Callie was left to imagine what her open-book mother could possibly be hiding. Apparently there were a few secrets in this house after all.

CHAPTER FOUR

Eleven years ago

Callie floated just beneath the surface of the lake, her hair fanning out mermaid-style. The late-summer currents caressed her skin, teasing her now and again with a hint of the cooler water below. She loved this moment between breaths, when she could watch the sun rise through the rippling, blurry surface of the water. Watercolor reds, oranges, and yellows streaked the sky. Callie ignored the burning sensation in her lungs so she could drift for a few seconds longer.

In the distance, she heard a muffled thudding, understanding too late that it signaled running feet on the dock. Something large crashed into the water beside her. She sucked in a mouthful of water. A muscled arm circled her torso and yanked her toward the shore, towing her in an unbreakable lifesaving hold. Her would-be rescuer dragged her onto the rocky strip of beach, scraping her lower back and filling her bikini bottom with sand and pebbles. She wrenched herself free, coughing and hacking to clear her lungs.

The shock of recognition made her gasp, then cough all over again.

Adam.

"What the hell were you doing?" he demanded.

She cleared her throat and grabbed on to her anger. It was easier to understand than the other feelings swirling beneath.

"I was floating," she snapped. "It helps me think. What the hell were you doing? You nearly drowned me."

Callie's voice ended on a squeak and she stifled a hysterical laugh. Had she conjured him up out of her subconscious? She'd been waiting for him all summer—he hadn't been back since Memorial Day weekend, when she had cut her face—and now here he was, ruining the last morning before school started again.

"I thought you were dead," he said grimly. The gravity in his voice took the wind right out of Callie's sails.

"Oh."

Both Callie and Adam were soaked to the skin, she in her bikini and he in his shorts and T-shirt, but she didn't care. It was a hot, muggy morning, and it felt good to be wet. The rising sun warmed her. Pebbles dug painfully into her backside, but she ignored them. She was alone with Adam. Nothing else mattered.

He wiped off his face with his wet T-shirt, and she had a tantalizing glimpse of his skin. He was pale—that stupid job had kept him inside all summer—but muscled, and a light dusting of hair trailed from his chest down into his shorts. She swallowed and looked away.

"What were you thinking about underwater?" he asked.

There was no way to answer the question without sounding like an idiot. She could feel the blush creeping up her neck.

"I saved your life," he observed, a hint of mischief in his voice now that he had calmed down, "so you have to tell me."

"I was worried," she hedged.

"About what?"

If she wanted to stretch out this moment with Adam, she had better say something—anything—even the embarrassing truth. She took a deep breath.

"I'm going on a date tonight." The words came out in a rush.

"So?" Adam just looked confused.

"It's my first date. Ever," she confessed.

"You must be joking," he said. "You're, what, seventeen?"

She could feel her blush grow hotter.

"Sixteen," she corrected.

"And you've never been on a date."

"Not by myself."

"Well, you can hardly go on a date by yourself," he observed reasonably.

She rolled her eyes. "I've only been on group dates. Never just me and a guy."

"So why the worry? Is he a jerk or something?"

She snorted. As if she would go out with a jerk.

"No, he's very nice. It's just. . . ." If she said it out loud, *she* would sound like a jerk.

"Stop thinking so much and just say it," he ordered.

"I want my first kiss to be good." The words tumbled out in a rush. "What if I'm terrible at it? What if he knows somehow that it's my first time?"

That shut him up. Judging by the stunned expression on his face, she should have kept quiet. She buried her face on her knees and wrapped her arms around her head. Crash position, because she was about to crash and burn.

"Don't say anything," she pleaded, her voice muffled. "It's ridiculous. I know. I'm a total cliché. 'Sweet sixteen and never been kissed.' I can't believe I just said that out loud. Forget it. Just forget that I said anything. I'm sure it will be no big deal. I should be grateful to get it over with. It doesn't matter if it sucks."

He didn't say anything. Of course he didn't say anything. How could anybody respond to such a pathetic admission? There was no good way out of this horrible moment. Maybe if she sat here long enough he would just go away.

She waited for what seemed like eons, but he didn't move. When she couldn't stand the suspense any longer, she risked a peek and found him looking at her, his expression serious. Worried, even. He probably thought she was out of her mind. She groaned and buried her face again.

She felt a hand on her shoulder, hesitant but nice in his attempt to offer comfort. Was this pity? She would take pity. If she were lucky, maybe he would even put his arm all the way around her.

"The first time for anything is scary," he began, sounding like a teen advice column. He accompanied the words with an awkward pat on the back. She would have laughed if she didn't feel so much like crying.

"Hell," he continued, "I was terrified on my first day of work. A real job in a real office. What if I sucked? What if I wasn't cut out for the hotshot world of finance? I still feel that way most of the time. What if I crash and burn and have to go back to delivering pizzas?"

She snorted at that—the idea was completely ridiculous. It took her a minute to realize he was serious. The guy was impossibly perfect, and he didn't even know it.

She might be powerless to stop tonight's train wreck of a date, but she could certainly talk some sense into Adam. She lifted up her head looked into his dark blue eyes. They were sitting closer together than she had realized.

"We've known each other for a long time, right?" she asked.

"Right," he replied cautiously.

He removed his hand from her back. She paused, worried she had said the wrong thing, but he didn't back away.

"We may not hang out," she continued, "because you're a lot older than me, but you've been coming up to the lake in the summers for as long as I can remember."

He nodded.

"So it's fair to say that I know you. You look out for your brother. You don't torture the little kids. You're pretty handy with a first aid kit. And you pay attention when I play my songs at the bonfire."

He smiled at that.

"I may not talk much, but I watch," she said. "You're smart, you work hard, and you really care about getting things right." She narrowed her eyes at him so he would know she was serious. "There's no way you'll crash and burn. It's just not possible."

He pinked up a little around the ears.

"I think that may be the nicest thing anybody has ever said to me," he said at last.

Now she was blushing. Again. She looked out at the water and shrugged one shoulder.

"It's true," she said simply.

"Thanks," he said, giving her an awkward side-hug.

They sat in a comfortable kind of silence watching the sun rise over the water. She should have been appreciating the gorgeous colors of the sky, but all she could feel was the warmth and the weight of his arm and his hand on her shoulder. All she could think about was how close they were, practically thigh to thigh. She wasn't even sure how they had ended up so close together, but she had no intention of moving. An idea occurred to her that was so impossible—so breathtakingly bold—that she didn't know what to do. There was one simple way he could help her with her problem. All she had to do was ask. If it worked, well, her scalp tingled just thinking about it. If it didn't, she might ruin things with Adam forever.

She opened her mouth before she could chicken out.

"You could help me with my problem," she said softly, still looking out at the water.

He took forever to answer, and she felt every second of it in the pit of her stomach.

"I don't think that's such a good idea," he said. At least he hadn't jumped up and run screaming from the beach.

"What if I'm terrible at it?" she said.

"You'll do just fine," he said roughly.

"But what if I don't?" she insisted, turning to look at him. Her eyes dropped to his mouth, but that made it hard to breathe, so she looked back up. They were so close she could see his pupils, and she could see his indecision.

"Stop thinking so much and just do it," she whispered, her heart thumping wildly.

But he didn't move. He wasn't going to do it. Her moment was slipping away.

So she kissed him.

It was clumsy, and stupid, and fast. She sat blinking up at him, holding her breath, wondering what the startled expression on his face meant. Had she done it right? Was she supposed to kiss him with her mouth open like in the movies?

He let out a half laugh and her heart crumbled. She could feel the heat of the blush that must be turning her face bright red.

"It was awful, wasn't it?" she asked.

He smiled and shook his head.

"It was very sweet."

She closed her eyes. "This is a disaster," she said, starting to feel sick. She had ruined everything.

"Hey," he said, reaching over to stroke her cheek. Little shivers raced from his fingers down her neck.

"When the time comes," he said softly, "don't worry so much. You'll do fine."

He kissed her earlobe. Her heart stopped beating, then started up again, this time fiercer and faster than before.

"Just relax," he said.

He kissed the corner of her jaw.

"Don't rush things."

Then her cheek. Then the corner of her mouth.

She couldn't breathe. She couldn't move.

Finally, his lips touched hers and she sighed. He was perfect.

He kissed her so gently, so softly, for maybe two heartbeats. Then he rested his forehead against hers.

"You'll be amazing," he said.

Somewhere along the way, her hands had crept up the front of his wet T-shirt. When she felt him begin to pull away, she tightened her grip.

"Callie," he said. She knew that voice. He was going to tell her to stop.

She leaned in and kissed him again, this time softly, the way he had kissed her. He held very still. He wasn't giving in, but he wasn't pulling away either. She kissed him again, this time on the corner of his mouth. Then on his cheek, and then on his ear, the way he had done with her.

Her heart thumped so hard in her chest she thought she might be having a heart attack.

"Am I doing it right?" she whispered in his ear.

He nodded, his movements jerky and his breathing ragged. She smiled and let her arms wind around his shoulders. When she brought her lips back to his, he groaned, pulling her closer and opening his mouth to devour hers. He wove the fingers of his other hand into her wet hair and held her tightly against him. She lost the ability to think. She fell in slow motion, supported by his hands, drinking in his kisses, her arms wrapped around his neck. Sensation overwhelmed her: the rough sand on her back, the cold wet fabric of his shirt pressed against her chest, the heat of his body, the frantic rhythm of their breathing.

Suddenly his mouth was gone. His forehead pressed against hers as they both fought to catch their breath.

"I'm so sorry," he whispered. He would have pulled away, but she held on tight.

"Don't you dare apologize," she answered fiercely.

"I have to," he said, shifting his weight onto one elbow so that the other hand could stroke her cheek, his fingertips tracing her faint scar from earlier in the summer. "If it had to happen—and let's be clear, this should never have happened—I should have kept it gentle." He demonstrated, kissing her softly while his hand smoothed her hair back. "I should have let you breathe." He kissed her again, achingly kind. His fingers trailed down her neck and traced her collar bone. She whimpered, arching her back to get closer to him.

He deepened the kiss, but not like before. He held back, and she growled with frustration.

"You're much too young," he said, his voice laced with regret. He kissed her one last time before resting his forehead against hers. "I got carried away. I'm sorry."

"Well I'm not," she declared. She would have wrapped her arms around him and kissed him again, but he pulled away, sat up, and studied at the sunrise sky.

"This has to stop," he said.

She stretched out long on the sand, her body on fire, feeling violently alive.

"Why?" she demanded.

He laughed. "You are a dangerous young woman, Callie James."

"Yes." She grinned. "Yes I am."

Was it wrong to be so pleased with herself? Despite the rocky start, this was *exactly* what she had been hoping for in a first kiss.

She lay silent in the sand for a few moments longer and then he pulled her up to sit beside him, right back where they started. He brushed the sand off her back. She leaned her head on his shoulder, he put his arm around her, and together they looked out at the water. Soon the joggers would be out with their dogs and the water skiers would break the calm, but for now, they had the lake to themselves.

"This can't happen again, Callie," he said. "You're sixteen. I'm twenty-two. Your parents would kill me if they found out, and then send my dead body to jail."

"I know." She gave him a crooked smile. "But it was totally worth it."

He caught her hand and pressed his lips to her palm, then nodded. She curled her fingers around the imprint of his kiss.

He stood, then offered her a hand to help her up, but she shook her head.

"I'm going to stay here for a little while."

He studied her for a moment.

"You okay?" he asked.

She smiled and nodded. 'Okay' didn't even begin to describe it. Blissful. Rapturous. Delirious. Ecstatic. She finally had a reason to use all those crazy vocabulary words from English class.

"Enjoy your first date, Callie James."

She watched him walk away until she couldn't see him anymore, then she looked back out at the lake. Adam had given her the perfect first kiss, and she would never forget it.

Adam woke abruptly, his heart pounding, unsure of what had yanked him so suddenly from the depths of sleep. Not the phone. Not a nightmare. The house lay still in the predawn light.

Then he heard it. The creak of a floorboard. The slow squeal of the screen door. Danny was sneaking out again.

Adam forced himself to be still, fought the urge to race after Danny and haul his ass back home. He needed to find out what the hell Danny did every morning, and there was only one way to know for sure.

Rolling out of bed, Adam grabbed a pair of jeans and a T-shirt off the floor, pulling them on as he moved through the dimly lit house. He jammed his feet into a pair of shoes by the back door and slipped out as quietly as Danny had just moments before, easing the door shut behind him. The chilly air cleared his mind and sharpened his senses. Although he couldn't see or hear Danny, he could just make out a trail of small footprints leading across the frosted grass and down the hill toward the lake. For once, Adam was grateful for the late spring.

When he reached the shore path, Adam paused to listen. He heard the scrape of a footstep and the click of a storm door coming from the direction of the commons. He approached slowly, finding a spot where he could spy on the summer house. What he saw stopped him in his tracks.

Callie had come home.

He recognized her silhouette, and the long blond curls shielding her face. She had a guitar in her lap, and he heard the muffled sounds of music coming through the storm windows. Danny sat in one of the wicker chairs, his back to Adam and his full attention on Callie.

Cold seeped through the thin cotton of his T-shirt, and he grew increasingly upset. He wasn't sure who frustrated him more, Danny and his flagrant disregard for the rules, or Callie and her power to knock him on his ass after so many years.

Did she consider that Danny might be out here without permission? Did she even know that Danny belonged to him?

Adam tried to set aside his turbulent emotions, but it wasn't easy. First he needed to accept that Danny had sought out the company of a stranger rather than turning to him. Then he had to wade through the confusion of Callie's return. His reaction to her was so strong that he was afraid to examine it too closely. Underneath it all was a layer of regret that had solidified over the years into something approaching anger. He couldn't tell if the anger was directed at Callie or at himself, so he tried to stick to the facts.

First, there was no way that Callie would be sticking around. He had followed her career closely enough to know that this was her moment. The band was poised to break into the big time. Only a fool would walk away right when all the hard work was about to pay off, and Callie was no fool.

Second, Adam didn't want Danny getting attached to a short-timer. Adam knew all too well how much it hurt to watch Callie walk away. The kid didn't need to go through that.

Adam wasn't sure how long he waited, spying on the pair of them from his chilly vantage point down by the shore. He couldn't see much, and he could hear even less, but he couldn't seem to tear himself away.

As the sun rose, the animal chatter grew louder, and Adam's stiff muscles began to cramp. He stretched, rubbing some circulation back into his arms, and finally retreated to the relative warmth of the cottage. He had uncovered the reason behind Danny's early morning disappearances, but instead of satisfaction, he felt only defeat.

CHAPTER FIVE

Callie accepted her guitar back from Danny and placed it gently in its case. She reached out to shake his hand.

"Thanks for a great jam session, my friend," she said. "Same time tomorrow?"

He lit up at the invitation. He shook her hand, clearly feeling very adult, and nodded enthusiastically, reminding her of a puppy whose tail wags its entire body. Roscoe yawned and stretched and then climbed to his feet, nudging Danny's hand until he got his good-bye head scratch.

After hearing Danny's story from her mother, Callie hadn't been sure what to expect this morning. The possibility that she could run into Adam again at any moment had also put her on edge. But Danny had turned up, still cautious, as if he expected her to send him home this time. They had played a lot of music and hadn't talked much. It seemed to be what they both needed.

"Same time tomorrow," he answered, his voice sounding less rusty than the day before.

Danny raced out of the summer house, the storm door slamming shut behind him, and she could hear the slapping of his feet on the path as he headed home. She smiled to herself and turned back to her instrument, ready to begin work on her own material. Roscoe resumed his napping position.

Callie continued working, caught up in the peace and sunshine of the morning, until the rumble of the school bus broke her concentration. Funny how she recognized the distinctive sound, even after all this time. She listened to the squeak of the brakes as it stopped to pick up Danny, then the roar of its engine as it lumbered on down the road. As the sound faded into silence, the peace was punctuated by a growl from her stomach. She laughed and began putting away the instruments. Roscoe understood that signal and stretched, then shook off his morning nap. Time for breakfast.

"Callie," said a deep voice from the doorway.

Her lungs seized up. She lost her grip on the fiddle and it tumbled onto the cushioned bench. She was grateful for the distraction it provided because it gave her time to recover from the shock.

Adam.

He didn't look anything like she had expected—not that she had really expected to see him again. But on those rare occasions when he had floated through her dreams, she had always envisioned him as Mr. Business Man, buttoned up in a suit, looking like the kind of guy who lives halfway around the world and flies on private jets.

The man standing before her was none of those things. Instead of a suit, he wore faded jeans, work boots, and a plaid flannel shirt over a white tee. She swallowed a hysterical giggle, realizing that he looked exactly like the Brawny paper-towel guy. The soft fabrics wrapped around the contours of his body in a way that a suit never would. The idea that once, long ago, she had wrapped herself around those contours seemed impossible, like something she had read in a book or seen in a movie. That memory must belong to somebody else.

Now he was here, in the flesh, and she could feel her blush rising and her throat closing up. Good grief, he was all man now, and more intense than she remembered. She had no idea what to say. Everything she could think of sounded silly or pathetic.

Electricity danced across her palms and she rubbed her hands together, trying to defuse it. She shot a hostile glance at Roscoe, the worthless watchdog, who hadn't bothered to sound the alert. Seriously? "The Road Not Taken" walks up and knocks on the door, and it doesn't even merit a growl? The dog didn't even have the sense to hang his head. He stretched forward, then back, shook his hind leg, and finally sauntered over to investigate. Rather than growling, as he should have, he began sniffing, as if Adam might have pockets full of treats. The traitor even began to wag his tail. She sighed in disgust.

Adam simply waited in the doorway, ignoring Roscoe and staring at Callie, arms crossed, his face serious. She had the uncomfortable feeling that he wasn't thrilled to see her.

"It's been a long time," he said. She couldn't read his face.

She nodded. "I'm sorry about your brother."

His jaw tightened, but he didn't answer.

She couldn't breathe properly. The air in the summer house seemed thick and hot.

"I need you to do me a favor," he said.

"What is it?" she asked.

How had she forgotten the color of his eyes? The same dark blue as Danny's, like the lake on a spring morning. Today they looked very cold.

"I need your help with Danny," he replied. "He's been sneaking out of the house every morning for weeks," he continued. "I'm sure you can imagine how disturbing it was for me to discover that he's been meeting—secretly—with a complete stranger."

She sucked in a breath, deeply hurt.

"Wait a minute," she said. "I only got here yesterday."

His mouth tightened. He would have spoken, but she barreled right over him.

"And even if I had been here the whole time," she continued, "I'm not some creepy pedophile that he met on the Internet." She choked down the lump in her throat. "I'm not a stranger. You know me."

"I did," he agreed, and the past tense hurt, "but you're a stranger to Danny." Adam's voice was cold. "He should know better than to talk with you, and you should know better than to let him."

Out of the hurt, anger was rising. She stood up and crossed the room to meet him head-on.

"Give me a break," she said, unable to connect the stranger before her with the Adam she had known so long ago. "Danny knows I live next door, so I don't count as a stranger. He and I play music together. There's nothing disturbing about it."

"It's disturbing to me," he said, "and I'd like you to stop."

"Just like that?" she asked, with a casual snap of the fingers. She thought about Danny's joy in playing, and how much she had enjoyed sharing the music with him. "We can't play music anymore?"

"Just like that."

"Who are you?" she whispered.

Callie felt sick. When had Adam turned into this coldhearted jerk? Did he not understand how important music was to his nephew? Taking music away would be like drowning him in all the big emotions that he couldn't control—emotions like her own rising indignation and outrage. Her self-control slipped, and her answer spilled out before she could stop it.

"No."

"Excuse me?" His eyes narrowed. Callie clenched her hands.

"No, I will not stop playing music with Danny," she repeated.

"Why not?" He seemed both annoyed and genuinely surprised. Either he wasn't used to people saying 'no,' or he really didn't understand that music was important to Danny.

"Danny clearly loves music," she said. "It's as necessary to him as breathing. If he wants to play music with me, I'm not going to turn him away."

"How can you say that?" he demanded. "You're not his parent. You hardly know him. How could you possibly imagine that you know what's best for him?"

"I would never hurt a child," she said, insulted that he would even think it.

"You know nothing about him! You could hurt him without even realizing it."

"You must have seen us playing music together," she said. "Did you hear him play? Did you see how happy he was? Why would you take that away from him?"

She had hit a nerve. His face closed up and his body stiffened.

"Won't you be the one to take it away from him?" he asked, his quiet tone more menacing than outright anger.

"What are you talking about?"

"I doubt you're planning to move back home," he said. "What happens to Danny when you leave?"

"I'll be here for a month," she answered cautiously. "We can play a lot of music in a month."

"And then what?"

"Then I leave," she admitted.

"That's what I thought," said Adam.

"So what if I can't promise forever?" she asked. "Nobody can. Not even you, and you know it."

He didn't visibly flinch, but she could tell by the clench of his jaw that she had scored a second hit.

"What I *can* do is be honest about how long I'll be here. You can't ask more than that."

"I can, and I will," he returned, and she didn't like the determination in his voice. "I can thank you for helping me discover that

Danny loves music, and I can find him another teacher, someone who will be here for the long term."

"But—"

"I won't risk it."

He stepped forward, close enough that she could feel the heat of his body, but she was too worked up to be intimidated. For a moment his mask slipped and she saw the pain behind those eyes, but, like Danny, he refused to let it out.

"I can't risk it," he said softly. "Danny needs stability more than music." He turned away. "I'll make sure he doesn't bother you again."

Before Callie could say anything, Adam walked away. She was left gaping at the now-empty doorway, sputtering, all the things she could have said—should have said—racing through her brain.

He disappeared down the lake path. Callie stared hard after him, willing him to reconsider, but he didn't turn around. She sat down hard on the cushioned bench, the very same bench where she had given herself body and soul to someone named Adam. She wouldn't corrupt the beauty of that memory by connecting it with the man she had met today. She didn't like the new Adam very much.

Muttering under her breath about the idiocy of men in general and one in particular, Callie finished packing up the instruments, gathered them up, and stalked up the hill toward the house. Roscoe trailed behind at a safe distance. When she got to the porch—more than a little out of breath—she unloaded the instruments and turned to look back down the hill.

"Arrrrggghhh!" Callie stomped her foot. She hated feeling powerless.

Dora poked her head out the back door onto the porch.

"Breakfast?" she chirped. "I was about to make some oatmeal."

"Later," said Callie. "Right now I need to deal with something."

She pressed her mouth into a firm line. Just because her own life was falling apart didn't mean that she couldn't fight for someone else.

She marched right back out the screen door, down the steps, and headed for the path through the woods that led next door, leaving Dora and her questions and the traitor Roscoe behind. She followed the path that led to the old barn, betting that she would find Adam there rather than at the cottage. He had updated it, painting it red so it looked like something out of a children's storybook. A sign mounted above the massive barn doors read "Reese Boat Restoration." The large doors must be the entrance for the boats. A smaller, people-sized door to one side bore a "Welcome" sign. She peeked in the window next to the door, but it was dark inside and she couldn't see much. Not very welcoming.

She began to feel foolish, standing outside the door and shifting her weight from foot to foot as she tried to figure out what to do. If she really intended to fight for Danny, she should barge right in and make her case. If her sister Mel were here, she would already be through the door and going head-to-head with Adam. Actually, Mel would have won the debate back at the summer house, with no need for a second round. Callie, however, was not Mel. She had used up most of her adrenaline on the march over and couldn't seem to make her hand turn the door handle. So she rang the bell.

She wasn't being a giant chicken, really, just polite. She jumped at the obnoxious clanging of a cow bell somewhere in the deep shadows of the barn's interior. Adam must have developed a weird sense of humor.

"Coming." The clipped voice came from somewhere in the barn. No turning back now. After a few seconds, she heard footsteps and then the door swung inward. He stood framed in the opening, his face in shadow.

"What." His voice was no more welcoming than his barn.

Callie took a deep breath and tried to imagine what Mel would do.

Adam wasn't sure what he was supposed to do with Callie, now that she had followed him to his last safe haven. He was still so frustrated with Danny for sneaking around, and with her for letting him, that he couldn't trust himself to be civil. The anger might be completely irrational and, perhaps, a little excessive, but it kept him grounded while all his other emotions ran amok.

What he really needed was a chance to cool off.

She opened her mouth to speak, and he realized that he just couldn't handle it. He turned on his heel and strode back to his current project, an old wooden Chris-Craft named *Speakeasy*. He shut Callie out of his mind and gave his attention to the boat in front of him. She was long and sleek and gorgeous, but all that beauty masked serious problems. He had stripped her down to the frame and found dry rot. The damage had accumulated over time, weakening the inner framework until repair was no longer an option. Minor problems he could fix, but the lower transom bow would need to be completely rebuilt. He would need patience to bring her back.

He heard footsteps behind him and stilled.

The work lights bathed the *Speakeasy* in an intense white glow, in stark contrast to the dimness of the rest of the barn's interior. He liked it that way. With the barn windows shut and the work lights on, he could focus entirely on the labor of love in front of him— and shut out the rest of the world. He could think about the things in his life that were going well, and forget for a few hours about his failings.

Callie moved through the shadows, circling the perimeter of his workspace until she reached the far side and faced him across the stripped-down shell. She stepped into the pool of light, her stance and her eyes filled with challenge. She was small—he had forgotten just how small—and so much more intense than he remembered. With her long honey-colored hair pulled back in a ponytail, she looked young, unpredictable, and slightly wild.

He leaned against an unused sawhorse and folded his arms, surrendering to the inevitable. In all the times that he had imagined running into Callie again, not once had he pictured this. Having a stilted conversation laced with regretful undertones, yes. Hooking up one last time before their lives swept them apart again, yes. But fighting? Never.

"I need you to do me a favor," she said, throwing his own words back in his face.

"What favor would that be?" he inquired.

"Let Danny play music with me," she answered.

Oddly, instead of raising his hackles, her words made him smile. *Stop thinking so much and just do it.*

They didn't need to fight about this. If he could just explain, if she would just listen, then maybe she would back off and help him instead of driving him crazy.

"Can we try this again?" he asked. He walked slowly around the stern until they were face to face, then held out a hand. "Callie, it's great to see you. It's been a long time."

They could manage a handshake after all this time, couldn't they?

"Adam," she responded cautiously, reaching out to take his hand.

They had touched each other in many different ways, years ago, but never a handshake. She had a firm grip, her skin cool and soft except for the callused fingertips. He held on longer than he should, unable to help himself. He let his fingertips slide to the pulse point on her wrist and felt the nervous stutter of her heartbeat before he released her hand.

"How are you?" he began, still trying for a fresh start.

"Why don't you want me to play music with Danny?" she interrupted.

He sighed. No fresh start.

"It's been a tough year," Adam replied, "for both of us. The last thing Danny needs is to get attached to someone who's just passing through. It's hard enough for him to connect with the adults that are already a part of his life and committed to him." Adam could feel himself 'getting intense,' as his brother used to say, and tried to ease up. "It's my job to protect him, and I don't want him to get hurt when you leave."

If Adam was hoping for sympathy, he didn't get any.

"So your answer is to stop him from doing something he loves? That makes no sense."

"I'm not going to stop him from making music," Adam protested, "but I do think it's important to know where he is, who he's with, and to steer him toward solid relationships. The only thing I know for sure is that you're going to leave."

The image of her walking away that night after the bonfire still haunted him.

"That an excuse," she said flatly.

"It's a fact. Danny needs people in his life who are going to stick around."

He stepped closer, intending to say more, but the hairline scar on her cheek distracted him. He remembered everything about that day. Evan showing off for Lainey. Callie trusting him to patch her up. That was the summer it all started, and Adam could only hope that Danny would remember how much his parents had loved him.

"What if I can help Danny while I'm here?" pleaded Callie. "Maybe he can relax with me because he knows I won't be around forever. Maybe I'm exactly what he needs."

"Maybe you are," he admitted, "but I can't take the risk. The stakes are too high."

Adam hadn't shared the details of the custody dispute with anybody other than the Doc, but he would tell Callie if he had to.

"Didn't you say that Danny has trouble opening up to the adults in his life?"

"I did," he answered. Nice of her to rub it in.

"Well he opened up to me," she said.

"Listening to music—even playing music—isn't the same as opening up," said Adam. He turned to walk away, just to put some distance between them. Then she lobbed her grenade.

"He talked to me."

Adam froze.

"I asked him where he learned to play," she continued, addressing her words to his back, "and he said that his dad taught him. They used to play songs together, and they would always play sad ones and make his mom cry."

Adam could feel his whole body tense. He put a hand on the stern of the boat, anchoring himself on the one solid thing in the room. After all these months of silence, Danny had spoken to a total stranger. Twin waves of relief and resentment swamped him. He closed his eyes and searched for the right words, speaking his reply to the darkness rather than turning to face her.

"Even if you can help Danny," he responded, measuring his words carefully, "at some point you'll leave. I know how it feels to watch you walk away. I don't want him to go through that."

He turned slowly to find Callie holding her ground, but her eyes had softened.

"It's not the same," she said softly.

Adam could see that this conversation was hard for her, too, and somehow that made him feel better.

"He would know right from the start that we only have a short time together," she continued. "What if this is his chance? What if he doesn't open up again for another year? Are you willing to risk that, too?"

Adam didn't answer. He couldn't answer. He could feel both sides of the knife, waiting to cut him. He didn't trust his judgment where Callie was concerned. He didn't want to be seduced by the possibility of a quick breakthrough when he had spent the last year trying to build trust with Danny. All that hard work could be lost if Callie's departure hit Danny too hard. But she was right. What if his way never worked? What if he lost Danny to Lainey's parents? What if Danny remained locked inside himself forever—until he found a different, more destructive means of escape? That was Adam's greatest fear, and his worst nightmare.

"Tell me again how long you'll be here," he demanded.

"At least a month," she answered. "I know it's not long, but maybe during that time I could get him to play some music with my Dad as well. It could smooth the transition when I leave."

Adam needed room to breathe, away from the intensity of her face. She glowed under the work lights in a way that made it hard for him to think clearly.

"At least consider it," she begged. "Please let me help."

Adam hated not knowing the odds, hated the fact that he needed help. He needed to think this through before he made any decisions, and it was hard to think around Callie.

"I'll consider it."

He frowned at Callie's rising smile.

"Let me be clear," he said. "You need to stay away from Danny until I have a chance to talk to the school psychologist. And—" he held up a hand to stop her from interrupting. "Once I make a decision, I expect you to abide by it, even if you don't like it. Understood?"

Callie's smile faded. He ignored an inexplicable stab of guilt and waited for her acknowledgment.

"Understood," she said shortly.

"Good," he said. "I'll let you know tomorrow."

He needed her to leave. He needed to think, away from those eyes that could see right through him. There was nothing more to say, so he turned away, grabbed a putty knife, and started hacking at an ancient layer of glue on the transom. After a moment, he heard her footsteps retreating. The cowbell clanged when she opened the door and left the building.

He stopped before he could damage the underlying wood. She had knocked him sideways, and he needed to find his footing. If Evan could see him now. . . . Adam shook his head. Thankfully his little brother would never see him like this. Adam was supposed to be the strong one, the one with the answers. But after losing Evan, all he had left were questions.

Callie closed the barn door behind her and leaned back against it, her heart still thumping in her chest. She had done it. She had stood her ground for the first time in years and it felt amazing.

She had always been courageous when it came to Adam.

The caress on her wrist, both unexpected and intimate, had taken her by surprise, reverberating through her body, confusing her. Unlocking memories buried years ago. But she had rallied. Instead of crumpling into a stuttering, blushing mess, she had channeled her sister Mel, imagining what Mel would say, and what Mel would do, and it had worked. No wonder Mel was so outspoken.

Pushing away from the door, she sprinted lightly back home, her spirits rising with every step. This new, grumpy Adam had tried to squelch her enthusiasm with his parting shot, but she wouldn't let him. She had earned her moment of triumph and she was going to enjoy it.

CHAPTER SIX

Ten years ago

He was back. Adam had finally come back. Callie spotted him from across the commons, surrounded by a pack of the older boys. She couldn't believe it had been an entire school year. Her junior year was over, and she had only one year of high school left before she could finally start her life. Adam had been out there in the real world this whole time. She wanted to hear all about it, but mostly she wanted to find a way to kiss him again.

It took forever to connect. The big barbecue on Memorial Day weekend was the kickoff to the summer season. Everybody wanted to catch up after the long winter. She was stuck with her girlfriends, he was stuck with his guy friends, and people would notice if one of them made a point of seeking out the other. The current flowing between them, as tangible to her as liquid lightning, seemed invisible to everyone else.

Only after the bonfire did he drift over to talk to her, when most everyone else had disappeared into the darkness in pairs and clumps. The fire had settled down to embers, providing just enough light for Adam to pick his way over the log benches and sit beside her. The moon, barely a sliver, didn't help much. The lampposts along the road were far enough away that the entire commons felt dark and private, perfect for all sorts of mischief.

Had he been paying attention? Had he recognized the song she had written for him? She hadn't exactly been subtle, calling it "A First Time for Everything." Nobody else knew about that kiss. Not her sisters. Not her friends. Definitely none of the boys she had dated this year. They would have no idea what inspired the song, but Adam should know. She had saved it for last—for him. The other boys could think it was about them if they wanted to. That's what they seemed like to her: boys. She tolerated their company because she wanted to go to the prom like everybody else, but they needed some serious practice when it came to kissing. She tried to avoid it if she could.

Her heart thumped painfully in her chest, as if it wanted to jump right out and into his lap. That's what she wanted to do. But what if he'd met some amazing woman in the city? A lot could change in a year.

They sat in silence for a few minutes and she relaxed. She wasn't imagining the energy that hummed between them. He felt it, too.

"I liked your new song," he said at last.

She smiled in the darkness.

"Thanks. I found our encounter . . . inspiring."

"Is that how you think of it? An encounter?" he asked, as he leaned forward to rest his elbows on his knees and stare at the fire.

"I try not to analyze it, or classify it, or categorize it," she answered. "Ruins the perfection of the memory."

He rubbed his forehead in a gesture she had come to associate with his internal tug-of-war.

"There are a million reasons we should try to forget about that day," he said.

"Such as . . . ?" she asked, curious to know what would be at the top of his list. In her mind, there were a lot of 'shoulds' warring with one overwhelming 'want.'

"I have the advantage of experience. If we got involved, it would be too easy for me to manipulate you."

"Hmmm," she said thoughtfully. "So you're worried that I might be overwhelmed by your manliness and become obsessed. Maybe stalk you?" She didn't bother to hide her snicker.

He gave her an irritated glance. "It's not funny," he protested. "Putting aside the legalities—which are a big deal—I don't want to be some creepy old guy who's corrupting you. You're supposed to be dating guys your own age, figuring this stuff out with them."

She gave a snort of disgust. "Yeah, that's been fun," she said, her voice low and sharp. "I've tried dating guys my own age this year. We're like the blind leading the blind and it sucks. They're too nervous to talk like normal human beings, and they're so drunk on hormones that they stick their tongues down your throat and try to dry hump you. It's nasty."

"Oh," he said.

"You can see why I might fantasize about an older guy who actually knows what he's doing."

"So now I'm a boy-toy," he groused.

She smiled.

"No, you're my man-toy. You should feel honored."

He grunted, not sounding pleased.

"Listen," she said abruptly, seizing her boldness before it evaporated. "I'm going to be up at sunrise for a swim. I'm going to make out with the first guy I see. I hope it's you."

With that, she stood up, grabbed her guitar case, and headed home, hoping every step of the way that her gamble would pay off.

He wasn't coming. The crushing weight of disappointment took her breath away, but she squeezed her eyes shut and scrubbed at her face, willing the tears to crawl back inside their tear ducts and stay put. If he was too chicken to acknowledge this thing between them, then that was his loss.

She ducked beneath the surface of the water one last time, then climbed on the dock, toweled off, and slid her feet back into her flip-flops. She hadn't taken two steps when she saw him standing on the shore path. The tears, already primed, came out in a rush, and she swiped them away with her towel. She marched down the pier, the boards thumping beneath her feet, and stopped a few feet away from him. Fury and relief and joy swirled inside her. He looked angry, which only unsettled her more.

"I thought you weren't coming," she said, hating the fact that her face must be all blotchy and he would know she'd been crying.

"I wasn't," he answered bluntly.

"Oh." She tried to sound like she didn't care. "What changed your mind?"

His gave her an assessing look. "I realized that if I didn't, you might hook up with somebody else."

She stiffened.

"Isn't that what you want?" she tossed back. "Maybe I would find someone more appropriate. Someone my own age." She threw his objections in his face, wanting him to admit . . . something. She must have scored a hit, because his face hardened and that caveman look came into his eyes. He stepped closer, so close that she had to tip her head back to see his face.

"I realized," he ground out, "that the local boys are no match for you, and that the only person in danger of being manipulated is me."

"I didn't—"

"Ah, but you did," he said, reaching up to cup her cheek. At his touch, the anger between them shifted, changing into a kind of heat. The river of emotion needed to pour out, and it did, flowing down her cheeks in hot streaky tears. "Intentional or not, it worked like a charm." He pulled her closer, so that the tips of her breasts brushed against him. "All I could think about all night was you coming up out the water in that ridiculously small bikini and throwing your arms around some other guy. I don't think I slept all night."

She hiccoughed, caught somewhere between laughter and sobs.

"I didn't sleep, either," she choked. "I've been here since before sunrise."

He leaned forward, touching his forehead to hers. "Is there somewhere we could go?" he asked, his voice suddenly hoarse. "We need to figure this out."

She nodded, then pulled away, grabbing him by the hand. She knew the perfect place. The summer house.

"Follow me."

Adam worked on the boat until he could barely stand. He returned to the house in search of food, drink, and another shower. Without the boat to hold his attention, his thoughts circled around and around the situation with Danny. He had to call Doc Archer, but how was he supposed to explain what had happened?

Oh, by the way, Doc, Danny sneaks out every morning, disappears to God knows where. Turns out he's been hanging out with the neighbors' daughter, playing music and talking up a storm. Who knew?

After all these months, the one place the kid never wanted to be was in the same room with Adam.

He poured himself a cup of coffee and sat down at the kitchen table. There was no denying the truth. He had failed. No matter how much he wanted to connect with Danny, his nephew still didn't trust him. Maybe Kat was right. Maybe Lainey's parents could succeed where he could not. He had to do what was best for Danny, even if it meant breaking his promise. Even if it meant letting Danny go.

From the depths of memory, his brother's voice bubbled up, so clear after all this time that it caught Adam by surprise.

'Come home for a visit. You could use a break, and some time at the lake. The company can survive without you for a week or two.'

How many times had he put his brother off because of some crisis at work? How many chances had he missed?

'It's Thanksgiving, man. Who does a deal over Thanksgiving? Book the flight home. You can stay with us. Shoot some hoops. Wrestle with the kids. It will be the opposite of the traditional Reese family Thanksgiving. I promise.'

If it weren't for Danny, Adam would have run from the memories months ago. He would have sold everything and moved far away. Fiji, maybe. But he was stuck, like Danny, in this life, here and now. Nothing could bring back the dead, and nothing could make the memories go away. He would have to find a way to survive without letting the guilt drag him under.

Adam shoved the memories away and grabbed the phone. Once he reached the Doc, he kept his explanation brief.

"I've got some progress to report, Doc, and a question."

"Great. Let's hear it."

"Turns out Danny likes music, and that he used to play guitar with his father. I had no idea, or I would have suggested it sooner."

"Better late than never," said the Doc. "So what are you going to do with that information?"

"That's what I wanted to ask you about. You know Mr. James, the music teacher?"

"Of course."

"His daughter Callie is in town for a month or so. Danny's been hanging around her whenever she plays music down by the water. Do you think there's any harm in letting them spend time together, even though she's only here for a short time?"

Adam didn't mention the fact that Danny had spoken to Callie. He wanted to keep that nugget of good news to himself for a while longer. He also left out his personal history with Callie.

"Well, we've talked about Danny's need for stability and predictability. You want the anchors in his life to be strong. But she doesn't need to be an anchor. She would be more of a catalyst for change. I see no harm in him taking music lessons while Callie is visiting, as long as he understands that she'll be leaving. You don't want her departure to come as a surprise."

"Understood," replied Adam. "Any other words of wisdom?"

Doc Archer laughed. "Sounds like you're on the right track. I'm glad that Danny's showed an interest in something. Maybe next you can come up with an activity for the both of you to do together."

"Right," said Adam. "Working on it."

Danny would be home from school any minute. While Adam waited, he needed something to do other than pace around the kitchen, so he went back up to the barn to assess the benches and seating from inside the *Speakeasy*. He had placed each piece carefully around the perimeter of his workspace during the tear-down and ignored them ever since. Adam loved working with wood, but leather and vinyl made him crazy. They were too pliable. Too unpredictable. Upholstery always put him in a bad mood.

Today, however, he was already in a bad mood, which made it the perfect time to take a closer look. After a quick survey of the wreckage, he concluded that the upholstery was a total loss—too many cracks and tears. But it was more than just a question of re-covering the existing cushions. The foam needed to be replaced as well. It had begun to crumble, and there was no cure for the musty smell other than starting fresh. He shrugged, resigned to the inevitable. Renewal takes time and hard work.

When he heard the sound of the bus coming over the hill, Adam turned off the work lights and headed out to meet Danny. They walked together back down to the cottage.

"So how was school?" asked Adam, holding the back door open.

He didn't really expect an answer. Doc Archer kept telling him to 'listen to Danny,' to 'ask Danny' and 'trust Danny,' which sounded great in theory, except for the fact that *Danny wouldn't talk to him.*

"Why don't you put your backpack in your room and I'll make you a snack," Adam continued, hoping that food would lure Danny back out. Thankfully, it did. Once the boy was settled at the kitchen table with a bowl of warmed-up ravioli, Adam brought up the early-morning music sessions.

"Danny, I know where you've been going in the mornings."

Danny stopped with a spoonful of pasta halfway to his mouth. He set the spoon down slowly and stared at Adam, waiting for him to say more. Eye contact at last.

"I'm glad that you found something you like to do," continued Adam, watching Danny's face closely. "I had no idea that you played the guitar, or that you might like music lessons."

A strange expression crossed Danny's face when Adam used the phrase 'music lessons,' as though he didn't like Adam's choice of words, but Adam pressed on, wanting to get to the heart of the matter.

"Callie and I talked this morning about her plans for the future. Did you know that she's only going to be in town for a few more weeks?"

Adam waited until Danny responded with a nod. It pained him to realize that this was the closest he had come to a conversation with Danny since before the accident.

"It doesn't make sense for you to work with her for a few short weeks. Now that I know you like music, I can arrange for you to have lessons with another teacher. Someone local, who will be here for the long term."

Danny shook his head no. He had turned white, his freckles standing out clearly against the pale skin of his nose. Adam continued with his proposal.

"She's very nice, and I can tell that you like her, but the more you work with her, the more you'll miss her when she's gone." Adam swallowed the lump in his throat. "I don't want that for you."

"No," whispered Danny.

The word hit Adam right in the gut. His heart started pounding, and he was grateful to be sitting down.

"What?"

"No," repeated Danny a little more firmly. "No music lessons. I want to play music with Callie."

He was talking. Danny was speaking to him for the first time in ten months. Adam was so happy to hear his voice again that it took him a second to absorb what he was saying.

"It's that important to you?" Adam asked gently.

Danny nodded. He didn't bother with any more words. The message had been sent and received.

"Well all right then," said Adam, clearing his throat and trying to sound normal. As if anything about this crazy situation were normal. "If you feel that strongly about it, I'll talk to Callie, let her know that it's okay with me. Shall I tell her you'll be over in the morning?"

Danny nodded again, and some of the color came back to his face. Then he gave Adam a hint of a smile, something Adam hadn't seen from Danny since—well, it was too long ago to remember.

"Why don't I go do that right now?" said Adam.

Danny's smile widened as Adam stood up and walked out the back door. He made it all the way down to the shore path before he lost it and sat abruptly on the steps leading down to the dock. He put his face in his hands as his shoulders shook with silent sobs. All the weight of the last ten months, all his fears of losing Danny—of failing him—all of it fell away and he was overwhelmed with a sense of hope.

Danny had looked him in the eyes and spoken. One way or another everything was going to be okay.

Callie wasn't expecting the knock on the porch door. She considered ignoring it. Roscoe shifted position and opened one eye—not that she would trust him to sense danger. She hadn't heard a vehicle, so it was probably Danny. Adam might not like it, but she wasn't going to blow him off.

In a way, the knock was a welcome distraction from yet another frustrating session of songwriting. She had made progress, but still felt stuck, dissatisfied with everything. Nothing sounded commercial, which meant that Brian was going to hate it. Also, most of her song ideas told stories from her own point of view. Twisting that into something Brian could sing grew more difficult every day.

But when Callie rounded the corner of the wrap-around porch, she saw Adam at the porch door instead of Danny. The shock of seeing him, even through the storm glass, made her pause. She hadn't had a chance to get used to being around him again. She wasn't sure she would ever get used to it. When she opened the door, he strode past her without waiting for an invitation.

"Come on in," she called halfheartedly to his back. She followed him back around the corner, where Roscoe the traitor welcomed him and sniffed his pockets. When it became clear that no treats would be forthcoming, Roscoe returned to his favorite spot, circled twice, and flopped down to resume his nap.

Watching Adam, she thought of the caged tigers at the zoo, pacing back and forth in their cramped sanctuary. Like the tigers, he was much bigger up close, and more intimidating. All that power coiled inside one man put her whole body on alert. She retreated to her comfy wicker chair, leaving the uncomfortable one for him, but he ignored it, walking over to the porch rail and leaning on it as he looked out over the lake.

"So what's the verdict?" she asked, when she didn't feel like waiting any longer.

He answered without looking at her.

"Danny would like to continue playing music with you," he said. She couldn't see his face, so she had few clues to his feelings other than the visible tension in his shoulders.

"And the psychologist?" she asked cautiously.

"Says it should be fine, as long as Danny knows from the outset that you're not staying."

"And you?" She didn't really care about the psychologist.

He turned to face her, his arms crossed, the afternoon sun highlighting every sharp angle and furrow on his face.

"It's what Danny wants," he said simply, as if that magically eliminated all his objections.

Callie studied him, wishing she knew what was going on in his head. She had been able to read the old Adam, but not this new model. She wondered if his own wounds, like Danny's, were still raw.

After a moment, he joined her, sitting across from her in the uncomfortable chair and leaning forward.

"If you and Danny are going to play music together," he began, "we need to establish some ground rules. For example, I'd like you to let me know when you're available, so Danny doesn't pester you at all hours. He needs to understand that there are boundaries."

Callie nodded. If he wanted to be all business, she could follow suit.

"I'm usually up before sunrise," she replied. Didn't he remember? "Danny can continue to visit in the mornings, if that's okay with you. Weekend mornings are fine, too. I'm always up."

Adam nodded, then continued outlining his terms as if they were negotiating a deal.

"If something happens, if Danny talks about how he's feeling, I need you to tell me."

Callie tensed.

"How can I build trust with Danny if I tell you everything?" she asked.

"It's critical that I understand Danny's state of mind. If you're not willing to work with me on this, then I can't agree to the lessons."

"But Danny won't talk to me if he knows I'm running back to you and spilling all his secrets," she objected.

"So don't tell him."

Callie opened and closed her mouth several times, completely at a loss. Finally she found her voice.

"I can't do that," she said firmly. She could see that Adam was getting upset. Holding up a hand to buy some time, she took a deep breath and started fresh.

"I understand that you want to protect Danny, and that you're worried about him. But you also want him to open up to me, right? You like it when he talks?"

"Of course," said Adam curtly.

"Great," she said. "So why not trust me on this one? I promise I'll let you know if he talks about anything major."

Adam thought about it for a few long moments, and Callie tried hard not to let the hurt show. Did he really find it that hard to trust her? She was the one who should have issues with him—not the other way around.

"Define 'major,'" he said at last.

"Why don't you define it," she countered. She wasn't going to help him be a control freak.

"Fine," he snapped. "If he talks at all about the accident, or his family, or about current or future custody arrangements, I need to know."

She raised an eyebrow at that. Custody arrangements? What was up with that? She thought Danny was settled here with his uncle.

"Agreed?" he demanded.

"Agreed."

She should feel good about this. In her Nashville life, she was the one to bend, while the others (especially Brian) got what they wanted. For some reason, she found it easier to stand her ground here at home. Maybe it was because she felt rooted, or maybe Adam brought out her strength.

"One last thing," he said.

She smiled faintly, waiting for the zinger. This would be where she compromised herself into nothingness.

"Before you play music with Danny again, I need to hear it. I need to know what kind of music you play with him."

She looked up at him in surprise.

"You want me to play for you?"

He nodded, completely serious. Her stomach did a mini-flip. Not once, all those years ago, had she played music just for him. At the bonfire, sure, but never when it was just the two of them. In fact, she had never played for an audience of one. She had jammed with other musicians one-on-one, and of course she had played just this morning with Danny, but that was collaborative—nothing like this.

"Now?"

He raised an eyebrow and half smiled, as if daring her to chicken out.

"Is that a problem?" he asked, glancing over at her guitar which lay in the open case, clearly ready to go.

"Of course not," she said, scrambling to think of something to play. "I'm surprised, that's all. I mean, you know what kind of music I play."

"I know what I hear on the radio," he answered, shaking his head, "but that's something else. That's not you."

She couldn't help smiling. There were only four other people in the world who understood how much she had changed her music to fit the band: her parents and her sisters. She had been wrong about so much with Adam, but she had been right about one very important fact. He knew her.

"Fair enough," she said, reaching for her guitar.

He leaned back in his chair, the pacing tiger relaxed, the coiled energy contained—for the moment, anyway. She pulled the strap over her head, got situated, checked her tuning. The polished wood felt solid in her arms, a shield between her and Adam. It wasn't that he was dangerous, just . . . intense. It was her own weak defenses she worried about.

His amusement at throwing her off kilter made her want to return the favor. She didn't much like this new, all-business Adam. She wanted to find out if the old Adam was still in there. But first, she needed to get her bearings.

"This is one of the songs that Danny used to play with Evan," she began. "He said it would always make his mom cry."

She probably shouldn't sing. Pushing her voice was one of the dumbest things she could do, but "Danny Boy" didn't pack quite the same punch without the lyrics. Besides, all the sleep and peace and quiet over the last couple of days had worked wonders. Her voice was still weak, of course, but no longer quite so raspy.

She kept her voice whisper-soft and focused on the meaning of the words. The music curled around them, intimate in a way that she hadn't expected. It reminded her of playing at the bonfire, where the music had swirled through the dark summer night and linked them all together.

When the last few notes of the song had floated away, she cleared her throat.

"We've also started to work on a song that's new to Danny, something happier."

He clearly recognized "Take Me Home, Country Roads" right away. She caught his eye and he smiled. She was pleased when he began tapping the rhythm with his fingers. The song lightened the mood between them, as she had hoped it would, and took her mind off the prickles of awareness dancing up and down her spine.

As she sang the familiar words, she made a covert study of his face. The years had changed him in subtle ways that fascinated her. His hairline had crept back. A few gray hairs dusted his temples. The planes of his face had an edge to them now. Harsh, but beautiful.

She could have ended the private performance after that song. She knew she had reassured him, and it would have been the safe thing to do. But she wanted to connect with the old Adam, and she knew only one way to do it.

"I'll probably play some of my own music with him," she said softly. "Being home brings it all back, if you know what I mean."

Callie tried to hold his eyes during the first few bars, but the memories overwhelmed her. She had played "A First Time for Everything" at the bonfire only once. Did he remember? It had been the prelude to a steamy summer. She had learned more about her body during their stolen hours together than she had in a lifetime of living in her own skin. It had taken some persuading on her part. He had refused to sleep with her, seeing as how she wasn't eighteen yet, but she had persuaded him to do just about everything else.

She let her eyes slide down to his jawline. The shadow of reddish-brown stubble made her want to stop playing and touch, so she let her gaze drift lower, following the line of his neck to the pulse point at the base of his throat. All she could think about was the scent of his skin, and the dusting of hair barely visible at the neckline of his T-shirt that would inevitably lead south. She jerked her gaze to the side, let it wander down his arm, finally stopping where his hand rested on his knee. He didn't tap the rhythm—it wasn't that kind of song—but he didn't twitch with impatience, either. She smiled to herself, finally relaxing, and serenaded his hand.

Only after the song ended did Callie raise her eyes. Nerves churning her stomach, she stayed silent, willing him to speak first.

His face was impossible to read, although she could see tension in the line of his jaw. Her stomach began to sink.

"That's still one of your best songs," he said softly.

She flushed and felt her world shift as she realized that the old Adam was in fact still in there somewhere, much as the old Callie still lurked inside of her. Feeling an odd mixture of relief and vulnerability, Callie used the excuse of putting her guitar away to break eye contact and the connection between them.

Adam stood and moved toward the door.

"So I should expect Danny tomorrow morning, then?" asked Callie.

He paused, looked back over his shoulder, and nodded. Then he disappeared around the corner of the house. The porch door swung shut with a snap and she shivered as she caught sight of him striding back toward the cottage. The old Callie very much wanted to connect with the old Adam, but she wasn't sure today's Callie was ready to risk those rapids again.

Adam forced himself to walk away, fighting the instinct to run. He couldn't seem to shake the raw energy that hummed along the surface of his skin. Danny wasn't the one he needed to worry about. Adam was the one who needed to stay the hell away from Callie. She was a siren, and he knew full well how dangerous she could be.

CHAPTER SEVEN

The next morning, Callie was still tuning up the instruments when she heard a light knock at the boathouse door. She smiled warmly at Danny, who took a tentative step inside. He didn't meet her eyes, and he hovered near the door as if things had changed, now that their meetings were official. Roscoe broke the ice by padding over and nudging Danny until he came the rest of the way inside. Then he resumed his napping position and thumped his tail a few times on the floor.

"Hey, Danny-boy," she said. "Come on over here and tune up your guitar." She patted the seat beside her, and Danny brightened. He seemed relieved, ready to follow her cues. Taking the lead was an odd role for Callie. She had been content for too long to follow the lead of someone else. Yet here she was, putting Danny at ease. It felt good.

He managed to get his arms around the full-size guitar, but she made a mental note to ask her father if they could borrow a smaller one from the school.

"Have you ever used one of these before?" she asked, holding up a tuning fork.

He shook his head.

"Well then you're in for a treat. We're going to tune our instruments the old-fashioned way."

He looked skeptical.

"Once you learn how to tune this way, you can tune anywhere, anytime, even if you don't have one of the fancy electronic tuners with you. Like now, for example. Do you have a tuner in your pocket?"

He shook his head again, looking sheepish.

"Me either. I guess we'll have to make do with this old thing. Okay?"

"Okay," he answered, lifting her spirits with a single word. She swallowed hard and continued the lesson.

"Hold it by the handle," she began, handing him the ancient tuning fork. "Try not to touch the top part, where it splits into two, or the ball on the end of the handle. And hold it gently—no squeezing—so it can vibrate."

He held it gingerly, as if it might break.

"Now hit the top part on something hard, like the back of the bench."

She laughed at the surprised expression on his face.

"Go on, silly. You won't break it."

He shrugged, then hit the top part on the bench, which started the vibration.

"Now touch the ball to your earlobe, while it's still vibrating."

Danny gave her a 'you must be joking' look.

"Seriously, touch it to your ear. Quickly, before it stops."

He clearly didn't believe her, but he lifted it anyway and touched the ball at the end of the handle to his earlobe. He jumped, startled, and then laughed.

"It works!"

Callie laughed, too.

"Of course it works. Try it again, but this time, after you hear the note, hum it back to me."

When he had mastered catching the note on his ear, she showed him another trick.

"This time, instead of touching the ball to your ear, try touching it to the body of your guitar."

He did as she asked, without the skepticism this time, and laughed delightedly when the guitar sang the note back to him.

"The tuning fork is giving you an A. Now all you need to do is make sure that your A-string matches it."

She gave him a few minutes to practice catching the note—sometimes on his guitar and sometimes on his ear—then humming it back and adjusting the tuning on the A-string.

"Can you hear the way your humming and the guitar oscillate together?" she asked.

"What's 'oscillate'?" he asked.

"It's the vibration of the note in the air," she answered. "Keep humming while you're tightening the peg, and listen to the way the two notes interact." She reached over to loosen up his string a bit. "Try it again," she instructed.

He did as she asked, and she let him listen before she continued.

"Right now, the notes are close but just different enough that it sounds like they're fighting with each other. Can you hear that?"

He nodded.

"Good. This time, keep listening as you tighten the peg. When it sounds like the two notes have relaxed together—like they're not fighting anymore—you'll know that they're in tune with each other."

His freckled face scrunched up as he caught his note and then concentrated on doing all three things at once: humming, tightening, and listening to the oscillation. After a moment, he looked up at her in triumph.

"I did it!" he crowed. "I tuned the A-string."

She grinned back at him.

"Yes, you did," she agreed, then jumped at the knock on the door. Roscoe barked halfheartedly from the floor, once again displaying his complete lack of watchdog skills.

It was Adam, and he was carrying a guitar case. For a moment, Callie had the sinking feeling that he was going to intrude on the lessons, but then she got a good look at the guitar case. She smiled, motioning for him to come inside. That was an awfully small guitar for a full-grown man.

"Good morning," said Adam. "I'm sorry to intrude, but I thought you might need this." He held up the case. Danny looked mystified. Callie wanted to hug him.

"What a nice surprise!" she exclaimed. "I was just thinking that my guitar was a little much for Danny. Why don't we take a look at what you've got there?"

Callie rearranged the instrument cases on the floor to make an open space in front of Danny, and Adam laid the case at his feet, snapping open the latches and revealing a gorgeous three-quarter-size acoustic guitar.

"It's perfect," she breathed, amazed that Adam would know how to choose the right guitar.

Adam got pink around the ears. "I had help," he admitted. When she raised a brow in question, he continued. "Your dad told me what to look for, which music shop would have it, everything."

She nodded. Of course her father would offer good advice on instrument selection, but when had they spoken? How had she missed it?

Danny picked the guitar up reverently and placed the strap over his shoulder. He reached for the tuning fork and immediately began tuning the A-string. Callie could tell that Adam was impressed by Danny's quiet confidence and his newly acquired skills.

Adam had remained on one knee after opening the guitar case, observing Danny without towering over him. Danny had eyes only for the guitar, paying no attention to the adults in the room. Once he had tuned the string to his satisfaction, he turned expectantly to Callie, anxious to learn the next steps. Adam stood abruptly, his expression closed.

"I won't stay," he said gruffly, ruffling Danny's hair. "Just wanted to make sure the guitar worked out." He moved toward the door and Callie's heart ached for him. He so clearly wanted to connect with Danny, but didn't know how to make it happen.

Callie poked Danny and gestured toward Adam, silently pushing Danny to say something. He looked confused, so she mouthed the words, "Say thank you!" to him.

He looked panicked, and shook his head no. She nodded vigorously back, determined to win the silent debate before Adam left. When Danny looked like he was going to be stubborn, she put her fiddle aside, leaned back, and crossed her arms, clearly signaling that she wouldn't play if he wouldn't say 'thank you.'

Adam was opening the door. It was now or never. Danny gave her a grumpy look, then cleared his throat. At the sound, Adam paused and looked back over his shoulder.

"Thank you," said Danny, his voice so soft that Callie could hardly hear him. But he had said it—out loud—and Adam had heard him. Several different expressions chased across Adam's face before he smiled at Danny.

"You're welcome," he replied. He met Callie's eyes and gave her a silent nod before making his exit.

When he had gone, Danny turned back to Callie and gave her a 'Happy now?' kind of look. He was clearly impatient to play. She placed her fiddle back in its case and picked up her guitar. Now that they had two guitars to work with, she knew exactly what they would play this morning.

Before they resumed the tuning lesson she said, "Thank you for saying thanks to your uncle. I know you don't talk much, but it's really important to let people know you appreciate them. Otherwise they might think you don't care."

He was quiet for a moment.

"Sometimes it's hard to talk," he whispered.

"I know," she said softly. "But when it's important, you need to speak up."

Instead of going back to the cottage, Adam headed for the barn. He couldn't sit still while his whole future rested in Callie's hands. He needed to do something.

He found himself fascinated by this all-grown-up Callie. She had always reminded him of a rushing stream, full of life and tumbling headlong toward her future, whatever it might hold. But she had changed. All that rushing and tumbling had filled a pool so deep and so still that he couldn't tell what she was thinking or feeling. He needed to know, and not just because of Danny.

He had made cautious progress on the *Speakeasy* over the past week, completing some smaller sections before he tackled the rebuild of the damaged stern. Adam chased away thoughts of Danny and Callie by getting to work. If he could fill his mind with the details of the restoration, there would be no room left for what-ifs or regrets. He removed the transom bow carefully. Most of the hardware had rusted, and the wood around it was crumbled and rotten, requiring him to get creative in order to remove it intact. Once freed, he cradled the wood gently so it wouldn't crumble before he could measure out the new planking for its replacement. Rather than steam-bending a large beam, he planned to laminate four three-quarter-inch mahogany planks together. The process would be simpler, and in the end the four planks working together would be stronger than a single beam on its own.

It was the layout tool that derailed him. He grabbed it without thinking, using it to pinpoint the holes for the dowels that would anchor the four planks together. As he marked the final hole location, he was distracted be the sight of his father's hand, holding the tool. He blinked and the hand was his own again, but the haunting image remained. His gut twisted, and he dropped the tool. He had to get the hell out of the shop.

Outside, the cool air helped, but he couldn't purge the picture from his mind. He strode to the crest of the hill and looked out over the water. He was not his father. He might have the old man's hands, and he might use the old man's tools, but that did not require him to follow the same path. It did not automatically make him a drunk, or a monster. Genetics was not destiny.

He could almost feel Evan's hand on his shoulder.

'Take it easy, man. He's dead. He can't hurt us anymore.'

Adam barked out a laugh of disbelief. He shrugged off his brother's comfort, as he had so many times when Evan was still alive, and headed down the hill. But Evan's ghost wouldn't give up so easily, dogging Adam as he hauled open the garage door on the boathouse and dragged out the kayak. It would take only another moment or two before he could escape onto the calm surface of the water.

'You can do this. I know you can,' Evan's voice whispered as he folded himself into the kayak.

Adam dug in with the paddle, his powerful strokes launching it away from the shoreline—and his memories—as fast as he could go.

'We're counting on you.'

The echo of Evan's voice chased him across the water, but he outran it, stopping only when he reached the center of the lake. He rested the paddle across the cockpit rim, his breathing ragged. He stared unseeing at the far shore. Instead of water and trees, he saw the dusty gloom of their secret hideout under the basement stairs. When things got bad—which they had on a regular basis—he and Evan would crawl through the gap in the drywall and wait out the storm. Mom would fade away to the land of happy-pills. Dad's rage would eventually blow over and he would pass out in front of the TV. While they waited, Evan and Adam would tell each other stories of the 'opposite life.' One day, they would both be free. They would get good jobs. They would marry strong, brave girls—girls who didn't run away from problems, or take pills to make them disappear. They would keep their children safe. They would never, ever hit their children. They would live in clean houses with sparkly kitchens like the ones on the TV commercials. Their refrigerators would be full, and they would never forget to make dinner. In fact, they would sit down to a family dinner every night. With dessert. On the weekends they would visit each other. Maybe they would even live on the same block. Their wives would make cookies for the kids, and Evan and Adam would teach the kids how to play basketball.

Adam shook off the memories, only to be confronted by a more recent image. He saw the hospital room where he had said good-bye to Evan, gripping his hand and promising that he would give Danny an opposite life, just like they had planned.

He could do it. Adam knew he could do it, but he didn't know how to do it alone.

Now Callie had come home, along with a boatload of memories, and thrown him a lifeline. But at what cost? Did it matter?

Turning the kayak back toward home, Adam made his decision. His best chance of connecting with Danny was to spend more time with Callie. Danny was different around Callie, and she might be the bridge that they needed. He would have to get comfortable with all his old baggage because nothing—not even the risk of ripping open old wounds—was more important than Danny.

Callie was just grabbing lunch when she heard a car coming down the driveway. Dora walked into the kitchen looking smug.

"That must be your sisters."

"Great," she said weakly, as her stomach sank down to her toes. After a year and a half of being treated like distant cousins, her sisters would not be satisfied with a nice chat over lunch. They would get her away from Mom and Dad and have her spilling her guts within the hour.

A car door slammed. The next few minutes were lost in a flurry of greetings and hugs and fussing over Roscoe. He could not have been happier.

When they were all settled around the kitchen table, Callie realized they had each taken their usual spots, seamlessly picking up the rhythm of family life that extended back as far as she could remember. Until this moment, she had felt disconnected from all her former selves, stretched too thin over too much time. But now, like the figures in a human paper-chain doll, all her former selves slammed back together in a rush. She felt like herself again, the last year and a half of self-imposed isolation somehow irrelevant.

She could sense her sisters' questions bubbling beneath the surface of the conversation, but they would have to wait. Mom and Dad didn't need to know all the details.

"You really didn't have to come up," said Callie, feeling unexpectedly weepy. "I could just as easily have come down to the city to see you."

Mel snorted. "Like that would ever happen."

Callie couldn't think of a snappy comeback. Really, what could she say? Mel was right. Ever since things with Brian had gotten really bad, Callie had pulled back, as if not talking about it would make things more bearable. Besides, there was a limit to how many times she could stand to hear 'I told you so.'

After lunch, her sisters insisted that they wanted to take advantage of the nice weather and build a bonfire down at the fire pit before dinner. Callie allowed herself to be dragged outside. She gathered an armful of logs from the woodpile while Tessa and Mel grabbed their jackets from the car. They grabbed something else as well: stacks and stacks of newspapers. Tabloids, to be precise. Callie groaned.

Not ready to discuss it, she marched ahead of them down to the fire pit and began arranging the logs. They didn't say anything either, at first. They simply twisted each tabloid into a neat tube and tucked it in between the logs. When they had finished, Mel pulled a lighter from her pocket, snapped the flame to life, and touched it to one of the tabloids. Then she sat back on the log bench and the three of them watched the fire grow.

Tessa was the first to break the silence.

"Want to tell us what's really going on?" she asked.

Callie thought about not answering. Somehow the feeling of shame and failure was stronger here, under a clear sky, than it had been down in Nashville. But she had been in denial for too long. The time had come to be honest, with her sisters and with herself.

"Brian and I have been living a carefully negotiated lie for a while now. We put on a good show for the press, but in private we've led separate lives. One of the terms of our truce was discretion in personal relationships. That's been easy for me. I don't have anything to be discreet about." She made a face. "Brian, on the other hand, can't seem to keep his pants zipped if there's a camera around. Frankly, I'm sick of playing the long-suffering, ever-loyal woman."

"What an ass," said Mel.

"What made this last time different from the others?" asked Tessa gently. Callie smiled at that. All the years of training to be a counselor had left Tessa unable to express an opinion. All she could do was ask open-ended questions.

"I don't know," answered Callie. "There's just something about not being able to use my voice that makes me crazy. So I left. My voice needs a break, and so do I."

"And then what?" asked Tessa.

"And then I go back," said Callie simply "This is our moment. I need to ride the wave with the band for a few years before I can strike out on my own. In the meantime, I need to stay strong."

"In the meantime," said Mel, "we need to kick Brian's ass." She poked at the fire and it blazed higher.

"Where did you get all these papers anyway?" asked Callie, neatly redirecting the conversation. Mel was a fighter. She would never understand Callie's need for harmony.

Tessa and Mel exchanged conspiratorial looks.

"The gas station," admitted Tessa.

"The one in town?" asked Callie. "Ugh. I didn't think the poison had spread this far north."

"We didn't want them corrupting local youth with stories of celebrities behaving badly," said Mel. Callie laughed.

"Speaking of local youth," said Tessa, "Mom said that you're giving music lessons to Danny Reese."

Callie stilled. A part of her really didn't want to talk about Danny—or Adam—with anybody, not even her sisters.

She nodded slowly. "That's right."

"Who takes care of Danny now?" asked Tessa. "We came up for the funeral last summer. . . ."

"Adam is taking care of Danny now," she answered, keeping her face expressionless.

"Well that's an interesting development," said Mel. Callie shot her a look, but couldn't be sure what she was implying.

"How do you feel about seeing Adam again?" asked Tessa, in full-on counselor mode.

Suddenly Callie felt surrounded. Suffocated. She had never told them anything. How could they possibly know?

"What are you talking about?" she asked, sounding too defensive. She had given herself away.

"We're not idiots, you know," said Mel. "Something happened between you and Adam. Sure, it was a long time ago, but these things leave their mark."

"I don't—I mean, we never—*arggghhh!*" sputtered Callie, burying her face in her hands. "How could you guys possibly know anything about it?" Her voice was muffled by her hands.

"We didn't need a full confession to know that something was going on," began Tessa.

"Of course we knew," said Mel. "Do you have any idea how many times we covered for your sorry butt?"

Callie picked her head up.

"You did?" she asked.

Tessa nodded.

"First we thought it might be Evan," continued Mel, "but he was always stuck on Lainey. It didn't take long to figure out who turned you into a space cadet."

"But I thought—"

"No, you really didn't," said Mel. "Adam would show up and your brain would shut off."

Tessa smiled.

"We worried about you when he left for that overseas job," she said.

"You did?" Callie couldn't quite absorb the idea that they had known all along.

They nodded.

"Oh," was all she could think to say.

"So I'll ask you again," said Tessa. "How do you feel about seeing Adam again?"

Callie would love to know the answer to that one.

"It's complicated," she hedged.

"Isn't it always?" asked Tessa.

"What do you want me to say?" asked Callie. "That I still have feelings for him? Fine, I do. I just don't know what they are. I'm not even sure I want to know."

"So how does this affect your time away from the band?" asked Tessa. "Would you call it a welcome distraction or an unwanted complication?"

"I don't know," said Callie. "Do we really need to answer that question today?"

Tessa backed off. Mel poked at the fire again. As Callie watched the flames climb higher, she thought about the tiny flame that had carried her nine-year-old wishes up into the sky. Technically, one part of her wish had come true. She made music for a living, and that was no small feat. Maybe, instead of whining about the rest of her life, she should focus on the things that had gone right.

Maybe she should write herself a theme song. "Down in Flames"? "Up in Smoke"? Maybe "Crash and Burn." She smiled wryly to herself. There was a song here in the fire somewhere. Maybe, once she had the damn thing written down, she could rise like a phoenix from the ashes and start over.

CHAPTER EIGHT

Kat Rodriguez closed the file she had been reviewing and rubbed the tension off her forehead. Today was definitely Monday. One of these days she would etch permanent worry lines between her eyebrows, like her mother's. She didn't share her mother's worries. She wasn't raising a child on her own. However, she did have thirty-six dysfunctional families in her active caseload and the frustrating knowledge that she wouldn't be able to help them all. Family law was a brutal, thankless corner of her profession. She had become a guardian *ad litem* for the county by choice, but she would burn out if she didn't pace herself.

She leaned back in her leather chair and, as Doc Archer had once advised over a beer, mindfully counted her blessings. She felt like an idiot, but she had to admit that it worked. Kevin Archer understood the dark side of her work like few other people, probably because he'd lived it.

Blessing number 1: Independence, in the form of her law practice. Never again would a stepfather or boss or boyfriend tell her what to do.

Blessing number 2: Prosperity, relatively speaking, after so many years of scrimping. Maybe it was wrong to enjoy nice things. Maybe she was overcompensating for growing up with nothing. It didn't really matter. She didn't want the Doc to explain it to her. She wanted to enjoy her leather chair and her lake view.

Her window had a great view of Main Street as it rolled downhill toward the water. The road ended at the lakefront park, and the lake stretched into the distance beyond it. A few early bulbs braved the changeable weather, but the view was still more brown than green. The starkness of the landscape, the wet browns and blacks against a pale gray sky, suited her mood perfectly. The world was a harsh, unforgiving place. Only the strong survived.

She watched the wind toy with her 'shingle,' which hung above the door and proclaimed "The Law Office of Katherine Rodriguez." That little piece of wood shouted her success to the world. She thought of the children she had helped so far, the cases where she had made a difference. They were all blessings that she could count, helping to balance the relentless stream of families falling apart.

The movement of a vehicle on the otherwise quiet street caught her attention. She recognized the SUV. Adam was about to step back into her life, but not in the way that she had hoped. She sighed, swallowing her frustration. There were so few intelligent, attractive, single men in her world. Last summer, after wrapping up Danny's case, she had promised herself that she would wait a year and then, when she was mostly clear of the ethical quagmire, reach out to Adam on a personal level. Dinner. A movie. Adult conversation.

The fantasy faded away as Adam got out of the car. She wondered briefly what he had been like as a teenager. She had grown up on a farm, light years away from the tight-knit summer crowd that gathered around the lake. She had been too busy with chores to realize what she was missing. Kat grabbed Danny's case file and carried it with her as she stepped out of her office and into the front room. Maybe it was for the best. Maybe they weren't destined to be together. Maybe. . . .

Adam pulled the door open, which set the bell jangling and filled the waiting room with a gust of chilly air. She smiled, even as her heart sank. There was no help for it. The man was tall, powerful, and gorgeous, and she had a huge crush on him. She would have to lock up her feelings until this case ended, but in this moment— just for one tiny second—she allowed herself to appreciate his gorgeousness and revel in the fact that she had worn her sexiest 'do-me' heels today.

"Good morning, Adam." Kat spoke slowly and calmly though her heart thumped double-time. "I was just looking over Danny's file. Can I get you some coffee?" He nodded, all business. Clearly his heart rate had not jumped. She waved a hand toward the armchair with its back to the window. He could admire the lake view another time.

Kat took her time getting the coffee, giving her heart a chance to slow down, and giving Adam a chance to appreciate the way her tailored suit enhanced her curves, especially from the back. Maybe there would be a spark between them this time around. Most men found her attractive, but last summer Adam had been completely oblivious. She had chalked it up to his grief and tried not to be offended by his indifference. Ten months later, maybe things would be different.

Kat turned and smiled, the folder tucked under her arm and a coffee in each hand. She crossed the room and handed him a steaming mug, watching him closely to see if he was watching her closely. He wasn't. She sighed.

Her graceful slide into the opposite armchair turned into more of a plop, complete with a splash of coffee landing on her lap, thanks to the 'do-me' heels. She smiled weakly and set down her mug.

"I met with Doc Archer last week," he began abruptly.

So much for small talk.

"Did something happen at school?" she asked. Kat scooted forward in her seat and almost dumped the case file on the floor. She set that carefully on the table in front of her and gave Adam her full attention.

"No. Danny's fine," he answered, his face difficult to read. "But the Doc wanted to let me know about the report he had been asked to prepare for the court—for you."

"I hope the request didn't surprise you," she responded cautiously. "Kevin will have a unique perspective on Danny's progress. He sees Danny almost every day."

Kat could read the tension in Adam's body. Professionally, she was under no obligation to reassure him, but she would try anyway. She would do her best to keep all the players calm in this high-stakes game. If she didn't, Danny would recognize and absorb their anxiety, and that was a step in the wrong direction.

"I see Danny every day, too," said Adam.

"I know," said Kat, "and I was planning to reach out to you after reviewing Kevin's report. Your call simply made that happen sooner."

He didn't look reassured.

"Look," continued Kat. "I understand how frustrating this must be for you. But think about it from the perspective of Danny's grandparents. Their hands are tied. They watch from the sidelines, and they see no progress. They're concerned that Danny needs more than you can give him." She held up a hand to forestall Adam's objection. "If your positions were reversed, you would have raised an objection long before now."

That shut him up. She could tell he was still frustrated, but she couldn't help feeling some frustration of her own. After working together last summer, didn't he know her at all? Had she not earned his trust by being open and honest and fair, and—most important—by putting Danny's well-being above everything else? His impatience and distrust rankled, and made her itch to prove him wrong.

"So what's our next step?" demanded Adam. "What can I do to demonstrate that Danny is where he needs to be?"

Had it been anyone else, Kat would have walked Adam gently through her process, explaining each step in detail and why it was important, but she had learned last time around that Adam had no patience for detail. He wanted the facts, only the facts, and he wanted them yesterday. This didn't bother her. She appreciated the directness of her interactions with him, and the challenge of communicating succinctly. It did make her wonder what it would be like to go on a dinner date. She suppressed a smile, imagining the rapid-fire exchange of personal details and pertinent medical information. Would he be as direct in the bedroom as well? Squelching that line of thought, she responded to his question.

"I'll spend time with each of the major players in Danny's life. I'll talk with one or more psychologists to get their thoughts on his situation. I'll review Kevin's report and discuss it with him. There will be no hearing until I fully understand Danny's situation, and you can rest assured that I will only recommend action that's in Danny's best interests."

"And in the meantime I'm supposed to just wait?" He looked like he might explode. Kat resisted the urge to roll her eyes. Where Danny was concerned, Adam could be intense.

"Of course not. You're supposed to continue to work with Danny. There is a simple way to solve this problem, you know, and it doesn't involve lawyers."

Adam gave her a skeptical look.

"I didn't say an 'easy' way," she continued. "I said 'simple.' If you can get Danny to start talking, and to express an opinion about his future, this problem goes away. That assumes he expresses a preference for staying with you. If he would rather live with his grandparents, well . . . then you're screwed."

Kat adapted her style to her clients, and Adam seemed to understand her better if she spoke plainly and swore for emphasis. To be honest, it was a nice change from the rest of her Rated G life. Most families needed gentle hand-holding, or compassionate mediation. Adam, in contrast, needed a kick in the ass. He had built up some thick armor—as well as a boatload of money—during his years in the brutal world of financial deal-making. He wasn't accustomed to taking advice from other people.

He smiled wryly, which was a long way from the spark of interest she was hoping for, but it was a start.

"If something doesn't change soon with Danny, then I'm screwed anyway. Might as well go down fighting."

She smiled back at him. "My thoughts exactly. Did Kevin have any useful suggestions for you?"

"That depends on how you define 'useful.'" He shook his head. "Only one way to find out."

Kat laughed at that. Watching this strong, capable man struggle to connect with a silent eight-year-old boy struck her as both funny and heartbreaking at the same time. Both were smart and both were stubborn. She knew better than to offer advice before Adam asked for it, but when the time came, she would give him an earful. In the meantime, he and Danny could continue to butt heads and see whose cracked first.

She needed to shift this conversation to a new topic, something unrelated to Danny. If she hoped to have a personal relationship with Adam a year from now, they would need to begin building the foundation now. The first step would be casual conversation before or after their discussions about Danny. It was too early in the day to suggest going to lunch, and a dinner invitation would be inappropriate. Damn it, the coffee had been a mistake. She should have skipped it, leaving an opening to suggest coffee at the diner next door. Now that would have to wait for another time.

As she opened her mouth to transition the conversation, he stood. She was losing him.

"I should get back to work," he announced.

"Of course," she replied, standing too quickly and swaying on her heels. "I wish you luck with Kevin's suggestions." She groped for something clever to say, something professional yet personal. "If there's anything I can do to help, legal or . . . otherwise, please let me know."

Adam stood as well, holding out a hand. She shook it. One of these days she would get past the handshake.

"Keep me posted on any new developments," he said as he put his coat back on and moved toward the door.

"Likewise," she said, holding the door for him. She watched him leave, ignoring the cold air and the jangling bell, thinking instead about her plan. The power of 'the plan' had carried her this far in life, one step at a time. Adam might not know it yet, but he was now a part of her plan.

'Small steps,' she reassured herself, tottering back toward her desk and the work that waited there. As she sank into her leather chair, she kicked off her shoes and smiled. Patience and planning would never let her down.

Callie sank into the comfy cushions of the wicker chair and admired the cherry sheen on her freshly painted toes. Not a bad job, considering she hadn't painted her toenails in years. Now all she needed to do was sit still long enough for the polish to harden. It shouldn't be difficult, if she could convince Roscoe to stay off her feet. She had her guitar at hand, a cup of tea on the table beside her, and nothing to do but stare out at the water. Her father was back at school today and her mother had retreated to the attic to paint. Callie planned to do a lot of nothing, apart from some songwriting, out here on the porch. The combination of direct sunlight and airtight storm windows made it the coziest room in the house.

She reached for the guitar and settled it into her lap, checking the tuning as she mentally reviewed her songs-in-progress. She toyed with a few melodies, but the soothing warmth of the sun soon relaxed her into a reverie, any residual tension disappearing with the morning mist.

Callie floated in a sleepy haze as the sun climbed up the sky. Then she heard the rumble of a vehicle engine, the scrape of tires on the gravel drive. She ignored it. As far as she was concerned, she was not at home. She heard the open and shut of a car door, a few footsteps on the gravel, and then the ringtone of a cell phone, a muffled voice as the new arrival paused to take the call.

Roscoe growled. They both knew that ringtone, and that voice. Brian had come looking for her.

As her stomach sank, Callie opened her eyes and sighed, lifting the guitar off her lap and placing it back in its case. In a way, his intrusion was her own fault. She had ignored his calls and voice-mail messages, replying only with a text message to say that she had arrived safely and she would see him in a month. Something urgent must have come up, something so important that he had left Nashville to come after her. Like an owner chasing down a runaway puppy, he had come to clip on the leash and lead her back home.

But what if she didn't want to go?

She took one last look at her cheerful toes, then rose to go deal with him. A cloud passed in front of the sun, taking with it the vestiges of her warm and fuzzy contentment. As she walked through the house toward the kitchen and the mudroom, Roscoe padding along beside her, she wished that she had taken a shower. With her hair twisted into a knot, wearing old sweats from high school, she felt defenseless, without the armor she needed to face Brian. Not that it would have helped much. He knew her too well. But still, she hated handing him the advantage.

Callie reached the back door in the mudroom and opened it, getting her first good look at Brian through the storm door as he finished up his phone call in the driveway. She could see the impatience in the lines of his body as he gestured to the unfortunate individual on the other end of the line. He must have flown to Chicago or Milwaukee and rented a car—actually, a truck—because she didn't recognize the vehicle. Only Brian would find it necessary to rent a pickup truck. Any normal person would have thought about the expense and chosen something more modest, but with Brian it was all about image. Whipcord lean, he wore his leather jacket and distressed jeans like a model. From his cowboy hat to the tips of his boots, Brian telegraphed 'rising star of country music.' It was all part of the act.

Roscoe planted himself beside her, growling every time Brian spoke into the phone. His support gave her the boost of courage that she needed. She reached down to rub his head, then pushed open the storm door.

Brian glanced up, still on the phone. He didn't smile, but Callie didn't really expect it. Given the circumstances of her departure, she expected him to go on the offensive and find a way to make everything her fault. He finished the call, then turned his full attention to Callie. In his eyes, she had done something wrong, and he was angry. Disappointed. She could see it in the hardness of his eyes and the tight line of his mouth. He would wait for her to speak first. To apologize. This was part of the game.

Callie sighed. She knew as well as he did how this would play out. She was the water. He was the rock. It was her role to go with the flow, to bend around his immovability, to fill in the gaps and smooth the way. After ten years, she had worn down a nice, deep stream bed for herself, and now she needed to lie in it. She breathed deeply and let the cool air brace her.

"Brian," she said. "I wasn't expecting you." She would play her role without groveling. "Would you like to come in?"

"No, thanks," he answered, crossing his arms and leaning back against the truck. He wore a leather jacket, while she was barefoot. Of course he preferred to keep her out here, where she would be cold. Always looking for the advantage. She chose to stay put, holding the storm door open, rather than leave the sanctuary of the house.

She glanced down at her defiantly red toes, then met Brian's eyes. The rage that had fueled her long drive through the night had cooled over the weekend and now froze into a kind of obstinacy. She no longer wanted to flow. She no longer wanted to bend. Brian needed something, and she found she was not inclined to give it to him—whatever it might be. In the past she might have asked him what he wanted or why he was here. Today, she simply waited.

When he realized she wasn't going to speak, an odd expression flickered across his face. But then he gave her a half smile, as if he were on to her tricks, and reclaimed the initiative.

"I was surprised by your abrupt departure on Thursday," he began. "You left a lot of unfinished business behind. It's not like you to be so . . . unprofessional."

Callie swallowed the flicker of outrage, refusing to let him bait her. He knew, better than anyone else, how much she valued professionalism, how it drove her crazy when the other members of the band blew off paperwork and rehearsals because they 'just didn't feel like it.' Brian was one of the worst offenders. It was a constant source of friction, and a button he was trying to push.

"You expected me to stay?" She tried to strike the right tone—offhand, casual, mildly surprised.

"I expect you to do your job." His voice lashed out at her, completely at odds with his relaxed stance.

The images flashed through her mind before she could shut them out: Brian naked in the studio, flesh to flesh with the three new backup singers. In one of the photos he had looked directly into the camera, unashamed. The girls had alternately posed for the camera and hidden their faces like naughty little children. And really, that's what they were. Technically adults, but so young they still thought life was a game.

So much for Brian's promises. So much for 'respect' and 'discretion.'

"And what exactly is my job?" she demanded. It sure as hell didn't include naked rehearsals. That phase of their relationship had ended years ago.

"It's whatever I say it is."

The cold fury behind his words knocked the breath right out of her. Buttressed by the doorway of her childhood home, she could feel in her bones how far off course she had gone. She sensed the shadows of her nine-year-old self and her sixteen-year-old self standing behind her, both shocked that she would let her boyfriend—let anyone—talk to her this way. Why was she speaking with him at all? But neither of those former selves could understand the complex web of relationships that bound her to Brian. Her professional existence, her career in the music industry, everything about her future depended on navigating these rough waters and charting a course forward.

"You may not be able to sing right now," he continued in a more measured tone, "but you can still carry your weight."

She noted the masterful use of another of her favorite phrases, another button pushed. When he paused for a response, she simply raised an eyebrow and kept her mouth shut.

"You need to come back to Nashville with me today. There's a mountain of work to be done getting ready for the tour and wrapping up the album. It's all hands on deck, babe. No slacking."

He sounded so reasonable, so rational, and yet—

"Besides, the new girls need a lot more rehearsal before they'll be ready for the tour."

Brian was still Brian. He wanted to dump all the shit work on her so he could spend more time 'rehearsing' the new talent. Well, he could screw them all he wanted, and he could screw himself as well.

Callie cleared her throat, feeling oddly as if she were about to experiment with cliff-diving. Had she ever refused a direct command from Brian? She felt light-headed as she opened her mouth, wondering if the word would come out.

"No."

"You don't think they need rehearsal?" Brian couldn't seem to connect her response with his statements. She smiled, and her voice came out stronger this time. Hoarse, but firm.

"No, I won't be going back to Nashville with you."

His mouth tightened. He seemed to consider his options, and it was a moment before he responded.

"I'm disappointed, Callie. I never thought you would be the one to let us down."

Callie's smile widened at that. Who exactly had done the letting down?

"I'm sure you'll recover nicely," she replied. *You always do,* she added silently.

"It's not me I'm worried about," said Brian. Callie didn't like the calculating look in his eyes. He wanted her to ask, and she couldn't help herself. She caved.

"What, then?"

"If you want to breach your contract, that's your business, of course," he drawled, "but I'm surprised you'd walk away. After all these years playing shitty little clubs, barely scraping by, it's finally time for the payoff. We're opening for one of the biggest acts of the summer. Big venues. Big money. And big-time promo for the new album. Opportunities like this don't come around twice. It seems like a strange time to quit."

The words 'breach your contract' pierced Callie straight through the heart. He might use the code word 'quitting' but she knew a veiled threat when she heard one. Was he crazy? She was a founding member of the band. She wrote all their material. She had earned her share of the band's success, and she damn well wasn't going to let him run her out just when they were hitting the big time.

"I didn't say I was quitting." She managed to keep her voice steady.

He lifted a shoulder. "That's what it sounds like to me."

"When Ron and Curry needed time for rehab, did you assume they were quitting?"

Brian said nothing. Callie could feel her indignation growing.

"When Ash had to do thirty days in jail, did you assume he was quitting?"

Brian pressed his lips together.

"No, you didn't. You told me to suck it up and pick up the slack. Remember?"

Still no answer from the self-styled King of the Band.

"Well it's my turn now, and you all can suck it up and pick up the slack."

She felt the thrill of defiance and wanted more. Her words, spoken in a weak, wounded voice, had power. They hung in the air, and she couldn't un-say them, even if she wanted to.

"Your professionalism overwhelms me," he responded.

Brian had retreated into sarcasm, and she enjoyed the unfamiliar sensation of holding the upper hand.

"As does yours."

"So how long do you plan to hide out up here 'healing'?"

She resisted the urge to roll her eyes when he made air quotes around the word 'healing.'

"At least a month."

He nodded curtly.

"And you plan to sit on your ass for a month?"

"If that's what it takes," she answered.

Brian considered her answer for a moment, then pushed away from the truck, taking a few steps toward her. She held her ground. It felt good, standing firm. She also liked standing on higher ground, looking down on Brian from a few steps up. For too long she had been tiptoeing in his shadow. Roscoe inched forward, his growl growing louder. Brian stopped at the foot of the back steps.

"June first," he said curtly.

She nodded.

"Full rehearsals for the tour start on the first. You have a month."

He looked at her for one last moment, then turned his back, returning to the truck. He opened the door but paused before climbing in.

"If you're not back on the first, I'll assume you've decided to walk away."

"I'm not walking away," she said calmly.

"Right," he said. "Just hiding."

Before she could respond, he climbed into the truck and slammed the door. He fired it up, peeled out, and left her in a cloud of dust. Roscoe chased the truck halfway up the drive, barking all sorts of insults and threats at Brian's retreating back.

"See you in a month, Bri," she called after him, grinning like a fool. As tightly as her future was tied to his, it felt good to loosen the knot and run free, if only for a little while. He would reel her back in soon enough.

The package arrived two days later. Funny how ten years of professional and personal history could fit into a single box. The accompanying note was brief: 'Sort this, then send it back. Record label attorneys need to review our past contracts, make sure all is go for launch. –B.'

Brian always had to have the final word. He had found a job she could do while 'sitting on her ass' and the note practically dared her to defy him again. She considered sending it back, but the thought of escalating the conflict exhausted her. Instead, she pushed the box into the hall closet. Brian would have his paperwork, sooner or later. Right now she was thinking 'later.'

CHAPTER NINE

Kat gave the Burroughs' attorney a firm handshake and the older couple, already outside and climbing into their Mercedes, a brief wave. She closed the door and turned to face Adam and Danny, who sat side by side on the couch. Did they have any idea how alike they looked? They shared the same intense dark blue eyes, the same stubborn chin, even matching ears. On Danny, the ears were too big, but it was clear looking at Adam that Danny would grow into them.

"I wish I could say that went well," Kat began, crossing the room to reclaim her armchair. "But we all know that's not true."

She sighed in frustration. Danny refused to talk, and Adam refused to listen. He refused to admit that Danny might possibly do better with someone else. She understood his commitment to his brother's last wishes, but at the same time wanted to shake him. When would he concede that something had to change? How many years would it take?

She addressed her next words directly do Danny, who stared at her but gave no hint of his emotions. "Let me be honest," she said. "Right now they make an excellent case for themselves."

Adam's mouth tightened but he didn't interrupt.

"Do you want to fight this?" asked Kat.

"Of course I want to fight," snapped Adam. "That's the whole point."

"I wasn't asking you," Kat replied, her voice calm and her eyes on Danny, who looked down at the table.

They both waited for any kind of sign from Danny, but Adam lost his patience first.

"Evan and Lainey only ever asked me to do this one thing," he said, his voice low and strained, "and I'm not going to let them down. I'm not going to let her parents railroad me because they feel like they know best. Danny stays with me."

Kat kept her eyes on Danny, looking for any sign of his thoughts or feelings, but he gave nothing away.

"Adam, would you mind giving Danny and me a moment alone?"

There. It wasn't much, just a flicker of his eyes up to her own and then back down again. She had startled him. Good. At least she knew he was in there somewhere. He was aware of the world around him, even if he chose not to engage.

When Adam didn't respond right away, she gave him a hard look, raised one eyebrow.

"Why don't you go wait in the car. I'll bring Danny out when we're finished."

The unspoken question was, *Do you trust me?*

Adam studied her, but she didn't look away. Finally he nodded and rose to leave.

"I'll be waiting," he said. The bell jangled as he pulled the door shut behind him.

Kat relaxed back in her chair and studied Danny. After a minute, he got tired of staring at the table and looked up at her. She cocked her head to one side and gave Danny a smile.

"You don't say much, but you listen."

She waited a long time for an answer. Finally he gave her a slow nod.

What she wouldn't give for a window into that brain. She needed to know more about Danny and what he wanted. Forget about the grown-ups. Danny held all the cards, if only he would show his hand.

"Do you understand that Adam and your grandparents are about to start a tug of war with you in the middle?"

He shrugged.

"Okay. You don't care. That's fine. You can go along for the ride on this one."

He looked surprised, as if he thought Kat would require him to have an opinion.

"Here's what I need you to understand," she continued. "If you care about where you live and who you live with, you need to tell me."

He shrugged again.

"Right, Got it. You don't care. But there may come a day when you do care." Kat let that idea sink in for a moment. "When that day comes—because it will, eventually—I need to know. I can't help you get what you want if you don't tell me. You need to speak up. Do you understand?"

Kat studied him for a long minute, trying to assess whether or not he was really listening.

He nodded, more firmly this time. He almost smiled, which made Kat wonder once again what was going on in that brain of his.

She smiled, too—the real kind of smile, not the professional kind.

"Good." She stood and walked over to the credenza. On the top, beside a fan of brochures about her law practice, sat a stack of business cards. Kat picked one up, turned it over, and wrote her cell number on the back. Then she handed the card to Danny.

"Here's my card. If you decide that you have an opinion about where you'd like to live, or who you'd like to live with, you call me. I'll make it happen."

He stood up, his poker face back on, and shoved the card into the front pocket of his jeans.

"You know how to use a phone, right?" asked Kat, wanting confirmation before she let him go. He was just young enough that he might not know how to call her.

He nodded again. Wow. Three nods and two shrugs. This was almost a real conversation.

"Good," she said. "You call me if you need me. Now let's get you out to the car. Your uncle must be wondering what we're talking about."

Together they walked out to the car. Danny had his windbreaker to protect him, but Kat found herself wishing she had grabbed her blazer.

She spoke to Adam through the window while Danny climbed into the back seat and buckled up.

"Anything I need to know?" he asked. Kat smiled at him, then winked at Danny in the back seat.

"Sorry, Adam," she said. "Attorney-client privilege and all that."

Adam looked like he was going to insist on full disclosure, but Kat put up a hand to forestall any further questions.

"I wanted to make sure that Danny understands the seriousness of the situation. He does."

When Adam still didn't look satisfied, Kat decided to nudge him out of his comfort zone.

"Why don't you get Danny back to school and then meet me back here. I'll take you to Lucy's for a cup of coffee and we can talk about next steps."

She gave him her warmest smile and stepped back, taking his 'yes' for granted. As she had hoped, he went along with her suggestion rather than continuing to press her for details in front of Danny.

"Right. I'll be back in ten minutes," he said.

As she watched him drive away, she tried to dampen her rising anticipation. He had agreed to coffee at Lucy's. This would add a personal dimension to their otherwise purely professional relationship. She wouldn't call it a date—couldn't, in fact—but it was a step in the right direction. All she had to do was not screw it up.

Callie parked on Main Street in front of the diner. She had played her very first gig at the diner the summer she had turned eleven, and it didn't look like much had changed since then. She leaned back in the driver's seat and stared at the carved wooden sign hanging above one of the doors in the row of shops. 'The Law Office of Katherine Rodriguez' occupied the storefront between 'Lucy's Diner' and 'BJ's Flowers and Found Objects.' It seemed right at home, tucked under the classy green awning.

Could it really be the same Kitty Rodriguez?

Never in a million years would Callie have imagined Kitty as a lawyer. A trophy wife, maybe, or a model, but a lawyer? Kitty had been the 'Jolene' of their generation. She could have had any man—okay, at the time it would have been 'boy'—she wanted, and she had broken most of the good-looking hearts in town. The rest of the girls had simply picked through the wreckage. Things had changed after her mom died and she moved away. Callie had never heard where she ended up. Back home, apparently.

Callie struggled to imagine Kitty building a life on her own, rather than attaching herself to a powerful man, but she couldn't quite picture it. Then again, Callie would never have imagined submerging her own dreams in order to support Brian's agenda, so who was she to judge?

This certainly complicated things. If Jim Stephens had retired, and Kitty Rodriguez was now the only lawyer in town, Callie might need to look elsewhere for advice. Jim had been an old friend of the family. She had imagined approaching him informally, asking for help understanding her legal obligations to the band, and—the really scary part—her options for a graceful exit, maybe a year or two down the road. But Callie couldn't imagine having that same conversation with Kitty. She wanted advice from a friend. No matter how much water had flowed under the bridge since high school, Kitty would never be an 'old friend.'

Why did everything have to change? Home was supposed to be her firm foundation, frozen in time. The idea of home had anchored her amid the crazy chaos of the music business, but the once-solid ground now kept shifting beneath her feet. Jim Stephens had retired. Kitty Rodriguez had grown up to be a lawyer. And Callie James had come running home when life got tough. Throw in her scraggly dog and broken-down Bronco, and she could write a great country song about her own sorry life.

She sat in the car for a few more minutes, pondering her next move. There must be a lawyer in one of the nearby towns. So what if she had to drive a little farther for advice? It would still be easier than trying to start fresh with Kitty. Between Google and the local phone book, she should be able to scrounge up a few candidates.

As she sat there, the door to Kitty's office opened and Kitty herself stepped out, looking amazing in some kind of power-lawyer getup. The slim lines of the suit showed off her still-spectacular curves. The wind whipped at the bottom of her skirt and mussed her casually upswept dark hair. She looked like a supermodel at a photo shoot: high heels, relaxed stance, thousand-yard stare, and a complete lack of self-consciousness. Callie didn't like to compare herself to this vision. Her casual, bohemian look couldn't compete, and that was completely ignoring the fact that she stood almost a foot shorter. A foot narrower, too, if she took her meager bra size into account.

Kitty raised a hand in greeting to a man who was getting out of his car. He had parked a few spaces down from Callie, and she couldn't tell who it was yet. Her view was blocked by the other cars. He strode toward Kitty, took the steps two at a time, and stopped when he reached her.

Callie inhaled sharply. Adam and Kitty? She slouched down, willing herself to be invisible, and waited to see if they would embrace, or kiss, or drop any kind of hint as to the nature of their relationship. A rush of possessive anger surprised her, and she gave herself a swift mental kick. If he wanted to spend time with Kitty, it was nobody's business but his own.

As she watched them interact, Callie marveled at the change in Kitty. The old Kitty had flirted as naturally as she had breathed. Sexual energy had infused all her interactions with men. But the new Kitty stood tall. She didn't flutter in response to Adam's arrival. She met him eye-to-eye and held herself as his equal. The transformation was remarkable, particularly since Callie considered Adam a prime example of the male species.

God, it was good to see him again. She could watch him all day. All night, too, if she could figure out a way to make it happen. She smiled grimly to herself. He had made that comment the other day about how hard it had been to watch her walk away, and she just couldn't get it out of her head. He was the one who had done the leaving, not her. If she didn't get a grip, she would soon cross the line from fondly nostalgic into stalker-land, and wouldn't the tabloids have fun with that? Still, she couldn't help feeling a shiver of awareness as he pulled open the door to Lucy's and gestured for Kitty to step inside. She would never forget the feeling of those hands on her body.

Callie let out her breath as the two disappeared inside Lucy's, leaving her to mull over her options. She could sit here in her car all day, pouting about the collapse of her half-baked plan, or she could go home and come up with something better.

Or, if she were feeling bold, she could go into Lucy's to pick up some doughnuts and casually bump into them. Maybe things with

Kitty wouldn't be weird after all this time. Maybe Kitty was the perfect person to help her. Maybe Kitty would explain that Adam was only her client. . . .

Callie snorted, imagining the scene. No way could she pull that off. Her sister Mel would do it in a heartbeat, but Callie lacked the necessary swagger. Performing in front of thousands of people? No problem. Gracefully handling awkward social situations? Not going to happen.

A knock on the car window had Callie jumping out of her skin. She found herself eyeball to eyeball with a less-than-prime example of the male species, Larry Hutchinson. With no clear escape route, she lowered the driver's side window.

"Hi, Hutch." She couldn't muster much enthusiasm for the greeting. Hutch's sudden appearance, combined with the cold air flowing in through the window, chased away any lingering warmth of sexual awareness. He was the human equivalent of a cold shower.

"Miss Callie James," said Hutch. "I heard a rumor you were back in town."

"Just for a visit," she clarified. "A short visit."

"Let's grab a cup of coffee," he suggested. "I've always wanted to go on a date with a rock star. We can catch up on old times."

"Ah, Hutch, I'm not a rock star. We play country music. And we're not even that famous."

He shrugged.

"Close enough for me," he said. "You're on the radio, right?"

"Um, yes." She scrambled for a graceful exit. "But I have some . . . errands I need to take care of this morning."

"Right," he drawled. "I guess we'll have to catch up another time."

How much could there be to catch up on? Larry still sported the same leather jacket that he had worn in high school. Same slicked-back hairstyle. Same moves (the casual lean, the knowing wink). Unlike Kitty, he hadn't changed much in the past ten years.

"I see you're still driving the old Bronco," he observed.

She sighed. If she were honest, she hadn't changed much, either. Same car. Same hairstyle. But she still didn't want to have coffee with him.

"Yep, this baby's still going strong after all these years," she answered weakly.

"So, what brings you to Main Street?" he asked. "Looking for Jim Stephens?"

How could he know that?

"No, of course not," scrambled Callie. "I was going to pick up some flowers for my Mom, but I just realized I left my wallet at home."

Her purse was sitting there on the passenger seat. He looked at it, then looked back at her.

"Right," he said again. "I hate it when that happens. I won't keep you then."

He straightened up, and she started the car.

"If you do decide to look up Jim Stephens, you'll need to go to Phoenix. He left for warmer weather ages ago."

"Oh."

"Kat's a great lawyer, though." Again with the winking. "If you need one."

"Thanks," replied Callie weakly. "I'll be sure to keep that in mind—if I ever need a lawyer."

Larry leaned back against the car next to hers and crossed his arms, watching her back out of the parking space. She held her breath until she was safely away. What a disaster. Even if Larry had no connection to Nashville, the last thing she needed right now was local gossip about why she might be looking for a lawyer. Her life was complicated enough.

"So what can I do to convince you that Danny should stay with me?" demanded Adam as he and Kat sat down at a table for two at Lucy's. Kat stared at him for a moment, blinking, as a dozen inappropriate replies chased through her mind. She busied herself with hanging her jacket neatly over the back of the chair. Adam didn't need flirting right now. He needed professional reassurance.

It was mid-morning, and there were only a handful of other patrons at the tiny diner, mostly retired police officers sitting at the counter listening to the scanner. As long as she and Adam kept their voices low, they could discuss the details of the case in relative privacy.

"Honestly," she began, "I don't think there's much more you can do. You've already made major life changes. You've left the intensity of your old job behind. You're putting down roots, for you and for Danny. It's not like you can magically conjure up a wife and a few ready-made siblings."

"You think my marital status is a problem?"

Kat hesitated. From her perspective, it was a huge bonus, but that had nothing to do with the case.

"It's not so much a disadvantage as an unknown. Danny's grandparents are the picture of stability. They've been married for more than thirty years. Your single status, on the other hand, implies a period of uncertainty for Danny as you date, and then adjustment when you find the woman you'd like to marry."

"So I won't date," he shrugged.

Kat snorted. She couldn't help it.

"For a while," he qualified.

This was not the solution that she would recommend.

"Putting your personal life on hold is one option, I suppose," she said carefully, "but not exactly a healthy example for Danny."

"And yet I don't see the dating scene as particularly kid-friendly."

Kat leaned across the table.

"It's not as if you would take Danny with you to a singles bar," she said. "You're entitled to your private life." She met his eyes. This was her moment to plant the seed, if she could only play it right. "There are a number of single women in the area. Smart, attractive, single women. I'm sure you could persuade at least *one* of them to date you."

She leaned back slowly, holding eye contact. Surely he couldn't miss her implication.

At that exact moment Lucy interrupted them.

"What can I get for you kids?" she chirped.

And just like that, the moment evaporated. Kat closed her eyes and took a deep breath before turning to Lucy with a bright smile.

"Coffee for me," said Kat.

"And me," said Adam.

"That's it? No doughnuts?" asked Lucy, looking offended. She was famous for her doughnuts.

"Two please," said Kat, before Adam could decline. The extra calories were well worth staying in Lucy's good graces. "Chocolate frosting, with sprinkles," she added, figuring she might as well go all the way.

Adam raised an eyebrow at her as Lucy walked back behind the counter to hunt up the doughnuts and the coffee pot.

"The price of good public relations," explained Kat. The chocolate should also help ease the frustration of Lucy's poorly timed interruption. "Look, Adam, all I'm saying is that you can be a parent and still have a social life. I wouldn't advise dating someone new every week, but you don't need to isolate yourself either. Just set a good example for Danny." She hesitated, then plowed forward. "At some point, you'll want a partner—and Danny will need a mother."

She held her breath, wondering if she had crossed the line. Adam remained silent for so long that she figured she had blown it. Finally he spoke.

"I understand that Danny needs to be a part of a family again, at some point, but I'm not sure he's ready yet." He rubbed away the deep furrows between his eyebrows. "I know I'm not ready, but one day I'd like to be able to give him the same kind of stability that Evan and Lainey were building together. Two parents that he can rely on. A little brother or sister. Family dinners every night. The real deal."

Kat slowly released her breath, not sure what to say. It was the most personal thing he had ever shared with her, but she could see from the way he straightened up in his seat that sharing time was over.

Before Kat could reply, the door opened and Larry Hutchinson strolled in. He sauntered over to the counter and took a seat near the posse of retired officers. Not too near, of course, given his awkward history with local law enforcement, but close enough to eavesdrop on the scanner. His overly casual demeanor tipped off Kat right away: Hutch was on the job. She had no idea what local squabble could possibly require the services of the town's only private investigator, but everyone in town could tell when he had a paying gig because he started to take himself very seriously. It would be entertaining if he weren't, well, Hutch.

Any hope of recapturing the moment evaporated with Hutch's arrival. Kat realized she was grinding her teeth and unclenched her jaw. Lucy returned, placing a small plate with two doughnuts between them and filling their mugs with steaming coffee.

"Cream and sugar's on the table," she said. Then she winked at Kat. "I'll give you two kids some privacy." She hustled back behind the counter to listen more closely to a burst of chatter on the scanner. Kat sighed. At Lucy's, it didn't matter how many degrees she had, or how many clients. She was still twelve.

"She thinks this is a date," stated Adam, his eyes following Lucy. "Why?"

"Please don't take it personally," said Kat. "Lucy has tried to pair me up at one time or another with every unmarried man in town under the age of fifty. And few over fifty, now that I think about it. She's just trying to be helpful."

Adam was new to small-town life. Though he had spent summers here, he had grown up closer to the city. More kids had attended his high school than lived in the entire village of Hidden Springs. There was little she could do to ease his feelings of paranoia. Everybody really was watching him.

"So we're starting rumors by having a cup of coffee together?"

"I wouldn't—"

"Are you sure this is a good idea?"

"What?"

"Going out in public together. I don't want to give people, particularly the judge, the wrong impression."

"Really, Adam, I wouldn't be concerned about local speculation. There's nothing improper about having a cup of coffee together."

"But why risk it?" he asked. "I don't want to have to start from scratch with a new GAL."

Kat separated herself from the unexpected hurt his words caused her. She tamped down on the flash of anger toward Lucy, who didn't deserve it and was only trying to help. This twist in her insides was her own fault. She had allowed her craving for a personal relationship to take precedence over the work at hand. Lawyer first, then life. She knew the rules.

"I understand your concern, although I don't share it." The words came out evenly, masking her growing frustration, but she couldn't help the tight edge that crept in. "This type of local speculation is very different from caught-in-the-act photos of you and some one-night-stand downtown."

She paused a moment to let her words sink in and to get a firm grip on her temper.

"For the moment," she continued, "let's enjoy our coffee and doughnuts. We'll fuel a lot more gossip by leaving abruptly than by finishing our coffee. After all, we have a professional relationship that provides a perfectly reasonable explanation for having coffee together."

Adam looked like he wanted to argue, but he kept his mouth shut. Given her darkening mood, that was a smart move. She shifted gears, trying to move away from the touchy subject of dating and relationships.

"Why don't you tell me how things are going at home? Maybe we can think of a new way to get through to Danny."

Adam's obstinate expression reminded her so much of Danny that she couldn't help smiling. Some of her frustration slipped away. She shook her head at his questioning look.

"Maybe if you put yourself in Danny's shoes . . ." she suggested. "Imagine that you're the one grieving and that you don't want to talk to anyone. What would be important enough to get you to speak up?" she asked.

"Basketball," he said thoughtfully.

She cocked her head to one side at the non sequitur.

"Evan and I used to play basketball together," he explained. "We never had heart-to-heart talks like girls do, but basketball seemed to work when things got tough. I never really thought about trying that with Danny. He's still so small, and I don't have the setup."

"But you can fix that," she observed, smiling slowly.

"Yes, I can," agreed Adam.

For the first time that morning, he gave her a genuine smile. Kat held on to a tiny thread of hope, both for Danny and for herself.

CHAPTER TEN

Late in the afternoon, Callie's cell phone sounded the ominous notes of Darth Vader's theme. She laughed. Tessa's suggestion of giving Brian his own special ringtone had been a stroke of genius. Now, instead of that sick feeling in the pit of her stomach, she had the giggles. She briefly debated blowing him off, but decided to take the call. Like ripping off a bandage, it might be painful, but better in the end to do it quickly.

"Brian," she said as she answered the phone. "What a surprise."

"Hey, babe," he said, as if nothing had changed between them. "How's the voice?"

"Improving every day," she answered, careful to keep her tone neutral.

"Great. That's great. Glad to hear it. And the files?"

Oh, right, the files that were still sitting in their box in the closet, waiting to be sorted.

"I haven't had a chance to sort them," she said. "Is there a deadline I should know about?"

"The attorneys called yesterday to follow up. I told them we needed a few more days. Tell you what. I'll send you the address. When you're done sorting, you send the box directly to them."

"We're sending them the originals?" she asked, mystified. That didn't sound like a smart move.

"Good point. You'll need to send them copies of all the documents. You keep the originals and bring them back home with you."

Callie swore silently. She should have kept her mouth shut and sent the originals. But making copies was easy enough, if time-consuming. The thought of going 'home'—whatever that meant —made her feel queasy. What the hell was she going to do?

"Callie, are you still there?"

"What? Yes. I'm here. Copies. Will do."

"Great. One other thing."

"Yes?" she answered cautiously, determined not to accept any more assignments.

"I've been talking with the label, and they want to know what we have in mind for the next album."

"The next one? We haven't even released the first one yet!" Callie knew that signing with a record label could be intense, and that they would push you to produce constantly, so that you always had something new and fresh. But seriously? Before the first album even came out?

"I know, I know. It's crazy. But that's the way they operate. They said that this quiet period before the tour is a great time to get a head start on the next album. And when they said quiet, I immediately thought of you, all quiet and secluded up in Wisconsin. What a perfect time to write new material."

Callie didn't respond. Yes, it was a perfect time to write new material. Her material. The songs she had been burning to write, the ones that Brian hated.

"Callie? You there?"

"Yes."

"Look, if you're going to bail on all your other responsibilities, the least you can do is crank out a few new songs. I mean, what else do you have to do all day? You never go anywhere."

Now, Callie knew that she didn't get out much, but how in the hell did Brian know that? Was she that predictable?

"I go out all the time, visiting friends, sailing, hiking."

He snorted, his disbelief clear even across the bad connection.

"Whatever. It's still time to get cracking on new material. Are we clear?"

Callie could feel herself stretching out again, with all her former selves lining up behind her, arms crossed, scowls on their faces. They didn't think much of the rationalization running through her head: 'It won't take all my time. I can still write my own songs, and work with Danny, and review the files. Of course, I'll need to step it up a little. Be more disciplined. But I'm the one who wants a music career. This is what it looks like to make it. Suck it up, sister, and enjoy the ride.' Her past selves might not like it, but they also didn't need to live in this moment, right now. She had to do that all by herself.

"New songs. Right."

She closed her eyes and let her head thump back against the cushions of the chair. So much for escaping.

"Excellent." Callie could hear voices on the other end of the line, higher in tone than Brian's but muffled. "Listen, babe. I need to run. Rehearsal is starting." A giggle. "I'll check in later this week, see how the new material is coming along." Some sort of scuffle, more giggles. "Let me know when you send the files."

"Sure. No problem," she said, looking out at the lake. She imagined that the water was warm and that she was floating in a sunny spot, her hair flowing around her like a mermaid's.

"Later," he said, and broke the connection.

She let the phone slide down into her lap and kept her eyes fixed on the water. If she focused hard enough, she could hold on to that feeling of floating, warm in the sunshine. As long as she could keep her head above the water, she would be okay.

"Hey, sugar," said Luke, poking his head out onto the sun porch where Callie sat in her favorite chair staring out at the lake, her guitar sitting unused in its case on the floor, her phone still in her lap. She had no idea how long it had been since the conversation with Brian.

"Hey, Dad," she said, looking over her shoulder to smile at him. "What's up?"

"I was going to ask you the same question," he said. "You've been out here for a while, but I haven't heard any music."

She looked back at the lake.

"I was thinking," she answered. "But I really should be working."

She knew her voice sounded defeated and that her father would want to know what was wrong. She should work harder to sound cheerful, because she really didn't want to talk about it. She sighed, wishing she could just play some music and forget about everything else.

"What do you say I get my guitar and we play something? You've been home more than a week now, and we still haven't played together."

She should have known her father wouldn't bug her to talk. He knew that—for the two of them, at least—the solution to just about any problem was music.

"Sounds perfect." she said, leaning forward and pulling her guitar out of its case. When he didn't immediately make a move, she looked back at him. "Well?" she asked. "What are you waiting for?"

They played for hours. When their fingers were raw, they stopped, watching the sunset burnish the water in fiery shades of red and orange. She felt light again, and free, her obligations more like filament bracelets than shackles.

"So what's this I hear about you not writing any music?" she asked at last, curious to know what had blocked her father. All her life he had been a songwriter. What had changed?

He sighed. "It's not easy to explain," he finally answered, and she laughed.

"Of course not," she said. "If it were easy to explain, it would be easy to fix, and you would have fixed it already."

"True," he said, chuckling at himself.

"Do you want to try to explain?" she asked, feeling the strangeness of the conversation. Coming back home, all grown up, put a whole new spin on their relationship, and it was disorienting.

"Let's just say that I'm having my midlife crisis," he answered. "Even though I always planned to retire from teaching after this year, it's still a big change. I guess I need to work through some baggage."

"Aren't you a little old for a mid-life crisis?"

He barked out a laugh. "God, I hope not."

"Sorry. I thought a mid-life crisis was something you do when you're forty. Not fifty."

"Fifty-four."

"Whatever," she answered, rolling her eyes. "Didn't you do one of these already?"

"Nope," he said cheerfully. "I've always been slow when it comes to the emotional stuff."

Callie considered for a moment, then had an inspiration.

"Maybe you need a red convertible," she suggested, trying not to laugh at the image of her dad zooming around in a shiny red car. "Or a Harley!" At that mental image, she did dissolve into laughter. "Oh my God, I have to call Mel and Tessa. That image is just too awesome not to share."

Her father actually harrumphed. "There's no need to tell your sisters about this. It's not a big deal."

As she wiped tears from the corners of her eyes, Callie took a few deep breaths and tried to settle down, but everything now struck her as funny.

"Don't tell your sisters," her father insisted.

"Fine, fine. I'll keep it to myself," she agreed. "For now."

He didn't look happy at that qualifier.

"Enough about me," he said, clearly still grumpy. "What's going on with you and the band?"

That shut down Callie's giggles quite effectively.

"Ah," he said. "So there is something wrong in Wonderland. What is it?" he asked.

"It's not easy to explain," she answered, twisting her lips at the irony of her response.

"I'll bet," he said. "Success changes everything."

"We had problems long before we signed the record deal," she said. Might as well be honest. If she spoke the words out loud, maybe a solution would be obvious.

"Such as . . . ?"

"Let's just say that success has amplified a bunch of small problems and interpersonal bullshit into much bigger problems and much messier bullshit."

"Do you think you can work it out?" asked Luke.

She sighed. "If I keep my mouth shut and do what needs to be done, if I continue playing mediator for all the growing egos in the band, then yes, we can work it out."

Luke was silent for a moment, considering.

"So what's the alternative?" he asked at last.

Tears filled her eyes so quickly that she could barely keep them from spilling over.

"I don't know," she whispered, then sniffled. Her father grabbed a tissue from the side table and passed it over. She blew her nose, grateful that he wasn't making a big deal out of her tears.

"Why not tell them to go to hell?" he asked. "Why stay?"

"How can I walk away?" she asked. "We've worked so hard and so long for this. I want my shot at the big time. I've always dreamed of making a living doing my music. So what if this isn't as wonderful as I had imagined? It's the only path forward that

I can see. If I can just get through the next few years, maybe I'll have enough credibility—enough connections—to strike out on my own. Until then, I need to suck it up."

"Are you sure it's worth it, sugar?"

"Yes," she said, knowing as she said it that she was lying. "No. Oh, I don't know. I can't bear the thought of going back. But I can't bear the thought of starting from scratch either. If I'm screwed either way, I'll take two years of hell over ten years of scratching my way back up from the bottom."

Her father didn't dive in with a bunch of stupid reassurances that everything was going to be okay. He just listened, and she loved him for it. She wondered, not for the first time, why he had left his own music career behind and retreated to rural Wisconsin to teach music.

They were both silent for a long time before he spoke again. The sun, sliding below the trees behind the house, left only a few last streaks of flame across the lake.

"Have you ever thought about recording a demo?" he asked.

"We just finished recording an album," she answered, confused. "We don't really need a demo."

"That's not what I mean," he said. "I'm talking about you and your music, not the crap . . . ah, I mean 'stuff' you write for the band."

She smiled wryly. "You like it that much, huh?"

"It's fine, but it's not you." He tipped his head to the side, giving her a speculative look. "A demo would be a concrete step toward leaving the band. Might make you feel better."

"I can't even wrap my head around that," she admitted. "My first thought is that it would be amazing. Of course, Brian would kill me if he found out. And I could never afford the studio time. And even if I kept it a secret, the second I gave a copy to a prospective label or venue, Brian would find out about it."

"It's risky, true. But so is doing nothing. Think about it," he said, as he stood up and stretched. "I better get started on dinner. I'll call you when it's ready." He ruffled her hair the same way he had always done. "Think about it."

Callie watched the last of the flames disappear from the water's surface, leaving the lake in shadow as day turned into night. She silently cursed her father for placing an almost unbearable temptation before her. Two competing concerns warred within her: How could she risk it? How could she refuse?

CHAPTER ELEVEN

Kat parked behind Adam's cottage and gathered her purse along with Danny's file. She had dressed carefully for this 'unplanned' visit, aiming for sporty weekend casual, like something from the J.Crew catalog. If the wind would cooperate by mussing her hair and putting some color on her cheeks, she would be all set.

As she approached the house, it occurred to her that she might not catch Adam and Danny at home on a Saturday. The morning had turned out to be sunny and beautiful and unusually warm for early May—the kind of day that a boy should spend out-side. But when she knocked at the door, Adam answered almost immediately.

She didn't need the wind to put color in her cheeks. One look at Adam, unshaven and barefoot, dressed only in flannel pajama pants and a white T-shirt, and she could feel the flush creeping up her cheeks. So he was a lazy-Saturday-morning kind of guy. Good to know.

He held the storm door open, welcoming her inside. She smiled up at him as she crossed the threshold and accidentally-on-purpose brushed against his chest. *Small steps,* she chided herself. *Don't blow it.*

"Morning, Adam," she said. "Sorry to interrupt your weekend, but I have an update and I thought you'd want to know immediately."

"You're not interrupting," he said. "Have a seat and I'll get you a cup of coffee." He gestured toward the kitchen table, then refilled his own mug.

"Do you ruin your coffee?" he asked after hunting down a clean mug for her.

"Definitely," she answered. "Cream, but no sugar. Milk's fine if you don't have any cream."

He shook his head, clearly a black-coffee drinker, and retrieved the milk jug from the refrigerator. As she watched him move confidently around the kitchen, she tried to remember the last time anyone had fixed her a cup of coffee. She had been on her own for so long now that she couldn't remember the last time she had shared a quiet cup of coffee at home with another human being. Her law practice had consumed her for the last few years, crowding out any hope of a social life. Before that, at the big firm in the city, she had always been the one to fix the coffee.

But she liked this. She could get used to this.

"So tell me the news," said Adam, placing the mug in front of her and sitting across the table.

"Nothing unexpected. Yesterday afternoon I received Kevin Archer's report, and he asked me to pass along a copy to you." She opened up Danny's file and pulled Adam's copy of the document. He took it without taking the time to read it.

"So what now?" asked Adam. "You know me. You've talked to Danny's grandparents. You have the report from the doc. What comes next?"

"I need to finish my research," she responded thoughtfully, "and try one more time to get Danny to express a preference. Then I'll be ready to make my recommendation to the judge."

She looked around, realizing that the house was too quiet.

"Where's Danny?" she asked. Maybe Danny would like to be a part of the conversation.

Adam looked uncomfortable, as if she had asked him if he wore boxers or briefs.

"He's having a music lesson."

"You're kidding," Kat exclaimed. "That's new. When did he express an interest in music? Where is he taking lessons?"

"This is all very new," said Adam. "Doc Archer suggested that we find an activity that Danny could do on his own, away from me. When I figured out that he liked the music he kept hearing from next door, it seemed a logical step to arrange lessons."

"So he's just next door?" asked Kat.

Adam nodded, then drank some coffee instead of elaborating.

"That's convenient."

It made sense. Luke James, the grade-school music teacher, lived next door. He would be a perfect choice to give Danny music lessons. Kat had the sense that Adam was holding something back, but she didn't want to push the issue. She'd rather wait and see if he opened up to her on his own.

"Well, I'm glad that you're working on this new angle with Danny. Whether or not it leads to a breakthrough, it shows you're trying, and that Danny is willing to try new things."

He didn't look encouraged, so she reached across the table and squeezed his hand.

"Every little bit helps," she said gently. She pulled her hand back before it could feel awkward and wrapped it back around the warm mug. There were too many ways to make a wrong move, and she needed to be careful.

At that moment there was a clatter at the back door, then Danny burst into the kitchen, proudly hauling a guitar case. Behind him was a slim woman, a curtain of wavy blond hair temporarily shielding her face as she navigated through the two doors.

Kat didn't need to see her face to know who it was. Only one of the triplets was in town.

Callie stopped short when she saw Kat sitting at the table with Adam, her mouth half open as if she had been about to speak. She recovered quickly, saying her farewells to Danny.

"Great job today, Danny-boy. Same time tomorrow?"

He grinned and nodded. When she offered her hand for a high five, he smacked it hard, then began lugging the guitar toward his room.

He waved at Kat as he went by, which under normal circumstances would have thrilled her, but she only managed a halfhearted wave back. She was too busy dealing with the avalanche of emotional baggage triggered by Callie's arrival.

Adam stepped into the awkward silence.

"Kat, have you and Callie met before?"

Kat forced a smile and held out her hand.

"It's a pleasure to see you again," she said, shaking the hand that Callie cautiously offered in return. "Callie and her sisters were a year behind me in high school," she explained to Adam.

Thank God it was Callie, the sister who never said anything. Kat had no desire to talk about the last time they had seen each other. It was beyond ironic that Callie was giving music lessons to Danny, who also never talked. Two mutes making music together. How oddly appropriate.

"So how did it go?" asked Adam.

Callie's eyes flickered toward the door through which Danny had disappeared, then back to Adam. She cleared her throat.

"Very well," she said in a raspy voice, as if she had a cold. "Danny is much more comfortable now, and he's really opening up about the songs he likes and the kind of music he wants to play."

"Wait a minute," interrupted Kat. "You mean 'opening up' as in he's talking? To you?" Callie nodded. Kat shot an irritated glance at Adam, who was also nodding.

She found herself caught between relief and annoyance.. This was great news—wonderful news—but how could he expect her to make an informed recommendation regarding Danny when he withheld vital information? How could he possibly excuse keeping this news to himself?

Kat stood abruptly. She needed to remove herself from this kitchen before she scolded him in front of an audience and completely destroyed her credibility.

"Adam," she said, striving to keep the irritation out of her voice. "Let's meet for lunch on Monday to talk about how this affects Danny's case." She put her purse on her shoulder and snatched up Danny's file. "I'm already running late," she added, mostly to make herself feel better. She might have no life, but she could create the illusion of one.

"Thanks for the coffee," she said as she reached across the table to shake hands with Adam. "Lovely to see you again, Callie."

Kat held herself together as she made her hasty exit and walked—as quickly as she could without giving the appearance of running away—back to the car. Only after she was safely cocooned inside did she give in to the frustration and slam her hand on the steering wheel. She started the car, fighting the pricking feeling in her eyes, and drove away without looking back.

Damn him for not trusting her. Damn Callie for dredging up unpleasant memories. But mostly Kat kicked herself for allowing that fragile seedling of hope to take root in her heart. Adam wasn't hers, not by any stretch of the imagination, and right now her chances of building a future with him looked bleak.

Callie stood in the kitchen, unsure of how to proceed after Kitty's—apparently now she went by Kat—abrupt departure. The undercurrents she'd left in her wake made Callie wonder again about her relationship with Adam. Despite the swirl of cool air that had swept through the back door, the room now felt smaller with only the two of them in it. Warmer.

"I hadn't meant to share the news of Danny's progress so soon," he began.

She raised her eyebrows. Was he blaming her for revealing secrets that she didn't know were supposed to be secrets? Her back stiffened in response.

"Not that I blame you," he continued. She didn't quite believe him. "But it complicates things. I didn't want to put any pressure on you or Danny to reach a major breakthrough."

Okay, so maybe he wasn't blaming her.

"I'm not worried about it," she said, "and I don't think Danny was paying any attention. He's still pretty enthralled with the new guitar." She smiled, and Adam's ears turned pink. He must hate that. He could probably feel it happening, the way she could feel a blush coming on, but really it made him so much more approachable.

"I'm glad," he said, taking a drink of his coffee. Then, realizing that she was still hovering near the door, he stood up and waved her inside. "Why don't you sit down," he said. "Do you want some coffee? Or something else to drink?" He moved toward the coffee maker, but she shook her head.

"No, no, I'm fine," she said, taking the seat that Kitty had vacated. It was going to take some time to get used to thinking of her as Kat. She took a deep breath. "I wanted to give you an update on our music session."

"Great," he said, reclaiming his seat across from her. "You gave me the headline earlier. Anything else I should know?"

The intensity of Adam's full attention made her even warmer, but she squelched the memories popping up in her mind and kept her thoughts on Danny. There was no point in getting all wound up about Adam until she knew if he was involved with someone else.

"Did he talk about his parents at all? Or the accident?"

"No," said Callie. "We just played music and talked about the music."

She shifted on her chair, wishing she had accepted his offer and had a cup of tea. It would have given her something to do with her hands.

"What do you mean, you 'talk about the music'?"

Callie wrinkled her eyebrows, wondering how to explain.

"I don't know. We talk about what parts of a song we like or don't like, which parts are tough to play. We talk about which song we should play next, or what's our favorite key."

She hesitated. He noticed.

"What? What else?" It was as if he could tell that she didn't want to tell him, and therefore this must be the most important part. It probably was.

"We talked this morning about how I write songs. He didn't say much, but he was really interested."

"Why?"

Callie wasn't sure she wanted to explain. She hadn't really talked about her songwriting with anybody other than her father, and the conversation with Danny this morning revealed as much about her as it did about him.

Adam looked like he was prepared to wait all day for her answer.

Callie sighed. Rather than looking at Adam, she watched her fingers tap out a silent rhythm on the edge of the table while she talked.

"I write songs to say the things that I can't say otherwise—the things that are too complicated or painful or scary to talk about face to face."

She stopped. He waited.

"When I play my songs for people, when I finally say exactly what I mean and they understand, well, there's nothing else like it."

Callie looked up and met Adam's eyes squarely, wanting to make sure that he understood this last part—even if it made her more vulnerable.

"If I didn't have music—if I couldn't connect to people through my music—I would be locked inside myself."

"Like Danny," he said, a muscle in his jaw working to hold back strong emotion.

She nodded. "Exactly. All his questions made me wonder if we should incorporate songwriting into our time together."

He stood abruptly, walking over to the sink and dumping the rest of his coffee. He stayed at the sink, his back to her, tension clear in the lines of his body.

"I thought this would be good news," she said, unsure of what was going on in Adam's head. "I thought this might be an opportunity to work through some of Danny's baggage, if it's okay with you and the shrink."

He sagged a bit, turned to face her. He leaned back against the counter and crossed his arms.

"It's a great idea," he said, his tone making it sound more like a funeral. "Screw the shrink. I think you should do it."

Callie wrinkled her eyebrows. She had known Adam once, but even if he were a complete stranger, she would still be able to tell that something was off about his reaction.

"What's going on?" she asked. "I bring you good news and you act like it's bad news. You're saying the right words, but the vibe is all wrong. I don't understand."

"How I feel isn't important," said Adam. "Leave it alone."

She could do as he asked. She could flow around these unexpected rapids and continue downstream as if nothing had happened. She could keep her present-day relationship with Adam much lighter and simpler than the one they had before. However, she had promised herself to stop going with the flow, and to speak up when she had something to say. It was time to walk the talk, to keep her promises to herself, even if she felt like she was going to throw up.

She stood, mostly to get Adam's attention and make sure she couldn't chicken out. Her knees felt shaky, so she braced herself by placing her hands on the table.

"No, I won't leave it alone. I think it's important to understand you and your relationship to Danny. You're a huge part of his life. If I don't understand you, then I can't understand Danny. What's going on?"

He waited so long to answer that she almost gave up. Finally he spoke.

"Ten months," he said fiercely, his voice pitched low so that it wouldn't carry to Danny's room. "I've been trying to connect with Danny for ten"—he swallowed an expletive—"months, and I got nowhere. Then you waltz in out of nowhere and reach him on the first day. You get him talking to me in less than a week. What kind of incompetent fool does that make me?"

Adam paused, taking a few deep breaths to get himself under control.

"I made a promise." He made a strange coughing sound, as though he were choking on the words. "I made a promise to my brother as he was dying that I would take care of Danny, and I'm a fucking failure. Danny's the only family I have left in the world and he doesn't want to be with me. That's what's going on."

The words hung in the air between them. Now it was Adam who didn't want to meet her eyes. He studied the table between them as if it held the answers he needed. She certainly didn't have the answers, but at least she had some perspective.

"Do you play music?" demanded Callie.

"No," he said, his voice full of regret.

"Did you know that Danny played music?"

"No."

"Then how the hell were you supposed to know that it would help?"

He finally looked up and met her eyes. She could his anger, all of it directed squarely at himself.

"I should have figured it out," he said evenly.

She snickered at that, and he narrowed his eyes, some of his anger now directed her way. But for some reason, it didn't scare her. It inspired her to give him some attitude right back.

"Okay, Superman," she said, rolling her eyes dramatically. "You really blew it on this one. I completely agree. If you don't have psychic powers, you don't deserve to build a life with this kid. I guess you'll have to give up and hate yourself forever."

"It's not funny," he said, his voice getting louder.

"You're right," she said, her humor fading. "It's not funny. Danny's hurting, and he needs music to help him heal. Can't you just be glad that you found a way to connect, even if it's through me? Your self-flagellation is not helpful."

"My what?" he said. Clearly he had heard her, or he wouldn't look so offended.

"You heard me," she said. "It's time to man up."

Callie could hardly believe her own boldness. Adrenaline hummed through her veins. If he wanted a fight, she was ready.

He laughed abruptly, and the tension in the room abruptly dissolved.

"You sound like my brother," he said.

"And that's a good thing?" she asked, uncertain how to proceed given the sudden mood change.

He smiled ruefully.

"It's a good thing."

She relaxed, let out a sigh.

"Well, that's a relief. I was running out of motivational one-liners."

He laughed, more naturally this time. Her adrenaline high mellowed into a happy glow. She needed to speak her mind more often. No wonder Mel said whatever was on her mind. It was liberating.

"So it's okay with you if Danny and I do some songwriting?" she asked again, circling back to their original topic.

"Yes," he said, looking much more relaxed about the whole thing. "And I appreciate you talking to me about it first."

"No problem," she responded. "I'm looking forward to it." She didn't really want to leave, but couldn't think of a reason to stay. She hovered for a moment, needing closure after the intensity of the last few minutes, but unsure how to make it happen. Should she shake his hand? Give him a hug? She wondered, given her hyped state of awareness, what would happen if they actually made physical contact. At a minimum, they would throw off very real, very painful sparks. Safer to back off, at least for now.

"So I'll see Danny tomorrow morning?" she asked, slowly retreating.

"I'm sure you will," he said. She gave him a wimpy little wave and escaped out the back door. If she could coast on the adrenaline high, it would be a very productive day.

When Callie returned to the house, she found a note from her parents saying that they had gone out to run errands. This provided the perfect opportunity to go on a treasure hunt. She had been thinking for days about reconnecting with her early songwriting. She could remember parts and pieces of her early attempts, but somewhere up in the attic were her music notebooks. The contents of those notebooks were more personal than a diary, and could provide her with the emotional memory she sought. She had squirreled them away in one of the cupboards under the eaves when she had left for college, not wanting anyone else to find them. Now all she needed to do was remember which cupboard, and she could open the door to her past.

She left Roscoe napping in a patch of sunshine and climbed the stairs to her mother's attic studio. This had been forbidden territory for as long as Callie could remember, which didn't mean she and her sisters had never sneaked up those stairs. On the contrary, they had learned quickly about the squeaky third and seventh steps. They had also learned to be cautious and to hide the evidence of their explorations.

Today, the mature choice would be to wait until her mother came home and then ask permission to root around in her private domain. But Callie also hoped to stumble across the flowered box her mother had been so anxious to hide. She would never get a peek at it if her mother supervised the search.

At the top of the stairs, she paused for a moment, her view of the studio obscured by layer upon layer of memories. She saw the original flowered wallpaper that her mother had stripped away when the girls were five. She saw the tiny windows, before Dad had opened up the wall and installed giant picture windows overlooking the lake. She saw the water damage from the year the skylight had leaked. And she saw the dress-up box still nestled in the alcove. When Mom had been desperate to finish a painting, she had allowed the girls play in the alcove as long as they promised not to bother her. The arrangement usually bought her an extra hour or two of painting time.

Callie's eyes widened as she surveyed the chaos that was her mother's present-day workspace. How in the world could the woman create art in the middle of all this clutter? Callie needed peace in order to create. Clutter was a distraction, tugging on her sleeve and demanding her attention. Yet somehow her mother managed to create dramatic and powerful pieces in the middle of a disaster zone.

Careful not to disturb anything, Callie worked her way around the edges of the room, checking each cabinet under the eaves for her notebooks. She clearly remembered writing KEEP OUT on the box with a red marker, on all sides, so it shouldn't be that hard to identify. But cupboard after cupboard yielded only art supplies, canvas, frames, and other random junk. No notebooks. Her heart sinking, Callie wondered if her mother had thrown the box out, not realizing that it was important.

In order to check the last cupboard, she needed to move aside her mother's 'resting chair.' The ancient, overstuffed armchair had an afghan thrown over it to hide the fraying upholstery. It faced her mother's current work-in-progress, which she had tented with a muslin dust cloth. Callie felt guilty enough about her unauthorized snooping. She didn't dare peek under the cloth. As she tugged the chair to one side, she did smile to herself at the memories it evoked.

When she was quite small, Callie would wake up first from the afternoon nap and creep up the stairs to spy on her mother at work. Her mother would be so deep in concentration that she wouldn't notice the creaking of the stairs or the little eyes peering around the corner. Eventually, she would take a break and step back, regarding her work. At that point she would notice Callie, who would demand to see the pretty picture. So she would sit in the 'resting chair' and pull Callie onto her lap, and together they would study the work-in-progress.

Callie checked the final cupboard, but there was still no sign of the notebooks. She would need to ask her mother about them—omitting any mention of the failed search, of course. First, however, she needed to cover her tracks. If she didn't put the 'resting chair' back in exactly the same place, her mother would notice.

As Callie stepped around the chair to move it back into place, her toe bumped something underneath. She pulled aside the fringe of the afghan and revealed the corner of a box. A flowered box. Her breath caught. Feeling mildly criminal, she bent to retrieve it. It was heavier than she had expected, packed full.

Callie scooted the 'resting chair' carefully back into place, then sat down on it with the box in her lap. She lifted the cover to find the box stuffed full of photos and letters. The ones on top appeared to be more recent than the yellowed envelopes toward the bottom, but they were all clearly from the same person—someone named Lauren Harrington. The return address was in New York City, and this Lauren had been using the same monogrammed stationery since the 1980s. Talk about consistency. It was the expensive kind of stationery. The envelopes were a creamy color, and they were lined in a dark green paper that matched the swirly H on the outside of the envelope.

Not sure how much time she had, Callie reached for the one on top. It was postmarked just a few weeks ago. This was probably the one her mother had been reading at the kitchen table, when she had looked so pale.

March 2

Dear Dora,

I am dying. I tell you this now, bluntly, because I am sick and tired of dancing around it. I was supposed to die when I was thirteen, and every year since then—43 of them!—has been a gift. We should be celebrating my triumph over the odds instead of tiptoeing around the truth. But the children are firmly planted in denial, unwilling to imagine a life without their mother. Even my doctors won't say it plainly. Only Barrett understands. And you, I hope.

Frankly, I'm relieved that I can see the end approaching, and that it is not cancer. I have been stalked by that invisible enemy for too many years. I swore to myself that I would never submit to chemotherapy again, and I meant it. But my new diagnosis means that I don't need to battle my physicians or my family, for there is nothing heroic they can do to save me. Thank God.

(It's congestive heart failure. Funny how the miracle that cured my cancer also sowed the seeds of my destruction.)

I write to you now, dear friend, because I would like to see you before I die. I would like you to see how our beautiful children have grown up. I would like us all to be together one last time.

The doctors tell me that I may have another year or two, but they are lying. (They call it optimism.) I know my body. I know my self. I will have one last summer on the bay, and then I will fade away.
    Would you deny a dying friend her last wish?
    Please come see me.

Love,

Lauren

Callie studied the letter for a long time, her mind filled with more questions than answers. Who was Lauren? If she was such a 'dear friend' then why had Callie never heard her name? And Lauren referred to 'the bay.' Could that be the same bay on Long Island where her mother had grown up? Was this a childhood friend? If so, why all the secrecy?

There were not supposed to be any secrets in this house.

For a horrified moment, Callie wondered if Lauren could possibly be a man. But she looked again at the handwriting, and the swirly H, and the text of the letter itself, and she relaxed. Lauren was a woman. Not, thank God, her mother's secret lover. Callie laughed out loud at the thought. Some things were just not possible.

Callie reached for the next letter in the stack, but the sound of a car coming down the driveway froze her hand. Heart pounding, she put the box back together and tucked it carefully back where it belonged. She smoothed the afghan and hurried downstairs, leaving no trace—she hoped—of her intrusion.

CHAPTER TWELVE

"Mom, do you remember seeing a box of my stuff up in the attic?"

Callie snuck the question in between bites of bagel, keeping the request casual. She pulled one of her feet out from under Roscoe and curled up more comfortably on the window seat.

Dora laughed. "Oh, no, dear. I booted that out long ago."

Callie's breath caught in her throat and her stomach dropped. She must shown her distress on her face, because her mother reached across the kitchen table and patted her hand.

"Don't be an idiot, dear. I didn't throw it away." The rush of relief left Callie feeling light-headed. "I put it on the top shelf of your bedroom closet," Dora continued. "I don't know why you worried so much that your sisters would snoop. Those old notebooks are only meaningful to you. They don't make sense to anybody else."

Dora returned to eating her cereal, while Callie thought through what her mother had just said and eyed her with suspicion.

"Mom, how do you know what's in the box?"

Dora looked up at her daughter, all wide-eyed innocence.

"Well, dear, I knew it belonged to one of you, but you didn't actually write your name on the outside of the box. All you wrote was KEEP OUT. Honestly, how could I put it in the right bedroom if I didn't peek inside? If you didn't want me to see it, you shouldn't have put it in my studio. I assumed that KEEP OUT didn't apply to me."

After that perfectly logical explanation, Dora took her last bite of cereal and then stood, carrying her bowl to the sink.

"How was your session with Danny this morning?" she asked, deftly changing the subject.

Callie knew a diversion when she heard one but couldn't help smiling.

"It was great," she answered. "We're building up a set of songs that we can play together. He taught me some. I taught him some. And we started on some basic music theory, so he can understand chord progression when he wants to write a song of his own."

Dora leaned back against the sink and regarded her daughter thoughtfully.

"You're very lucky, you know. Both of you."

"What makes you say that?" asked Callie, her mouth full of bagel.

"You found Danny at just the right time. Who else could have discovered his love for music? And don't say your father. He feels badly enough that he didn't figure it out months ago. No, there's something about the connection between you and Danny that's very special. Look how much progress you've made with him in such a short time."

Callie would have spoken at that point, but Dora steamrolled right over her.

"And you needed Danny. Yes, you did," she said in response to Callie's raised eyebrow. "You needed someone who would accept you just as you are. Only a child can do that. Everyone else brings their baggage and their expectations to the table."

"I think Danny has more baggage than most adults," said Callie wryly.

"Fair enough," agreed Dora. "But you know what I'm getting at. He doesn't tell you what kind of songs to write, and he has no idea if a song 'sounds like you' or not."

Callie nodded slowly, realizing that even her father had a set of expectations about her music and what it should be.

"Anyway," said Dora. "I wanted you to realize how lucky you are. To step out of your life, to put aside all that baggage and focus on the act of creation—it's a rare opportunity. It can't last forever, of course, but this is a special time. Enjoy it."

Her mother sounded so wistful that Callie wanted to ask why, but this did not seem like the right moment. Dora had begun a brisk clean-up and jumped immediately into a new stream of chatter. Questions about her art, her life, and the choices she made along the way would have to wait.

"You'll be on your own today, dear. I'm off to Chicago to replenish my supplies before the final push to finish my current project." She gave her daughter a sidelong look. "I'm meeting your sisters for lunch. Do you want to join us?"

The distraction of a field trip was tempting, but Callie was on a good run with her songwriting and hated to lose momentum.

"I'll stay here and work," she answered, "but give them a hug for me." She paused, suddenly suspicious. "Do they even know you're coming?"

"Not yet," her mother answered with a sly smile. "But they'll make time for lunch with their mother."

"Mom, you can't just—"

"I can and I will," said Dora firmly. "If you have a problem with my methods—if you would deny me a nice, relaxing lunch with my daughters—then you can come along and keep me company instead."

Callie shook her head.

"I thought not." Dora grinned, full of mischief. "In that case, have a lovely day, get lots of songwriting done, and I'll see you at dinnertime. It's your turn to cook, you know."

Dora threw that last comment over her shoulder as she headed upstairs to get dressed. Callie rose slowly and followed, intent on tearing apart her closet to find the notebooks. Maybe later, with her mother safely in Chicago, she could have a second look at her mother's box of memories.

Kat watched the clock as it ticked past ten. She realized that her foot was tapping. If Adam wanted to keep secrets and blow off meetings, then he would have to live with the consequences. She couldn't believe that he would be so cavalier with Danny's future.

The file lay open on the desk in front of her, the report from Doc Archer on top of the stack of papers. It was brief, but covered all the basics. Danny had settled into a comfortable routine that included a refusal to talk. Nothing had altered this routine since the beginning of the school year. All the people in his life had adapted to Danny's choice, rather than pushing Danny to adapt to the world around him. Until something jolted him from this comfortable routine, perhaps a more aggressive intervention or a change in the custody arrangement—or both—Danny had no incentive to rejoin the world.

And now Danny had started talking, but to Callie, of all people. Doc Archer's report was now obsolete and Adam's case a hundred times stronger. The James sisters certainly had a knack for disrupting people's lives. If she were superstitious, she would make the sign of the cross every time she saw one of them.

The jangle of the bell yanked Kat out of her thoughts. She hadn't even noticed Adam drive up, park, and walk past her window. She needed to get her head in the game. It was smart of him to show up, but it didn't get him off the hook for keeping secrets. She met him in the waiting room.

"Adam, I'm so glad you could make it," she said, extending her hand for a firm handshake. "Would you like to join me next door for coffee? Or would you prefer to meet here?" she asked, acknowledging his concerns from their previous coffee date, but reminding him that she didn't share those concerns.

"I think it's important that we meet here," he answered, taking off his coat.

"As you wish." Kat turned and walked back into her office, leaving him to follow or not as he liked. No casual meetings in the waiting area today. She needed the solidity of the desk between them, and the reinforcement of her leather chair.

When they were seated, Kat swallowed the angry lump in her throat.

"From this point forward," she began, all business, "I would appreciate it if you would let me know right away about any change in Danny's status. If he stops talking, if he opens up to anyone else, if he does anything at all out of the ordinary, I need to know. And so does Doc Archer."

Adam looked like he was going to object, but she needed to be firm on this point.

"I can't make an informed recommendation, nor can Doc Archer offer an honest assessment, if we don't have the facts. If you can't trust me, then I can't trust you, and we have a problem. Do I make myself clear?"

Adam hesitated, then nodded curtly.

"Excellent. Now let's talk about the case. The fact that Danny is talking changes everything. You've made a clear breakthrough and you should take credit for it. I wouldn't recommend any changes to Danny's situation as long as he's making progress and you're providing a stable environment."

"Of course I'm providing a stable environment. I thought we had already established that."

"The custody arrangement is being reviewed, so everything gets a second look. I have to consider all the usual factors," said Kat. "You're a single parent, with all the related challenges, as we've discussed. I also need to consider the other people in Danny's life and whether or not they are a strong link in his support network. Then there's your work situation and whether or not it is compatible with raising a family."

"My work is extremely child-friendly."

"Certainly, if you consider it work. Some might view your business as more of a hobby, and worry that you will get bored and want to go back to the high-powered job you were doing before all this happened."

"Some people like you?" he asked.

She nodded.

"That's not going to happen." Adam's answer had the intensity of true conviction, but Kat still had her doubts. How could a man of his intelligence and drive settle for a quiet rural existence restoring wooden boats? She didn't quite buy it.

"If you say so," she said.

Adam looked dissatisfied with her answer, but he turned his attention to a different point.

"What people would you evaluate other than me? I'm really the only person in Danny's life."

"And that's precisely the problem," returned Kat. "You'll need to expand Danny's support network over time, once he's comfortable talking with a wider range of people. Obviously Doc Archer and I would be considered part of his network now. With the introduction of the music lessons, Callie James becomes a factor as well."

Kat didn't bother to hide the skepticism in her voice. She was under no obligation to like Callie.

"You have a problem with the music lessons," stated Adam, direct as always.

"No, I have a problem with the teacher."

"And that is?" he prompted.

"She's not stable," said Kat. "She's an unknown element in delicate situation. You don't know how long she'll be in town. She has no experience working with children. And a simple Google search will fill you in on some of the more salacious details of her life as a professional musician."

If this last statement surprised Adam, he hid it well. If anything, his face hardened and became more difficult to read.

"And yet she is the one person who has connected with Danny," he challenged. "She's the key to this whole thing."

She had made him angry, but it was her job to be straight with him.

"I think it's risky," she insisted. "It may turn out to be the right choice, but it's my job to make sure you've thought it through." She paused, giving him a hard stare. "Clearly you have."

He didn't back down, leaving them in an odd kind of emotional stand-off.

"I'm keeping close tabs on the situation. If I have concerns, I'll pull the plug," he said. "And of course I'll notify you immediately," he added.

She mentally torched her step-by-step relationship plan.

"Is there anything else I can do to prove my worthiness?" he asked. "Shall I sign a statement swearing off women until Danny turns eighteen?"

Kat forced a smile. "You could try," she answered, striving for a lighter tone. "But I doubt anybody would take you seriously."

"Why is that?" he asked, giving a cynical laugh. "Relationships are a pain in the ass. I'm happy to put it off for a few years."

Kat wished she could smack him across the face on behalf of every single, thirtysomething woman in the world.

"Give me a break, Adam. You're a healthy man in the prime of his life. Nobody will believe you if you claim celibacy. It's like advertising the fact that you're planning to sneak around."

She put up a hand to stop him when he tried to object.

"Let me put this another way," she said. "If you try to convince the judge—who is single, by the way, and not that much older than you—that you are going to be celibate for the next ten years, she will laugh in your face, declare you certifiable, and give custody to Danny's grandparents."

"So you think I should hit the local dating scene?"

"You already know my opinion on this subject. I think you should put some reasonable boundaries on your personal life such that it has minimal impact on Danny. Engaging in open, honest relationships with women from the local community would be perfectly appropriate."

"You seriously think I should start dating."

"If it's someone local and stable, then yes."

"Fine," he said. "I'll be sure to let the judge know I plan to 'shop local.'"

"Great." She ground out the word through clenched teeth. "You be sure to use just those words."

He laughed. "I will."

And just like that the tension disappeared, leaving the ragged edges of her temper flapping in the breeze.

"So what happens next?" he asked.

"In a week or so, once we're sure that Danny's progress is going to stick, I'll submit my report to the judge and we'll wait until a date is set for the hearing. Could be anytime in the next two months."

"And in the meantime?" he queried.

We have a *normal conversation* over a cup of coffee.

"Keep doing what you're doing," she answered. "And, if you don't mind, I'd like to have a meeting with Danny. Maybe now that he's talking, he'll let us know how he feels about the current custody arrangement."

"It's worth a try," said Adam.

"How about tomorrow?" asked Kat.

"So soon?"

"Now that he's started talking, the sooner the better."

CHAPTER THIRTEEN

While her mother was showering and getting ready for the day downtown, Callie went hunting for her old music notebooks. Her mother had said that she'd put the KEEP OUT box in Callie's bedroom closet, but the closet was so jammed full of old clothes and random junk that Callie couldn't find a thing. As much as she wanted to find the notebooks, she feared that if she pulled out any single item, the rest would tumble down in a dusty, feathery mess.

When she finally spied the corner of a cardboard box on the top shelf, far back in the corner, she knew what she needed to do. Gritting her teeth, she began unloading the top shelf onto the bed. Little Mermaid sleeping bag. Milk crate full of mermaid and princess costumes. Another milk crate full of hats, some with feathers, and several feather boas. Extra comforter for the bed (mermaid, of course). Milk crate full of grade school memorabilia. Knitting bag overflowing with yarn and a single, yet-to-be-finished project. The yarn had tangled on something at the back of the shelf, something Callie couldn't see. Tugging gently, Callie dragged the object forward.

She had snagged a picture frame. Lifting it down, she realized it was the photo of her first real gig. Her mother had placed the five-by-seven print in a sterling silver frame, now tarnished, that featured elaborate loops and swirls. The yarn had hooked on one of the swirls. At the time the photo had been taken, she had felt unbearably mature and professional, but looking now at her eleven-year-old self, she couldn't help but smile. So young, and so fearless.

She had played, coffeehouse-style, during the after-church rush at Lucy's. That first gig had gone well, so she had continued, playing every Sunday from eleven thirty to one thirty for the whole summer. Her father would pull up in the minivan just after one o'clock, slipping in the door to listen while she finished up the set. He would wait patiently while she gathered up her gear, accepted payment from Lucy and (every time) turned around and used the money to buy doughnuts. Lucy had offered to pay her in doughnuts, but Callie had loved being able to say she had a paying gig. Then the two of them would drive home, talking about music, one professional to another.

It was all she had ever wanted to do: play music, get paid, buy doughnuts. Callie laughed quietly to herself. Why couldn't life be that simple? And why hadn't she been back to Lucy's for doughnuts yet?

Her smile faded as she remembered the day she had put the photo up on the closet shelf. It had been during her sophomore year of college. She had brought Brian home for the day, to meet her parents and see her lake, imagining an afternoon of playing music with her two favorite people—Brian and her father. She and Brian had just formed the band. They were in the first flush of dating, feeling the rush of discovery, dismissing each other's faults as endearing little quirks. She had wanted the opposite of Adam, and she had found him.

The day had not gone as well in real life as it had in her imagination. Brian and her father had been stilted and awkward together, and she had never found the right moment to suggest that they play music. Her mother had asked a million questions, making Brian defensive. Her father hadn't said a word. So she and Brian had retreated to her room—leaving the door open, per the house rules—where she had hoped that, if nothing else, they could reconnect with each other.

She had never seen her bedroom through the eyes of a stranger. As they entered the room, she felt herself grow younger as he grew older, the gap between them widening by the second. Suddenly the Little Mermaid poster on her wall seemed childish rather than classic, the matching comforter mortifying. Even the gauze draped over her four-poster bed, which she had thought so bohemian and shabby-chic, looked stupid.

Brian had carefully seated himself on the bed, as if he were afraid the Little Mermaid images would permanently tattoo his rear end. His smirk said more than she wanted to hear, so she had turned her back on him and walked to the window, staring out at the lake and trying to ignore the ache in her chest.

"What's this from, open mic night?" he had asked. She had turned to find him holding the picture of her first gig, which he had picked up off her night table.

"It's nothing," she had answered, swallowing the lump in her throat. "My Mom just likes to take pictures." She had grabbed the frame from his hands and shoved it between two milk crates on her closet shelf, as far back as she could reach.

The whole idea of bringing Brian home had been a mistake, and she wanted to get it over with as soon as possible. So she had turned back to him, arms crossed, and pulled the plug.

"Let's get out of here," she had said, her bleak mood turning darker when he visibly brightened. "It's not what I thought it would be."

He had laughed. "You've totally moved on, babe. This place has nothing to do with who you are. This is who you were. Let's blow this joint and get back to reality."

And that was the last time Brian had visited her childhood home—until this summer, of course. She hadn't been a frequent visitor herself. She had hit the major holidays, most years, but they had been working so hard to build a reputation, always touring or rehearsing or recording, and the band had always come first. Brian had always come first. Whenever she had gone home, whenever she had walked into her bedroom, she had remembered the feeling of being there with Brian, and home hadn't felt like home anymore.

It was time to exorcise some demons. It was time to connect the Callie of today with all her former selves. It was time to open the box.

She placed the framed photo gently on her night table, where it belonged, and returned to the closet. Standing on tiptoe, she reached into the back corner and caught hold of the KEEP OUT box, dragging it toward the center of the shelf, then tipping it down into her arms. It wasn't all that big, but it was surprisingly heavy. She set it down on the floor and sat cross-legged beside it, opening the top and breathing a sigh of relief when she saw all her notebooks tucked safely inside.

Callie ran her fingers along the wire spirals. She had filed away her musical life so neatly, the colorful assortment of spiral-bound school notebooks arranged in perfect chronological order. She pulled out the last one, which should be the first, chronologically speaking, and checked the cover. Sure enough, she had written '1996' in black marker on the teal cover.

She laughed when she opened the cover and saw what she had written on the first page:

'Warning: The music and lyrics in this notebook are the property of Callie James and you do NOT have permission to use them in any way. Close this notebook immediately and return it to Callie James.'

As she paged through the notebook, she understood why her mother had found it so confusing. The pages were more of a mental map than a carefully edited collection of songs. There were snippets of lyrics, notes about song concepts, guitar tabs, melody lines, sketches of song structure, even a few doodles. None of it would make sense to an outsider—only to her.

She flipped through page after page, notebook after notebook, retracing ebb and flow of her high school experience. Her heart began to ache, then her throat, and then her eyes blurred so that she couldn't read anymore. She set the notebook aside and wrapped her arms around her legs, resting her forehead on her knees and letting the tears fall. She cried for the first time in years, mourning the brave, passionate girl she had been and lamenting the quiet, compliant woman she had become.

She might have stayed there all day, wallowing in self-pity, but for a light knock on the doorframe as her mother breezed in.

"Well, dear, I'm off to the big city—" Dora stopped midsentence. "Oh, sweetie, what's the matter? Are they ruined? Did they get wet?" She dropped to her knees beside Callie and wrapped her arm around Callie's shoulder. "Oh, sweetie, please don't cry."

Callie sniffled and turned her red, bleary eyes on her mother.

"I'm fine, Mom. Really. And the notebooks are fine. I just . . . I wasn't prepared for this particular trip down memory lane."

She wiped her eyes with the hem of her T-shirt and slowly climbed to her feet, grabbing a tissue from the box on the desk to blow her nose. Dora stood also, stepping back to study her daughter.

"You don't look fine to me," said Dora, putting her hands on her hips.

Callie gave a watery laugh. "Mom, please. I needed a good cry. Now I've had one, and I'll wash my face and get on with my day."

"Maybe you should come with me to Chicago," suggested Dora, clearly uneasy at the thought of leaving Callie alone.

"Stop it," insisted Callie, blowing her nose one last time. "I'm all done crying. You have your day in the city. I'll have my day in the country. Then, over dinner, you can tell me the latest from Mel and Tessa and I can tell you about all the cool stuff I found in my notebooks. Okay?"

Callie was prepared to hustle her mother out the door if necessary, but in the end Dora went willingly.

"Promise me you'll call me if you need me," said Dora as she backed slowly out of Callie's room.

"Go. Have fun. I promise I'll call if I need you." This last promise did the trick, and Callie breathed a sigh of relief as her mother finally walked away. This mini-breakdown would only add fuel to the fire when her mother and sisters dissected her life over lunch today, but at least Callie could finish airing out her emotions privately, without fear of interruption.

When her mother had driven away, Callie returned to the notebooks. Leafing through them now, she felt lighter, better able to embrace her teen angst with compassion rather than grief. She may have lost the intensity of those years, but she had not lost the core of herself. She had submerged it beneath a pool of very deep, cold, still water. All she needed was a dose of sunshine and she would be fine.

In the last notebook, the one from freshman year of college, she found what she had been seeking. Not that she had been looking for one particular song, but if she wanted to reconnect with herself, the easiest way to do it would be to pick a work-in-progress from all those years ago and, in essence, collaborate with herself to finish it.

The song wasn't complete. It was more a jumble of notes and ideas, but the core of it was there. She had barely begun the transition from concept to creation when she had brought Brian home for that visit. When they had driven away, she had left the notebook behind. There was no way she was going to finish a song inspired by homesickness called "Find My Way Back Home." She was moving on, not going home.

Ten years later, back home—really back home—Callie felt a tug as she read the title. She studied her notes carefully. She had written lyrics for the refrain, strong lyrics that still felt right.

I press my face against the glass
I watch the miles go rolling past
I know where I would rather be
The only place I feel like me
The only place I call my own
It's time to find my way back home.

She wouldn't change them. There was a decent sketch of the song structure, but she would rewrite the hesitant attempts at verses. She could draw on a richer pool of experience now, and she had learned a lot from her time away. As she studied the tabs, and her scribbled melodies, she realized that she could work with the building blocks she had left behind. She didn't need to start from scratch.

Setting the notebook aside, Callie replaced the top on her KEEP OUT box and stretched, her muscles stiff after sitting in one position for so long. She got to her feet and surveyed the chaos she had created by unloading the closet. Then she glanced out the window and saw the sunshine dancing on the water.

It was a gorgeous day. The mess could wait.

A loud crash from next door, followed by a steady a stream of curses, caught Callie's attention on her way down to the lake. She detoured across the lawn and slipped through the fence, weaving through the shrubs until she could see what was going on. She found Adam wrestling with a long metal pole, one end of which was supported by a sawhorse, the other end near a hole in the ground full of something gray, possibly wet concrete. As she watched, he coaxed the one end toward the concrete, but the other end—the one on the sawhorse—slid as well, threatening to crash onto the ground again. When he saw her, he paused, resting the near end of the pole on the ground and wiping the sweat from his face with the bottom edge of his T-shirt.

The stolen glimpse of his abs struck her nerves like a tuning fork, sending a shiver through her entire body. For the first time in her life, Callie fully appreciated the term 'treasure trail.'

She swallowed hard and called out to him.

"Everybody okay over here? I heard a crash."

"I'm fine," he answered tersely. "Nothing to worry about. Just lost my grip."

He didn't look fine. He looked like he was trying to do a two-man job by himself. Were all guys idiots? Or only the ones that she knew?

"What are you doing?" asked Callie.

"I'm putting up a basketball hoop for Danny."

"Really?" she asked, surprised. The pole looked awfully long. "Will he be able to reach the basket?"

"It's adjustable." said Adam. "And four feet of the pole will be in the ground."

"Oh," said Callie. That made much more sense.

"Can I help you get it up?" she asked, then flushed when she realized what she had said.

He grinned. "How can I possibly refuse?"

She blushed harder and crossed her arms. Maybe she would just watch him struggle with it and wait for him to wipe his face again with his T-shirt.

"If you can lift from that end, I'll guide the pole into the hole."

She caught his smirk, but couldn't think of a response. There was no way to talk about poles and holes without making some sort of innuendo.

"All you need to do is walk it up slowly," he said. "And be gentle."

She snickered, unable to help herself, then walked over to her end of the pole and got a strong grip.

He seemed distracted, just stood there staring at her hands wrapped around the pole.

"Tell me when you're ready," she said. He snapped out of it.

"On three," he said. "One . . . two . . . three."

She did exactly as he had asked, lifting her end slowly and smoothly while he guided the pole into the concrete. In less than a minute the job was done.

"That was easy," she said, now standing beside him and steadying the pole. He knelt at the base and secured a metal collar brace with four massive bolts.

"You were hoping it would be harder?" he asked, looking up at her over his shoulder.

She laughed.

"No," she answered, struggling to keep her expression serious. "I thought it would take longer. I don't like to be rushed."

They were actually flirting. She had seen other people do it, but couldn't remember ever doing it herself. She and Adam had been too intense for flirting, and Brian was more into biting sarcasm.

Adam pulled a level out of the back pocket of his jeans, checking to make sure the pole stood straight, then rose slowly to his feet. His movement brought them face to face, just inches apart. In that moment, the humor slid away, leaving only the buzz of awareness in its wake. Callie let her hand fall away from the pole.

"Thanks," he said softly.

"Anytime," she answered.

They stood frozen for a few heartbeats, a shared breath, and then he stepped back, giving her a half-smile.

"For the record, I don't like to be rushed either."

She blushed at that and dropped her eyes, unable to keep up the banter. She remembered all too well that he liked to take his time.

"Well, I guess I'll see you later," she said, turning back toward the opening in the fence. "Hope your pole stays up," she called over her shoulder. She giggled. Flirting was fun. Maybe she should do it more often.

She had reached the fence when he called out to her.

CHAPTER FOURTEEN

"Callie, wait."

The words were out of his mouth before he had any idea what he planned to say. She stopped at the opening in the fence and looked back at him.

"Where are you headed?" he asked.

"Down to the lake," she called back. "I need to clear my head."

His mind filled with images from long ago. The minuscule bikini. The unnecessary rescue. The talk that had followed. Their "encounter" had branded him in a way that he was only now coming to understand.

"Isn't it a little cold for a swim?" he asked.

"I was just going to sit by the water," she answered. "I need some lake time."

"Why don't we take out the canoe?" he asked.

She cocked her head to one side.

"Don't you have other things. . . . I mean, you don't need to rearrange your day for me."

"No worries. Give me a sec to find a jacket," he said. "It will be cooler on the water."

He stepped into the cottage before Callie could back out. It didn't take long to strip off his sweaty T-shirt, find a clean one, and grab his jacket off the hook. He was back outside in less than a minute.

"Come on, let's go," he said. Callie hesitated for only a second before following him down the hill.

The dock rested in pieces on the shore, stacked like a set of white Lincoln Logs. They would have to do this the old fashioned way, launching the canoe from the shore in front of the boathouse, which formed a natural ramp. He hauled up the garage door on the boathouse and hoisted the canoe off its rack, carrying it a few feet and dropping it gently half in and half out of the water.

"Could you grab the paddles, please?" he asked, pointing to where they hung on the wall. She nodded, bringing them to the boat and laying them gently inside. Adam hung on to the end of the canoe, making sure it stayed put. He didn't want to have to go wading into the lake after it.

"Have you been canoeing before?" he asked, hoping the answer was 'yes.' Just because she had grown up on the lake didn't mean that she had tried every single water sport.

She didn't bother to answer, hopping nimbly into the stern, picking her way up to the bow and grabbing a paddle along the way. She sat in the front properly, with her rear end resting on the bench and her knees on the keel of the boat. She looked back over her shoulder at him.

"Well? Are you coming or what?"

He grinned. This was going to be fun. He leaned down to shove off, timing his push and his leap so that he landed gently in the boat as the stern slid into the water. He had no desire to get his shoes wet, or to humiliate himself by tripping. Like any male over the age of twelve, he wanted to impress the girl.

"Let's go this way," she called over her shoulder, pointing down the shoreline to her left. "I'll show you one of my favorite spots."

"Lead on."

She paddled with quiet confidence, and he matched her, stroke for stroke. They did rather well, considering they had never canoed together before. For Adam, the most challenging part was keeping his eyes up and his attention on the sunshine, the water, and the steady rhythm of their paddling. With each stroke, Callie leaned forward slightly, revealing a swath of pale peach skin below her windbreaker and above the waistband of her jeans. As much as he enjoyed the view, he needed to pay attention to what he was doing.

"So how are things with the band," he asked.

Her back stiffened, and it occurred to him that a canoe was not the best place to have a conversation. He couldn't tell much about what she was thinking by looking at her back.

"They're fine," she said, but the way she said it didn't sound like things were fine.

Adam waited for a few strokes, but she didn't expand on her answer. This was almost as much fun as trying to have a conversation with Danny.

"Aren't you guys touring this summer?"

"Mm-hmm."

"Any new music?"

"The first album just came out," she said. "That's what we'll be playing on the tour. I'm supposed to be working on the second one right now."

"Is this what you do when you're writing new music?" he asked. "You come back home?" What he really wanted to know was how often she might be back. The idea that he might run into Callie on a regular basis threw a whole new variable into his calculations. Talk about an unknown quantity.

"Usually I stay in Nashville, but I need some time to rest my voice and recharge."

So this was a kind of sabbatical for her. A break from her life rather than a change in course. It explained her raspy voice, but not her lack of enthusiasm.

"So you like the life?" he asked. "Seems like it would be rough to be on the road all the time."

"We're not on the road all the time," she answered. "We take breaks to rehearse new music and record in the studio."

"You don't have daydreams about settling down?"

She snorted. "You sound like my mother."

Adam sighed. This was not going well. He just wanted to connect the Callie in front of him with the Callie that he remembered, and he couldn't find the thread that joined them. She seemed like a different person—one who played a vitally important role in his future with Danny.

"What do you want to know, Adam?" Callie's direct question surprised him.

"What do you mean?" he asked.

"If you want to know something, you should just ask. We know each other well enough for that, I think."

He really wished that he could see her face.

"Nothing. Everything." He sighed. "It's been nearly a decade. A lot has happened."

"The questions can wait," she said firmly. "We're here."

They had reached a shallow, sheltered spot where the shoreline curved. A screen of trees helped to calm the water and protected them from the wind. Callie placed her paddle across the gunwales of the canoe. Adam did the same, and they drifted for a moment before coming to rest beneath the bare hanging branches of a stand of willow trees.

Callie turned her face up to catch the sunlight that filtered through the willow strands. Her long blond curls streamed down her back, the sunlight dancing along the highlights in her hair, much the same way that it sparkled on the ripples in the water. He envied her tranquility, her ability to sink into the moment. He wanted that for himself.

Callie could have stayed in that moment all day, with her face tipped toward the sun, eyes closed, the canoe gently rocking in the water. But she wasn't alone. She could sense the solidity of Adam's presence behind her, waiting. He had questions, and she wasn't sure how to answer him.

When she felt calm and centered, she opened her eyes and, pivoting carefully, turned fully around to face him. The sun highlighted the contours of his face but revealed nothing of what he might be feeling. She took a deep breath, then began.

"There's no way to compress the last nine years into a neat little story for you. There was college, and the band, and then the long, hard slog to get where we are today. It's not exactly fodder for a family movie."

"Fair enough," he answered. "But if you're spending time with Danny, I'd really like to know more than just the tabloid headlines."

"Oh, God."

"That bad?" He raised one eyebrow, clearly intrigued.

"You read that crap?" she hedged.

"Let's think about it from the perspective of a parent choosing a music teacher for a child. Where should I get my information?"

"From me," she said, appalled at the idea that the tabloids could have the final word.

"So fill me in," he said.

She sighed. Where to begin?

"The reality of life with the band is pretty boring, but the press is always looking for a story. We've only made the majors a few times—the tabloids you see at the supermarket checkout. If you Google us, you'll mostly find the gossip from Nashville, the tattle websites, that kind of thing. A couple of the guys in the band have struggled with drug and alcohol problems. They've been in rehab a few times, and Ash did some jail time."

"But you never got caught up in any of that?" probed Adam.

"Of course not," she said. "I can't stop them from being idiots, but I can walk away from it myself."

He nodded, his face impassive.

"What else?" he asked.

He waited while she struggled to find the words. How do you reduce ten years of Brian to a few sentences?

"Until recently, I was involved in a relationship with our front man. We formed the band in college."

That was a good start. Keep it simple. Stick to the facts.

"Brian has trouble saying no to women," she continued, making the understatement of the century. "Although we weren't married, I had certain . . . expectations regarding fidelity. He did not share those expectations."

"I saw some headlines last week," said Adam, his voice gentler than it had been a moment before.

She closed her eyes. "You saw that," she repeated.

"I did."

She sighed.

"The recent coverage was both national and ugly. You'll find articles that question the status of our relationship and what a breakup would mean for the future of the band. This round included 'caught in the act' naked pictures of Brian with our three new backup singers." She cleared her throat, drawing strength from a rising tide of anger. "For me, it was the last straw."

"So you left."

She nodded.

"You're not really having a problem with your voice?" he asked.

"No, that part is true. It's the reason we hired the backup singers in the first place." She smiled, hating the fact that she had become cynical already. "I auditioned them myself, hand-picked my own replacements."

Callie finally broke eye contact, staring across the water. She couldn't quite reclaim that feeling of tranquility from a few moments before, so she asked the one question burning in her mind.

"Do you want me to stop my sessions with Danny?" She stared at the far shore, waiting for his verdict.

"No."

She looked up at him in surprise, relief swamping her turbulent emotions.

"Really?" she asked, a smile breaking through. "I thought for sure you'd pull the plug."

"Are you trying to change my mind?"

"No! I mean . . . I just. . . ." She took a deep breath. "Thank you. I appreciate your trust."

His mouth twisted ruefully.

"Let's call it a calculated risk."

"I can work with that," she replied, her smile widening.

"So why is this your favorite spot?" asked Adam, shifting his position so that he sat on the bench rather than kneeling.

She breathed a sigh of relief, grateful for a change of topic and happy to talk about something other than paparazzi and cheating boyfriends.

"In the summer," she began, "when the willow branches hang down low, this spot reminds me of that scene from *The Little Mermaid*."

He raised his eyebrows.

"It's silly, I know," she said.

"I have no idea what you're talking about," he said. "I've never seen it."

"Seriously? It's a classic. It's animated, based on the fairy tale, and there's a scene set in a place like this."

"And why do you like that scene so much?" He seemed honestly curious, without the judgment she had come to expect from

Brian. *And now for the embarrassing part,* she thought, scrambling for an explanation that did not shed too much light on her preteen fantasies.

"Well, the mermaid and the prince are in a rowboat, and there's this great song. . . . Anyway, the girl—she can't talk, because of this curse—she's trying to find a way to communicate with the prince, but he doesn't understand."

She wasn't making any sense, and the mystified look on his face made her want to laugh.

"We're talking about a kids' movie, right? Rated G?" He raised an eyebrow. "What exactly happens on this boat?"

"Not what you're thinking!" Callie couldn't hold back the laughter. "It's one of those perfect moments. Sunset. Music. They're about to kiss, and the whole world stops, but then the minions of the bad guy—bad witch, technically—tip over the boat, and the moment is ruined."

"Minions?" he asked.

Her breath hitched, and she looked up at him sharply. Brian would make a snide remark at this point, squelching the effervescence of the moment.

"I like that word," he said, tipping his head to the side as if giving the matter serious thought. "Much better than 'henchmen.' If I were a villain I would definitely have minions."

She relaxed and dumped all thoughts of Brian overboard. She was living her life in this moment, with this man, and she didn't want to ruin it by thinking about Brian.

"So let me get this straight," he said, resting his hands on the gunwales and leaning toward her. "The prince is leaning forward, right?"

She nodded, suppressing a smile. They were going to flirt again. It was lovely, this feeling of being attractive and clever and . . . wanted. It had been much too long.

"And the mermaid—wait, does she have a tail and everything?" Callie shook her head.

"Right. No tail. Mermaid with legs. Got it." He readjusted his grip, which rocked the boat. "So she's leaning forward, too."

Callie nodded, but she didn't move.

"Lean forward," he said in a stage whisper. Her eyes widened.

"You're not going to tip us over, are you? I mean, I love the scene, but I have no interest in living it. The water is really, really cold." She leaned forward anyway, scooting her hands along the gunwales until they were a few inches from his paddle.

"No, I'm not going to tip us over," he said. "I'm just trying to get a feel for the scene."

He looked up at the willow branches and then down at the sparkling water before looking back in her eyes, which were now inches away from his. Even though she knew they were only flirting, she found it hard to breathe properly.

"Very romantic," he decreed. "Did you ever bring a boyfriend here at sunset to make out?"

She shook her head. She had thought about bringing Adam, all those years ago, but they had run out of time.

"Good," he said softly.

She held her breath, unmoving, clutching the sides of the canoe for balance. The moment seemed to stretch out in time, suspended. They were so close she could feel his breath on her lips. She blinked, her gaze dropping to his mouth, not quite brave enough to close the gap between them, but hoping for a wave of courage. Were they really going to open this door again?

"You know," she whispered, her eyes still on his mouth, "they never did kiss. This is the moment when the boat tips over."

She watched his lips twist into a rueful smile. He didn't pull back, but he didn't close the gap, either.

Sunlight infused the moment with color, searing it into her memory. She looked back up into his eyes, sinking into the dark blue depths. She didn't think about the past or the future. Only this moment mattered.

So she kissed him.

Callie lost all sense of time. The world was reduced to sunlight, water, and Adam. She drank him in, breathed him in, wanting more. She tried to lift one hand, but felt the balance of the canoe shift beneath her. She grabbed the side again.

He laughed against her mouth. She inched closer so she could explore his jawline. He kissed the hollow at the base of her neck. She found the tender spot where his jaw met his ear and inhaled the subtle scent of his neck.

A gust of wind brought them back to reality. With a groan, he pulled back, breathing hard. She swayed toward him, off balance, unwilling to let him go so soon.

"Wait," he said hoarsely.

"Why. . . ."

"I can't—"

The boat swayed again, and she swayed with it, closing the gap between them. She could sense his hesitation, feel him holding back. She didn't want to hold back. She had wasted too many years of her life already. So she let go of the boat and grabbed his shoulders, the boat rocking wildly. She scooted closer, so that only the narrow shaft of the paddle separated their bodies. There was no way for him to pull back without dunking them both.

"Callie," he breathed, when her attention strayed to his neck. He bent his head, his mouth pressing against her temple. "Callie, please, we have to—"

She lifted her head just as he ducked lower.

"Ow!" He jerked back, one hand going to his nose, the other still gripping the gunwale. The boat lurched. Callie could feel it start to roll and grabbed for the sides. Adam moved at the same time, in the same direction, throwing them even more off balance. The canoe flipped, dumping them both into the freezing cold water.

"Cold, cold, cold!" shrieked Callie as she flailed in the shallow water, trying to find her footing.

They scrambled to their feet at the same time, Adam spitting curses as he grabbed for the canoe. The water barely reached their knees, but it burned with a fiery cold that could quickly become dangerous. He needed to get Callie back home—and fast.

"Your paddle," he barked, reaching for his own which had started to float away. She grabbed hers, anchoring it between her knees, then got a firm hold on the bow of the canoe. He met her eyes and she nodded.

"On three," he said. "One . . . two . . . three."

They lifted the upside-down canoe out of the water, then flipped it, so that it landed upright in the water with an icy splash. His hands were already going numb, but he gritted his teeth and steadied the canoe while she climbed in. She was small and would feel the effects of the cold first. Her shaking hands could barely grip the paddle. He climbed in behind her, dripping, and wrapped his stiff fingers around the handle.

They raced back, the furious pace warming them just enough to keep going. With a final burst of speed, they grounded the boat on the rocky beach. Callie hopped out first and held the prow steady as Adam made his exit. He yanked the boat out of the water, leaving it beached at the entrance to the boathouse.

She moved to hang her paddle back on the wall, but he stopped her.

"Leave it," he said, taking the paddle from her and dropping it in the boat. "I'll deal with it later. We need to dry off and warm up."

She nodded, her lips blue and her teeth chattering. She looked like she was going to fall over, so he wrapped an arm around her shoulders.

"Come on, let's get you home."

He half guided, half dragged her up the hill to her back door. Her hands were still shaking, so he opened the screen door and the inner door, shepherding her inside. He started unzipping her wet jacket, but she stopped him.

"I've g-g-got it," she protested, pushing his hands out of the way and clumsily pulling down the zipper.

"Are you sure?" he asked, wondering if she would be able to turn the water faucet in order to run a bath or take a shower. "Is anybody else here to help you?"

She shook her head. "G-g-go home, already. You need t-t-to get warm as m-m-much as I d-d-do. I'll b-b-be fine."

He hesitated. She was peeling the wet jacket off her arms and revealing the wet white T-shirt underneath. He couldn't help but notice the fact that she was very, very cold. A part of him wanted to stay, to make sure that she was able to remove all that wet clothing and start the shower. What if she couldn't unhook that lacy bra? Or turn the faucet? They both needed to get warm. If they shared body heat, maybe—

"Unless you want t-t-to join me?" she asked, looking hopeful.

He shook his head. Even though his body (and most of his brain) was shouting 'Yes!' a small part of him still knew better. His life was complicated enough.

"I'll be back in an hour to check on you," he said as he stepped back outside. "Go get warm."

She frowned, but he shut the door in her face.

He turned toward his cottage, walking, then breaking into a jog. If he were honest with himself, he would have to call it running away.

Only later, when his hot shower had faded to lukewarm, did he let himself think about that kiss, that wet T-shirt, and how much he would have liked to help Callie get warm.

As promised, Adam showed up on her doorstep an hour later.

"Are you warm again?" he asked. His hair was still damp, and he wore a few more layers than were really necessary. He noticed that she was overdressed as well, her face flushed.

She nodded. "Nothing like a bath to warm you up from the inside out."

He could think of a much better way to warm her up from the inside out, but pushed the thought aside. He needed to stop this thing between them before it could go any further.

"Callie, I can't do this."

"Do what?"

"This," he said, moving a step closer so that she had to look up to meet his eyes. "Us. Kissing."

"Oh. That." Her eyes dropped to his mouth and she smiled slowly. "I'm sorry about that. I don't know what came over me."

"I do."

He must have surprised her, because her breath hitched, but she kept her eyes fixed on his mouth. He couldn't stop thinking about her mouth, either—thinking that the mistake had already been made. There couldn't be much harm in one last kiss.

He reached up to weave his fingers through her hair until he clasped the nape of her neck in his hand. He tipped her head back so that their eyes met.

"I know exactly what came over you."

Before she could react, he covered her mouth with his, tasting, teasing, gently biting her lower lip, then exploring her jaw, her ear, and the sensitive hollow behind it. With his other hand he caressed her cheek, his fingers trailing across her scar before they too plunged into her hair. She grabbed on to the front of his jacket with both hands, making him grateful for solid footing.

He stilled, resting his temple against hers. There was no cold water to bail him out this time.

"I still can't do this," he breathed against her ear.

Neither of them moved.

"Why not?" she whispered fiercely, nipping at his earlobe.

He groaned, one hand tracing her spine down her back and then pulling her hips against him.

"It's complicated. There's a custody issue and I can't—" He pulled back slightly, so that his forehead rested against hers and he could look into her eyes. "I won't risk getting involved with you. Not while this custody thing is still unresolved."

"What makes me so risky?" She pulled back, insulted, but he didn't let go. When she backed into the doorframe, he moved with her, hips moving forward to grind against hers. Her legs parted, just a little, and one leg slid up to wrap around his thigh.

"You're leaving," he growled.

"True," she whispered, leaning in to bite his lower lip, "but not today. In fact, I'm on my own today. Nobody home but me."

"You have no idea how much I would like to take this inside."

She wasn't making it easy for him. He placed his hands on her shoulders and took a decisive step back. When he dropped his hands to his sides, she continued to hang on to his jacket.

"So show me," she suggested, tugging him closer.

He kissed her firmly before pulling away again, this time retreating as far as the driveway.

"I can't. I need to be on best behavior until this custody thing is sorted out. And then, well, by then you'll be gone."

"But nobody would need to know. . . ."

He laughed. "Callie, this is a small town. Somehow, one way or another, everyone would know."

She couldn't argue with that. She had grown up here, and knew all too well what he was just coming to understand: small-town gossip travels faster than anything else in the universe.

"So that's it?" she asked. "We pretend this never happened?"

"I don't like it any more than you do, but yeah. That's the plan."

She crossed her arms, still leaning on the doorframe, looking like a kid who had been given a time-out. Then she smiled, and he started to worry.

"Fine."

"That's it?" he asked warily.

"If you change your mind," she said, turning to go back inside, "you know where to find me."

This time, she was the one to close the door in his face.

CHAPTER FIFTEEN

Nine years ago

Callie felt his presence before she saw him. The hair on the back of her neck rose, and her entire body began to tremble. She had tried to sleep. Really, she had, but there was just no way she could relax when she knew he would be arriving late tonight. She had tiptoed out of the house at two a.m., hoping that he might have the same idea. They had made no plan, arranged no secret rendezvous, but last year they had made the summerhouse their own, and she desperately wanted to find him here again.

She turned to find him silhouetted in the doorway, the full moon casting his face into shadow. The trembling grew so strong that her knees nearly buckled, but she managed to stumble across the room and meet him halfway. They wrapped their arms around each other and just stood there, holding on tight. Her trembling eased. The solidity of his body, the heat—the reality of Adam—was almost more than she could handle after so many months apart.

"I'm eighteen." She spoke the words into his chest, but he heard them. He pulled back, his expression grim.

"I know."

"You don't look happy," she said. "Why?"

"There's something important we need to talk about."

He had found someone else.

She tried to pull back, but he wouldn't let go. She pushed against his chest, but found herself imprisoned within the circle of his arms. Her eyes burned, the tears ready to fall, but she squeezed her eyes shut and used her anger to hold the floodgates closed.

"Just say it." She spoke the words to his chest. "And then let me go."

If anything, he held her more tightly.

"They're sending me to Singapore."

His answer was so unexpected that it took her a few seconds to understand.

"On a business trip?" she asked.

He slid his hand around the nape of her neck and gently eased her head back so that she looked into his eyes rather than at his chest.

"On a five-year assignment."

The weight of the words made it suddenly difficult to breathe.

"Five years is a long time," she said softly.

"I know."

He sat in one of the wicker armchairs. She curled up in his arms, wishing fiercely that she could make him stay.

"When do you leave?" she asked.

"Tuesday."

She choked on the news. "So soon?"

His arms tightened around her. They sat in silence for a long time while she absorbed the full meaning of his news.

"Are you okay?" he finally asked.

She nodded, but didn't try to speak through the lump in her throat. He shifted position so he could see her face.

"You don't look okay," he said, a crooked smile on his face.

She swallowed hard.

"I was the one who said 'no plans, no promises,'" she whispered, "but I couldn't help it. I just thought, now that I'm eighteen, and Madison really isn't that far from Chicago. . . ."

"I thought about it, too," he admitted.

"I can wait for you." She couldn't imagine doing anything else.

"You have no idea how much I want that," he said roughly, "but I won't let you do it."

"You don't get to decide."

Crazy as it seemed, she felt completely at peace with the idea putting her life on hold for five-years.

"Please, Callie. You've talked so many times about getting away from here and playing your music for other people. You need to do that. You need to go after what you want—not sit around waiting for me."

She didn't respond. He would be halfway around the world. If she wanted to wait for him, there was nothing he could do to stop her.

"Callie?"

She leaned forward to give him a swift, hard kiss. "If this is going to be our last weekend together, then I have only one request," she said.

"What's that?" He sounded suspicious.

"I want my first time to be with you."

He went completely still, but she could feel the electricity race through both of them. Every muscle in his body tensed, and she was fully aware that one particular part of his anatomy thought this was a fantastic idea. That wasn't the part she would have to convince. It was his brain that was going to cause problems.

"I'm not going to claim you like some prize and then walk away," he said. "I'm not that much of an ass."

"No," she agreed. "That's why I'm the one who's going to claim you as my prize, and then I'll walk away."

He choked on a laugh, then said, "It's not funny."

"I'm not joking." She climbed off his lap to stand before him in the moonlight. She didn't want to waste a second of their time together. Grabbing the hem of her T-shirt she stripped it off, pleased to hear his swift intake of breath.

"I'm a grown woman and—quite legally—I can do whatever the hell I want."

She slipped her thumbs inside the waistband of her pajama pants and would have stripped them off as well, but he leapt to his feet and grabbed her wrists. She laughed.

"Slow down," he growled, holding her wrists behind her and pinning her body against his.

She found his chin with her mouth and kissed her way along his jawline, the harsh stubble burning her lips. When she reached his ear, she began whispering all the things she would like to do now that the legal barriers to their physical union had disappeared. He maneuvered her until her back hit the wall, then pinned her wrists above her head. He claimed her with his mouth, pressing the length of his body against hers and kissing her until she gasped for breath.

Desperate for more, she shifted her upper body, teasing both of them by brushing her breasts against his chest. He had taught her well last summer, and she used every lesson against him. He groaned, then adjusted his grip so that he could hold her wrists with just one hand. With the other, he grabbed her breast and held her body still, teasing the tip with his fingers until she whimpered his name.

He let go of her wrists. She wound her arms around his neck and wrapped one leg around his waist, locking him against her in case he had any stupid ideas about leaving. But he didn't. He slid his hands beneath her hips and lifted her to meet him. She hooked her feet together, anchoring herself to him, and gave herself over to the fire.

She wasn't the only one who had learned a lot last summer. He knew the secrets of her body, and he used them to his advantage. After so many months untouched, the combination of his hands kneading her backside and his erection grinding against her center had her shuddering in his arms within moments.

He scarcely gave her a chance to breathe before carrying her back to the chair. She curled up again in his lap, but this time he kissed her senseless. Each time she tried to peel off his shirt, he distracted her with his hands. He caressed her everywhere, his hands stroking up and down her back, her legs, and between her thighs, until she gasped his name and shuddered in his arms a second time.

When she had recovered, she climbed off his lap and stood before him with her hands on her hips.

"My turn," she said. She reached for his hands and pulled him to his feet. "Take off the shirt."

He obeyed her order with the half-smile that she loved. She moved into the circle of his arms and distracted him with a kiss while she pulled his wallet out of his back pocket. When she stepped back with her prize, he raised an eyebrow in question.

"Please tell me you have a condom in here," she said. "You are not getting out of this with some lame excuse about not having condoms. Now do you have some, or do I need to go get mine?"

That got his attention. "I thought you said—"

She grinned at him.

"Don't be an idiot," she said. "I knew you were coming."

Now who was having trouble breathing? She opened his wallet and sure enough, there were three condoms tucked inside. She calmly ripped one condom from the chain, tucked the remaining two back inside, and tossed the wallet onto the chair.

He held himself very still, his breathing uneven. While he fought a losing battle with his conscience, she went about her business, unbuttoning his shorts and then slowly unzipping them, easing both his shorts and his boxers down his hips until they fell to the floor around his ankles.

She ripped open the condom. He put his hands over hers, whether to help or to stop her she didn't know. It didn't matter. She rolled the condom onto him all by herself, and by the time she had achieved her goal, both of them were struggling to breathe.

She led him over to the long, cushioned bench where they had so often stopped short of this milestone. He would have eased her back on the bench, but she turned them around and gave him a gentle shove. He lay back instead, pulling her on top of him.

She had waited so long for this moment that she wanted to move fast, but he slowed her down with his kisses and his hands until she grew impatient. He held her hips against his and she knew that, if she let him, he would pleasure them both without ever coming inside her. She dragged herself up to a sitting position.

"Please, let me have this," she said.

He cradled her face in his hands, and she knew then that he would give her this gift, because that's what it was: a gift that she would remember forever. She lifted herself up and positioned him so that she could torture them both by lowering herself ever so slowly back down. He took a strangled breath and grabbed her by the hips. She smiled.

"Can't wait?" she asked.

Instead of answering, he shifted his hands so that he could touch her center with his thumbs. She whimpered. The more she tried to lower herself onto him, the stronger the pressure of his fingers. Damn him, she was going to come before he was inside of her.

No more slow and easy. She was so wet and so close to coming apart that she barely felt the breaking of her barrier as she took him fully inside her. He groaned and his hands tightened reflexively, sending glorious shocks radiating from her center outward. She rolled her hips, experimenting, and he groaned again. She leaned forward, which also felt good, and he shifted his hands, so that he held on to her backside, helping her to rock against him again.

They moved together, finding their rhythm, until she could feel herself filled to overflowing. She clung tightly to him as her body tightened around him and he finally let go. In that moment, she knew that they belonged to each other.

Together they watched the darkness fade to dawn. Callie decided that she hated the sunrise. She hated all signs of time passing. One night gone. Only two remained.

"So how do we do this?" she asked. "Monday morning, at sunrise, what do we do?"

"I guess we say good-bye," said Adam. "We've done it before."

"And then? When will you be back?"

"I just don't know," he said softly.

At least he was honest. She thought about it for a minute.

"We won't say good-bye," she said. "We'll just say, 'Until I see you again.' We don't need to worry about exactly when that might be."

He smiled. "Because we'll see each other again."

She smiled back. "Yes, we will."

Callie couldn't believe she had shut the door in Adam's face. She was standing up for herself for the first time in years. She was throwing out challenges and playing with fire again. She leaned against the door, her nerve endings still zinging from the kiss. Who was this brave new woman inhabiting her body?

For so many years she had been faithful to Brian, or at least to the idea of their relationship. She had built a wall around herself, setting herself apart from the world, avoiding the temptations that Brian craved. But something had changed. She had changed.

Callie pushed herself away from the door and headed for the phone. She needed to talk to someone or she would explode, but she stopped halfway through dialing Tessa's cell phone. She could imagine all too easily the scene on the receiving end of the call. Tessa and Mel were probably still at lunch with their mother, dissecting her life over salad. Sure, she wanted to talk, but not on speakerphone to all three of them at a restaurant. She put the phone down and stared at it for a moment.

There was nobody else she wanted to call.

She was too restless to write music, or even to play. She needed to move. She prowled the house, then grabbed her jacket. It was time to get out, to go somewhere, do something. Anything to get rid of this adrenaline rush.

But she stopped short at the door. She knew exactly what she needed to do, and it was right here in the house. Throwing her jacket toward the pegs on the wall, Callie marched back through the kitchen and took the stairs two at a time until she reached the attic studio.

It was time to open the box.

Callie flopped down in the resting chair and reached around the side. Sure enough, the flowered box was still there, hiding beneath the fringe of the afghan. She pulled it out and opened it on her lap, guilt and curiosity swirling inside her. For better or worse, the guilt wasn't strong enough to stop her.

Best to start from the beginning. Callie tipped it so that the most recent letters fell against her stomach, giving her easy access to the earliest materials at the bottom. She quickly leafed through them until she held the first one in her hand. The postmarked dates went back almost thirty years.

September 29

Dear Dora,

I miss you. We all miss you. Even the babies know that something is wrong. I understand your reasons for leaving, but are you sure it's the only way? We are a creative bunch. Perhaps we can come up with a better solution than severing all ties.

You know I will support you, even if you continue down this road, but please reconsider. We just don't feel like a family without you.

Love,

Lauren

October 16

Dear Dora,

I must beg your forgiveness for sending that letter in September. You are absolutely right. It was incredibly selfish of me, and I won't do it again. You deserve to lead your own life, and to find your own happiness, rather than simply playing a supporting role in mine.

Enclosed is a photo of the twins. I will try to send one each month, so you can watch them grow. Please write when you can. I want to hear all about this new life of yours.

Love,

Lauren

The enclosed Polaroid showed two babies, perhaps six months old. At the bottom Lauren had written "Ellie" and "James." The pink bow on Ellie's fuzzy head helped to distinguish girl from boy, but otherwise the two babies looked much the same in their one-piece pajamas.

Callie puzzled over the relationship between her mother and Lauren as she skimmed the next few letters in the series. Lauren had kept her promise. She had not repeated her plea for Dora to come back, and she had enclosed a photo in each letter. The letters grew longer as Lauren recounted funny little stories about the growing babies. After the first six months, the letters came less often, although each contained several photos. From time to time, Lauren would mention someone named Barrett (her husband?), but generally she talked about the children. Dora had clearly responded in kind, but her half of the conversation was missing.

Callie frowned in frustration. This was like reading a mystery book with pages missing and the end torn off. Who were these people? Why had her mother never mentioned them? There was an easy way to get answers to all her questions, of course. All she had to do was ask.

Right. Like she was going to admit to her mother that she had been snooping around. Even as she reached for the next letter, Callie knew that what she was doing was wrong, but she couldn't seem to stop herself. The idea that her mother had lived a whole other life, one that she had never mentioned to her daughters, completely blew her mind. Callie simply had to know more.

As the years passed, the notes became less frequent, but they were still stuffed with snapshots. Callie found herself fascinated by the parallel story of these twins in New York City, only a few years older than she and her sisters. They had suffered the same fashion disasters, the same unfortunate hairstyles, but the pair in New York did it with more flair and more money. The girl had even gone to a debutante ball when she was sixteen.

By the time Callie had caught up to the present, late-afternoon sun streamed through the studio windows. She studied the most recent photo, sent just before Christmas. Ellie and James were all grown up now, responsible adults back home for the holidays. It was Thanksgiving, if the turkey on the table was any indication. No spouses yet, but surely it wouldn't be long. Both twins were attractive and, according to Lauren's maternal bragging, extremely successful in their chosen careers.

Callie tucked the photo back into its envelope and reached for the final letter, the one that had piqued her curiosity in the first place. She re-read it, hoping for insight now that she had more context.

March 2

Dear Dora,

*   I am dying. I tell you this now, bluntly, because I am sick and tired of dancing around it. I was supposed to die when I was thirteen, and*

every year since then—43 of them!—has been a gift. We should be celebrating my triumph over the odds instead of tiptoeing around the truth. But the children are firmly planted in denial, unwilling to imagine a life without their mother. Even my doctors won't say it plainly. Only Barrett understands. And you, I hope.

Frankly, I'm relieved that I can see the end approaching, and that it is not cancer. I have been stalked by that invisible enemy for too many years. I swore to myself that I would never submit to chemotherapy again, and I meant it. But my new diagnosis means that I don't need to battle my physicians or my family, for there is nothing heroic they can do to save me. Thank God.

(It's congestive heart failure. Ironic how the miracle that cured my cancer also sowed the seeds of my destruction.)

I write to you now, dear friend, because I would like to see you before I die. I would like you to see how Ellie and Jamie have grown up. I would like us all to be together one last time.

The doctors tell me that I may have another year or two, but they are lying. (They call it optimism.) I know my body. I know myself. I will have one last summer on the bay, and then I will fade away.

Would you deny a dying friend her last wish?

Please come see me.

Love,

Lauren

Callie had a better perspective on the letter now, but no idea how her mother might respond, or if she had responded already. She wished that she could meet Lauren. After reading all these years' worth of correspondence, she wondered how her mother could have hidden a rich and vital friendship for so long. She wanted to know the mysterious Barrett, and the model children, Ellie and Jamie. More than anything else, she wanted to know if Dora planned to visit Lauren before it was too late.

The sound of a car coming down the drive startled Callie so much that she jumped to her feet. The box tumbled to the floor, letters and photos flying everywhere. A quick glance out the window confirmed her worst fear.

It was her mother.

Frantically, Callie scrambled to pick up the evidence, tossing it all back into the box in a jumble. She would have to come back later to sort them neatly in order to hide her tracks. But for the moment, she needed to get the letters back in the box, and fast.

When she had collected them all, she jammed the lid back on the box and slid it under the resting chair. The slam of a car door propelled her down two sets of stairs and out onto the sun porch, where she opened her guitar case, plopped into a chair, and began thrashing out a hard-driving rhythm, one that could plausibly explain why she hadn't heard the car.

A few moments later, Dora stepped onto the sun porch.

"Hi sweetie, I'm back."

Callie didn't need to fake her start of surprise. She had been playing so loud that she really hadn't heard her mother open the door.

"Hi Mom. How was lunch?"

"It was lovely to see your sisters, but we missed you. How did the songwriting go?"

"Great," answered Callie, too quickly. It had been a bizarre day, from finding her notebooks to getting dunked to uncovering her mother's secret past. The one thing she hadn't done all day was write music. "I had a very productive day," she said.

Her mother looked at her oddly—the woman had an excellent bullshit detector—but didn't ask any more questions.

"Don't forget, you're on for dinner."

"I know. I'll be right there." Callie began to put away her guitar.

"I can help," said Dora, opening the door to head back inside. "I just need to put my shopping away. Oh! And don't let me forget." She paused in the doorway. "We need to talk calendar. At lunch, your sisters and I cooked up a plan for a girls' weekend in New York."

Callie's head snapped up, but her mother had already gone back into the house. Now Callie had a dilemma on her hands: Should she tell her sisters?

CHAPTER SIXTEEN

Callie could tell that Danny wanted to say something. He lingered after their session, taking way too long to put his guitar away. Then he stood in the doorway, shifting from foot to foot.

"Spill it," she demanded.

"What?"

"If you have something you want to say, then say it. I don't bite. You know that."

He was quiet for a minute, and she wondered if she had been too blunt. At least he didn't panic and run away.

"Callie, can you show me how to write a song?"

Callie caught her breath. She hadn't expected him to ask outright. She thought she would have to coax him into it.

"I can try," she replied.

"How did you learn?"

She smiled. "My Dad taught me. Did you know that my Dad is your music teacher at the grade school?"

Danny nodded.

"I can't exactly remember how I got started, but I'll ask him. You know, he writes music, too."

"What kind?"

"Mostly country music songs," she answered, "kind of like mine, but . . . happier, I guess."

"I don't want to write happy songs," he said, completely serious.

She choked back a laugh.

"No, I figured you might have some sad stuff to write about first."

"Yeah." He seemed pretty matter-of-fact about it. "I want to write a song for Grace."

Who was Grace? Callie set the question aside. She could ask Adam later.

"I'll talk to my Dad today and get his advice. We can get you started tomorrow. Does that sound good?"

He nodded again.

"Okay, then. You need to head home or you'll miss the school bus, but I'll see you tomorrow. Bring a notebook."

"Thanks, Callie." He said it softly, but she heard him.

"Anytime, kid."

When he had gone running in the direction of the cottage, his guitar case swinging wildly in one hand, Callie leaned back and sighed. This was news, and she needed to share it with Adam. She had planned to give them both a few days of breathing space before seeing him again, but a promise was a promise.

An hour later, she found Adam in the barn, working on the boat. This time it seemed to be in more pieces, and he was using a very loud tool of some kind. He hadn't heard the cowbell clang, nor had he heard her call his name. He worked, shirtless, a sheen of sweat highlighting the muscles of his back under the work lights. There was even a tool belt slung low around his hips. She leaned in the doorway, content to watch and wait. She drifted into a daydream, fantasizing about all the tantalizing ways that this meeting could play out.

Sudden silence jerked her out of her reverie. She straightened up, shook off all those inappropriate thoughts, and called out to him.

"Adam."

He spun around. She had startled him.

"Callie, what are you doing here?"

Callie looked at his eyes, not his bare chest, and definitely not at the dusting of hair leading down into the front of his jeans. She ignored the play of muscles as he lifted the heavy tool and set it on a nearby workbench.

"Nothing," she stammered. *Definitely not staring at your half-naked body.* "Everything's fine. I just wanted to give you an update."

He gave her a skeptical look and grabbed his T-shirt off the workbench, pulling it on over his head.

"Great. Go ahead." His curt tone of voice told her more than she wanted to know. Sure, she had been expecting a little awkwardness after their last encounter, but this was ridiculous. Apparently he thought she had come over here on some flimsy pretext in order to seduce him. Maybe that was plausible given their past history, but he was the one wearing a tool belt and parading around without his shirt on.

"You remember when we talked about incorporating songwriting into my sessions with Danny?" she began.

He nodded, arms crossed as he leaned back against the work table.

"I was planning to introduce it gradually, but he asked me point blank today if I could help him to write a song. I thought you would want to know."

Ha. Now he would feel like an idiot, because she had a totally legitimate reason to be here. Clearly she had no intention of seducing him. That was wishful thinking on his part. She was here with an actual update on Danny, a report of even more progress.

"Thanks," he said, uncrossing his arms and resting his hands on the edge of the workbench. "You're right. This is exactly the kind of thing I'd like to know."

She smiled, pleased that he had admitted it out loud. But then she remembered the other critical question.

"I did want to ask you about one thing. Who is Grace?"

She tried to ask gently, in case the name brought back memories, but apparently not gently enough. He stiffened, the arms crossed again, and he wiped all expression off his face.

"What did he say about Grace?"

"He said that he wants to write a song for Grace."

Adam opened his mouth, but no words came out. He walked over to a small refrigerator and pulled out a bottle of water, drinking half of it before he faced her again.

"Grace was Danny's little sister. She was three when she died in the accident."

"Oh my God." They were both silent for a moment. "I thought Grace might be a friend, or maybe his grandmother. Not his sister. It hurts just thinking about it."

She felt like she might throw up, so she leaned against the doorframe and closed her eyes. She must have gone white, or done something else alarming, because Adam walked over to her and clasped her upper arms, propping her up.

"Are you sure you can handle this?"

Callie's eyes snapped open and she straightened up under the warm weight of his hands. Her body might welcome the extra support, but she resented the implication that she wasn't strong enough.

"Of course I can handle it. If Danny can stand to work through this, then I can certainly handle listening."

"This is rough stuff," he persisted, "and I need to know that you're not going to freak out and run away halfway through. If you start this, I need to know you can finish it."

"I'm not going anywhere." She met his eyes squarely and didn't flinch.

"For now," he qualified.

"For now," she agreed, hating that she needed to hedge her answer, but it was true, and he was right. He studied her for a moment more, then dropped his hands, breaking the intense connection between them.

"I have a request to make, on Danny's behalf," she said.

"What?"

She struggled to find the right words to explain. Everything that came to mind sounded stupid, or insulting.

"Writing a song is a risky undertaking—for anyone, not just for Danny. When you finally share that song with someone, you make yourself vulnerable in a way that's hard to describe to someone who's never done it before."

"Okay. So what do you need?"

"When Danny's ready to share the song with you, I need you to listen without judgment."

"I'm not going to criticize his song, Callie. I'm not an idiot. Or an asshole."

She flushed, but didn't back down. He was taking this as an insult, but it wasn't about him.

"That's not what I mean. This is his first attempt. It's likely to be a little clumsy, a little cliché."

"So?"

"So a typical reaction to that would be to smile a little, or maybe pat him on the head when he's finished. But he's not an idiot either. He'll be hypersensitive, and that little smile, that pat on the head, will feel condescending." She took a deep breath and started over. "Listen, if you find that you're distracted by Danny's inexperience, I need you to use your best poker face. Don't smile. Don't pat him on the head. Be completely serious. Can you do that?"

Adam smiled, which ticked her off.

"This is a big deal. I can't believe you're not taking this seriously."

He laughed, then laughed harder as she became more and more outraged.

"Calm down," he said through his laughter.

"This is exactly what I'm talking about," she bit out the clipped syllables through clenched teeth. "If you smile, or laugh, or do something else stupid and inappropriate after hearing Danny's song he may never speak to you again."

Adam finally managed to stop laughing.

"Give me some credit here. If Danny chooses to share a song with me, I'll be as terrified as he is, and as vulnerable. I'm not going to ruin it."

She opened her mouth to argue, but he raised his hand to stop her. It was his turn to be serious.

"What you need to understand is that this is about far more than a song. This is about Danny and me and our ability to stay together as a family. I'm fighting for us to stay together, and I need to know if Danny is with me in this battle."

He was waiting for some kind of response, but she had no idea what to say.

"Has he said anything to you about what he wants? About the future?"

She shook her head, and he sighed. He must have been hoping for more, but she and Danny rarely talked about Adam, or about this custody issue. They concentrated on the music.

"So we move forward from here. You help him write a song for Grace. I'll fight to keep him with me. Maybe, when he's done working through the past, he'll be ready to talk about his future."

"I'll do what I can. I'm sorry I can't do more." She reached up to squeeze his forearm, wanting to offer some comfort.

He reached for her as well and threaded his fingers through her hair, much as he had done the other day. She tipped her head back into his hand, hoping that maybe, just maybe, he had changed his mind.

"You're doing more than you know," he said, giving her a gentle kiss on the forehead. Then he pulled away, returning to his work on the boat, leaving Callie standing alone in the doorway.

Adam turned back to the boat, determined to steer clear of temptation, but simply being in the same room with Callie undermined all his good intentions. He needed to stay focused on the long-term goal, which was to create a healthy, stable family for Danny. An opposite family. Callie could never be a part of that. She had chosen a very different path. At best, they could have a fleeting affair before she returned to her real life. A part of him wanted that, no matter what the risk to the custody battle or to his own sanity, but he refused to put himself first. Right here, right now, his world revolved around Danny, and Danny needed to come first.

"Thanks for meeting with me today," began Kat. She studied Danny, who sat across the desk from her with his arms crossed, looking down at his feet. She sighed. Given a choice, she would have preferred to meet with him in the waiting area and send Adam to the car, like last time, but Adam had steamrolled them into her office and here they sat, Principal and Delinquent, while Adam waited outside the door. She couldn't think of a way to break the ice.

There was no reason to stay behind the desk. It was only making the tension worse. Kat stood and walked around the desk to sit in the other guest chair next to Danny. He finally looked up, thank God, and she took her opening.

"Look, Danny, I know you don't talk to everyone, but the time is coming for you to speak up. You know that your grandparents want you to live with them?"

He nodded.

"And your uncle wants you to stay with him?"

He nodded again.

"What do you want?"

He shrugged, broke off eye contact and looked back down at his feet.

"Still no opinion, and that's fine. Here's what you need to know: I'm going to make a recommendation to the judge. Right now, there are strong arguments to be made for both sides, but if you speak your mind, your opinion will matter a lot."

He looked back up at her. Excellent. She had piqued his curiosity.

"You heard me. Your opinion can make the difference, but only if you speak up. If you choose to say nothing, the judge and I will make the decision for you."

Kat held his eyes for a moment to make sure he understood, then she rose and walked toward the door to the outer room. Before she opened it, she looked back at Danny one last time.

"You still have my card?"

He nodded.

"When you decide what you want, call me. Anytime. Day or night. Wake me up in the middle of the night if you want. But call, okay?"

He smiled at the idea of waking her up. If he thought prank phone calls were funny, then there was definitely hope. She smiled back and opened the door. Adam jumped up from his chair and joined her in the doorway.

"We're all set here. Danny has some things to think about, and he knows what to do when he reaches a decision. Right, Danny?"

Kat held his eyes until he confirmed with a nod.

"Great. I'll let you know as soon as I hear about a date for the hearing. In the meantime," Kat directed her words at Danny, "keep talking."

He gave her a brief smile before ducking in between her and Adam and heading out to the car. Kat couldn't help but be insulted that he seemed so relieved to escape her company, but at least he had kept her card. Small steps were all she needed, so long as they were headed in the right direction.

She put her hand on Adam's arm to stop him before he followed Danny out the door. A part of her longed to ask him out to a nice, adults-only dinner, but things between them were still tense. Besides, he was still off-limits. Dinner, for the moment, was not an option.

"I'll call you later this week," she said, "to see how things are going with the music lessons."

"That's fine," he said curtly, and then he left.

Kat sighed. Still no faith in her judgment? She could feel herself getting caught up in Adam's opinion of her and mentally shook it off. She would never go down that road again. She was not that naïve, needy girl anymore, desperate for approval from the men in her life. She had changed. Never again would she be that vulnerable.

That afternoon, Callie knocked softly on the door of her Dad's office. The door was ajar, so she poked her head inside. She needed his advice before her session with Danny tomorrow morning. Sure enough, he was there, but he was listening to the other side of a conversation on the phone. He waved her in, motioning for her to sit in one of the chairs.

She was glad she hadn't barged right in, the way she had always done as a child. The old presumptions about this house being her house, in which she had unfettered access to every room and could interrupt any conversation, had fallen away. After her intrusion into her mother's memory box yesterday, she was feeling the need to be on her best behavior.

"Stay cool, man, and let me know what you think about the new material," said Luke, then joked around a bit before saying good-bye. When he talked to his music-industry buddies, he always sounded like a cool cat from the seventies, which made Callie giggle.

It was easy to forget, in the routine of day-to-day living, that her father was more than a music teacher. He kept his songwriting private, even from Callie. The family never saw that side of him, except for rare glimpses like this into his other world.

"What can I do for you, sugar?" he asked, leaning back in his chair. "The music doctor is in."

She smiled, loving the 'cool cat' talk, and plopped down in the recliner in the corner.

"Dad, I need help. You know I'm working with Danny every morning?"

He nodded. "How's that going?"

"Better than I ever expected. He wants to learn to write music, and for the life of me, I can't remember how I learned. Any advice?"

He leaned back, sighed, and reached for his guitar, which sat right next to his office-type chair on a stand. He settled the instrument in his lap and fingered the strings, absently plucking out a melody while he thought about it.

"Well, first you need to know the basics."

Callie laughed. "I know that, Dad. I was hoping you could break it down You know, step one, step two. . . ."

"When you and I first started writing songs together, you had a pretty solid background in music theory. You may not have thought about it very much, but you had been taking piano lessons for a few years, and playing guitar since you were strong enough to press down on those strings. You knew your major and minor chords, and how to add a seventh, and generally knew how a transition was supposed to sound. How much music does this boy know? If he already speaks the language, it will be a lot easier to help him learn to write it."

Callie considered what she knew of Danny's training.

"He knows a lot of material—more than I would have expected, but it's mostly in G. He knows a few chord families, knows how to improvise a little, but that's about it. I don't think he's tried any other instruments, and I don't think he reads music at all."

"So you keep it simple. If he wants to write something, he'll need to stick with what he knows. He'll end up writing something that sounds like a folk song, and that's okay. Over time, his vocabulary will expand, and he'll be able to develop more complex stuff. But for now, you start him off easy."

"He's going to focus on the lyrics, I think. He's got a lot to say, and he doesn't have another way to say it." Her father smiled, and there was a lot more loneliness in that smile than Callie had ever noticed before. "That's why music gets written, sugar."

"I'll see if he can get words down on paper, so we have some raw material."

"Start with the chorus. Whatever is circling around and around in his head and he can't get it out—that needs to be the chorus. Everything else is just verse. Oh, and save the kicker for the bridge."

Callie refrained from rolling her eyes at that bit of advice. She must have been five years old the first time he had told her to save the kicker for the bridge. In fact, she could still remember that first song she had ever written. Sure, it was a simple little thing, but it had come from the heart and it sure had helped her feel better.

"Thanks, Dad. I have some ideas about how to get started."

Callie rose and started toward the door, wanting to give her father more work time, but his words caught her before she could get away.

"Have you thought any more about cutting a demo?"

"I thought we agreed it was too risky." She leaned against the doorframe, needing the extra support. The sudden thought of leaving the band made her feel light-headed.

"No. *You* said it was too risky. I said you should keep thinking about it." He paused, his lips curving into a smile. "What I meant was that you should keep thinking about it until you came around to my way of thinking, which is that you should do it. And I know just the place."

"Around here?"

"Yep." Luke looked very pleased with himself. "My buddy over at the local radio station was bragging to me the other day about their new, state-of-the-art recording studio."

"You're joking. State of the art?"

"Well, he may have been exaggerating, but it is fairly new. Certainly adequate to record a demo."

Callie stood in the doorway, her mind spinning with all the possibilities and implications. Between the lightheaded feeling and all the spinning, she thought she might be sick.

"Think about it. We're an awfully long way from Nashville, and nobody would need to know. If you want to give it a try, I can make it happen."

Adam's words echoed in her mind: *'This is a small town. Somehow, one way or another, everyone would know.'* But would it matter, this far from Nashville?

She pushed herself upright. This was not a decision she needed to make today. It could wait, until she figured out exactly how much risk she could handle.

CHAPTER SEVENTEEN

Adam definitely felt like a fifth wheel. He had accepted the invitation to a Sunday-afternoon barbecue at the Jameses' house mostly because he wanted to watch Danny interact with other people. The hearing could be scheduled anytime now, and he needed some idea of how Danny would behave.

The afternoon had been a revelation. Danny had munched on snacks, listening to Dora's stories about Callie and her sisters when they were little. She'd told tales about all the summer kids, including Adam and Evan and Lainey, and Danny hadn't been able to get enough. Once he'd relaxed, he'd behaved like a perfectly normal—if quiet—eight-year-old boy. By the time they had finished eating and were all seated on the porch watching the sunset and pulling out instruments, Adam had become the outsider.

Dora's constant chatter had put Danny completely at ease. With her, there were no awkward silences—in fact, there was no pressure to say anything at all. Danny adored her, and she adored him right back. Danny seemed a bit in awe of Luke, perhaps because he was a teacher at school, or more likely because he was the father of Danny's idol, Callie. He had studied Callie as she interacted with her sisters. The concept of identical triplets fascinated him, and he'd asked all sorts of questions about it. The comfortable companionship of the group highlighted Adam's failure. Of course Danny needed more than just Adam in his life. Why had he not realized this before? What else had he missed?

The thought made Adam sick to his stomach, so he took another sip of cold beer and watched the sunset. Dora must have sensed his mood, or maybe he wasn't doing a very good job of hiding it, because she came over to sit beside him on the wicker sofa, patting him on the knee and launching into yet another story.

A loud fanfare on the guitar interrupted Dora, for which Adam was grateful. The musical portion of the evening was about to begin. The players had all tuned their instruments, Danny included. He had brought his guitar 'just in case.' Now that they were really going to play music all together, he glowed.

The next hour was one of the most difficult of Adam's life. Danny's clear voice, shy at first, then gaining strength as he grew more comfortable, cut through Adam's defenses and left him completely exposed. After so many months of struggle, Callie had reached right into Danny's soul and healed him. He would be forever grateful to her for doing what he couldn't. He should be feeling only joy now, and relief—and he did—but the weight of his failure pressed down on him until he couldn't breathe.

Just when Adam thought he could stand no more, Danny took a deep breath and said, "I have a song."

"Are you sure?" asked Callie, and Adam realized what Danny intended. Somehow, he had written a song already. Adam closed his eyes, searching for the reserves he knew he was going to need. Damn Callie for not warning him about this ahead of time.

"I'm sure."

Adam opened his eyes and put on his poker face just as Callie looked over to assess his readiness. He nodded to her, and apparently he was faking calm well enough that she turned her attention back to Danny. She hovered over him like a lioness guarding her cub, but when he was ready to play she backed off.

God, what a song. Simple, but powerful, it had the feeling of a spiritual. Danny sang about his family. He knew they were on the other side, waiting for him, but he couldn't see them, and they couldn't see him, except in his dreams. He sang about searching for them every night, waking to find himself alone again. He sang about the silence that filled his days, and how he waited for night to come again, so that he could go to sleep.

> *I remember her laughter.*
> *I remember her face.*
> *And I will keep searching*
> *until I find Grace.*

Adam could feel the knot tightening in his throat, and he wasn't sure that he could make it through the end of the song. Callie was as lost in the music as Danny, unaware that Adam was about to self-destruct. She had heard the song before, probably helped him put it together. For them, this moment was all about release. But for the rest of the small audience, this moment was a revelation.

Danny had found his voice.

As the last few chords faded into the sunset, Adam worked to control his throat. Danny looked up at Callie, and she grinned down at him, the two of them glowing like a pair of light bulbs. Luke squeezed Danny's shoulder, and Dora bubbled over with praise for Danny's first song. Everyone else basked in the moment, but Adam couldn't engage. He could feel himself begin to crack, the fault lines splintering through his body. He was going to shatter into a thousand tiny shards, and someone was going to get hurt.

Adam stood up and walked out.

Callie stared after Adam, stunned and hurt. He had promised —promised!—to handle this moment well, and he had let her down. Worse, he had let Danny down, leaving her to clean up the aftermath.

"Oh, poor thing."

At first Callie thought her mother was talking about Danny, and she was ready to yell at her for saying something so condescending right in front of him. But one look at her mother's face told her Dora was talking about Adam.

"Are you crazy?" Callie was furious.

"Pipe down," reprimanded Dora. "That was quite the stunt you two pulled. I don't know why you're so surprised."

She caught Danny's eyes and directed her next words to him.

"You wrote a powerful song, young man. You weren't watching your Uncle Adam's face during the song, but I was. You ripped his heart wide open, brought back all sorts of memories. Of course he's upset, and he's not the type to fall apart in front of other people. He needs some time to recover, and we're going to give it to him."

Callie was so churned up inside that she wanted to hang on tight to her anger, but her mother was right, damn it. Danny had taken to songwriting like a fish to water, and he had stirred up a storm of emotion with a single song. Danny wasn't the only one who had lost family in that accident.

Callie turned to Danny.

"Why don't I go find your uncle and make sure he's all right. Maybe talk a while. You stay here, okay?"

Danny nodded. Callie squeezed his arm, then stood up.

"Would you mind putting my guitar to bed?" she asked Danny. He looked like he needed something to do.

"Okay," he whispered.

She knelt back down in front of him, forcing him to meet her eyes. He looked lost, and she feared that he would crawl right back inside himself and never come out again.

"Honey, your uncle is going to be fine. I'm going to go make sure of it. This is not your fault, and I don't want you to change anything about your song. It's perfect. Do you understand?"

He nodded solemnly, and his eyes looked less wild.

Callie rose and handed Danny off to her mother, who immediately launched into another triplet story. She caught Tessa's eye and motioned for her sister to follow her outside. It was very handy to have a licensed counselor on hand during a time of crisis.

"Any suggestions?" she asked, pitching her voice so Danny couldn't hear them.

"Just listen," said Tessa. "Try not to judge. He's probably been playing the strong, silent type for the past year when he should have been grieving. You don't need to fix him. Just listen."

Callie nodded, more than a little intimidated but ready to help if she could.

"Will you help Mom with Danny?" she asked.

"Of course," said Tessa, "especially if it means Mel has to do the dishes."

They grinned at each other, and then Callie slipped away into the long shadows of the sunset. Heading toward Adam's cottage, she hoped that the right words would magically come to her. Right now her mind was a blank. She stepped through the fence and into Adam's yard, turning toward the cottage but then doing an abrupt about-face and heading for the barn instead. She had a hunch that Adam was in his man cave. Maybe cornering his in his man cave was a stupid idea, but she was in no mood to wait patiently until he was ready to talk.

Callie pushed open the office door. The cowbell, as usual, announced her presence. She followed the sound of power tools and found Adam working on the boat. This time he had kept his shirt on, but in her mind she could see the play of his muscles as clearly as if he had stripped down. She liked the solidity of him, the raw power. She wished that he would use that power for something other than locking up his own feelings.

Callie realized that she was stalling. She was going to have to say something.

"Adam." Her voice came out as a wimpy little croak. She cleared her throat and tried again. "Adam."

This time he heard her over the whine of the equipment and switched it off, standing still for a moment before turning around. Her stomach clenched. What the hell was she doing? She had no idea what to say, and she couldn't exactly whip out a guitar to express herself in song. She suppressed a hysterical laugh at the mental image.

She should have walked Danny home and let the two of them sort it out, or maybe sent Tessa over to talk him off the ledge, but then she gave herself a mental kick. She was a big girl, and she could certainly handle one difficult conversation. Danny didn't need to deal with this.

Callie squared her shoulders.

"Um...Hi, Adam."

"Hi Callie."

Great. Brilliant start. This was going to go really well.

"We...ah...we were worried about you, after you walked out like that."

"Well as you can see," said Adam, spreading his arms wide, "I'm fine, thanks."

Callie could feel her spine stiffen at his condescending tone. She narrowed her eyes. If Adam was itching for a fight, she could think of a few things that needed saying.

"And Danny? Do you think Danny is 'fine'?"

Ha! Direct hit. She could see the involuntary flinch before he closed up his face again. Take that, Mr. Tough Guy. His eyes slid away from hers and he looked at a spot somewhere over her shoulder.

"I'm sure Danny will be fine by morning. In the meantime, I'm the last thing he needs."

"Yeah," said Callie, sarcasm giving her voice an edge. "If I were baring my soul to the only father I've got left, I'd want him to run away, too. I mean, who wants a father figure around when things get tough?"

Callie took an involuntary step back as Adam closed the distance between them. Maybe she had crossed the line with that last remark. She had definitely blown her instructions to 'just listen.' As he left the glare of the work lights, his face fell into shadow, making him look even more menacing.

"Oh, that's rich, coming from you," he growled. "Do you remember that we were going to talk about Danny's music? Do you remember how you were going to 'keep me posted' and 'fill me in' on anything important?"

She retreated until she bumped up against the wall of the barn. She had to look up to see his face, and this close she could see that he was furious. She quickly looked back at his throat. Much safer. Callie felt like prey, and she didn't like it.

"Tonight wasn't the first time you heard that song. How long have you two been cooking up this surprise? How the hell did you think I'd react?"

Callie sucked in a breath. Anger rushed through her, making her taller and stronger. She met his eyes, ready for battle.

"Frankly, I thought you'd be thrilled. Not only is Danny talking about the accident—finally—but he's talking about how he feels. Now. Today. Not stories about what he used to do or feel, but stories about how he's coping today. This is a big deal, and you're missing it. You're wallowing in some weird kind of self-pity because I didn't keep you in the loop enough, but the truth is that you weren't paying attention. I told you that he was talking about his parents. I told you that we were playing music together. And I told you that he was going to try writing a song for Grace."

Callie punctuated her remarks with her finger, poking Adam in the chest for emphasis.

"What more did you need to know? Danny cares about you. He cares what you think. And when he revealed his innermost feelings to you, you walked out. You left. Like his family left him. So good luck winning his trust. After the stunt you pulled tonight, I wonder if that will ever happen."

Callie put both palms on his chest to shove him away, but he put his own hands over hers and held them there, against his heart.

"Don't say that," Adam said, his voice rough.

"Don't say what? Don't tell you the truth?" She tried to tug her hands free, but he wouldn't let go.

"Don't take away my hope."

Her breath caught and she could feel the sting of tears at the back of her eyes. Damn it, she needed her anger back again. But it was gone, leaving her defenseless.

"I know I was an idiot tonight, but that song—that stupid, amazing song—caught me by surprise. What was I supposed to do? Have a breakdown right there in front of everyone?"

Callie shook her head. She couldn't speak.

Adam looked down at her small hands imprisoned by his large ones. He didn't meet her eyes.

"I need your help." He said it so softly that Callie wondered if she had misheard.

"What?" she whispered.

"I need your help," he said, anger returning to his voice. How he must hate asking for help from anyone. She smiled, sympathy softening her expression.

"It's not funny," he said, and she laughed. She couldn't help it. He looked so outraged.

And then he kissed her.

Callie wasn't sure exactly what had happened. One second he was glaring at her, and then the next his mouth was on hers, their hands still clasped between them. Only now the backs of his hands burned into her breasts, and her head scraped against the wall behind her. She didn't really care. Her attention was focused entirely on his mouth and the electricity coursing through her body.

Callie didn't want it to stop. She had waited too long.

Adam pulled away, abruptly ending the connection between them, but her body continued to thrum with energy. She stared at him, wide-eyed.

"What was that for?" she asked, breathless.

"You were talking too much."

"Oh." She smiled. "I could do it again. I have a lot to say, you know."

He laughed. She hadn't seen him laugh like that since forever. Open. Vulnerable.

Then he kissed her again.

After that, Callie couldn't think very clearly. Her conscious mind shut down and all that remained was feeling. Heat, hunger, and lust roared through her, tearing away all the trappings of civility. Her single, mindless goal was to consume this glorious man, to draw him inside of her in every way possible until they were one being, and to do it now.

She tugged her hands free of his and wrapped her arms around his neck. His hands slid around her body to grab her behind and lift her up. Suspended between Adam and the plank wall of the barn, Callie wrapped her legs around his waist and gave herself to him.

His hands were everywhere, beneath the fabric of her shirt, her bra, drawing her breasts to a painful arousal. His mouth devoured her jaw, her ear, her neck. When he shifted his arms to get a better grip, then moved to carry her somewhere else, Callie blinked away the haze.

"Adam," she murmured into his ear.

He didn't respond, just kept carrying her down the hall toward the office.

"Adam," she said again, this time louder.

Again no response, so she wiggled until he lost his grip and she slid down the front of his body to rest her feet on the floor. That friction almost distracted her from the problem at hand. It certainly distracted Adam, who nudged her against the wall and began kissing her again.

She hugged him, hard, so that he couldn't kiss her senseless anymore, and said firmly, "Adam, we need to go back and get Danny."

He stilled. At least he had heard her. After a moment he responded.

"I'm not sure that's such a good idea."

She hugged him tighter.

"You need to talk to him tonight. No excuses."

She felt him sigh. He pulled back and she released him, looking up into his eyes as he rested his forehead against hers.

"I don't suppose you'll join us for the conversation? Act as translator?"

She smiled.

"You guys are going to be fine. Now come on," she said, grabbing him by the hand and pulling him toward the door.

"Wait," he said, holding her back.

"What?" she asked, exasperated at this new delay.

He grinned, the light of mischief in his eyes.

"You might want to button your shirt first."

She looked down, horrified to realize that her shirt was hanging open, and her lacy bra was on display for all the world to see. When had he . . . ? Never mind. She raced to button it up, then grabbed him by the hand again and pulled him out the door.

They found Danny standing on a stool at the kitchen sink, helping Mel. Dora kept up a running commentary. The woman was truly a world-champion talker. Danny glanced up when they came through the back door, but immediately looked back down at the sink. Adam's last shreds of optimism faded.

Callie gave his hand one last squeeze, then left him to go distract her mother, giving him a clear path to approach Danny. He walked slowly over to his nephew.

"Hey, Danny. It's time for us to head home. Could you please say thank you to Mrs. James?"

Danny stilled but didn't look up. He carefully handed the slippery wet plate to Mel. Wiping his hands on a towel, he stepped down from the stool and walked over to Dora.

"Oh, sweetie, is it time for you to go already?"

Danny nodded.

"Well, thank you so much for helping with the dishes. I really appreciate it. And I hope you'll come over and see us again soon."

Danny nodded again. Adam walked up behind him and placed a hand on his shoulder, a gentle reminder of what he was supposed to say. The boy tensed under his hand, but he did remember to mutter, "Thank you," even if he said the words to his shoes.

"You're welcome, sweetie," answered Dora. "We'd love to see you anytime."

She reached over to ruffle Danny's hair, then met Adam's eyes. He turned away from the compassion he saw there and guided Danny toward the door.

"Thanks again, Mrs. James," he called over his shoulder. "Good night, everyone."

He held the storm door open for Danny, and the two of them stepped out into the twilight. Danny took a few steps toward the break in the fence, but Adam stopped him.

"I thought we could go down by the water for a few minutes," he suggested, "so I can explain what happened earlier."

Danny shrugged. Not exactly an enthusiastic endorsement of the plan, but Adam would take what he could get. They picked their way down the hill, then found a place to sit on the stacked white pier lumber, looking out over the lake. The far shore had fallen into shadow so that you couldn't see where the water ended and the trees began. Soon enough the piers would go in and the summer people would arrive, but for now they had the lake to themselves.

Danny swung his feet, tracing patterns in the dirt with the toes of his sneakers. For a long time, they sat in silence watching the colors change in the sky. Adam liked to imagine that his brother was up there somewhere, looking down on him and Danny. Adam sent up a plea for assistance, hoping for a flash of inspiration. The sun had long since set. The surface of the water danced in the darkness, but the sky still glowed orange behind them. The dark blue of night crept up from behind the far tree line, arching over their heads, and slowly chased the orange from the western sky. When he could wait no longer, Adam broke the silence.

"I'm sorry I ran out on you earlier," he began, feeling all the awkwardness of the moment. "Callie had mentioned that you were working on a song for Grace. . . ." Adam cleared his throat. "I thought I was ready to hear it, but I was wrong." He listened to the tree frogs sing for a minute before continuing.

"I know you miss your family. I do, too," admitted Adam. "But I don't let myself think about them very often. Maybe I should."

Danny stopped scuffing his toes. At least he was listening.

"To be honest, when you got to the end of your song, I thought I was going to cry right there in front of everyone, and I panicked. I needed to get away for a few minutes until I could pull myself back together."

Danny looked up at him then, his expression masked by the dark. "Doc Archer says that crying is good for you."

Adam barked out a laugh.

"I'm sure Doc Archer is right," he said, "but I'm a grown-up. I'd still be embarrassed if I cried in front of Callie and her parents."

Danny thought about that for a minute.

"You can cry in front of me," he offered. "We're family."

Adam put an arm around Danny's shoulder and squeezed.

"I know, buddy. And I should have brought you with me when I got the hell out of there."

"Yeah, you should have," agreed Danny. "And by the way, you're not supposed to say that."

"Say what?" asked Adam.

"H-E-L-L," answered Danny. "It's a swear word. If you say it at school you get in trouble."

"Oh," said Adam. "Good to know."

"You swear a lot," said Danny.

"I do?"

"Yeah. But I don't care. My Dad swore a lot, too."

Adam chuckled.

"He did, didn't he?"

"Yep. I know all the swear words. Even more than the other kids at school."

"Great," said Adam, imagining the trouble in store now that Danny had started talking. "Maybe you can keep that knowledge to yourself."

Danny snickered. "Maybe."

"Troublemaker," said Adam, giving Danny another squeeze. "Let's get back home. It's a school night."

As they climbed back up the hill, Adam sent a 'thank you' up to his brother, grateful that he and Danny had found a way to muddle through.

CHAPTER EIGHTEEN

Callie jumped at the knock on the summer house door. She had been so deep in her music, thinking through a tricky transition, that she hadn't heard the footsteps approaching. Roscoe stretched, rolling over to chase his patch of sunlight on the floor, and gave a belated bark.

"Nice watchdog," observed Adam from the doorway. She felt the low rumble of his voice vibrate through her, as though she had touched the tuning fork to her ear. She shivered, then leaned over to scratch Roscoe's ears affectionately, anchoring herself on Roscoe's calm energy.

"He knows you're not dangerous."

She straightened up and began putting her instruments away. Roscoe clambered to his feet, stretching and shaking off the nap.

"How did things go last night with Danny?" she asked. "He didn't say anything about it this morning, so I didn't ask. He seemed peaceful, though."

Adam stayed rooted in the doorway. Maybe he wanted to pretend their little encounter last night hadn't happened, but she remembered quite well. She snapped the last case shut.

"Better than I expected," he finally answered.

"That's good, right?" she asked. "Why the long face?"

"Let's say that it wasn't my finest moment," he said. "I hate feeling like I don't know what I'm doing."

He stepped into the room, giving Roscoe a chance to slip out the door and go exploring. He walked over to sit beside her on the bench. Did he remember all the toe-curling things they had done on this bench? He leaned forward, resting his elbows on his knees, clasping his hands, and staring out at the lake.

"Look, I didn't mean to interrupt your work time. I just wanted to thank you for last night." He sat back and met her eyes. "Danny and I really made a breakthrough, and we could never have done it without you."

She smiled. "You're not interrupting. If you hadn't stopped by, I would have come to see you." She took a deep breath, gathering her courage. "I'm glad that things went well with Danny, but that's not why I wanted to see you. I wanted to know if you had changed your mind." She leaned forward to cup his jawline with her palm. She let her whole body sway toward him, pausing when she could feel his breath on her lips. She waited there for his answer, impressed with her newfound audacity.

"I still think it's complicated," he said, but he didn't pull back.

She nodded, hope bubbling up inside her.

"I still think it's a bad idea."

"Aren't we always?" she asked.

She let her hand steal around the nape of his neck, her thumb tracing the curve of his ear.

"But I'm beginning to think we should do it anyway," he said.

She smiled, breathing in the heady mix of Adam and hope.

"So what are you waiting for?" she whispered. "Stop thinking so much and just do it."

At her words, something inside Adam snapped. For so long he had kept his emotions tightly leashed, submerging his own needs in order to build a life for Danny. Not anymore. This was his moment. Screw the consequences.

He closed the gap between them, pressing her back against the cushions of the bench, taking her mouth with a fierceness that matched hers. She shifted beneath him, wrapping her arms around his neck and hooking a leg around his hips. He growled his approval.

He gained a new appreciation for flowing skirts and blouses as he discovered how easy it was to shove them out of the way, revealing the delicate skin beneath. She quickly tugged off his work shirt and the T-shirt beneath, refusing to let him slow down. He would have lingered, chasing her elusive scent from the hollow of her neck across her collarbone, but she would have none of it, wriggling free of her underwear and struggling to free him from his button-fly jeans.

They found themselves laughing, breathless, as the last barriers fell away and then silent, stunned, when she locked her legs around him and pulled him deep inside. They balanced in that moment, forehead to forehead, breath to breath, absorbing the reality of their raw, physical connection. With each pulse, he could feel her surround him, until the connection overwhelmed them and they tumbled over the edge together, faster and faster, until the release slammed into them, wave after wave of it, leaving them spent, motionless.

He felt his world shift beneath him, subterranean plates heaving and sliding to make room for Callie. This moment had altered the geography of his life. He needed a new plan, because he refused to imagine a future without her.

He said nothing. For now, it was enough to breathe with her, to feel their hearts beat together. Plans and promises could wait until tomorrow.

CHAPTER NINETEEN

Callie woke to the chirp of a text message. She groped for the phone on her night table, found it, and checked the screen. Of course it was from Brian. Who else would text her at five in the morning?

She rolled onto her back and closed her eyes, wanting more than anything to ignore him. After the emotional roller coaster of the last few days, the last thing she wanted this morning was another wild ride.

Groaning, she rolled onto her side and read the message.

Check your e-mail. Now.

She sighed. What could possibly be that urgent? She had already blown yesterday making copies of all the band's legal documents. The morning's surprise visit from Adam, followed by their headlong plunge into complicated, had left her in a generous frame of mind, more than happy to spend her afternoon taking care of band business. She had made a copy of the documents for herself, just in case, shipping the originals back to Brian and the first set of copies to the record-company lawyers. She had e-mailed Brian the tracking info. What else could he possibly want?

Callie gave up hope of falling back to sleep, despite the fact that the sky outside was still dark. There would be no rest until she followed through and checked her e-mail. She sat up, grabbed her sweatshirt from the foot of the bed, and pulled it on over her pajamas. Then she leaned back against the pillows and switched over to e-mail on her phone.

She found a message from Brian right at the top of the list, followed by a bunch of junk mail. She opened his message.

This is unacceptable.

Below the words were a link to a web page. Callie's heart sank when she saw that it led to a Nashville gossip column. This could not be good news.

Did she really want to know? Maybe if she deleted his message, the problem would go away. Waiting out the gossip cycle was usually the best way to handle these things, anyway. Because, realistically, what could she do about online gossip? She couldn't care less what some Nashville gossip columnist said about her. It was unlikely to affect her life in a meaningful way.

Then again, why would Brian bother to forward it?

She touched the link and her phone brought up the web page.

Under the headline 'Splitsville for Deep Trouble?' was a slideshow. Callie's stomach twisted. The first image clearly showed Callie and Adam kissing in the canoe. Her finger twitched, swiping reflexively through the images. The second showed the two of them dripping wet, heading up to the house. The next, taken later, after they had warmed up, showed them kissing at her back door. Her stomach twisted tighter as she understood what the next photos might reveal. As she flew through the rest of the slideshow, her stomach began to churn and she realized that she was going to throw up. She bolted for the bathroom. Luckily, her stomach was empty, so after a few dry heaves, she sank slowly to the bathroom floor and curled into a ball.

The idea that someone had been watching them—photographing them—during those intimate moments ripped away the hazy afterglow and left only the taste of bile behind. She felt naked and exposed and angry. This was her home. The safest place in the world.

Or at least it had been, until now.

As the sky outside began to turn pink, she brushed her teeth and crawled back into bed. She read every word of the article, stared at every picture, checked every caption. It was bad. There was no denying it. But it wasn't as bad as she had first thought. The photographer—no, the stalker—had been so far away yesterday morning that the shots of her and Adam in the summer house were grainy. The storm windows had distorted his view enough that readers could see her breasts, sure, but they couldn't see her nipples. She choked, realizing that she was trying to find a bright side in all this. Really? The best she could do was 'no nipples'?

The columnist flattered her, in his sideways fashion, implying that the band would collapse if she defected. She couldn't help but laugh at the idea. He had clearly never met Brian or felt the force of his ambition. He also had no clue that their romantic relationship was purely fictional now, a poignant storyline for the PR machine. As far as the media was concerned, she and Brian had founded the band together, they wrote all their songs together, and without the foundation of their partnership, the band would fall apart. Brian's history of infidelity, contrasted with her own steadfast loyalty, gave the talking heads something to talk about. These photos showing her own indiscretion might screw up the agreed-upon storyline, but they also might sell more records.

Brian wasn't angry because she had slept with somebody else. He didn't care. He was angry because he could feel her slipping away. More than anything, Brian valued control.

She sighed. If she defected, Brian would have some story-spinning to do, and he would actually have to pay a songwriter, but none of it would stop him from achieving his goal. The question was, would he take her down? It would be all too easy for him to paint her as a psychotic harpy, and to scare off anybody who might consider working with her. He would do it just to teach her a lesson.

More important than her own uncertain future was the fact that there was no mention of Adam by name. The last thing he needed right now was his name in an online gossip column. In the images, only the back and side of his head were visible. If someone knew Adam, and knew about her connection to him, then they could certainly guess his identity. But thankfully her stalker had not bothered to find out, and it was unlikely anybody in Nashville would feel the burning need to know. To them, all that mattered were the implications of her affair for an up-and-coming band.

Brian could be as angry as he liked, but she had made it clear that things were over between them long ago. If she wanted to have a wild fling with her next door neighbor, that was her own business. If they needed to adjust the PR storyline, so be it.

Perhaps she needed to make their relationship more clear to him.

Callie searched the site for the older article. Similar in format to the one about her and Adam, this one showcased the naughty 'caught in the act' photos of Brian and the three new girls in the band. And he thought her discreet affair with Adam was unacceptable? She copied the link to the article and pasted it into her reply.

So is this.

My life is my own.

Deal with it.

Callie held her breath and hit send. As the e-mail whooshed away into cyberspace, she stared after it, amazed at her own daring. Something about the distance made it easy for her to say exactly what she wanted to say, and screw the consequences.

And there would be consequences.

Kat rapped sharply on the kitchen door of Adam's cottage. Danny should be off to school by now, so she could talk with Adam privately. What they had to discuss was not suitable for Danny's ears.

"Kat, what are you doing here?"

She had caught him in sweats and a T-shirt, unshaven, barefoot. It didn't matter how rumpled and appealing he might look. They had business to discuss.

"May I come in?" she asked, not bothering to keep the edge out of her voice.

"Of course."

Adam ushered her inside, then poured two cups of coffee and sat at the kitchen table. He even remembered that she took cream in her coffee, but she didn't let that soften her up. She couldn't bring herself to sit down across from him, so she stayed on her feet, keeping the table between them.

"We need to talk," she said tersely, fanning out a stack of pictures on the table in front of him. Then she stepped back, crossed her arms, and waited.

She saw the flash of recognition in his eyes.

He flipped through the images, but she kept her eyes on his face. She didn't need to see the pictures again. She had memorized them. Adam and Callie kissing, in a canoe of all places. Adam with a hand on Callie's cheek, his fingers starting to slide into her hair. The two of them locked together in the doorway of her house, her leg wrapped around him. And worse. Much worse. She had no desire to see them again.

Thinking about it was making her sick all over again.

"Where did you get these?" he demanded.

"On the Internet." It figured that he would go on the offensive.

Adam sat heavily in one of the kitchen chairs and rested his head in his hands, kneading his temples. Kat pressed her lips together, refusing to ease this moment for him. He was the one with the explaining to do.

"I don't understand. Why would there be pictures of me on the Internet?"

"It's not about you, Adam. It's about Callie. These pictures showed up on a country-music gossip site." The 'I told you so' was implied.

"But how did you find them?"

"I set up an Internet alert on your name and another one on Callie's name. I get an e-mail whenever something new pops up about either of you online. I found this little gift in my in-box this morning."

Adam sighed and leaned back, meeting Kat's eyes. He had screwed up and they both knew it.

"How bad is this?"

Kat relented a bit, uncrossing her arms to pull out a chair across from him. She could be professional and pissed off at the same time. Adam might be an idiot, but that didn't mean she needed to be one, too. She stacked the photos neatly and turned them face down.

"Look, Adam, I can't ignore the photos. Even if I could, you can be sure that the attorneys for Danny grandparents will bring them to my attention. You're not named in the captions or the article, but that doesn't make them go away."

"Understood."

"So now I need to figure out what this means for Danny," she said, "and how it changes my understanding of you."

"You were the one who said that I didn't need to sneak around," he challenged.

"If you recall," she bit the words out, "I have consistently recommended that you have an open, above-board relationship with someone local and stable. Callie is the opposite of those things."

"She's local," he objected. "She grew up here."

"Does she live here now?" asked Kat. "Will she be a part of Danny's day-to-day life?"

He didn't answer. No surprise there. She pressed her advantage.

"And what happens when it all falls apart?" she asked. "Does that mean no more music lessons for Danny, even when she's back in town?"

Adam's jaw tightened. At least he was listening.

"I need you to think about what you're doing, because this isn't about what you want. It's about Danny. You need to be sure that you handle your personal life in a way that doesn't hurt him."

"I would never—" began Adam.

"You already have. You put your own needs ahead of his, both by interfering in Danny's relationship with Callie and also by flaunting what can only be a temporary fling. Only time will tell if you've done any damage."

She waited while he thought about the implications of what she had said.

"Is there anything I can do?" he asked.

"I would say 'keep your pants on,' but it's a little late for that, isn't it?" she replied.

Was that unprofessional? Frankly, she didn't care. Nor did she care if she made him angry. Judging by the look on his face, she was doing a good job of that.

"I'm sorry," he said curtly. "I've complicated things. It was . . . unintentional, and I'll do what I can to mitigate the damage. In the meantime, I'll be sure to keep you posted on Danny's progress."

It wasn't quite groveling, but she would take it.

"Of course," she responded, keeping her tone crisp and professional.

She stood and headed toward the door, leaving the photos behind. God knows she didn't want to touch them again. Maybe he would check the facts, do the Google search on Callie to see what turned up. Maybe he would admit that he was an idiot for getting involved with her. At this moment, however, she would bet that his only regret was getting caught.

"By the way," Kat said as she paused in the doorway, "it looks like the hearing will be on June first. You should get the official notice tomorrow. That's in two weeks. I've already asked Doc Archer to do a re-evaluation of Danny in light of his breakthrough."

Before Kat could leave, Callie appeared at the back door. Kat gave her a tight smile. How perfect. Really. It was the perfect way to cap off a perfect morning.

"Oh, hi. Sorry. I didn't mean to interrupt. I had a quick . . . never mind. It can wait. I'll come back—"

"No, don't leave," said Kat, neatly swapping places so that Callie now stood in Adam's kitchen and Kat could escape. "I need to run. Oh"—she paused—"Callie. I saw an ad for your band's summer tour. Congratulations. Looks like you guys are finally breaking into the big time."

"Ah, yeah, thanks."

"Do you think you'll be around for the next few weeks, or will you need to get back?"

"I should be here for a few more weeks," answered Callie cautiously. "Why?"

"Just curious. Danny's doing so well with his music lessons. We'll have to find him another teacher after you leave." Kat shut up, leaving the best parts unsaid.

Enjoy him while you have him, honey, because it won't last forever.

"See you later." With a cheery wave, Kat slipped out the door, leaving Callie and Adam to sort out the mess they'd made.

Callie stared after Kat, wondering what the hell was going on. The room swirled with undercurrents. She turned to see Adam leaning back in his chair, his face inscrutable. Gone were the openness and vulnerability of the last two days.

He knew.

That would explain the undercurrents.

"Did Danny get off to school okay?" she began. "Because we need to talk."

"He did," answered Adam, "and yes, we need to talk." He turned over a stack of photos on the table. She slumped into the chair opposite him.

"I'm so sorry," she whispered.

"So am I."

She stared at the stack of photos, hating the fact that her career could taint the waters here in Hidden Springs.

"In two weeks, there's going to be a hearing," he continued. "A judge will decide whether or not I'm doing a good job with Danny. His grandparents want custody, and they're going to bring forward as much evidence as they can to show that I'm doing a terrible job."

Callie looked up at Adam's face, and felt even worse. Adam had mentioned a custody issue, but she had no idea things were this bad.

"The judge will rely heavily on the recommendation of Danny's guardian *ad litem*. That's Kat. If I can't persuade her, then I lose him."

More than anything, she wanted to reach across the table and squeeze his hand, but the kitchen windows were large, the blinds open. A simple gesture could end up being another incriminating image on the Internet.

"It's not like I would never see him again, but it wouldn't be the same." He took a deep breath. "I want to make this work.

For Danny. For my brother. For me. Danny's the only family I have left."

"Adam, you're doing a great job," she protested. "Danny has finally started talking, and now he's writing music. Why would the judge agree to a change right when things are getting better?"

"I don't know," he sighed. "But the photos are certainly a complication."

"I understand," she said, staring down at her hands. "And I really am sorry." She took a deep breath and held it for a second, looking up as if the ceiling could take away her tears, then exhaled on a big sigh. "This is my fault. I thought we were far enough from Nashville that I could relax. I let down my guard. I was wrong, clearly, but don't worry. I'll stay away. There won't be any more pictures. And if we need to stop the music lessons, I understand." She swallowed. "I'll hate it, but I understand."

He reached across the table and took her hands in his. When she glanced meaningfully at the windows and tried to tug them away, he held on tighter.

"You have done so much in such a short time," he said. "You're making a difference with Danny, which is the most important thing."

"But the pictures—"

"What's done is done." He squeezed her hands. "We can't make the pictures go away. Even if they come up during the hearing, I'll simply argue that I'm entitled to my personal life."

Callie quirked a smile. "That may be true, but I'm not exactly Marian the Librarian."

"Who cares?" he shrugged, cradling one of her hands in his and turning it palm up so he could trace circles on the inside of her wrist. He smiled when she shivered, cocking one eyebrow. "The whole 'sexy librarian' thing has never been a turn-on for me, anyway."

"Really?" A wave of relief crashed over her. They were going to be okay.

He pulled her hand and close to his face and kissed it, his unshaven skin rough against her palm.

"I'd be happy to demonstrate."

Callie melted. She struggled to remember why she shouldn't crawl across the table and into his lap.

"But the photographer—"

"Can go screw himself." Adam stood, tugging her up to her feet as well, and pulled her toward the hallway. "Come on. I have something I need to show you."

"What?"

"My bedroom."

Later, they lay entwined in Adam's sheets. He traced lazy circles on her back, and she imagined the song she would write about him. Most of her ideas so far were not appropriate for younger audiences—much like those pictures.

"What are you thinking about?" he asked.

"The photos." She grimaced. "I wish I could shrug them off the way you have, but I hate the feeling of being stalked. It's bad enough in Nashville, where I know I need to be on best behavior in public, but to have this follow me home is excruciating."

He kneaded her lower back, erasing some of the worried tension, and replacing it with a pool of heat. She stretched, content to let him clear her mind, and turned his own question back on him.

"What are you thinking about?" she asked.

"The hearing," he admitted. "Would you mind talking to the school psychologist this week? He needs to revise his report on Danny for the judge, and I think he should hear about the lessons from you."

"Of course."

"Thanks."

She nodded, enjoying the odd contrast between good manners and naked skin. They lay quietly for a few moments before he broke the silence.

"What happens when you go back to Nashville?" he asked softly.

"What do you mean?"

"Will you stay with your band? Even after everything that's happened?"

"Of course," she responded, surprised by the question. "I don't have a lot of other options."

"Why not?"

She shrugged.

"The usual reasons. We've made commitments, signed contracts, recorded an album. Someday, maybe, I'll have the connections to strike out on my own, but that's years away."

"You've never thought of getting out of the business completely?"

She stilled, turning the familiar question over in her mind. At some point they had all asked her this: her mother, her sisters, even her father. It always made her sad. Didn't they know her? Only Brian had never asked.

"It's all I've ever wanted," she said simply. "It's who I am."

He absorbed her answer, silent for so long she thought she had lost him. Then before she realized what was happening, he rolled her over onto her back, pinning her against the mattress.

"We'll have to make the most of our time together, then," he said.

"I know," she laughed, once again swimming in relief. "So what are you waiting for?"

CHAPTER TWENTY

"We need to talk."

Callie choked back a laugh when she heard Brian's pronounce-ment crackle through her cell phone. At least the Darth Vader ringtone had put her in the right frame of mind. Starting with Brian's text message this morning, the whole day had been one crazy roller coaster ride.

"You're right," she returned. "We do need to talk." Ignoring the knot in her stomach, she set her guitar aside and walked to the sun porch windows, hoping to draw strength from the water.

"Your voice sounds fine to me," he accused "It's time for you to get back to reality."

"My voice sounds better because I've been resting it," coun-tered Callie, "something I won't be able to do back in Nashville. I need to stay here through the end of the month as planned."

He let out a cynical laugh.

"I know exactly what you're doing up there, and it's not rest-ing. Enough playtime."

"I'll come back when I'm ready, and there's nothing you can do about it." Callie held her breath, shocked by her own combat-iveness, and waited for Brian's response.

"Now, babe, that's where you're wrong. You should have read those contracts more closely while you had them." He paused for effect. "I own you."

The sweeping statement knocked the air right out of her, and anger rushed in to fill the void.

"Are you threatening me?"

"I'll do more than threaten you if you don't get your ass back down here. I gave you this ticket to the big time, and I can just as easily take it away."

He hung up.

Callie sputtered into the disconnected phone, then threw it back into her bag, disgusted. Even if he was right about the contracts— even if he did own her—he was wrong about one very important thing. He had given her nothing. She had earned her place onstage, and she wouldn't give it up without a fight.

Rather than picking up her guitar again, she marched into the house, straight to her father's office. She barged in without knocking and strode over to his desk. He looked up in surprise.

"I want to record the demo," she said bluntly.

He leaned back in his chair and gestured toward the recliner in the corner. She shook her head and started pacing instead.

"What prompted the change of heart?" he asked.

"Brian," she spat, as if his name were a curse. "For now let's call it 'creative differences.' I need to have all my ducks in a row before I go back to Nashville."

Her father raised his eyebrows, but didn't comment. Instead he picked up the phone, called his friend Gib over at the radio station, and within minutes had reserved the studio for Thursday. She took several calming breaths while he finished on the phone, but it didn't work. Instead of feeling calm, by the time he hung up she felt like she was going to be sick.

"You okay, sugar?"

"I don't know," she wailed, sinking into the recliner and burying her face in her hands. "I just don't know anymore."

She scrubbed her face, determined not to cry because of Brian. Adam's question from the morning floated through her mind again. Have you ever thought about getting out of the business? *Yes, damn it.* She thought about it all the time, and the thought of walking away hurt almost as much as the thought of sticking it out.

She looked up suddenly.

"Dad, why did you get out?"

He understood the cryptic question instantly, and considered for a moment before answering.

"I wanted something more."

"How does leaving your career behind and moving to the sticks get you more?" She needed a real answer, not a platitude.

He sighed. "I'm not like you. I don't light up when I get on a stage. It was fun, and I was good at it, but there were other things I wanted so much more."

"Like what?"

"Like a life. A family. Times were different then, and things were . . . complicated. Besides, you can't raise a family if you're on the road for months at a time. It's a recipe for disaster."

"But lots of musicians have families." She couldn't quite suppress the flutter of panic in her voice.

"Sure they do, and sometimes it all works out. But in those days—not so long ago, mind you—the music scene scared me. So many friends destroyed by drugs, and then AIDS." He sighed. "I had to walk away. I wasn't strong enough to stay."

It was more information than he had ever offered before, and for that Callie was grateful. But she looked down at her callused fingertips, knowing that he couldn't answer the questions that consumed her. Why she couldn't be like everyone else? Why couldn't she be satisfied with a normal life? Why couldn't she walk away?

Sometimes she thought of music, and her connection with the audience, as an addiction. No matter how high the cost, she couldn't seem to give it up.

"Are you thinking about leaving?" her father asked gently.

She shook her head, still looking down at her hands. "There's nothing else for me. If I stop performing, I stop breathing. If I walk away, I cut out my heart and leave it behind."

"Maybe there's another way."

She looked at him then, so earnest in his concern for her happiness, and sighed. She couldn't follow his lead on this one.

"Not for me, Dad. Songwriting alone isn't enough."

"I get that," he said, "but staying with the band might not be the right move either."

"It's the only move I have. Leaving the band will take time and planning. Even with a demo in hand, I can't just cut and run."

"I know, I know. But when you're ready, I can make some calls. Make sure that demo gets a fair hearing."

Callie smiled. "Dad, that's sweet, but I don't think there's much you can do from here."

"You'd be surprised," he replied, completely serious.

She stilled, her family radar picking up something new and unfamiliar.

"Dad, what are you not telling me?"

He laughed at that.

"There's a lot that I'm not telling you. Parents are people, too, you know. Just because I'm your Dad doesn't mean you know everything about me."

Now he was making her nervous. Mom had secrets. Dad had secrets. She had secrets. Next thing she knew, her sisters would be calling her to confess that they had secrets, too. It was all too much.

"Relax," he said. "It's nothing scary. I've kept in touch with a few friends who stayed in the business, that's all. When you're ready to circulate your demo, I can call them."

She breathed a sigh of relief. He was trying to be helpful.

"Thanks, Dad," she said, standing up and leaning over the desk to give him a kiss on the forehead.

"Anytime," he replied with a wink. "That's what Dads are for."

"No fair! You're using your right hand!"

Danny waved his arms wildly, trying to block Adam. Adam shot the basket, using both hands, then caught the rebound just above Danny's fingertips and spun the ball on his left index finger.

"You're right, I did."

Danny stopped trying to reach the ball and planted his fists on his hips.

"That basket doesn't count, then."

"True." Adam still spun the ball up above Danny's head.

"And I get a free throw."

"You do?"

"Yes," stated Danny definitively.

"Fine." Adam tossed the ball up into the air, and Danny caught it on the way back down. He ran over to the chalk line on the driveway and prepared to make his shot.

Adam marveled at the change in Danny over the past few weeks. He had progressed from total silence to arguing like a lawyer. Doc Archer said he still wasn't talking at school, but that it was just a matter of time.

"Move away from the basket," Danny ordered. When Adam didn't immediately move out of the way, he repeated his command. "I know your tricks. Your arms will 'accidentally' block the shot. Now move it, or I win."

"Okay, okay, I'm moving."

Adam grinned as he moved to the side of the 'court.' Danny was right, of course. If he was close enough to the basket, he would indeed mess with Danny's shot. Over the last few days he had

stopped tip-toeing around Danny and discovered the power of joking and teasing to bring Danny out of his shell.

Danny celebrated his winning basket with a whoop and a fist
pump. Adam challenged him to an extremely high five. Danny
leaped to slap his palm, then jumped again to brush his fingers on
the underside of the net before racing into the cottage.

Adam slapped the pole as he passed and wondered if Callie
would stop by again tomorrow morning. He hoped she would.
What a great way to start the day.

Danny had already grabbed a bottle of water. Adam found him
on the front porch, kicking back in one of the chairs and staring the
lake. Adam followed suit, resting his feet on the porch railing and
chugging his water. He and Danny might not share music, but they
could share basketball, and—if they were lucky—this summer they
could share the lake. Danny giggled when water ran down his chin
and onto his shirt, then laughed even harder when a giant belch
caught him by surprise.

Adam looked at him out of the corner of his eye, and Danny
managed a belated "'Scuse me" in between all the giggles.

Would Lainey's parents understand a eight-year-old boy?
Or would they be appalled by the burping and farting and the
endless bodily-function jokes? Now that Danny was opening up,
Adam kept having flashbacks to his own childhood, and his adven-
tures with Evan. No matter what the judge decided for Danny's
future, it would be lonely without siblings, and that made Adam
ache for him.

When Danny had calmed down a bit, Adam brought up the
custody issue.

"Hey Danny, you know that the hearing is coming up soon,
right?"

"I know."

"The judge is going to ask you what you want."

"I know."

"Have you thought about what you're going to say? Do you know what you want?"

Danny was silent for a long time, so long that Adam feared he had made a mistake in bringing it up.

"I want to go home."

Danny spoke the words so softly that Adam could barely hear them. When their meaning sank in, he reached over to squeeze Danny's shoulder.

"I wish that were possible. More than anything." He sighed, trying to imagine what Evan would have said. "But we can't go back. We have to play the hand we're dealt. Over the next week or so, you need to think about what you'd like your future to look like."

Danny nodded.

"I wish Callie could stay," he said, his eyes still on the water.

"Me, too, buddy," he whispered. "Me, too."

CHAPTER TWENTY-ONE

Callie parked in front of Lucy's but didn't get out of the car right away. She was ten minutes early. If she were feeling more social, she would go on inside, grab a table, and drink a cup of tea while she waited for her dad to walk over from the school on his lunch break, but the last thing she wanted right now was light chitchat with semi-strangers. Her entire body hummed with adrenaline. The idea of leaving the band—now, not in two years—consumed her.

As she leaned back in the driver's seat, tapping out a rhythm on the lower curve of the steering wheel, her gaze came to rest on the sign for "The Law Office of Katherine Rodriguez." She dismissed the idea before it could fully form. Kat was not feeling very charitable toward Callie right now, not after those photos. Callie had made Kat's job more difficult, and that was not a good way to make friends.

The problem was that Callie had run out of options. She had looked for other area lawyers, but each time she picked up the phone to call one of them, she put it right back down again. The idea of choosing a lawyer at random—rolling the dice with her future—didn't make any sense. This was too important.

Maybe in this case, the devil you know. . . .

Callie glanced around, wondering if her tabloid stalker lurked in the bushes, or sat drinking coffee at Lucy's. Thinking about it made her angry all over again. She could hear Brian's words echoing in her mind. *'I own you.'* Nobody owned her. Not Brian. And not some sleazy photographer.

Callie opened the car door before she could chicken out, moving quickly toward Kat's office. She didn't pause to reconsider. She hopped up onto the sidewalk, crossed the distance to the door, and pushed it open to the jingle of a bell. The time had come to take action.

Only when Kat emerged from the private office did Callie have second thoughts. Once again, Kat looked like a lawyer from a TV show, smart and sexy and dangerous. And once again Callie felt childish in comparison, in her flowing skirt and cowboy boots. To make matters worse, she stood at least six inches shorter than Kat in those power heels.

But a little adrenaline goes a long way. Callie used every ounce of it to stand tall and lift her chin.

"Callie, what a surprise."

Kat said the words, but to Callie she didn't look surprised. Must be all the lawyer training.

"Do you have a minute?" Callie asked.

"Of course." Kat was all poker-faced politeness, even as she checked her watch. "Is this about Danny?"

"No."

Kat motioned Callie toward the upholstered chairs right there in the waiting area. Callie chose a seat with a view of the street, so she could keep an eye out for her father through the window. Kat took the opposite chair, facing her across the low coffee table.

"What can I do for you?" asked Kat in a tightly professional voice.

"I need a lawyer. I was hoping you could help."

Now *that* was a look of surprise. Callie smiled.

"It depends on the nature of your problem," responded Kat cautiously. "I specialize in 'domestic relations,' which is really anything that affects families. Divorce, custody, adoption, wills, estates, trusts, that kind of thing. But this is a small town, so I also do some real estate and small business work. What kind of help do you need, exactly?"

"You know that I'm in a band. I need to get out."

Kat didn't even blink.

"So what's stopping you?"

Callie laughed helplessly. She had only asked the obvious question.

"It's complicated," she said.

Was there even a way to explain in words all the different ropes that bound her? Ten years of hard work. The force of Brian's ambition. Her signature on the contract with the record company. The possibility that they would struggle without her. The fear that walking away would mean the end of her music career. The fear that Brian was right.

"Of course it is. That's why you need a lawyer."

Mindful of the fact that her father would walk past the window at any moment, Callie summed up as quickly as she could, outlining Brian's threats of legal action and his claim that he 'owned' her. All the rest was just emotional baggage.

"So what you're telling me is that you signed a band agreement when you were eighteen and naïve, you've lived with it all these years, and now you want to figure out how to end it. You're afraid that he'll sue you, or that he or the record company can somehow compel you to stay. Does that sound right?"

"You have a talent for brevity."

She smiled. "Goes with the territory."

"So what do you think?"

"I think I need to see the contract. Can you leave the band? Yes, of course. Nobody can make you stay. Will it be messy? Probably. But I can't tell you anything for sure until I see the documents."

Callie could feel the little bubbles of hope fizzing and popping inside. She didn't care how messy this got, as long as there was a way out.

"So what happens next?"

"You bring me whatever you have. I'd like to see any sort of paperwork that relates to the band. Contracts for gigs you've played or are going to play, copyright notices you've filed for songs. Bank records. Whatever you've got, I'd like to see it. Do you have access to those records?"

"As a matter of fact, I do." Callie spoke calmly, but inside she did a shameless victory dance. Brian had handed her the keys to her prison cell. If he'd had any clue, he never would have done it.

"Get those to me as soon as you can and I'll see what I can do," said Kat.

"So you don't need to be a music industry lawyer to help me? I was afraid I'd have to see a specialist."

This was the perfect excuse for Kat to step aside, saying something like 'You're right, maybe it would be best if I referred you to someone else,' but she didn't do it.

"You might, but maybe not. You want to find a graceful way to leave a partnership. Unless there's some music industry twist to your case, I should be able to help. And if I can't, I can help you find someone with the right skills."

Callie saw her father approaching from the direction of the school and rose from her chair. Kat followed suit.

"I need to meet my father for lunch, now, but I can bring the papers over later," said Callie.

"Sounds good," said Kat.

Callie paused by the door, unable to leave without saying something about the past.

"I'm sorry," she said softly. "I didn't get a chance to say it that night, and I know it's been years, but I'm sorry about your Mom—about everything."

Kat didn't pretend to misunderstand.

"Thanks," she said. "Sometimes it seems like a million years ago, and sometimes it's right here with me, like it just happened."

"Why did you come back?" asked Callie. "Wouldn't it have been easier to put down new roots somewhere else?"

Kat sighed.

"So many reasons. To honor the memory of my mother. To make sure I never forget. To make sure it never happens again." The answer was unexpectedly raw and honest. "When I work with teenagers, I tell them that they'll be free of their past one day. I guess I need that to be true for me, too."

"So do I," agreed Callie.

Kat offered a hand and Callie accepted, sealing their unexpected connection with a handshake.

Callie ducked out of Kat's office, Brian's threats no longer weighing her down. She treasured the fragile little bubbles of hope rising within her. Perhaps, if she collected enough of them, they would carry her through.

"Hey, Dad." Callie caught up with her father as he was opening the door to Lucy's.

"Hey, sugar, where did you come from? I saw your car and thought you were already inside."

Callie grinned and slipped through the open door.

"My secret."

"We'll see about that," he muttered with a smile.

"Sit anywhere," called Lucy from behind the counter. "I'll be right over." She offered warm-ups to the usual crew of retired officers and turned up the volume on the scanner. They had beaten the lunch rush, and the only other person in the diner was Callie's old 'friend,' Larry Hutchinson. Thankfully, he stayed put at his tiny table in the far corner of the room. He couldn't seem to resist winking at her, but she pretended not to notice.

Callie and Luke chose a table with a view of Main Street. As they got settled, she realized that her father might be even more excited about her demo recording session tomorrow than she was. Maybe he always buzzed with energy during the school day, but she could practically see it crackling off his skin.

"So are you ready for tomorrow?" he asked.

"I think so. I've got a working song list, and it's a nice mix of moods and tempos. My plan is to lay down a solid recording of each song before I do anything fancy. If I have time, I'll go back and layer secondary instrument tracks, or backing vocals, but the most important thing is to get all the songs recorded."

"I agree. In fact, I was thinking—"

"Luke James, where the hell have you been? It's been months since you came in here to see me."

"Lucy," he answered, "I don't know how the time got away from me. Forgive me?"

"Don't let it happen again," she said. "And where's Dora?"

"Painting."

"Well, make sure you bring her with you next time. And you," she accused, turning her attention to Callie. "How many years has it been since you came to see me? Five?"

"Six." Callie ducked her head to avoid a swat from Lucy's order pad.

"Six years! Unbelievable. I guess that's what happens when you make the big time. You forget the people who gave you your first break."

"I did not!" Callie couldn't tell if Lucy was kidding or not, but she was insulted either way.

"Well, then, you should come play here again one day."

"I will."

"Great. How about Sunday?"

"Sunday?" Callie squeaked. She shot her father a 'rescue me' look, but he leaned back in his chair and smiled, enjoying himself way too much. She nudged him—well, okay, kicked him—under the table.

"Actually, Callie is only in town for a little while longer," he observed. "Two more weeks, right?"

She nodded, eyeing him suspiciously. Was he going to rescue her or throw her under the bus?

"If you want her to play, I'd go for Memorial Day weekend. It'll give you more time for publicity, and you'll get more of the tourist crowd."

Callie glared at him. This was no rescue. She had just been thrown to the wolves—and by her own father.

"Oh, that would be perfect!" crowed Lucy. "Eleven thirty on Sunday, just like the old days?"

"Of course," answered Luke.

Callie clamped her mouth shut, vowing to give him a piece of her mind as soon as they were alone. If she were a conspiracy theorist, then Lucy would be on the suspect list, too, but she couldn't be sure. He might have cooked this one up all by himself.

"Wonderful." Lucy fluttered away, already plotting. "I'll make posters. Oh! And I can put a notice in the paper." She turned back abruptly. "Oh, I almost forgot, what can I get for you?"

After they had ordered, and Lucy had disappeared into the kitchen, Callie laid into her father.

"How could you? You planned this! 'Let's meet for lunch, sugar,'" she mimicked. "'We haven't been to Lucy's for ages.'" She dropped her voice to a fierce whisper. "How am I supposed to keep a low profile if I'm playing public gigs?"

He laughed, not bothering to deny her accusations.

"Relax. This is the local diner. You played your first gig here when you were, what, eleven? twelve? Of course you would come back here to play again. Nobody will think it's a big deal."

She groaned and buried her face in her hands. Should she tell him about the tabloid stalker? Of course, that would involve admitting her involvement with Adam, and she wasn't quite ready to share that with her dad yet. This was supposed to be a vacation, not a soap opera. Where had her quiet, restful escape gone?

"So about tomorrow. . . ." He moved on to the next subject as if she were done lecturing him. "I was thinking that you might need an extra pair of hands."

"Why?" she asked, confused.

"We booked the studio time, but you won't have any help."

"Won't there be a tech?" She let him get away with the distraction. She really, really wanted things to go well tomorrow.

"Not unless you count Gib. He'll get you rolling, but after that you'll be on your own. He's got a radio station to run."

"Great," said Callie. Now her demo was going to take twice as long to record and it would probably suck if she was tweaking all the equipment settings herself.

"So I've arranged to take the day off."

"You what? But, wait, can you do that? What about your classes?"

"That's what subs and personal days are for." He reached across the table to squeeze her hand. "This is important, and I'd like to help you make it good."

"Wow. Thanks," said Callie, almost willing to forgive him for plotting with Lucy. But not quite.

He grinned. "Just trying to help."

CHAPTER TWENTY-TWO

Callie and her father burst into the kitchen, still overflowing with energy after their day in the studio. Her mother had made a pot of chicken stew for dinner. Callie didn't even need to look under the lid to be sure. The kitchen smelled amazing.

Roscoe came padding into the kitchen, still stretching as he trotted over to greet them with a friendly tail and too much licking. He could sense that something exciting had happened.

"You're right on time," called Dora from the stove. "Dinner's basically ready. It just needs to simmer for a bit." She covered the pot and turned the dial on the stove. "In the meantime, I thought we should have a celebratory cocktail."

She beckoned for Luke and Callie to follow her outside, where she had set out some cheese and crackers and put a bottle of champagne on ice. The perfect end to a perfect day. Callie felt the sting of tears and wrapped her arms around her mother.

"Thanks, Mom," she whispered.

Dora patted her gently on the back. "I never liked Brian, anyway."

Callie choked on a laugh as she pulled back. "I know." She rolled her eyes. "Trust me, I know."

"So let's toast your first step toward leaving the band!"

Dora filled champagne flutes for all three of them, and they raised their glasses. Callie spoke first.

"To freedom!"

"And music," added Luke.

"And love!" Dora's last-minute addition to the toast came as Callie took her first sip. She breathed in a few too many champagne bubbles and spent the next several minutes coughing and blowing her nose. When she had recovered, Dora patted her on the knee.

"I know you're not ready to think about love again, sweetie, but sooner or later it will find you." At Callie's wary expression, she pressed on. "Love makes the world go round. Without love, there would be no music, no art. Everything would be gray and boring."

"Mom, this is not the time to write me a fairy tale." She gave her father a pleading look, but he leaned back in his chair and took another sip of champagne. He knew better than to interrupt Dora when she got on a roll.

"I don't need that kind of distraction," Callie insisted.

"Distraction," scoffed Dora. "What kind of an attitude is that?"

"The kind of attitude that will make me successful in the music business."

"Sure, successful, miserable, and alone."

Callie squared her shoulders, ready to go head to head with her mother if necessary, but Luke saw the warning signs and stepped in.

"Ladies, do we really need to debate this now? How about we celebrate today's step forward and leave the larger issues of life, love, and happiness for another day?"

Dora gave a dissatisfied *hmmph.*

"Fine," said Callie coolly as she refilled her glass.

"I was thinking . . . ," began Luke.

Callie looked up at him in alarm. Whenever he began a conversation with those words, trouble was sure to follow. Dora evidently had the same thought, because she turned her full attention to Luke and narrowed her eyes. He cleared his throat and began again.

"I was thinking that I should make a phone call."

"To whom?" asked Dora.

"Zeke."

Callie wasn't sure how to interpret her mother's reaction. Dora clearly knew who Zeke was, and had mixed feelings about Luke calling him. Callie asked the obvious question.

"Who's Zeke?"

"He's an . . . old friend of your father's," answered Dora carefully, her eyes on Luke. "He runs a small record label out of Nashville."

Luke nodded. Callie sucked in a breath.

"Wait, you don't mean Zeke—"

"Yes," interrupted Dora. "That Zeke."

"Oh my God. You never told me. . . ."

"I didn't want Brian to pressure you."

"What?"

"The music you were doing with the band would not have been right for Zeke's label, but if Brian knew that you had an 'in,' he would have pressured you to use the connection anyway. I would have said no. Rather than deal with all that mess, I never told you that I knew him."

"But you're telling me now."

Luke nodded, and his whole face lit up. "The music you're doing now is perfect for him. All I need to do is make a call. I can't guarantee that he'll sign you, but I can guarantee that he'll listen."

Callie felt a wave of dizziness sweep over her and carefully set her champagne glass on the table. Then she dropped her head and rested it on her knees. Dora reached over to rub her back, and Luke squeezed her hand.

"Are you okay, sweetie?" asked Dora. "If this is all too much, you don't have to do anything." From the tone of her voice, Callie suspected that her last remark was directed squarely at Luke. She kept her head down and let them argue it out.

"This is her moment, Dora, and I can help her seize it."

"If she's not ready, then you're not to push the issue, Luke." She dropped her voice. "You don't need an excuse to reconnect with Zeke. If you want to call him, you should just call him."

"This is not about me," insisted Luke, also in a low voice. Did they think she couldn't hear them? She wasn't that dizzy. Callie kept her head down and waited to see what other interesting things they would say.

"Bullshit," returned Dora. "We both knew that this day would come. We weren't sure when or how. But it's here, now. And you have some thinking to do."

Luke didn't respond, at least not verbally, and Callie longed to pick up her head, but the moment she did, her parents would lose the thread of their mysterious conversation. Luke broke it off anyway, returning his attention to Callie.

"Sugar, are you okay?" Luke squeezed her hand again, and his voice was gentle. Callie slowly picked up her head.

"I'm fine, Dad. Really. Just overwhelmed."

"Your Mom's right, you know. I won't call Zeke if you're not ready. I don't want to push you."

Callie smiled and squeezed his hand back.

"You're not pushing me. I'm ready. And if I'm really going to do this, I'll need to find a way to control the story before Brian turns it to his advantage. If you really think that my demo is good enough, I'd love it if you would call . . . Zeke. I still can't believe you're on a first-name basis with him. But I'll get over that. In the meantime, yes, please, make the call."

"Really?" Luke bounced like a kid ready to race outside for recess. He paused and looked at Dora, waiting for something.

She smiled and nodded, but she looked sad. Luke gave her a swift kiss on the cheek and left the porch, presumably to make the call right this second. Callie thought about the box of letters in the attic. How much of her parents' story did she really know? She was still getting used to the idea that her parents were people living their own lives, not supporting players in hers.

Dora leaned back in her chair and looked out over the water, sipping the last of her champagne. Callie took a sip of hers as well and then asked Dora the question that had been on her mind for days.

"Who's Lauren?"

Dora didn't visibly react, though she did pause for a second, champagne glass in midair. Then she carefully set her glass on the table and folded her hands in her lap, looking down at them briefly before meeting Callie's eyes. Callie had never seen her mother like this, all her fluttering energy concentrated into an intense stillness.

She had asked the question out loud, and the words could not be unsaid.

"What do you want to know?"

Callie swallowed, then took a deep breath.

"Are you going to visit her while we're in New York on the girls' weekend?"

"Yes."

"Are you going to introduce us?"

"I don't know."

"Why not?"

"I don't know if I'm ready."

Callie digested her mother's cryptic answers. Before she could form another question, her mother posed one of her own.

"How do you know about Lauren?"

"I found your letters."

"Did you read them?"

"Yes."

Her mother looked away for a moment, but she didn't lose her composure or her energy.

"And what did you learn from the letters?"

No accusations? No recrimination? This unfamiliar stranger looked like her mother, but felt like a completely different person.

"I learned that you have a lifelong friend that you kept a secret from your family—or at least from your daughters."

As she spoke the words, Callie felt smaller and smaller. She had breached her mother's trust, and now Dora must feel even more exposed than Callie had felt after seeing the stalker photos. The thought made her feel sick all over again.

"You're right. I have never talked about Lauren with you girls. She represents a thread in my life that I set aside before you were born. When I received her most recent letter, though, I knew that the time had come to pick up that thread again, and to weave it back into my life."

"She's dying."

"Yes."

"How can you be so calm about that?"

"She was dying when I met her. It's not exactly news."

Callie floundered, full of questions but unsure how to interact with this version of her mother. Dora rose to her feet, effectively ending the conversation.

"Please don't mention this to Luke. He has enough to think about right now."

"Okay," Callie whispered, feeling the tremors in the foundation of her world. She wished she had never opened her mouth.

"I'm going to get dinner on the table. I'll call you when it's ready."

"But—"

"I'm not ready to talk about this now. Your questions will have to wait."

Callie snapped her mouth shut. Dora disappeared into the house. As the sun set, the trees cast long shadows across the lawn. Callie closed her eyes and shut out the beauty of the view, wishing that she could rewind the last ten minutes. Given a second chance, she would keep her mouth shut and leave her mother's secrets undisturbed. Actually, if she were serious about second chances, she would rewind the last ten years and start fresh. Every choice she had made since that first meeting with Brian needed to be undone. She should have stayed on her own, making her own music and singing her own songs. Every compromise, every concession, had eaten away at her soul until only a hollow shell remained. She had made some progress toward filling it again, but it would take time. Her past choices would cast their shadows over her life for years to come.

This must be what regret feels like. Perhaps, down the road, she would know wisdom, but for now, she just felt foolish.

CHAPTER TWENTY-THREE

"I can't believe I agreed to this," said Callie.

Adam laughed as she wrapped a wool blanket around herself and huddled behind the windshield of the passenger seat on the *Speakeasy*. Now fully restored, she was finally ready for a test run on the lake, and he had brought Callie along to share the moment. The sunny, sixty-degree day had seemed plenty warm on shore, but once they had launched the boat and moved into open water, they discovered the true meaning of the words 'wind chill.'

A small part of him still couldn't believe he was trading a warm morning in bed with Callie for this chilly boat ride, but truthfully he was sick of lying low. If he couldn't spend time on the water with a beautiful woman—whatever her future plans—then he needed to make a change. There had to be some balance between Danny's life and his own. How could he ask Danny to be a whole person, embracing life, if he wasn't willing—or permitted—to do the same?

"It's freezing out here," she muttered. "Tell me again why we're doing this?"

"Wimp," he called cheerfully. "Come over here by me. I'll warm you up."

She didn't immediately take him up on his offer. Not a good sign.

"Do you think that's wise?" she asked. He didn't like the shadow that crossed her face. She shouldn't have to worry about stalkers. "Not to be paranoid, but that photographer could still be following me around."

"Get over here. I could care less about the photographer."

"But the case. . . ."

"Our secret's out. We can't make things any worse. Might as well enjoy ourselves."

She smiled, then shrugged and slipped into the circle of his arms. They continued like that for a while, Callie standing in front of Adam, her head tucked under his chin, her body wrapped in the blanket, and his arms reaching around her to clasp the boat's steering wheel. When they reached the middle of the lake, Adam slowed the boat. Leaning down, he spoke softly in her ear.

"Do you want a turn to drive?"

"That would mean unwrapping the blanket." She tugged it more tightly around her body.

"I know," he laughed. "And I'll repeat the question. Do you want to drive?"

He could tell that she was tempted, but she needed a nudge.

"Are you chicken?" he asked.

"What?" she said.

"I knew it."

"I am not." She sighed dramatically. "Give me the wheel, city boy. I'll show you how it's done."

"And I'll keep you warm," he said, adjusting the blanket and holding it in place so that she had her arms free to drive. He sat down in the captain's chair, bracing her hips between his thighs and giving her more room to maneuver. She placed her hand on the throttle and thrust it forward. The boat leaped in response, propelling them forward through the chop. She drew a large, lazy circle in the center of the lake, then cut back through her own wake to make a series of figure eights. Finally, she straightened out their course and headed down the length of the lake, keeping her pace steady, her hand firm on the throttle, adjusting her course as needed in response to the ever-changing water.

He had never been so turned on in his life.

The blanket slipped a bit. He changed his grip so that he held the blanket in one hand, leaving his other hand free to do mischief. He let it stray downward, snagging the waistband of her long flowing skirt so that he could slide it down over her hips. Her breath hitched as it pooled around her feet.

"Adam, stop it. I'm driving here." She swatted at his hand. "It's cold!"

"I know," he chuckled. "Hands on the wheel, please."

She gasped as his cold hand met her warm belly, then began sliding upward. In seconds, he had unclipped the front clasp on her bra and begun torturing her breasts with his icy fingertips. He liked the way her nipples responded immediately to his touch, but he wanted more. The blanket certainly added to the challenge, but he was, to put it bluntly, up for it.

As his hand warmed, and he let it roam more freely, caressing the soft skin of her belly and then moving across her hips, encouraging her underwear to follow her skirt to the floor. When she realized what he was trying to do, she wriggled in protest, but it was too late. He moved forward to the edge of the seat and pressed himself against her curves, now sheltered only by the scratchy wool blanket. Anchoring her hips against him, he slid his hand slowly down her belly until his fingers reached their goal. She shivered and leaned back against him, her hands still clutching the wheel.

"Adam," she warned, her voice coming out more like a moan.

"Yes?" he answered softly, his fingers circling around and around her center.

"Adam, please, I can't . . . think."

"Good thing there's nobody else out here on the water." His fingers grew more insistent. Her breath came in pants. He anchored her more firmly as his fingers demanded more and more of her.

"Adam," she cried, her entire body wracked with shudders. He held her steady, pressed hard against him, until her breathing slowed and he thought she could stand on her own. She still clutched the wheel, but her legs were steady as he slowly, gently, withdrew his hand.

She reached over and pulled the throttle back, slowing the boat until they idled, drifting gently in the waves. She cut the motor, and the sudden stillness caught him by surprise. They had covered nearly half the length of the lake, but were still out in open water, enjoying more privacy than they were likely to find on land.

"Hold this," he whispered in her ear, nipping at her earlobe as he secured the blanket around her and tucked the edges into one of her hands.

"Mmmm-hmmm," she murmured dreamily.

Adam smiled. If she was dreamy now, she would be reeling soon. He slid from the captain's seat and moved into the bow, yanking the seat cushions off the benches and piling them on the floor. He grabbed a few towels from the stack in the back and laid them across the cool vinyl. Then he tugged Callie toward him.

"Are you thinking what I think you're thinking?" she asked, eyeing the makeshift bed with equal parts interest and skepticism.

"Definitely," Adam said, reaching beneath the blanket to run his hands up her bare legs, encouraging her to sink down on top of him. He wanted her now, before her dreamy haze faded. He managed to escape his jeans before her knees capitulated and she melted down onto him. He caught her hips and met her as she closed the gap between them, plunging into her as the wool blanket floated down to cover them both.

She arched her back, clinging to the benches for support. He gripped her hips and they rode the waves, slowly at first, rising and falling with the rhythm of the water. But the waves grew bigger. They struggled to keep pace, crashing together, again and again, until they both collapsed, spent, and tumbled helplessly in the surf.

"Adam," she said softly. He smiled into her neck.

"You're irresistible," he whispered in her ear, then nipped at her earlobe with his teeth, making her shiver, and the hair on the back of her neck stand up. "You've always been irresistible."

"And you're trouble," she sighed. He laughed.

"The best kind of trouble."

They lay in silence for a few minutes, sheltered from the cold wind, until he remembered why they had launched the boat in the first place.

"How do you like the boat?"

"I love it. She's a thing of beauty."

"I agree," he answered as he kissed his way down her neck. "She's unforgettable."

Callie lay in the circle of Adam's arm, lulled by the rocking motion of the boat on the water. If only this moment could last forever. Forget Nashville. Forget stalkers. Forget custody battles and careers. In this moment she had found peace, and she didn't want to let go.

Adam made it all too easy to imagine a new life. Instead of starting over in Nashville, she could start over here in Hidden Springs. She and Adam and Danny could be a family. She and Danny could play music together every morning. During the day, with Danny off to school, Callie could work on her music while Adam worked on his boats, but of course they would have to break for lunch at some point. Lunchtime would quickly become her favorite part of the day.

From time to time she would travel to Nashville for meetings and recording sessions. During the summers she would have to tour. Maybe Adam and Danny could join her, sometimes. The road would be lonely on her own, but she would know, even during the long stretches away, that she had a real home waiting for her. A real family. Love.

The word hovered, suspended in her imagination, and she built sand castles and dreams all around it. It was too soon for daydreams like this, too soon to let the word 'love' float around unsupervised, but she couldn't help it. Adam had always given her the courage to dream big.

Kat was saying good-bye to a client when she saw Adam's SUV pull up. He was hauling a gorgeous, dripping wet wooden boat. She laughed softly to herself as she waved good-bye to the family. What kind of idiot takes a boat out on a blustery May morning? It was barely sixty degrees outside, and probably colder out on the water. She shivered just thinking about it.

Her smile faded as she got a closer look. Adam had a passenger, and it looked like Callie. They talked or . . . something . . . for a few moments, then his passenger—yes, it was Callie—hopped out the passenger door and Adam drove away. Kat sighed. If Adam intended to keep a low profile in the weeks leading up to the hearing, he was going about it the wrong way.

As Callie approached, Kat straightened up and put on her best professional smile. She smoothed her jacket and pushed open the door, ushering Callie inside. Kat might not be rosy-cheeked and windswept from a morning on the water, but she had just this morning helped a family finalize the adoption of their foster child. With a dose of perspective, the knot in her stomach would loosen and the queasy feeling would go away, right?

"Hi Kat," chirped Callie as she stepped inside. Kat let the door close on its own, the happy little bell jangling her nerves.

"Good morning," Kat responded, her voice cool. "I'm glad you could make it."

Kat directed Callie to her private office. Call her petty, but she wanted the reinforcement of the chair and the desk today. Kat took her time pulling out Callie's file and a notepad. Neither of them broke the silence with polite chatter. Kat picked up her pen and tapped out a sharp little rhythm.

"I've looked over your documents, particularly the band agreement. Here's where you stand. You signed an agreement that favors the interests of the band over the interests of the individual members. All the songs have been copyrighted in the name of the band, not the songwriter. The real kicker, though, is the exit clause. It's harsh."

"I was afraid of that," Callie admitted, "but I couldn't remember the details. How bad is it?"

"That depends on your perspective," answered Kat. "The exit clause, as written, says that you can walk away at any time. You have rights to your share of the band's current assets, including money—"

"That sounds good," Callie interrupted.

"—up to a maximum of five hundred dollars."

"Oh."

"And you leave behind the rights to all the songs. Those stay with the band."

"Oh."

Kat watched Callie, curious to see how she would react. When Callie didn't seem inclined to speak, Kat continued.

"Keep in mind that you could dispute this agreement. If nothing else, we could challenge the copyright on the songs. Those were done as work-for-hire for the band, which is unusual."

"But that costs money."

"Yes."

"And it could generate some ugly publicity."

"I suppose."

While Callie mulled over the situation, Kat wondered what kind of client Callie would turn out to be. Was she itching for a fight? Looking for an excuse to sue? Maybe hoping to jumpstart a solo career with a burst of publicity? Or did she plan to fade away, retire to small-town Wisconsin, and start a new life? Kat caught herself as she was about to roll her eyes. Wouldn't that be a bitch, if she stayed? Callie could swoop right in and lock up the only eligible bachelor in the entire county.

Which made Kat an idiot for facilitating the process.

"What do you want, Callie?" she asked abruptly, preferring a solid answer to a lot of speculation. Callie cocked her head, confused, so Kat clarified her meaning.

"What's your goal here?" she asked. "Are you going to stay in the music business? Do you want to burn bridges? Do you want publicity? Do you want privacy? What are you looking for?"

"I want out," Callie sighed. "No drama. No publicity. I want to be done with the band. After that, yes, I want to stay in the music business. I'm working on making that a real possibility. But in the meantime, I need to understand how to get out of the band, and how long the process will take."

"That part's easy," said Kat. "All you need to do is tell them in writing. The resignation can be effective immediately."

"That's it?" asked Callie, clearly surprised. Kat smiled. Non-lawyers always expected things to be complicated. Sometimes they were very simple.

"I can't promise they'll take the news well," qualified Kat, "but technically that's all you need to do."

Callie smiled. "They will definitely not take it well." She thought for a moment, then asked, "Can you help me do this? The writing part, I mean. I don't want to screw it up."

"Sure," answered Kat. "Do you want to get together on Monday and I'll have a draft letter for you to review?"

Callie let out a big breath and nodded.

"Thanks," she said. "This is turning out to be a lot easier than I thought."

Kat smiled cynically, feeling the weight of every one of her twenty-nine years.

"Don't worry. It will get harder."

CHAPTER TWENTY-FOUR

"I received your resignation letter today. You can't be serious."

Callie could feel the lash of Brian's voice through the phone line, and it cracked all the pleasure out of the day for her. She had picked up the freshly-pressed copies of her demo CD this morning and floated home filled with hope, ready to conquer the world. Gib had stopped her before she left the studio, asking if he could have the honor of breaking one of her songs on the radio—whenever she was ready.

She could have kissed him.

"Callie, are you listening?" Brian snapped.

"I'm here," she sighed. She stepped outside, Roscoe at her heels. He stuck close, protective, as if he knew who was at the other end of the line.

"We agreed that you would return to the band next week. We have concerts coming up. You made a commitment," he spat out the word, "and now you pull a stunt like this."

Callie struggled to remember Kat's coaching. Stay calm. Breathe. He can't force you to stay. She paced back and forth on the lawn, kicking the grass every now and then. Roscoe paced with her, inspecting each of the divots she made with her foot.

"It's not a stunt, Brian. I'm leaving the band."

"Like hell you are."

"You don't need to like it, Brian, but you need to accept it. There's nothing you can do to change my mind." Thank God Kat had prepared her for this conversation. Without rehearsal, she would never have found the words on her own.

"If this is a play for a bigger percentage, it's not going to work. We can do this without you, but what can you do without us? Are you planning to move in with one of your sisters and play coffee houses? Or even better, move back home and teach music lessons?"

His sarcasm came all too close to her daydreams of domestic bliss with Adam. Her eyes pricked with tears and she squeezed them shut, wondering what the hell was wrong with giving music lessons. Or, more to the point, what was wrong with her for not wanting to teach music lessons.

She didn't bother to respond to Brian's questions, and he laughed.

"Don't worry. I already know your plan. Little birdie wants to fly solo."

Callie didn't comment, but he knew her well enough to make his barbs sting. The sarcasm hurt. It shouldn't have, but it did.

"Oh, please," he sneered. "Well, if you want to give that a try, be my guest. But," and his voice got dangerous, "if you even think of playing the band's music, of stealing those songs, I'll bury you."

Callie gasped. They were her songs. Hers. She had written every one of them.

She tried to calm her racing heart. He was pushing her buttons, and she was letting him do it. She needed to stick to the script.

"Brian, my reasons for leaving the band don't matter. My future plans don't matter. What matters is that I'm leaving, and the best thing for all of us is to handle the situation professionally."

Callie held her breath, waiting for him to respond. This was it. If he believed that she truly was leaving, then she had a very short window of time to get her demo in front of the right people before Brian could sink her. She would need to move fast.

"You'll regret this." Brian's voice was quiet, dangerous.

"I doubt that." She had already decided that there would be no more regrets.

"I guess we'll see soon enough who's right—and whose career is over," he threatened.

"Fine," she responded calmly.

"Fine," he threw the word back at her like a five-year-old.

"Fine." She laughed, and hung up. For once in her life, she would have the last word.

"Arrrffff," barked Roscoe, and Callie laughed harder. Apparently it was Roscoe's turn to have the last word.

Adam watched, fascinated, as Callie prepared the sailboat. Somehow, in all the summers he had spent at the lake, he had never gone sailing. He'd been water-skiing, canoeing, kayaking, even paddle-boarding, but never sailing. From time to time she gave him orders, using unfamiliar technical terms, but he generally got the idea. Put the sticks—battens—into the little pockets on the sails. Put the hook through the grommet on the top of the sail and then feed the edge of the sail into the channel on the mast. Callie hauled on a rope and the sail climbed to the top. She tied all the knots, saying it would take too long to teach him how to do it right.

Before he knew it, they were pushing off, catching the wind and heading toward the middle of the lake. He had never traveled so fast over the surface of the water without the roar of a motor. The relative silence took his breath away. It was magical. So magical, in fact, that he stopped paying attention to Callie and her orders. Big mistake. If not for her shout of warning, he would have been knocked overboard by the boom when she turned the boat. From that point forward, he paid more attention to his captain, and to his job holding the rope that controlled the little sail. The jib sheet. Why a rope was called a sheet he had no idea.

The wind died down in the middle of their run, leaving them adrift in the middle of the lake. He could see the newly installed dock in the distance, but they would need a lot more wind before they could make their way back. This, then, was the downside to sailing. Adam felt no need to break the silence with meaningless chatter. He was content simply to soak up the sun and listen to the lapping of the water against the hull.

"I resigned from the band."

Adam turned around so fast to look at Callie that he almost fell in the water.

"You're serious?" he asked, his mind swimming with all the new possibilities this presented.

"Absolutely," she answered, her focus still out on the water.

"Congratulations," he said, throttling back his enthusiasm. He didn't want to scare her off. "So what happens next? Do you still need to tour with the band this summer?"

She shook her head. "The backup singers are already covering for me, so they're set for the tour. All I needed to do was send my official letter of resignation and I'm free to pursue my career on my own terms."

"It's that simple, even with the recording contract?" Adam asked. It seemed odd to him that the record company wouldn't have any objections, but maybe the music business played by different rules than the rest of the business world.

"It's not like I'm walking away with anything of value. All the money, and all the songs, stay with the band. Brian isn't happy about it, but there isn't anything he can do to stop me."

The look of calm determination on her face made him pause. He didn't want to be a buzz-kill, but he didn't want her to get hurt either.

"Are you sure Brian won't do anything? Sometimes people do stupid things—vicious things—when they're angry."

"That sounds like Brian," she said with a sigh. "I don't know what exactly he could do, but if he can find a way to prevent me from being successful on my own, he'll do it."

"Do you have any leverage?" he asked.

She cocked her head for a moment, considering the question, then outlined the terms of her separation in more detail. It certainly sounded like a clean break, but he thought about what he would do if he were involved in the deal and wanted to derail it.

"He might sue you, even if he has no real grounds to do it. That would be one way for him to generate bad publicity and create the perception that you're not a good bet for investment by another record company."

She shrugged, and he regretted dampening her spirits.

"I wouldn't put it past him," she said. "He'd do it just to wipe out my savings, so that I don't have any seed money."

"Have you got anything on him?" asked Adam.

She thought about that as the wind picked up and they started moving again. He found it amazing that they were moving forward even though the wind blew in their faces. Something about the angle of the sails and the strength of the centerboard allowed them to race toward the wind.

"I've already taken away the thing he wants most, which is my songwriting. I'm the one who writes—wrote—all the songs for the band. Now he's going to need to pay someone else to do it, and it's likely they won't sign the copyright over to the band the way I did."

"Does the record company know that you're the only actual songwriter in the band?" asked Adam, intrigued. This could be the leverage that she needed.

She shook her head. "I don't think so. They had a lot of questions about the copyright on existing songs, but they didn't dig into the specifics of who wrote what. Mostly they wanted to make sure nobody was going to come along later demanding money."

"That's it then," said Adam, feeling a little more smug than he probably should.

"That's what?" asked Callie.

"Your leverage."

"How do you mean?"

"First of all," began Adam, "you can threaten to tell the record company that the only songwriter is leaving the band. Brian could say you're lying, but the truth would become obvious at some point, and he knows it."

"True," said Callie, her expression brightening.

"And second," he continued, "you could threaten to sue the band to regain control of the songs."

She laughed at that. "That would never work," she protested. "Brian would know it's a hollow threat. I don't have the money to sue, and even if I did, I have no case."

"Maybe," Adam agreed, "but the point is not to win. It's not even to sue. The point is to make a credible threat. If Brian believes you're crazy enough to sue, if only to publicize the fact that you are an amazing songwriter, then you've got your leverage. He doesn't want to jeopardize this summer's tour or the possibility of a second album."

"Interesting . . . ," she murmured, her attention back to the water and the wind. He let her mull over his suggestion while they turned the boat again, this time heading away from the wind, back toward home.

Taking the boat in a new direction required a change in tactics. They let the sails out wide, taking full advantage of the wind at their backs. As they sliced through the chop, jolted from time to time with a spray of icy water, Adam admitted to himself that he was more than ready for a change in the direction of his own life. Maybe Callie, newly free of her obligations, could be persuaded to stay. He already knew he didn't want to let her go again.

"So how does this affect your plans?" he asked. "Is there any need to go back to Nashville?" He glanced back at her but couldn't read her expression. Her eyes were on the waves and the water. He wasn't even sure she had heard him, but after a minute or two, she finally answered.

"I need to get back soon," she said flatly. "There will be a brief burst of publicity about me leaving the band, and then people will start to forget. I need to make my move now, while I'm in the spotlight."

"Make your move to what?" He needed to know more about her plan before he could hope to change it.

"A deal of my own. I want to write and record my music on my own terms. I've cut a demo and this is my chance to get people to listen to it." She shrugged. "Besides, all my stuff is still at the loft. If I wait too long to clear it out, Brian will change the locks, or get rid of it. I need to close out that chapter of my life. No loose ends."

Callie abruptly shifted gears, calling instructions to him as they approached the dock. In the flurry of activity that followed, further conversation was impossible. Adam did not want to end up in the lake, so he paid attention, but in the back of his mind he was already planning his campaign to get Callie to stay. All he needed to do was persuade her to follow a new dream instead of an old one.

CHAPTER TWENTY-FIVE

Danny burst through the kitchen door, full of energy from the morning music session and the mad dash back up the hill. Adam knew, in the logical, rational part of his brain, that he had once possessed that kind of energy, but he couldn't remember it. Not viscerally.

He could, however, remember quite well how his mother used to yell at him and Evan for running in the house, running on the stairs, jumping in the kitchen, and generally bouncing off the walls. He now understood why people longed for their youth. It wasn't about beauty or strength. It was about energy.

These days, he got his energy from coffee.

"How was music today?" he asked Danny.

"It was awesome! Callie played her awesome new song for me, and it's . . . it's just . . ."

"Awesome?" supplied Adam.

"Yeah, awesome. I can't wait to hear her try it out at the diner. She said you can never tell with a song until you try it in front of a crowd."

Adam nodded knowingly, as if he had a clue. What was he going to do if he couldn't convince Callie to stay? He would need to beg Luke to take on the role of music teacher for Danny. It wouldn't be the same, but at least the arrangement would preserve a link back to Callie. The problem was that both Danny and Adam wanted more than a tenuous connection to Callie. They wanted her here, with them, for the long haul.

Adam toyed with that thought as he helped Danny assemble his usual school-day breakfast of cereal and juice. He turned it over and around in his mind, considering it from all angles. What they had was so fragile. If she hadn't walked away from success on her own, he could never have asked her to abandon her music career for this . . . thing that bound them together. But now he wouldn't be asking her to give anything up. He would simply be asking her to stay.

For so long his own dream of an opposite life had been just that—a dream. Evan had been the lucky one. He had found Lainey early in his life and, for a brief time, made the dream a reality. Adam hadn't been so lucky. He had found Callie too soon and figured it out too late.

Now he had a second chance. Callie was starting over. Why not start over with Adam? Her father had found a way to build a music career here in Hidden Springs. Callie could follow in his footsteps. All Adam needed to do was find the courage to ask.

Danny chattered as he ate, the floodgates now wide open, and Adam tried to focus on the here and now, on the boy in front of him. What mattered was Danny and the hearing. Adam's dreams could wait a few more days. There was a moment of silence while Danny took a breath and a bite of cereal, and then he piped up again.

"I think we should ask Callie to stay," Danny announced. He stated it as matter-of-factly as he could with his mouth full.

"What?" Adam choked on his own cereal. Since when could Danny read his mind? "Please don't talk with your mouth full," he said. Then he had to wait, impatient, while Danny finished chewing.

"I think we should ask Callie to stay," Danny repeated, his mouth clear this time. "I don't want her to go."

Adam cleared his throat again, choosing his words carefully. "It's not our decision to make. It's her decision, and if she wants to go, we have to let her." He ignored the tiny knife-twist in his gut. "I don't want you to go either, but it's not my choice. What if the judge thinks you should stay with your grandparents? Then you're the one who will be leaving."

"No, I won't," answered Danny, as if it were a done deal.

"How can you be sure?"

"Kat told me."

Adam almost choked again. "She what?"

"She said that if I knew what I wanted, then I should speak up. That she would listen, and the judge would listen."

Adam sputtered, questions tripping over each other in the rush to get out. He closed his mouth, marshaled his thoughts, and started fresh.

"So you know what you want?" he began. "You want to stay?"

"Yep." Danny took another huge bite of cereal, serene, as if they were discussing the weather. Adam could feel his jaw start to clench.

"Were you planning on letting anybody know?" Once again, he had to wait for Danny to finish chewing.

"Well, yeah. Eventually." Danny took another huge bite while Adam reeled from the combination of relief and frustration. He dropped his forehead into his hands, hoping that Danny wasn't planning to drop any other bombshells today.

"So can we ask her?" Danny repeated.

"Callie?" Adam looked back up at Danny, feeling like he was one step behind in this entire conversation.

"Yeah," said Danny.

Adam took a breath, carefully locking down his emotions.

"Sure," he shrugged, poker face ready. "There's no harm in asking."

Danny paused in his chewing and cocked his head, looking at Adam oddly. Adam took a bite of cereal, despite the turmoil in his stomach. There was no reason for Danny to know how badly Adam wanted Callie to stay. Danny would never understand why his uncle suddenly felt like sprinting down to the lake and diving in—anything to release the tight coil of tension that used to be his stomach.

"Good," said Danny abruptly, as if that settled the matter. "I'll talk to her about it in the morning."

"Sounds good," said Adam, the coil tightening its grip. "Let me know what she says."

Was it a cop-out to let Danny ask her? Maybe. But then again their chances might be better if the request came from him. Now that Danny was talking, he was pretty irresistible.

Maybe she would say yes. God, he hoped she would say yes. He wasn't sure he could safely guide Danny through the next ten years on his own.

Callie had just stepped out of the shower when she heard the doorbell. At this hour of the morning, it was unlikely to be a delivery, but it might be Adam. She smiled, imagining all the different ways that she could greet him at the door. Her mother was up in the attic studio, totally absorbed in her painting. Her father was at work. However, she wasn't willing to put on a show with the paparazzi in the neighborhood. She let her X-rated thoughts float away on a laugh. Any welcome would need to be rated G.

The morning's music lesson had gone well. Maybe Adam wanted to check in on Danny's progress. Hoping it was really him, she quickly dried off and threw on a bathrobe. The thick terry covered her completely, but should get him thinking about what might—or might not—be underneath.

Her damp curls bounced against her back as she padded down the stairs. So far so good. No groan of the UPS truck chugging back up the drive. Maybe it really was Adam. She hurried to the back door. Roscoe caught up with her in the mudroom. The sound of the bell must have disturbed his morning nap. He trailed along at her heels, but hung back growling when he reached the mudroom.

Not Adam.

Brian.

She had no opportunity to regroup or get dressed. She had already pulled open the back door and only the storm door separated them.

"Callie," he drawled. "You're looking fresh this morning."

She swallowed, tried to get a grip. She refused to give in to the rush of panic that threatened to overwhelm her. Clearing her throat, she pushed open the storm door.

"Brian, what a surprise."

She didn't move aside. She had no intention of welcoming him into her home. Roscoe tried to push past her, so she held him by the collar. As satisfying as it would be if Roscoe bit Brian, she wouldn't give Brian yet another tool to use against her.

"You knew I would come for you," he stated, as if it were a foregone conclusion. The scary thing was, he was right. She had known, deep down, that he would never let her leave without a fight.

"Actually, I was hoping we could be civilized about this." Callie straightened up as much as she could while still keeping her grip on Roscoe.

Brian took a step forward, as if he could waltz right into the house. This would be the last time he took her acquiescence for granted.

"You can stay outside, thanks."

Roscoe growled in support.

He gave her a tight smile and stepped back.

"Callie, I'm not going to have this discussion on the back steps. Am I coming in, or are you coming out?"

Talking to Brian was difficult enough without holding on to Roscoe the whole time. Besides, she didn't want to drag her mother into this.

"I'm coming out."

She took her time settling Roscoe down. Brian could wait. Luckily, there was clean laundry stacked on the washer in the mud room, so she ducked into the bathroom and threw on jeans and a T-shirt. Shoving her feet into a pair of flip-flops, she stepped out the back door. It was chillier than she had realized, her wet hair making it feel even colder, but she decided to gut it out. She wanted Brian gone.

Brian walked over to the truck and pulled open the passenger door.

"Let's go for a drive," he said. At the sound of his voice, Roscoe started barking from inside the house.

"We can talk right here," she said. Better to deal with him on her own turf.

"Callie, it's cold, and I can't hear you over the damn dog. We need a quiet space to talk. The truck works fine. Let's go."

She debated her options, making him wait for an answer.

"Fine," she agreed tersely. She couldn't think or hear with Roscoe barking anyway. One last compromise wouldn't change the outcome, and it would keep her feet from getting any colder.

She climbed into the passenger side of the rental truck and slammed the door, waiting for Brian to climb in on his side. They had spent a lot of time over the years riding from gig to gig together in a truck. It was the perfect place to end their relationship.

Brian started up the engine and slammed it in gear, pulling away from the house and roaring up the driveway. She fastened her seatbelt.

"So what's left to talk about?" she asked.

"I heard about your new demo."

"You heard it? How?" She didn't like the idea that he had gotten his hands on it. She couldn't even imagine how it was possible.

Brian laughed. "I didn't need to hear it. I heard *about* it. You played that folksy, coffee-shop crap that you love so much—the stuff that will never sell."

He smiled, and Callie, watching his face in profile, didn't like the nasty feeling that came with it.

"Don't worry," he continued. "I'll still take you back, even if everyone is laughing at you behind your back. You're too useful to throw out because of one mistake. It's a big mistake, granted, but I can overlook it."

Callie held her breath until she had herself under tight control. Brian was poison, and she couldn't listen to him. He hadn't heard the demo. He had no idea what he was talking about. He only wanted to hurt her.

"How did you hear *about* the demo?" asked Callie, forcing her voice to be calm and even. If nothing else, she needed to know how he was following her life up here so closely.

He leaned over and popped open the glove box. Inside she found a stack of pictures and flipped through them. The ones at the top of the stack she already knew from the gossip website, but the rest were new. Viewing them one by one was like watching a stop-motion movie of her life. There she was entering the radio station, then leaving with the demo CDs. There was even a close-up photo of one of Lucy's posters advertising her special appearance.

"Oh my God, have you been stalking me?"

"What?"

In a moment of genuine surprise, Brian's mask slipped and she glimpsed, briefly, the old Brian—the direct, driven guy he had been before the pursuit of fame changed him.

"I don't have time for that." He shrugged off her accusation like an autograph request from an unattractive fan, and the glimpse disappeared. "I hired a private investigator. He was more than happy to follow you around this month."

She stared at him a long moment before it dawned on her. "Hutch," she finally said. "You hired Larry Hutchinson."

"That's the one," confirmed Brian, displaying no remorse whatsoever.

"But if you hired him," she argued, "why did the pictures end up on the gossip site? Did Hutch sell you out?"

"I sent them." He laughed at her stunned expression. "Free publicity, baby."

She started to feel queasy. Was she that naïve? Had she ever known Brian at all?

"So the pictures of you with the new girls?"

"Yeah, those too." The smirk on his face was making her nausea worse.

Callie thumped her head back against the headrest and wondered how she could communicate with this stranger. She also started to wonder where the hell he was going on this 'drive.' Instead of sticking to the shore road, he was heading through town toward the highway.

"Where are we going?"

Brian didn't answer, but his smirk faded.

"If you want to talk, then let's talk," she said, "but I've had enough of driving around."

He still didn't answer. The nausea in Callie's stomach veered toward panic. She needed to get out of this truck.

"Brian, you can't just kidnap me."

Ahead, past the picnic area, was the entrance to the highway.

"Brian. Listen to me." She reached over to squeeze his arm. "Whatever it is you're thinking, stop. We need to talk, not drive."

His fingers tightened on the wheel. Callie's breath stopped as he accelerated toward the entrance ramp.

"Brian—"

He slammed on the brakes and swerved. Her hands flew out to brace herself, one catching the dash and the other the door. The tires squealed as the truck fishtailed into the gravel parking lot and came to a halt in a cloud of dust.

Thankfully, the picnic tables were unoccupied.

Callie let go of his shoulder and slipped out of the truck. The stones in the gravel lot bit into her feet through the thin soles of her flip-flops, and the wind whipped her wet hair around her face, but she didn't care. She was fine as long as she was out of that truck. She picked her way over to one of the weather-beaten tables and sat on top of it. Wrapping her arms tightly around herself, she waited for Brian to admit defeat.

It took about ten minutes.

At least, that was her guess. She didn't have a watch. But after a long, cold eternity, Brian climbed out of the truck and walked slowly in her direction, his hands shoved into the back pockets of his jeans.

"The band needs you," he admitted, unable to meet her eyes.

She smiled. "The band needs a babysitter. It doesn't have to be me."

"Who will write our new material?" He sounded like a whiny kid.

"There are lots of songwriters out there. You'll find one you like."

"We keep all the music, you know. You don't get to take it with you."

"I know," she shrugged. "You can keep it. I'm not going to fight for it."

"Damn straight."

"Unless you're an asshole," she warned, narrowing her eyes. "Then I might change my mind."

That shut him up, for a minute anyway.

"I don't understand why you would leave. Why now, when we're about to break out?"

"You mean, apart from the fact that I can't stand to live a lie anymore?"

"Yeah, apart from all our personal bullshit."

Callie had to smile. He could dismiss their twisted ten-year relationship with the wave of a hand. It was their business relationship that he couldn't imagine ending.

"I guess I'm sick of changing my music to fit the band, you know? I like that folksy crap that doesn't sell."

He gave a short, harsh laugh.

"You know," he said, "I chose you because you were adaptable."

She cocked her head to one side.

"What do you mean, you 'chose me'?"

"I found you, at that open-mic night, and we talked for hours. Remember?"

She nodded.

"I wanted to start the band even then, but I needed someone practical, not some starry-eyed 'artist' planning to sacrifice success for the sake of the music. Someone real, who wanted to make a living in the business. Someone who would let the business drive the music and not the other way around. What's the point if you're not in it to win it?"

Callie kept nodding. There didn't seem to be much point in arguing with him. All this time, she had thought they had a connection, flawed though it might be, when really she had been one more building block in his career plan. The truly scary part, the thing that made her worry about her future, was the fact that she had fallen for it in the first place.

Was her judgment really that bad?

"I thought that person was you," he continued, unaware that her attention was wandering. "I thought I could count on you. And yet, here we are, ten years later, about to make it, and you're blowing me off for the sake of the music."

He seemed to be waiting for a response.

"It's not just the music, Brian. It's everything."

"What the hell is that supposed to mean?"

"It means that I'm a person, too. For ten years I've been living your dream. Now I'm going to live mine."

"Right," he scoffed. "We'll see how that works out for you."

"I'll be fine," she answered, her voice strong. For the first time in a long time, she felt strong.

They stared each other down, but neither gave any ground.

"I could ruin you," he threatened.

"You could try," she agreed, "and then I could ruin you."

"Is that a threat?"

She smiled.

"It's a simple statement of fact," she observed. "As a courtesy, I sent a copy of my resignation to the record company attorneys. You'll notice that I did not emphasize my role as the sole songwriter for the band." She paused for effect, just as Adam had suggested. "That can change."

Her smile widened when she saw his jaw tighten. Brian didn't deal particularly well with insubordination. From her perspective, though, it felt pretty good.

"So we're through, then," he said.

"Looks that way."

Finally they were getting around to the parting words. She was cold and really wanted to get back home.

"Fine," he said. "Don't expect any favors." He turned on his heel and walked toward the truck. As he climbed in he called out, "And don't come crawling back."

Callie jumped to her feet as he started the truck and peeled out of the parking lot. By the time she realized what was happening, he had made the turn onto the highway ramp and was gunning the truck up to full speed. She watched him disappear into the distance, her mouth hanging open. He had left her on the side of the road, quite literally in the dust.

Jerk.

She picked her way back to the picnic table and sat down again, rubbing her arms to get some circulation going and ignoring the wind as best she could. She was mulling her options when a police car pulled into the parking lot and drew up alongside her. The officer rolled down the window. She laughed helplessly. Could things get any worse?

"Good afternoon, miss," he drawled. "Everything all right here?" He removed his sunglasses and surveyed her summery attire, fighting a smile.

"Hi, Jack," she said. There was no way she was going to call him 'officer.' "How's Sally?"

"She gets into a lot less trouble these days. I wonder why that is?"

Callie narrowed her eyes.

"Maybe because her big brother leaves her alone?"

He laughed.

"Maybe because the James sisters left town?" he suggested, all innocence.

Callie pursed her lips. He was probably right about that one. They had gotten into plenty of trouble, and dragged poor Sally along every time.

"Possibly," she admitted.

"You were expecting warmer weather for your picnic, Miss James?"

"Ha. You don't even know which sister I am."

"Of course I do. Everyone knows that Callie—and only Callie— is back in town. I'm a cop, you know, and a highly skilled investigator." He smirked. "In fact, if I use my detecting skills right now, I would say that you've been dumped by the side of the road. Angry boyfriend?"

"Ex," she ground out through clenched teeth.

"Ah. . . ." He leaned over and opened the passenger door. "In that case, hop in. I'll give you a lift home. It'll be just like old times."

How many times had Jack driven Callie and her sisters home when they were teenagers? Her twelve-year-old self demanded that she stomp her foot and tell him to buzz off. However, her too-old-for-this-crap self was freezing her ass off. As annoying as Jack might be, he had wheels, and she needed a ride. So she climbed into the police car and let him drive her home.

Talk about full circle.

CHAPTER TWENTY-SIX

Adam tried to act casual, leaning against the counter and sipping his coffee, but his insides were unsettled. Before Danny had gone off to his lesson this morning, he had repeated his intention to ask Callie to stay with them.

"She said yes," Danny announced as he breezed into the kitchen.

Just this once, Adam wouldn't have minded if Danny dropped his guitar in the kitchen instead of being responsible and putting it away immediately in his bedroom.

"Really?" Adam called after Danny. He forced himself to be still. He didn't want to worry Danny by pacing around the kitchen.

"Uh huh," yelled Danny from the bedroom. Adam heard the thump of the guitar case hitting the floor, and a moment later Danny reappeared in the kitchen. He sat down at the table and began pouring cereal. Adam waited, but no further details were forthcoming.

"So . . . what exactly did you ask Callie?"

"I asked her if she would be my music teacher forever."

Adam released the breath he had been holding. It came out as half laugh, half cough. That wasn't the phrasing he would have used.

"And how exactly did she answer?"

Danny concentrated on pouring the milk into the bowl, then looked up at Adam.

"She said that she couldn't be here every day, but that she would always come back, and that whenever she was here she could play music with me. Every day."

His insides stabilized, leaving him with the realization that some conversations were best left to the grown-ups. It was time he started acting like one.

"That's good news."

Danny nodded.

"Did she say how long she was staying in town?"

Danny nodded again, but his mouth was full.

"How long?"

He waited, hiding his impatience, until Danny finished chewing. "She leaves on Monday."

Adam closed his eyes. He had the weekend to convince her to stay.

Eight years ago

Adam waited until the crowd thinned around the bonfire. He used the time to strengthen his resolve. Memories of Callie had tortured him all evening, but he refused to cave in. He would do the right thing even if it killed him. Callie had been subdued tonight, and she hadn't met his eyes. He was fairly certain that his Christmas card had done the trick, but he needed to be certain—or maybe he needed this one last excuse to talk with her. Whatever the reason, tonight he would make sure that she had moved on.

When he sat down beside her, she stiffened, but she didn't walk away. She wove her pick into her guitar strings, snapped the case shut, and stared into the fire.

"Hi, Adam," she said. Her voice was so distant he might as well be back in Singapore.

"Hi."

He knew what he needed to do, but had no idea what to say.

"We got your Christmas card," she said, "and the photo. She's very pretty. What's her name?"

"Charlotte," he said. He didn't trust himself to say more.

"How did you meet?" she asked.

"Do you really want to know?"

She waited a moment, then shook her head.

The urge to confess overwhelmed him. *She's just a friend. I didn't want you to wait for me.* But he held himself ruthlessly under control, determined to see it through.

"How was your first year of school?" he asked.

"It was great," she said brightly, but her voice sounded brittle. "I joined a band, and I'm dating the lead singer. His name is Brian."

"A lot can change in a year."

She nodded.

He couldn't think of anything else to say. His Christmas card had worked exactly as planned. Deep down he wanted to pound her new boyfriend into a pulp and then drag her back to Singapore with him, but that was just a fantasy. Callie had moved on. He would never ask her to put her life on hold for him. She deserved better.

"So I guess this is good-bye," she said, looking at him for the first time.

He nodded. The shadows in her eyes cut him to the bone. He had done that to her.

"Good-bye," she said, then grabbed her guitar and rose to leave. He watched her walk away until she disappeared into the darkness.

It was done.

Adam followed the sound of music to the boathouse, wishing with every step that he had tackled this conversation earlier in the week while Danny was at school. It would have been much easier to have a soul-baring conversation when the body was already naked. But Callie had been different yesterday. More intense than usual. And he had still been reeling from Danny's pronouncement that he wanted to live with Adam. Between that relief and the distraction of Callie's bare skin, he had missed his best—and possibly last—chance for a naked conversation. With Danny home from school today and through the weekend, their opportunities for private time would be limited.

Adam hesitated before knocking, not wanting to interrupt, but Roscoe barked a welcome and she stopped playing. He had never been particularly good at 'we need to talk' talks, so when she met him at the door and wound herself around him, he welcomed the delay, sinking into her lips and inhaling in the scent of her skin.

She began to pull away.

"Stay," he whispered. The word slipped out before he could stop it. She smiled and then leaned back into him for another kiss.

"Don't worry," she murmured against his mouth. "I'm not going anywhere."

He tried to disappear into the kiss again, but couldn't quiet his mind. She was leaving. This time he was the one who pulled back, just enough to see her face. She met his eyes and he held still, memorizing the moment. The morning sunlight swam in the blue-green of her eyes and warmed her hair. He savored her slow, quizzical smile and tightened his grip on the gentle curves beneath his hands.

"Stay here with us," he repeated. "We need you. Don't leave on Monday."

Callie could feel her heart stop, then start again in a hard driving rhythm.

"Are you serious?" she breathed, wrapping her arms more tightly around him. "You've got so much going on, with Danny and the custody case. I wasn't sure you were ready for us to be . . . real."

He eased back a little and rested his forehead against hers.

"I can't imagine anything more real than this. I need you. We need you." He kissed the tip of her nose. "You and me and Danny, we make a family. We should be together."

She laughed. It bubbled up from deep inside her and there was no way she could hold it back, even if she wanted to.

"I can't believe it," she laughed helplessly. "I honestly never thought that you and I . . . that I could be part of a family and still be able to do my music. It's just . . . inconceivable."

"Why?" asked Adam, his breath warm on her ear. "Your father did it. Why not you?"

She leaned her forehead against Adam's shoulder. What he said was true. Her father had found a way to combine a music career with a family, but the way Adam said it made her pause. She and her father were very different people.

"My father is a teacher at heart," she said softly, directing her words at Adam's shoulder, "and a songwriter. He's not a per-former." She pulled back so that she could see his eyes. "I am. The songwriting isn't over until I have a chance to share my music with an audience. That means getting out on the road from time to time. Doing my music means performing my music."

She tried to lose herself in his eyes, but it didn't work. She couldn't ignore the wrinkle of concern between his eyebrows, or the stubborn quirk of his mouth as he prepared to object. Her chest tightened and her hope began to fade.

"What do you mean?" he asked, his confusion all too real. "I thought you said you wanted to stay."

"I do," she whispered.

"But we need you to really stay. Not just visit," he explained, tension tightening his voice. "Do your music here. If it worked for your father, it can work for you."

She closed her eyes. "It's not the same."

"Danny and I are ready to build a family. If you're not—"

"I am," she insisted. "I want this, more than you know. Just because I can't be here every day—"

"I won't do that to Danny," he interrupted. "He deserves stability. He shouldn't have to adjust to a parent who floats in and out of his life. I don't want that for him." He paused and took a breath. "I don't want that for me."

"But we can talk on the phone," she pleaded, clutching at the last fragments of the dream. "Or we could set up the computer to . . ." Adam was shaking his head even as the words were coming out of her mouth.

"Callie, I don't want that kind of life." His arms tightened around her as if he were trying just as hard to hang on to his own dream. "I promised myself years ago that I would have a real family, the kind with a bunch of kids and a couple of dogs. I want to eat dinner together every night and barbecue on the weekends. I made that promise again to my brother before he died. I don't want to break that promise—to him or to myself." His voice cracked, but he continued anyway. "Please stay here. I don't want to do this without you."

She swallowed hard, wanting more than anything to dive into his arms and never come up for air. But she wouldn't do this to herself again. She wouldn't compromise her dream away.

"Adam, I made a promise, too," she whispered. "I swore I would give my music a chance. I'm finally free to do it. This is my moment. How can I walk away now?"

"I don't want you to give up," he said, his voice low and intense. "But please, think about what you really want. Have you considered that your dreams might be different now? You're not the same person you were ten years ago. What do you want today?"

"I don't know," she choked, pulling out of his arms. "I don't know."

His question hurt, and she hated that it made her doubt all the things she had been so certain about until this moment. She shook her head, but he was still there, waiting for his answers, so she ducked around him and ran out of the summer house. She needed to escape, to breathe, and to think.

Adam collapsed into the nearest chair, unable to believe what had just happened. For a moment, before she had pulled away, he had thought the dream was theirs. How could she walk away from this? He needed her. Danny needed her. And clearly she needed them.

The what-ifs tugged at him. This was all his fault. If he had found a way for them to be together all those years ago, they wouldn't be struggling to stay together now. He had pushed her away with that stupid Christmas card. What if he had begged her to come with him? What if he had asked her to wait? What if he had never gone away? Ultimately it didn't matter because all the what-ifs in the world couldn't help him now.

He waited for what seemed like hours. Roscoe had loped out the door after her, but he shuffled back after only a few minutes, head hanging low. Adam let him in the door and scratched him absently behind the ears. Together they waited, but she didn't come back, and Adam couldn't wait forever. He had to go back up the hill. Danny would be worried.

He took a deep breath and marshaled his thoughts. This was a setback, but he refused to admit defeat. He simply needed a new approach. Clearly a big part of Callie wanted to stay. What would it take to convince the rest of her? His strongest weapons in this battle were Danny and the lake. The time had come to use them. He gave Roscoe one last belly rub and then headed back up the hill to the cottage.

Callie ran down the lake path, putting as much distance as possible between herself and Adam. She stopped when she reached the sheltered cove and the stand of willow trees where they had capsized the canoe. She bent over, her hands on her knees, and tried to catch her breath, but she couldn't. Her breath came in hitches and gasps until the sobs finally broke through. She sat down hard on the grass, wrapped her arms around her knees, and let it all out.

Only later, when the storm had passed and Callie could breathe normally again, did she realize that she had made her decision. If she didn't fight for her dreams, nobody would. If she didn't value them, nobody would. And if she didn't pursue them now, she would miss her chance to make them real.

No matter how desperately she wanted to build a life with Adam and Danny, she couldn't trade in her dreams to make it happen. No relationship could weather the subversive 'what-if' whispers that would inevitably follow. When times get tough you need to be sure of each other, without any lingering doubts.

If Adam didn't want all of her, he couldn't have any of her.

She blew her nose on the hem of her shirt and wiped her eyes with her sleeves. The next two days would be a bitch, but she would get through it. She had survived the loss of Adam before. A second time wouldn't kill her.

CHAPTER TWENTY-SEVEN

"Hi sweetie. I just checked in with your sisters. They're driving up in the morning. How was the music lesson?"

Callie stopped short at the kitchen door, dismayed to find her mother in the kitchen instead of closeted in her studio. It was too late to wash off the evidence of her tears. Too late to sneak in the side door. Way too late to avoid the interrogation.

"Great. Wonderful. We had fun." Callie tried to duck into the microscopic bathroom off the kitchen, but Dora's sharp gaze had already assessed Callie's face. Her eyes narrowed and her lips pressed together.

"Then why have you been crying?"

"I haven't—" she began, but Dora wasn't buying it. "Okay, fine, I've been crying. It's not a big deal."

"Right," Dora snorted. "I'll get the tea. Sit," she ordered, pointing at the kitchen table. Callie complied, hoping she could keep this conversation short, or at least, shorter than her mother's usual heart-to-hearts.

Dora must have had the kettle going recently because less than a minute later she brought the tea, sat down across from Callie, and plunked a box of tissues on the table. She gave Callie a chance to blow her nose and then the interrogation began.

"Why have you been crying?"

"Because it's been a crappy day, and it's not even noon."

"Brian?"

Callie laughed a little even as she sighed. Her mother really didn't like Brian.

"No. Not this time."

"Then Adam."

Callie nodded, eyes down, searching her mug for an escape route.

"Did he call off the affair, then?"

That got Callie's attention.

"How did you know—"

"I'm not an idiot, you know. And I have an excellent view from the attic."

Callie flushed. She was a grown woman, for Pete's sake. If she wanted to take a lover, she didn't need her mother's permission or approval.

"So he broke it off?"

"No." Callie cleared her throat. "I did."

Dora raised her eyebrows, but to Callie's surprise did not comment.

"He wants me to stay here." Callie said the words as if they were a death sentence.

"Ahhh. . . ." Dora leaned back in her chair and waited. She didn't have to wait long. The dam broke and the rest of the story rushed out.

"What am I supposed to do?" Callie wailed. "I want to stay, I really do, but not every single day for the rest of my life. Adam's got some kind of mental block. For him it's all or nothing. There's no compromise. So now I'm screwed no matter what I choose. I just have to pick a flavor of miserable."

Dora was silent for a few moments, studying Callie and sipping her tea. Then she put her mug down and reached across the table to pat Callie's hand.

"Maybe he'll come around."

Callie snorted. "So far it's pretty clear cut. I can stay and have love, or I can leave and have music. But I don't get to have both." She glared into her mug, then muttered, "No wonder songwriters write so many depressing songs."

Dora laughed. Callie shot her a look.

"This isn't funny, Mom. This is my life you're laughing about."

"I know, dear," she said. "I know. And I don't mean to laugh. I'm just so happy that you and Adam found each other. I always liked him. Don't give up on him yet."

"And if he's given up on me?"

Dora sobered at that thought.

"Then you pick up the pieces and move on," she said. "Love isn't a one-shot deal, you know. If things don't work out now, that doesn't mean you're cursed forever. It means the timing is off."

"But I want this to work out." Callie's voice hitched and she paused, clamping down on the tears that wanted to come flooding back. "I don't want to wait for another chance."

Dora sighed. "What I'm saying—not all that eloquently—is that sometimes things *don't* work out for a reason."

Callie raised her eyebrows and gave her mother a skeptical look.

Dora smiled gently. "I'm terrible at giving advice. Why don't I tell you a story, instead?"

"Okay," answered Callie slowly, wondering where this was headed.

"Your father is a wonderful man," her mother began. "We've built a great life together."

"But . . . ?"

Dora's smile faded.

"A long time ago, there was someone else," she said softly.

Callie held on tight to her mug and waited for her mother to continue.

"His name was Barrett. We met the summer I turned nineteen. I was still living at home then, in Sag Harbor, out on Long Island."

"Barrett?" asked Callie. "From the letters?"

"Lauren's husband," said Dora. "They were already married when we met."

Callie's stomach tightened. This was not a good way to start a story.

"But they have kids," she said, not even sure what she was objecting to.

"They do." Dora nodded, her eyes remote. "I was there when the twins were born."

Callie could feel her heart pounding in her chest, even though there was no logical reason to be upset. They were talking about things that had happened thirty years ago.

"I got to know both of them that summer," Dora continued. "I worked at the yacht club. They were members." She smiled. "Lauren wasn't much of a sailor, so I helped Barrett whenever he wanted to take the boat out. Sometimes it was the three of us. Sometimes just Barrett and I. We became friends."

"More than friends?" asked Callie, afraid to hear answer.

"Yes."

"Mom!"

Dora laughed. "Don't sound so shocked."

"Good grief, Mom, a threesome?" Callie sputtered.

Dora burst out laughing. When she could catch her breath she clarified, "Not a threesome, dear." She chuckled before continuing. "No dear, just a regular old twosome. Barrett and I."

Callie realized that she now felt relief knowing that her mother had 'only' had a traditional affair, rather than a soap-opera-worthy entanglement. Shock was really a matter of perspective.

"I just . . . it's hard to imagine you as the other woman," she said.

"I didn't really feel like one—at the time, I mean," said Dora.

"But I thought you were friends with Lauren."

"I was," answered Dora. "I am."

"You mean she still doesn't know?"

"She knew from the very beginning."

Callie shook her head, confused. "I don't get it. The whole situation sounds . . . messy."

"It was. Messy. Complicated. In the end, I had to walk away."

"Why did you say that Lauren was dying when you met her?" asked Callie.

"Because everyone thought she was," answered Dora matter-of-factly. "She had battled leukemia in her teens. Doctors back then had fewer tools to fight it, and the fact that she had survived so long was considered something of a miracle."

Callie reflected on the concept of her mother as the 'other woman' in some kind of Hamptons love triangle. Maybe her own tabloid troubles wouldn't shock her parents as much as she had feared.

"Have you seen Lauren since you left?"

"No. We kept in touch the old fashioned way."

"Why have you never talked about this before?" asked Callie, not sure she really wanted the answer.

Dora sighed.

"Sweetie, this isn't the kind of thing you share with your children. It had no bearing on your life until now. And if you hadn't seen the letters, we wouldn't be talking about it at all. Look, I just wanted to let you know that love isn't a once-in-a-lifetime opportunity. Yes, I'll always have a soft spot in my heart for Barrett, but we had no future together. So I left. And yes, it hurt. But what else could I do? Destroy a family? Accept that I would never come first? No. I couldn't love Barrett and still be me."

"That's my problem," Callie confessed. "I can't be what Adam needs me to be. I want to, but I can't."

Dora squeezed Callie's hand.

"I know it hurts now. I know it's not easy. But I stayed true to myself and look how well things turned out. I lost Barrett, but I found your father. We've raised three beautiful daughters, and we've been together for thirty years. What more could a girl ask for?"

Callie reached for the box of tissues, blowing her nose again in an attempt to avoid total meltdown.

"How about a happy ending?" Callie gave her mother a watery smile.

Dora smiled. "You know, I've always thought of a happy ending as more of a journey than a destination."

"And I've been on the wrong road for ten years," said Callie. Her mother patted her hand one last time, then rose to leave the table.

"Let's call it a detour, sweetie, and be glad that you're back on track."

Callie put on a smile for Danny, who waved to her from his perch at the bow of the *Speakeasy*, but she didn't join him. She knew from experience that his preferred seat would be both windy and wet on a day like today. No matter how sunny and warm it might be on land, the brisk wind kicked up choppy little waves and the spray would be freezing cold. She stayed in the first mate's chair, opposite Adam.

Despite the unanswered question hanging between her and Adam, she refused to regret joining them for an afternoon boat ride. This might be their last opportunity to spend time together. The words 'as a family' echoed in her mind. As much as she might daydream about having a normal life, the hard truth was that she could not build a career and a family at the same time—not her kind of career, at any rate, with Adam's kind of family.

Callie watched Adam pilot the boat. He stood, one hand resting casually on the throttle, tall and strong and confident. If only she had

started out with confidence like his—bone deep and unshakeable—
she wouldn't need to start over. Even in the face of losing Danny,
he had remained determined. Her own newfound confidence
seemed more like an evening wrap: gorgeous and wonderful, but
so light and insubstantial that it kept fluttering out of her grasp in
the slightest breeze. Callie sat up straighter and lifted her face to
the sun. She was learning, the hard way, how to stand on her own.

They crossed to the far shore, which was more sheltered and had
less chop. Once there, Adam slowed the boat and turned to her.

"Do you want to drive for a while?"

"No, thanks." Callie shook her head emphatically. She remembered all too well what had happened the last time. Not that the
same thing would happen with Danny on board, but why torture
herself by reliving the memories?

He grinned knowingly.

"Chicken?" he teased.

What was he trying to accomplish here? Why did he insist on
tormenting her? Did he really think it would change her mind?

Danny piped up from the bow. "Callie's not afraid of anything.
Are you, Callie?"

She pursed her lips and narrowed her eyes at Adam. He didn't
bother to hide his amusement. This whole thing was a setup.

"Of course not," she called to Danny. "I'd be happy to drive."
She cleared her throat before pitching her next remark in a low
tone, solely for Adam's ears. "I'd hate to disappoint Danny."

Adam's grin widened.

"Woo hoo," shouted Danny as Callie stood up. "Drive fast, Callie! Really fast!"

"I think I'll start out easy and see how it goes," she called back,
wondering if Adam would understand her subtle message just for
him. Probably not.

Rather than vacating his spot, Adam sat down and gestured for
her to come stand in front of him. He raised an eyebrow, daring her

to back out. She ignored him and took her place at the wheel. Any torture would surely be mutual, and he deserved every second of it.

She accelerated up to a gentle cruising speed, following the shoreline and enjoying the heat that radiated from Adam's body. She fit perfectly against him, her head tucked just below his chin. It made her wish the world away, just for the day, or—if she were feeling greedy—the entire summer. Nothing had ever felt better than standing in the circle of his arms, and she hated the fact that it would end.

Danny jumped up and shouted "My turn!" and Callie started, nearly knocking out Adam's teeth. He was apparently dissatisfied with her leisurely pace and wanted to crank things up a notch. He tugged her out of her spot and took the wheel, trying —and failing—to shrug off Adam's assistance. She sank back into the opposite seat. Danny accelerated as much as Adam would let him, and Callie held on tight until Adam declared Danny's turn over and reclaimed the wheel. As the ride mellowed again, Callie stared out at the water, thinking about the two very different paths that lay before her. On the one hand, she could revel in her newfound freedom, both personal and artistic, and pursue her music. On the other hand, she could stay here and explore this wonderful, fragile thing growing between her and Adam and Danny. Together they would be a family. She could still write music, of course, and she might even give music lessons to local children, but she would probably never tour again.

It was such an idyllic vision, this small-town life, such a perfect future laid before her. Why did she hesitate? What was wrong with her?

"What are you thinking about?" asked Adam, loud enough for her to hear him over the sound of the motor, but not quite loud enough for Danny to eavesdrop. He knew the answer, of course. He must know.

"You and me," answered Callie, "and our discussion this morning."

"I'm glad you're thinking about it," said Adam.

She kept her gaze on the water.

"And?" he prodded.

"And I don't know," said Callie.

Adam was silent. Callie debated how to proceed, and wondered if there was anything she could say to change his mind.

"My life is complicated right now," Callie began.

"Mine, too."

"So maybe we should take things slowly," she said. "I can visit again in a few weeks and we'll see how we feel."

He shook his head.

"What's wrong with starting slow?" she demanded in a whisper.

Adam met Callie's eyes for a long moment before he turned his attention back to the water.

"If you're not sure about this," he answered, his voice low, "then I'd like to end things now. I don't want to drag it out. I don't want Danny to build up hope, only to have it crushed later. Better to make a clean break."

"But you're ripping me in half." Callie choked on the words, her emotions pressing on her chest so that she struggled to breathe.

"How do you think I feel?" he demanded, his voice low and harsh. "There's more than one way to incorporate music into your life."

"And there's more than one way build a family," she responded fiercely.

"Not for us," said Adam. "I want the real thing, and Danny needs the real thing. Two parents who can be there for him. Two parents he can count on." The tension spread from his voice to his body until his hands clenched the wheel.

"There must be another way," she pleaded softly, unable to stop herself from begging.

He shook his head. "You don't know how lucky you were, growing up with both your parents around all the time. Not just around, but paying attention. They loved you, and they would never hurt you. I know what happens when parents don't get it right, and it sucks. I won't do that to Danny, and I won't do it to me. I've waited my whole life to find the right person, and you're it. If we're going to do this, we're going to do it right. We're not going to half-ass it and hope for the best."

Callie's heart clenched up in her chest and she held her breath, swallowing the tears that threatened to overflow. She didn't want to hear the determination in his voice—the finality. She fought to keep herself together, praying that Danny wouldn't turn around.

Deep down she found a tiny seed of anger. She anchored herself on it, pouring all her energy into it until it grew to fill the hollow place in her gut. Adam was wrong to give her an ultimatum, and wrong to demand that she give up her dreams. In his own way, he was no better than Brian. She had submerged her dreams for years in order to support Brian's vision of success, and look where she had ended up. Full circle. Now she had to choose, but should she choose Adam's vision, or her own?

She closed her eyes and felt the chill of the breeze on her face and neck. She pulled the cold deep inside herself, hardening her heart against the pain to come. Adam had asked her to change her dreams in order to fit his vision of the perfect family, but she just couldn't make herself do it.

"You know," she said, "You told me once that I shouldn't put my dreams on hold for you."

"That was a long time ago," he said.

She smiled sadly.

"Feels like yesterday." She cleared her throat and pitched her voice louder, so that Adam would be able to hear her clearly. Adam, but not Danny. "I can't give up on my music," she continued. "If I try to be what you need, I would only end up hating you." She swallowed hard and swiped tears out of her eyes. "I'm sorry."

The silence pooled between them, cold and hard.

"So am I," responded Adam at last. "So am I."

"This is boring," shouted Danny, shattering the moment. "It's my turn again."

Adam let Danny drive them back home, and for that Callie was grateful, because there was nothing more to say.

"I thought I might find you here."

Luke draped a blanket around Callie's shoulders and sat down beside her on the dock. The night had grown chilly, though she didn't realize she was cold until the blanket settled around her. She had come to watch the sunset, and to get away from her phone. Her sisters knew something was wrong and they were taking turns trying to get through, but Callie couldn't deal with them right now. Too much sympathy and she would crack. So she had escaped down the hill and had been staring at the dark water for hours.

She sat in silence for a while beside her father, neither of them in the mood for words and with no instruments at hand. Finally Callie spoke.

"How hard was it to walk away?"

Luke didn't pretend to misunderstand.

"Not that hard." He spoke softly, his gentle words floating out over the water. "You need to remember that I was a kid, not even twenty-five, when your mom and I got married. I hadn't had much time to build up my career. And the music scene was . . . ugly. If you think the drugs and the sex are bad now, you should have seen it back then. The AIDS scare was just beginning—most people still didn't believe it could affect them. It was impossible to imagine a career in music being in any way compatible with getting married and raising a family."

"You knew you wanted that?"

"A family? Yeah. I love kids. Always have. But there was no way. . . . Let's say that when I met your mom, the path forward became clear. I walked away and never looked back."

"That simple, huh?"

"For me. But I'm a songwriter, first and foremost. I don't need to be on stage. I'd rather connect one-on-one with people—give a music lesson—than perform. You're not like that."

"No," she admitted. "One-on-one stresses me out."

"Exactly. But when you're onstage, in front of a crowd, you light up."

"I can't give it up," Callie whispered.

"I know." Luke squeezed her shoulders.

"But I want . . . more." She shook her head, defeat washing over her. "Is it so wrong for me to want more? When I'm not performing, when I'm not on the road, I'd like to have a home. A family. Other people have that. Why can't I have that?"

"I don't know, sugar," said Luke. "Is that the problem you're working through with Adam?"

Callie snorted in disgust. "We're not working through anything. He wants a full-time partner in his life and let's face it: I'm a part-timer at best."

"You're going to give up?"

"What do you mean, 'give up'? This isn't a fight, Dad. It's a relationship. If Adam doesn't want to continue, then it's game over, and thanks for playing. There's nothing I can do about it."

"So you're content to let him find someone else? You're not going to try to change his mind?"

Callie hated it when her father talked in that calm, teacherly voice. It inevitably meant that he was going to lead her into a logic trap from which there was no escape other than admitting she was in the wrong. Just hearing that reasonable tone made her back stiffen. But she was *not* in the wrong, damn it. She was the one *being* wronged.

"He's made up his mind. Of course I hate the idea of him with someone else, but he's a grown man, perfectly capable of making his own decisions. I can't stop him. And I won't have to watch, will I? I'll be on the road." Most of the time, anyway. The rest of the time—well, that was something she'd need to figure out.

"And you can live with some other woman taking on the role of Danny's mother?"

Callie had to grit her teeth to keep from cursing.

"If Adam keeps custody of Danny, then yes, eventually someone else will be his mom," she replied.

"And if this new mom has no clue about music?"

"So be it," said Callie, her jaw clenched.

"Well, if his mind can't be changed, I guess that's it," said Luke, clambering to his feet and stretching out his legs. The boards creaked as he took a few steps back down the dock toward shore. He paused briefly and said, "You can drive away on Monday and never look back. Never wonder what might have been."

"Exactly." Callie clipped out her words. "That's my plan." She hated the petulant tone that had crept into her voice, but couldn't help it. All of her former selves had joined in tonight's pity party, including the pouty eight-year-old.

"You ready for Lucy's on Sunday?" asked Luke. "She's expecting a good crowd, given that it's Memorial Day Weekend."

"I'm ready."

"Great. I'm heading up. You coming?"

"In a minute."

"Good night, then," he said softly.

"Good night," she whispered.

Callie thumped her head on her knees. He was wrong. He had no idea. There was no use fighting a stone wall, no way through or around Adam's basic objection. She refused to torture herself with hope. It was time to suck it up and move on.

One last lesson with Danny tomorrow morning, and then she would be through.

CHAPTER TWENTY-EIGHT

Callie waited until she and Danny had put their instruments away before breaking the news.

"Hey, Danny, we need to talk."

"Okay," he answered. He stopped rubbing Roscoe's belly and looked up at her. Roscoe nudged Danny's hand to get him started again. No human conversation could possibly be as important as Roscoe's belly rub.

"You know that I'm going back to Nashville on Monday, right?"

"Yeah."

"And I've got that performance tomorrow at Lucy's."

"Yeah."

"So I was thinking that today should be our last lesson together."

"What? Why?" Danny jumped to his feet. Roscoe followed suit, only a lot more slowly.

"Well, I need to rehearse tomorrow morning. For the show."

Now he looked like she had stomped on his heart.

"But you promised that we could play together every morning, whenever you're here. And you're still here." His accusation hit home. She winced.

"True." Callie hadn't anticipated this particular argument. She could picture her father laughing at her for making a promise to a kid and then trying to weasel out of it.

"Besides," Danny argued, "you asked me if I wanted to play in your show, and I've decided that I do." He crossed his arms, his expression daring her to object. Roscoe sat right beside him and gave her an equally challenging look.

"What?"

Callie hadn't been serious when she had asked Danny if he wanted to perform. She had intended to plant a seed for the future, maybe next summer.

"I want to play. I'm ready." He seemed insulted at her surprise.

"Of—of course!" she said. "Sometimes I get distracted by the fact that you're only eight. But if you feel ready, then you're ready. Are you sure?"

"Yes. And I'm almost nine. My birthday is in July."

"Well, okay then." She admitted defeat. He had totally out-maneuvered her.

"So I think we should play together tomorrow morning," said Danny, circling back to win the argument. "We need to rehearse."

"Yes, we do," Callie conceded. "And we should discuss this with your uncle." Ready or not! "He doesn't like surprises."

"No." Danny thought about that for a minute, then giggled. "No surprises for Uncle Adam."

Adam was clearly surprised to see Callie trailing Danny through the kitchen door. Had he expected her to slink away, never to be seen again? If he had any regrets, he hid them well behind a polite mask. She didn't even have to worry about awkward moments because Danny filled the room with excited chatter about tomorrow's performance. Adam got the gist of it, despite Danny's scattered explanation. Danny wanted to perform his song—the one that had clobbered Adam—as part of Callie's show tomorrow.

She couldn't tell if he liked the idea or not. In fact, she couldn't tell if he felt anything at all, and that started to piss her off. If she had to walk around with gaping wounds in her heart, then he could at least give her the courtesy of a small outward sign of his inner pain. One chip in his sculpted granite exterior would be enough to soothe her, but he gave away nothing.

She wanted to poke around, hunting for evidence of heartbreak, but first they needed to make a decision about tomorrow.

"Danny," said Callie, "the crowd at Lucy's tomorrow will be bigger than usual. It's Memorial Day weekend, and she's been putting up posters all over town. I'd love for you to play with me, but honey, I don't want to freak you out."

"I won't be freaked out," he pleaded. "I promise."

He bounced around the kitchen like a popcorn kernel ready to explode.

Adam picked up the thread of her argument. "I know it doesn't seem scary now," he said, "but sometimes, in front of a crowd, the nerves can sneak up on you."

"They won't get me," he insisted.

Callie met Adam's eyes across the kitchen. Now, with Danny's happiness on the line, he displayed some cracks in his cool façade. He looked even more concerned than she felt, and—to be honest—she could understand that. She had learned over the years that normal people do not find performing for an audience to be a comfortable experience. For her, it was magical, but normal people just want to throw up.

"How about this," said Callie. "When I'm done with the show, but before I play an encore, I'll look over at you. If you want to go for it, then you give me a thumbs-up and start to take out your instrument. We'll have it all tuned up and ready to go. But if you change your mind, you shake your head and we'll skip it. Nobody will even know. What do you think?"

Danny stopped bouncing long enough to consider her proposal, then nodded.

"That sounds good. I know that I'm going to do it, but you're not sure, and that's okay. Playing at the end will be perfect."

Adam nodded his agreement. Callie squeezed Danny's shoulders, then let go so he could start bouncing again.

"Okay then," she said. "Danny, I'll see you tomorrow morning to rehearse. Adam, you be sure to get there early so that you can snag a table by the front. In fact, I'll give Lucy a heads-up and see if she would be willing to reserve one."

"Sounds like a plan," said Adam.

"Yessssss," said Danny, doing a victory elbow-pump.

"Hey, Danny," said Callie. "You mind if I talk to your uncle in private for a minute?"

Danny hefted his guitar and grinned at her before heading toward his room. "He's all yours," he drawled.

She shook her head, smiling. Danny was going to be fine.

She, on the other hand, was not. But for her own peace of mind, she was going to give Adam a piece of her mind, whether he wanted it or not.

She motioned for Adam to follow her outside. Not only did she want some distance from Danny, she wanted to be as far from Adam's bedroom as possible.

"What's up?" he asked curtly.

"This sucks," she threw back.

"And?"

"I think you should reconsider your concept of the perfect family."

Adam crossed his arms, not looking particularly receptive to an alternative worldview. Fine. She would say her piece and walk away, knowing that she had done everything she could.

"It's like this." She took a step toward him, stopping just over the edge of his personal space. "There is no perfect family. You have this vision of a mom and a dad living together in perfect harmony and raising Danny, maybe having a few kids of their own, and that's beautiful. But it's not real. Maybe you could find that with someone else, someday." Saying the words out loud made her feel sick. "Maybe that only exists on TV. But it's not your only option."

She took another step toward him, her breasts now so close to his tightly crossed arms that she could feel his body heat.

"You and me? This is real. Me and Danny? Real. Just because I won't be around every second of every day doesn't make me any less real. It means that we need to make our time together count for something. And I think it does." Callie fought the tears. She needed to finish this. "I think that what we have is worth fighting for. If you want to throw this away," she choked, "then that's your choice. Your mistake. But let me be clear. I'm not the one giving up on us. You are. And I think you're wrong."

Callie meant to walk away. The moment called for a dignified exit, but she couldn't do it. She reached for him, caressing the stubble on his cheeks and pulling him closer for one last kiss. If this was it—if they were really over—she wanted to make it memorable.

She sank into him, pressing herself against his crossed arms, and savored every last second. His lips tasted like coffee. When she nipped at his lower lip he groaned, finally opening his arms and pulling her close, devouring her right there in the open air, one hand sliding into her hair and the other tracing her spine from top to bottom and pulling her hips tight against his.

A sudden breeze chilled the back of Callie's neck, rousing her enough so that she could pull away. Adam held on for a moment longer, but then let his arms drop to his sides.

"Don't give up on us," whispered Callie. Then she made her escape.

Kat cleared her throat before answering her cell phone. She didn't want to advertise the fact that the phone had woken her up, especially not to Adam. She wondered what would prompt a call on a Saturday morning.

"Good morning."

There was nothing but silence on the other end of the phone. Had he pocket-dialed her? Did they have a bad connection?

"Hello? Adam?"

Still silence, and then finally a voice.

"Is this Kat?"

"Yes." Her brain clicked on and she realized who was on the other end of the line. "Is this Danny?" Kat kept any hint of shock out of her voice, although she was scrambling out of bed and pulling on a robe.

"Yes."

"Is everything okay, Danny?"

"Yes."

She waited for him to tell her why he was calling, but silence filled the line. She rolled her eyes. Great. This was going to be a challenging conversation.

"So . . . where's your uncle?"

"He's outside."

"Is he okay?"

"Yes."

"What's he doing?" This was like pulling teeth.

"Kissing with Callie."

Oh, of course. Wonderful. Very discreet.

"Was there something you wanted to tell me, Danny?"

"Yes."

She waited. Nothing.

"What did you want to tell me?"

She heard the sigh on the other end of the phone and reminded herself that this was a big deal. Danny had picked up the phone and found the guts to call her. She needed to find the patience to hear him out.

"Take your time." While she waited, she slid her feet into her slippers and padded into the kitchen. She switched on the coffee maker, which was prepped and ready, and found a bagel in the fridge. By the time she popped the bagel into the toaster, Danny had found his voice.

"I know what I want. I want to stay with Uncle Adam."

"Oh." His answer, abrupt and direct after all that delay, startled her. "That's great. Do you think you'll be able to tell the judge how you feel?"

"Yes."

"Great. I know it can be scary to speak up, but when you do, people listen."

"I wish Callie could stay, too," he whispered.

Kat ignored the heart-clench.

"Did you tell her that?"

"Yeah."

"And what did she say?"

She was not prying into Adam's personal life. She was looking out for Danny. Big difference.

"She said she had to go, but that we could play music together whenever she came back to visit."

Kat breathed a sigh of relief. Maybe that made her a bad person, but she didn't care.

"You spoke up for what you wanted, and that's all you can do. She has to live her own life, even if it doesn't fit together with yours."

"I know."

"You sure you're okay?"

"Yeah. She's going to let me play with her at Lucy's tomorrow, so that will be cool."

Kat digested this news, not sure she had understood him.

"Are you saying you're going to play music with her during her performance at Lucy's? In front of all those people?"

"At the end. I'm going to be her encore."

"Oh. Wow. You don't think you'll be nervous?"

"Maybe a little, but I really want to do it."

"That's. . . ." Unbelievable. Amazing. Scary. ". . . cool. Mind if I come watch?"

"You totally should. But come early, because I heard that it's going to be really crowded."

"Right. Of course. I'll be early. Maybe I'll bring some friends."

"Good idea," chirped Danny. "Make sure you stay all the way until the end. I don't play until the end."

"I know."

"Good. See you tomorrow."

"See you—"

Danny had already hung up. Kat stared thoughtfully at her phone. What an odd conversation. Hard to believe he had gone nearly a year without talking. But it gave her an idea.

CHAPTER TWENTY-NINE

Callie was putting the finishing touches on her hair and makeup when the doorbell rang, followed by urgent pounding. What the hell? She hurried downstairs, worried that something had happened to Adam or Danny, but found neither of them at the back door.

"Brian? What the hell?"

He pushed past her into the mudroom and then into the kitchen. She followed, worried that he might be losing it, but mostly concerned about getting rid of him and making it to Lucy's on time.

"We need to talk."

Callie couldn't stop the helpless laughter that bubbled up. She sank into one of the kitchen chairs and laughed until tears leaked from the corners of her eyes. The box of tissues was still on the table from Friday night, so she blew her nose and wiped her eyes, and tried to regain control.

Brian watched, confused, as he leaned against the kitchen counter with his arms crossed.

"Callie, snap out of it. This is important."

"Of course it is," she said, still hiccupping. "It always is. What do you need?"

He moved over to the table, sitting across from her and opening a FedEx pack full of documents.

"The record company needs some additional reassurance that this is a friendly separation. We need to get these papers signed and notarized today so I can get them to the record company ASAP. Otherwise they'll start pulling back on the publicity for the tour and the album. I can't risk that."

She shook her head. "I can't do this now. You'll have to wait."

"Callie, we need to take care of this."

"No," she said, pushing herself up to stand and looking down at him. "I have a gig this morning. When I'm finished, I'll give my attorney a call. If you're lucky, she might be available to meet this afternoon. But for now," she paused for emphasis, "you need to wait."

"But—"

"It's time for you to leave."

"But—"

"Oh, for goodness sake. Follow me there, if you must. Enjoy the show. But if you bug me again I'll refuse to sign the papers until next week."

Brian stood to face her.

"I don't appreciate your attitude."

She grinned.

"I never liked yours either."

Adam fought the urge to turn around and scan the room. The last thing he wanted to do was make Danny nervous by shifting around in his seat, but the itchy feeling between his shoulders wouldn't go away. By the time he and Danny had shown up, the two remaining seats at the reserved table left him with his back to the door. He was nervous enough on Danny's behalf. The seating arrangement only made it worse.

His nerves didn't seem to be rubbing off on Danny, though. For a kid who hadn't talked for nearly a year, he was awfully eager to be heard. Granted, the moment of truth had not yet arrived, but the kid looked like he was going to follow through.

Lucy worked the counter, commanding an army of inexperienced summer wait-staff. She must be loving the packed house. What a way to kick off the summer season.

Dora, Luke, and Danny chattered away, and listened raptly to some guy named Zeke tell stories about the music business in Nashville. Adam still hadn't figured out what the guy was doing here, but he seemed to know Luke from way back. Tessa and Mel whispered to each other but refused to speak with Adam. Callie had clearly briefed them on the status of their relationship.

So Adam ate some food and, when that excuse ran its natural course, drank his coffee. He saw no need to disrupt the flow of conversation around him.

He did another casual scan of the room, this time twisting in the opposite direction. He pulled something in his neck doing a double-take. No, he was not mistaken. Kat was sitting at corner booth with not only Doc Archer, but also Danny's grandparents.

Adam's first instinct was to march over to their table and give Kat a piece of his mind, but the sheer number of people in the room made that impossible. Besides, no matter how bizarre the adult dynamics in the room, he wanted to keep things simple for Danny. Surprise guests and an impromptu confrontation would not help Danny get through the next hour.

So he sat. And stewed. And finally pulled out his phone.

He kept it casual. He pretended to check something—e-mail, or the time—and when he was certain that nobody at the table was paying attention, he typed the text message:

What the hell?

He stretched so that he could see her reaction, keeping it small and, again, casual. Kat had felt the buzz of her phone over the chatter of the crowd and was pulling it from her pocket. She glanced across the room and met his eyes. Damn it, she had known exactly where he was sitting. If she knew he was here, why the hell hadn't she given him a heads-up?

She kept her movements subtle, but he could see that she was replying to his message:

Trust me.

Furious, he shoved his phone back into his pocket. There wasn't a damn thing he could do about the situation, but he didn't have to like it, and he damn well didn't have to trust her. Why should he? She certainly hadn't trusted him enough to tell him about this little stunt.

To be fair, he hadn't warned her that Danny might perform. Chances are she would be pissed as all hell when Danny took to the stage. The thought made him smile and took the edge off his temper.

Apparently they would both need to trust each other.

Callie slipped through the back door of Lucy's after seeing the packed house and the overspill of people outside waiting for a table. She kept reminding herself that this was Lucy's, the people in the audience were tourists, and there was nothing high stakes about the performance—but her stomach didn't believe it, churning and clenching as if she were about to play a stadium.

Not that she minded being alone onstage, but today she felt oddly exposed and unsure of herself. Maybe it was because she was leaving tomorrow, heading into the unknown. Maybe it was because she was going to play her own music after so many years of twisting it to fit the band. Maybe it was because she would be playing for Adam.

Or maybe it was nerves. Whatever the reason, she needed to get over it.

She lifted her guitar out of its case and stepped into the main room, moving with purpose to the alcove where she would play. The spot felt like home, and she started to relax. She settled onto her stool, propping one foot up on the crossbar and resting the weight of her guitar on her thigh.

She checked the tuning on her guitar using her tuning fork. The novelty of it helped to catch the attention of the diners, and the vibration of the ball on her earlobe connected her to the music in a solid, tangible way. When she finished, she looked up at the crowd. A hush spread across the room, but it was Danny, with his infectious grin, that set her to smiling. Her heart swelled and she could feel the extra punch of courage and love.

Callie took a breath and began to play. Something about launching into a song helped Callie transition into her professional mode. She knew that she could keep going no matter what happened, because during the years of touring with the band, anything that could happen *had* happened, and the show had always continued. Well, all except for that time in Oklahoma, but you can't argue with a tornado warning.

As Callie continued to play, she began to feel her audience. Of course she could sense her parents and Danny and Adam, sitting only a few feet away. She wondered briefly about the stranger at their table, but let the thought drift away as she broadened her view to include the rest of the room. It was almost as if a part of her could reach out and touch each person, connecting with their hearts, so that she knew how to play each song—how to communicate with them. She moved seamlessly from song to song until she had almost reached the end of her set. She paused before beginning the last song to speak to the crowd, letting them know that this next song would be her last song, but that she hoped to play for them all again soon. She smiled at Danny and winked. This was his cue to get ready.

As she played the last song, she tried to draw the feeling of home deep inside, so that in the months ahead she would be able to find it again. She sang to Lucy, still behind the counter, who had stopped her cleanup mid-wipe to listen to the music. She sang to Brian, lurking in the corner by the door, and to Hutch, leaning against the counter with his mouth full of doughnut. She sang to Kat, who shared a booth with an odd assortment of unfamiliar faces. She sang to her parents, and Danny—but most of all to Adam.

He had turned in his seat to face her, and she took this chance to meet his eyes, to sink in, and to open herself one last time to the painful intimacy between them. She would miss this. She would miss him. He, of course, refused to be the one to look away, so she did it for him, letting her gaze roam unfocused over the crowd as she finished the song.

When the last of the notes faded to silence, the crowd broke into loud applause. She smiled, nodded graciously, then escaped into the hall. She waited a moment, then two, making sure that the crowd did indeed want to bring her back out again.

When she stepped back into the room, the crowd quieted immediately. She smiled, feeling the familiar thrill of connection.

"Thank you. Really, it's been a pleasure to play for you today. If you like, I could play one or two more before I go."

She got a quick round of applause and a few whistles in response. So she took her place again and waited until the room grew quiet.

She took her time with the lead-in, the intricate finger-picking leaning more toward flamenco than folk. She wanted that sense of the far-away to strengthen the feeling of coming home. This was the song she had been working on ever since she had found her notebooks—the song that she had abandoned after Brian's visit all those years ago. After so many years away, she could finally embrace the idea that 'there's no place like home.'

Her gaze traveled over the faces in the room, many of them familiar. She let her eyes slide past Brian. She no longer cared how he might react to the song. He was, perhaps, too scarred to carry any fragment of home in his heart. She smiled at Lucy, communicating her gratitude for . . . everything. And she made sure to nod to her parents, letting them know that this song was as much about them as it was about her.

Over the last few weeks the song had become a tribute of sorts to Adam and Danny, who had given her a taste of what home could mean. It didn't need to mean going back, running away, or hiding from the world. Home could also be a touchstone, a place of serenity at the heart of the chaos. Even if she and Adam never found a way to move forward together, he had forever changed her idea of coming home, and she was grateful for that.

The only person in the room who had heard the song before was Danny, and she smiled as she met his eyes. He looked like he might explode. He could hardly stay still in his chair. She smiled as she rolled into the last chorus. He was about to have his chance.

> *I press my face against the glass*
> *And watch the miles go rolling past*
> *I know where I would rather be*
> *The only place I feel like me*
> *The only place I call my own*
> *It's time to find the road back home.*
>
> *I don't care how far I go 'cause I know*
> *There's no place like home.*

A final round of finger-picking, this time more folk than flamenco, and she let the song drift away into silence.

Danny leapt up to start the applause. She grinned at him and motioned for him to come join her. They got him settled on a chair beside her, and as the clapping quieted, she offered an explanation.

"Ladies and gentlemen, please welcome my good friend Danny Reese, who has graciously agreed to help me wrap up the show today. We'll be performing one of Danny's songs. It's called 'Until I Find Grace.'"

There was a bit of a commotion back at Kat's table, but Callie ignored it. Danny was looking at her, making sure she was ready to go, and she nodded. Her role today was solely moral support. She was going to throw in some harmonies they had been practicing, and add some richness to the accompaniment with her guitar, but this was Danny's show now, and she swelled with pride as he stepped up to the challenge.

Adam needed to get a grip. Danny was about to start playing, and Adam was still reeling from Callie's performance. He had heard her play around the bonfire countless times, but he had always assumed that the intimacy came from the firelight and the darkness and the magic of the summer night. He had never seen her perform in front of a real audience, in front of strangers. She was different onstage.

She took his breath away.

He had never known another performer, never seen anyone else make the transformation from regular human being to something more. Music had poured out of her, filling the room. There had been no whispers, no fidgeting, no clatter of dishes. She had held them, rapt, as she'd played one song after another. In a way, it had been even more intimate than the time she had played for him alone, the day he had agreed to the music lessons. Rather than holding back and keeping her eyes down, as she had for him, she had opened herself completely to the audience, and in her vulnerability had captured them all. Only after the last song faded into silence did she smile and release them from her spell.

The sound of Danny's voice, uncertain at first, then gaining strength, pulled him out of his thoughts and back to the present. Adam hadn't heard Danny play his song since that night. Was it only a few weeks ago? So much had changed. This time, despite the emotional punch of Callie's performance, Adam felt prepared. He smiled when Callie gave him a sharp look, checking to make sure he wasn't going to lose it again. He deliberately relaxed, leaning back in his chair, and gave Danny a thumbs up. There was no way he was going to screw up this moment for Danny.

And really, it wasn't nearly as painful the second time around. Adam could sidestep the giant abyss of pain and move beyond it, focusing on the song itself and appreciating what Danny had accomplished. Not only had he found the words to express his loss, but he had set them to music and created a tribute to his family. Adam found himself humbled by the clear-sighted compassion of this woman who had taken Danny by the hand and walked with him through the darkness. He couldn't imagine a future without her.

The song ended, followed by much applause, and then the crowd began to move. Callie put her arm around Danny and gave him a squeeze, then gestured for him to lean his guitar safely against the back wall. Adam stepped forward, both to shield Danny and to give him a hug. He crouched down so they could speak face to face, and so Danny could hear him above the babble of voices.

"Nice job," he said, man-to-man. "You seem pretty comfortable up on that stage."

"Yeah. I like it."

"We'll have to make sure you get another chance, then."

"Really?"

"Yep. And now I think there are some people who want to see you."

Adam would have brought Callie with them, or at least thanked her, but she had been drawn into conversation with her parents and their friend. She gave him a wave as he and Danny began to weave through the crowded room toward Kat's table at the back, and he hoped she would follow when she could. They had to stop every few seconds so that people in the crowd could congratulate Danny. Adam didn't have the heart to cut these conversations short, because with each compliment, Danny glowed brighter.

The room had cleared slightly when Adam and Danny finally arrived at the booth where Kat and Doc Archer sat facing Lainey's parents, Susan and John. Adam ushered Danny into the empty seat beside Kat, and he took the remaining spot next to Doc Archer.

Susan had been crying, as evidenced by her red-rimmed eyes and the small mountain of used tissues on the table in front of her. She couldn't reach Danny to smother him in a hug, so she reached across the table and squeezed his hands instead.

"That was lovely, dear. Did you really write that song all by yourself?"

Danny looked uncomfortable at being the center of his grandmother's attention. Like Callie, he seemed to find it easier to open up to strangers, but he was kind enough not to yank his hands away.

"Callie helped," he answered, "but only when I got stuck. I did all the words myself."

"That's wonderful," choked Susan, starting to cry again. "Don't mind me." She waved her hands around in front of her face and then blew her nose. "It's been an emotional morning."

"It's nice to hear your voice again, son," said John gruffly. He didn't have a mountain of tissues in front of him, but Adam would bet he had wiped his eyes a few times in the last twenty minutes.

Susan got herself back together and finally met Adam's eyes. "I forget sometimes how much you look like Evan."

"I know," Danny chimed in. "You get used to it, but sometimes it still hurts to look at him."

Adam felt the twin knives of guilt and grief twist in his gut. All those months he had thought Danny's refusal to look at him had been because he'd hated him. Only now, months too late, did he understand.

Kat cleared her throat.

"I asked all of you to meet me here this morning because I thought it would be helpful to see the progress Danny has made in the last month. We all worried about you for so long." She patted Danny on the shoulder. "It's great to hear your voice and know that you're doing better."

Danny flushed and looked down at his hands.

"I also thought this would be a great opportunity for us to talk informally ahead of the hearing this week. John, I understand you've been having some health issues lately?"

Danny's grandfather coughed, as if in response to Kat's question. Susan stepped in to answer.

"John has been having some heart trouble." She leaned against him, and he put his arm around her shoulder. "It's not an emergency, yet, but it has got us thinking about the future."

Adam felt a flutter of panic at this news. It was one thing to fight for custody of Danny, quite another to imagine raising Danny completely on his own, without even the support of grandparents.

"Doc Archer, would you mind sharing your thoughts?" Kat asked. Adam had to admire the skill with which she was orchestrating this meeting. He gave up the last vestige of his anger with her.

The doc had been leaning back, observing the interplay among all the interested parties at the table, but now he leaned forward.

"Danny has made amazing strides over the last few weeks, to the point that I have no serious concerns about his current custody arrangement. In fact, given his progress, I would hesitate to recommend any changes in his custody at this time."

"And Danny, isn't there something you'd like to say?" said Kat. She gave him a smile of encouragement. He squared his small shoulders and looked his grandparents in the eyes.

"I've been thinking about my future, too," he said, "and I'd like to live with my uncle, if that's okay with you. I could still visit you, but I like living with Adam."

John squeezed Susan's shoulders as she started to cry again.

"Of course, honey. We can do whatever makes you happy." She reached over to hold his hands again. "We were just so worried about you."

Kat surveyed the faces at the table, then nodded, apparently satisfied.

"Excellent," she pronounced. "If everyone is comfortable leaving the current custody arrangements in place, at least for the time being, then there may be no need for a hearing."

Susan and John nodded their agreement. Doc Archer did the same, reaffirming his position. Danny smiled tentatively. But when her gaze came to rest on Adam's face, she pursed her lips.

"You don't seem appropriately happy about this turn of events. Do we have a problem?"

"No." Adam moved quickly to reassure Danny, who had looked up at him with a panicked expression on his face. "It's just. . . ." He sighed. He had no experience with negotiation in a family context, and he hated floundering through unfamiliar territory when the stakes were so high.

"I don't want to do this alone." He met John's eyes, since Susan was reaching for the tissues again. "I'd like to think that we're in this together. Danny needs all the family he can get."

John nodded. If they had been standing, there might have been a man-hug, or at least a warm handshake. Susan nodded while blowing her nose. Doc Archer gave him a real smile.

"The judge will be thrilled to know that Danny's grandparents will be an integral part of his life," said Kat.

"They will," said Adam.

Danny grinned, and Adam reached over to rub his red hair. This unexpected resolution had left Adam feeling lightheaded with relief. He glanced across the room to see Callie still deep in conversation. She should be a part of this moment. She was the one who had made it possible.

"We'll worry about the paperwork on Monday," said Kat. "In the meantime, I think we need some doughnuts to celebrate."

She headed toward the counter to order the doughnuts, and Doc Archer chose that moment to make his farewells. When Adam turned around again, Callie was gone.

CHAPTER THIRTY

Callie secured her guitar safely back in its case as Adam congratulated Danny on his performance. She needn't have worried about Danny on stage. He was a natural. She intended to tell him as much, but her parents were beckoning her over to their table. When she turned to look for Adam and Danny, they were halfway across the room. She gave them a wave and resigned herself to making polite small talk. Tessa and Mel had disappeared, probably in search of more doughnuts.

"Callie, come meet Zeke," said Luke. She blinked. This couldn't possibly be the Zeke of Nashville fame. He looked completely normal. A little pudgy, even.

Dora suppressed a smile and pulled out a chair for Callie. "Come on, sweetie. Sit down."

Callie reached across the table to shake hands and then sat, still bewildered by this turn of events. What was Zeke doing here? And why hadn't her father given her a heads-up?

"Nice show, young lady," said Zeke. "You have a raw, honest sound that I like."

"Ah . . . thanks," answered Callie. She wondered if Brian was still in the corner and hoped he would stay there. The last thing she wanted or needed was for him to sabotage this unexpected meeting.

Hutch, however, could take as many pictures as he liked. She peeked over her shoulder and sure enough, he was holding his cell phone at an odd angle, the tiny camera lens pointed directly at her table. Excellent. Time for the tabloids to give her some positive press.

"Zeke and I were talking about how tough it is for a new artist to get a break these days." Her father's comment snapped her attention back to the table.

"You mean a break like playing for Zeke Williams?" she asked.

Luke laughed. "Exactly. Who gets a break like that anymore?"

He exchanged a meaningful glance with Zeke. Callie wasn't sure how she felt about her father living vicariously through her career. Not that she didn't appreciate the effort, but Zeke Williams traveling all the way to Wisconsin to listen to her play in a diner? Was there blackmail involved? The whole thing felt surreal.

"May I ask what brings you to town, Zeke? I have to assume it was more than my little gig here at Lucy's."

Zeke glanced at both Dora and Luke before responding.

"An excellent question. I've been after your father for ages, trying to convince him that he needs to be in Nashville. We've made a lot of money together over the years, but a songwriting talent like his can't stay buried in the hinterlands forever. It's not good for the soul—or the business. I need him in Nashville to train the next generation."

Callie shot a glance at her father, but he had his poker face on, as did her mother. She struggled to connect all the dots.

"But Dad, I thought the songwriting was something you did as a hobby, just for yourself."

Dora actually giggled. "Honey, do you honestly think we could have put you three girls through college all at the same time on your Dad's teaching salary?"

"But you never . . . I mean, what songs did you . . . ?" Callie sputtered to a halt, her entire world turned inside out. Zeke stepped in to fill the gap.

"So when your Dad sent your demo CD—"

"When he what?" She shot her father a horrified look. They were supposed to discuss giant steps like this *before* taking them, not after.

Luke held up his hands in mock surrender, and had the good sense to at least look sheepish.

"Sorry, sugar. Your demo deserved to be heard, so I sent it to Zeke."

As far as Callie was concerned, her father should be feeling a lot more guilt. Downplaying his songwriting all these years. Hiding industry connections. And now, to top it off, sending off her demo without permission. It was almost as bad as . . . well, as reading a box of someone's private letters. It was an invasion of privacy, pure and simple.

"You like to do things the hard way," he explained, "and frankly I think you've paid your dues. It was time for your lucky break."

While Callie chewed on that logic, Zeke continued his story.

"I figured I could kill two birds with one stone. I could see if your music was as good live as it was on the demo, and I could lobby in person for your father to come to Nashville." He grinned at Luke. "Face to face, I can be pretty persuasive."

Callie felt her world tilt even further off balance. The man had just announced his plan to lure her father to Nashville, and her mother, who should be freaking out, was smiling an odd little smile and looking at her father as if she were simply curious to see how he would react.

Before Callie could re-orient herself, Brian appeared at her elbow and tugged on her arm.

"Callie, let's go. We have unfinished business."

Callie shook off his hand.

"Excuse me, but I'm in the middle of a conversation."

"It can wait," he said flatly. "I can't."

That comment earned him three cold stares from Dora, Luke, and Zeke. Brian ignored them, but then did a beautiful double-take when he recognized Zeke. Of course he would recognize a mover and shaker from Nashville. This was the type of thing he lived for. She sighed and waited for the charm to ooze forth.

"Zeke Williams," he said, recovering quickly and holding out a hand, "I'm Brian Tate."

"I know who you are," answered Zeke, keeping his arms crossed above his paunch. "What's so all-fired important that it can't wait?"

"Some legal paperwork related to our upcoming album," replied Brian smoothly, dropping his hand when it became clear that Zeke wasn't going to touch him. He shrugged off the slight as if Zeke were simply being eccentric. "We need to get everything squared away before I head back to the airport. Perhaps we're on the same flight back to Nashville?"

"Nope. I'll be staying in town for a few days." Zeke's words were directed more at Luke than at Brian.

"Of course."

Brian wasn't faking smoothness as well as he usually did. Zeke's surprise appearance must really be throwing him off his game. Callie saw Kat over at the counter, talking to Lucy. Perhaps this was the right time to deal with Brian, so she could sort out the last of her baggage, as well as her own shock, before talking with Zeke and her father again.

"If you all don't mind," said Callie, cutting Brian off as he was about to say something, "I'll take care of this paperwork with Brian so he can make his flight. We can continue our conversation later, back at the house."

She pushed away from the table before they could object and hustled Brian over to the counter. She conferred briefly with Kat, who handed Callie her office keys and said she'd be there in ten minutes. Before Brian could think of a new way to corner Zeke, Callie had him out the door and safely tucked into Kat's waiting room.

Kat wove through the crowd, doughnuts held protectively above her head, until she reached the booth again. She found Danny deep in conversation with his grandparents while Adam looked on. The furrow in Adam's brow worried her. For a man who had won a custody battle, he seemed awfully somber.

She placed the doughnuts in the middle of the table and Danny threw a 'thanks' her way before diving in. He continued chattering away to his grandparents with his mouth full, and they were too overwhelmed to care about his manners. She smiled, so grateful for this happy ending. She couldn't save everyone, and she knew it. In this case, they had achieved the best possible outcome, and she was determined to enjoy it. She chose a doughnut for herself and studied Adam while she savored the moment.

"What?" he asked irritably, when she had been looking at him for several minutes.

"You won. Relax. Smile," she said.

He harrumphed at her. There was really no other word for it. She stifled a laugh.

"What's bugging you?" She kept her voice low, so that Danny and his grandparents wouldn't overhear. "Why aren't you enjoying this?"

He was thoughtful for a moment.

"Have you ever achieved a goal, only to discover that something has changed along the way, and achieving that goal is no longer enough?"

To anyone else, Adam's remark might seem cryptic, but she had seen enough of him and Callie over the last few weeks to have her suspicions.

"So you have a new goal? A new vision of the future?" She asked even though it made her throat feel tight. It was always better to know the facts.

"I want something I can't have."

He said it without bitterness, but it was the acceptance in his voice that surprised Kat. He had been so determined to retain custody of Danny, it seemed out of character for him to give up on anything without a fight. But then, if his relationship with Callie had fractured so easily, perhaps it wasn't meant to last.

"She's not ready for a relationship?"

Kat couldn't quite believe she had asked the question, but there was no taking it back now. She had officially crossed the line from professional to personal. At least she had waited until the case was over.

"I need someone who can commit to staying here. She can't."

Kat's eyes widened.

"So physical proximity is a deal-breaker for you."

He nodded. Kat's fingertips tingled, her entire body on alert. This was not the time for a deeply personal discussion, with Callie and Brian waiting next door and Danny and his grandparents sitting a few feet away. But she couldn't resist one little zinger before leaving.

"In that case, you should remember that some of us have already made the commitment to living here full time."

She stood and made her farewells to Danny and Susan and John, leaving Adam to think about her parting words.

Once inside Kat's waiting room, Callie crossed her arms and waited for Brian to speak.

"Callie, how in the hell did you get Zeke Williams up here?" he demanded. She didn't care for the way he got in her face, so she held her ground, and her silence, until he backed off.

"He's an old friend of the family," she explained, omitting the fact that she had never met him before today.

"Old friend!" he choked. "How dare you hold back a contact like that for all these years? Do you have any idea how much he could have done for us? You don't waste a contact like that. You use it." He shook his head in disgust. "Maybe it's a good thing that you're bailing on the band. Unbelievable."

She nodded.

"I couldn't agree more," she replied. "You and I have even less in common than I once believed, and I think we'll both be happier if we part ways."

"Let's get on with it then," he said, tossing an envelope down on the coffee table. "You sign these papers and we're all set."

She remained standing. She wouldn't be signing any papers until Kat had a chance to look them over.

"What is the purpose of the papers?" she asked, curious but not particularly concerned.

"The record company wants you to waive all rights to the band's songs, so you don't try to sue for money or copyright later."

"I see," she replied. Adam's instincts had been right on target. "And have you told them yet that you don't have a songwriter for the next album?"

"No need," shrugged Brian. "We'll find someone."

The sad fact was that he could probably find some poor, insecure songwriter to accept whatever deal he offered. The promise of fame and fortune could cloud anybody's judgment.

She sighed. She would do her best to warn off any prospects, but she wouldn't be able to protect everyone from Brian's ambition.

At that moment, Kat entered through the main door, setting the bell jangling.

"Thanks for meeting with us on such short notice," said Callie. "I'm hoping that this will be quick, because I know we all have things we'd rather be doing today."

"Agreed," said Kat. She scooped up the envelope from the coffee table and turned to Brian. "Please, have a seat," she said, indicating the waiting-room couch and chairs. "If you'll excuse us, we'll take a moment to review the documents." She ushered Callie into her office, closed the door, and took her seat behind the desk. Callie followed suit, sitting across from her, thinking that it felt pretty good to leave Brian cooling his heels in the other room.

Kat took her time looking over the documents before giving Callie an overview.

"It's pretty simple," she said. "They want you to confirm that you have signed away all your rights to the music, the recordings, and any future income. They also want you to waive your right to sue down the road. I'm not surprised. I would have asked the same thing if I were on their side. So let's talk about what you want."

"Didn't we already do that?" asked Callie.

"Think of this as your second-chance sweepstakes," replied Kat. "Have you had any second thoughts? Do you want to keep some leverage? Are you okay with cutting all ties to the band and moving on? It's up to you." With that, Kat leaned back in her chair, looking as if she had all the time in the world to wait for Callie's answer.

Right or wrong, Callie had to admit that she was tempted to hang on to this last little bit of power. A part of her enjoyed watching Brian squirm. But more than power, Callie wanted closure—no strings, no ties, and no regrets.

"It's time to move on," she said firmly. "I don't care about the money. I don't care about getting credit for the songs. I want a clean break and a fresh start."

"Done," Kat responded with a brisk nod. She slid the documents across the desk to Callie. "Read it, let me know if you have any questions. When you're ready, you can go ahead and sign it."

Callie skimmed the legalese, but Kat had already explained the important points. Everything made sense. Callie signed in various places and they returned to the waiting area to find Brian leafing through a magazine. He tossed it aside and crossed his arms.

"Well?" he asked.

Callie tipped her head to one side and studied him, wondering how she had ever found him attractive. Hopefully her judgment had improved over the years. She looked at Kat, who nodded. The time had come. Callie handed the envelope back to Brian.

"It's done," she said quietly. "I signed them."

"Great," he snapped, pulling the documents out of the envelope and double-checking the signature and date on each copy.

"That's it then," said Callie. "We're done." It was hard to believe, after all these years. Instead of feeling angry, or bitter, or even sad, she simply felt empty. "I'll stop by next week to pick up my stuff from the loft."

Brian didn't seem to care about the final details, as long as the papers were signed. "Whatever." He shrugged. "See you around, Callie," he said, turning to head for the door.

"See you around," she echoed. He stepped outside, accompanied by the jingle of bells. The door swung shut and he was gone.

"Well," said Callie thoughtfully as she turned back to Kat, "that was kind of a letdown."

Kat studied Callie's face, searching for any sign of imminent breakdown. She saw nothing but serenity. A part of her wanted to ask what Callie intended to do about Adam, but she couldn't think how to phrase the question. *What are your intentions toward the only eligible bachelor in town?* (Hutch clearly did not qualify.) *If you break Adam's heart, can I pick up the pieces?* She left her questions unasked and turned her attention to business.

"Trust me," she said. "A cold, calm meeting is much better than a lot of drama. Those never end well."

"I'll bet," Callie replied, flopping back on the couch.

Kat sank into the end chair.

"So what happens now?" asked Callie.

"We shake hands and part ways," answered Kat with a smile. "I'll send you a bill." She paused, realizing she didn't have an address for Callie. "Where should I send the bill?"

Callie laughed. "Good question. Send it to my parents, I guess. If I'm not there, they'll know where to find me."

"So you're definitely leaving, then?" asked Kat, careful to keep her voice neutral and the flutter of hope firmly caged.

"That's still the plan," Callie said slowly. "Why, had you heard something different?"

"No." Kat could dance around her question, or she could just ask. She decided to ask. "But I've seen you with Adam, and with Danny. I couldn't help but wonder if you might decide to stay."

Callie's mouth tightened, and she looked up at the ceiling. "I don't know," she said, "but I still need to go to Nashville. Adam needs some time to think, and I need some time to plan." She gave up on the ceiling and turned her gaze back to Kat. "I'm going to find a way to make things work with Adam, but he's not quite ready to think outside the box."

Kat smiled tightly, her last flutter of hope wilting away and leaving only a dull emptiness behind. She had chosen to come home to face her demons, but she hadn't anticipated how lonely it would be.

"I want to thank you," said Callie, abruptly changing the subject, "and to apologize."

"For what?" asked Kat. Callie couldn't possibly know that she had just destroyed the last of Kat's daydreams about Adam.

"Thank you for helping me," answered Callie, "and I'm sorry for messing with your life back in high school." She looked down at her fingernails, then back at Kat. "It all happened so fast, and then you never came back to school. It must have been rough."

Kat let out half a laugh as she shook her head. "It was awful," she agreed, "but it also saved me."

"Really?"

"More than you know," said Kat softly. "More than you know."

CHAPTER THIRTY-ONE

Callie watched Danny bounce back toward the cottage, shaking her head. Now that he knew she would be in town for two more days, he had grand plans to write another song before she left. Ambitious, perhaps, but not impossible. Before too long he would be giving her a run for her money on the songwriting front.

She had decided to roll with this lucky break, to stick around for a few more days and return to Nashville with Zeke. If things continued to go as well as they had yesterday afternoon, she might have herself a recording contract before she got back to Nashville. As Brian had pointed out, you don't blow a connection like that.

If she had used this family connection when they were first starting out, it would have felt like cheating, but she had spent the last decade paying her dues and felt no need to pay them again. Besides, it wasn't as if Zeke would sign a deal with a no-talent hack simply as a favor to an old friend. Her father's influence had gotten her a hearing. Everything else was up to her.

The biggest surprise of the last twenty-four hours was how light she felt now that she was truly free of Brian. Yesterday's meeting with Kat had only confirmed what she already knew: it was time to leave. The prospect of success had amplified Brian's

need for control, turning an annoying quirk into a disturbing afflic-
tion. If she had to promise up and down not to sue for the rights to
her songs—songs that she never wanted to sing again anyway—in
order to be rid of him, then she'd happily sign as many copies of
the damn documents as they needed.

She picked her way through a few familiar tunes, not quite ready
to go back up to the house. There was something about playing
music with her bare feet up on the wicker table and staring out
over the lake. More than anything it made her want to play all the
old favorites, work her way through all those layers of memories,
until she surfaced again in the present. Here at the lake her life felt
deep and rich in a way that new experiences and new places never
could. She had been pondering this richness for weeks now, and
she had come to the conclusion that she needed to spend time here,
in between all the other demands her career might place on her.
And if she was going to be spending more time here, she would be
running into Adam over and over again.

The thought made her smile.

Adam might not be ready to imagine a family with one vaga-
bond for a parent, but she could. Given time, and patience, she
fully intended to change his mind. Today, for example, she would
drop by to give him an update on Danny's progress. He had asked
for updates, after all. And if she happened to be wearing a particularly attractive sundress, maybe a little makeup, and had freshly
painted toes, well, that would just be a happy coincidence. If
Danny happened to learn that there were freshly baked cookies
at Dora's house, he might decide to run right over and beg for
one. And then, if Dora—by chance—needed Danny's help in the
garden all afternoon, well then Adam would just have to deal with
Callie all by himself.

Her smile widened. He didn't stand a chance.

Adam sat alone at the kitchen table, staring into his cup of coffee and wishing it held some answers. Of course it didn't. There were no easy answers to this dilemma. He and Danny needed stability and commitment. Callie needed the freedom to grow. There was no way that he would cage her, but he wasn't willing to compromise either. If it were just him, maybe things would be different, but he had Danny to consider.

Danny startled him by banging through the kitchen door, guitar case thudding against the doorframe.

"How was your last lesson?" Adam kept his voice neutral, his expression clear. No need to involve Danny in his personal drama. He would simply be grateful that Danny had managed to squeeze in one last lesson before Callie left today.

"Awesome. And it wasn't the last one."

"What?" Adam clamped down on the surge of irrational hope. He had no reason to believe that Callie had changed her mind.

"Two more days," called Danny as he disappeared down the hall.

Adam groaned silently and rubbed his forehead. This was like ripping the bandage off slowly. The longer it took, the more it hurt. He needed her to go already. Instead she lingered, torturing him.

By the time Danny returned to the kitchen Adam had collected himself and was pulling out Danny's favorite cereal, a bowl, a spoon, the milk. The normal business of breakfast occupied them for a few minutes, but all too soon, Danny was chomping away, and Adam found himself unable to fill the silence.

"You don't have to be sad, you know," said Danny through a mouthful of cereal. The comment took Adam by surprise.

"About what?"

"About Callie leaving. It's not like she'll be gone forever."

Adam smiled sadly.

"I know."

"She said she would be able to visit a lot."

Would the torture never end?

"That's nice."

"Maybe one time she could do a sleepover."

Adam choked on his coffee.

"What's that again?"

"A sleepover. You know, when somebody spends the night at your house?"

"Right. I know what a sleepover is. I just . . . never thought about it."

"It would be awesome. We could play music until late, and then play again first thing in the morning. And we could all have breakfast together." Danny finally swallowed so that he was speaking with a clear mouth. "We would be almost like a family."

Adam tried to imagine how his brother would want him to respond. *Evan, if you're out there somewhere, I could really use a hand.*

"It would be nice," he agreed cautiously. "But it would also be hard because we couldn't be a real family forever. Eventually she would have to go away again."

"But she would come back," Danny countered.

"True. But families are supposed to be together all the time. Not just sometimes."

Danny snickered. "Who told you that?"

"I just know," said Adam defensively. Some truths were self-evident. This one he had learned the hard way. *Evan? A little help here. . . .*

"Maybe that was true when you were a kid," said Danny. Adam could almost hear the unspoken 'in the olden days.' "These days families are weird. Some have one parent. Some have extras, if they're divorced. Sometimes both parents work, sometimes just the mom or just the dad. Carol Lee's mom is a pilot, and she goes away all the time, but she always comes back." Danny shrugged. "My mom says that love makes a family, nothing else. I mean 'said.' She said. She used to say that."

Danny ducked his head and took a huge bite of cereal. Adam couldn't speak, and not just because he didn't have the words. There would be no getting past the giant lump in his throat. Danny was right. It was as if Lainey had whispered the words in Danny's ear just when Adam needed to hear them. She had thrown him a lifeline when he was drowning. He wouldn't let her down. He wouldn't let Evan down.

"You're right." Adam cleared his throat and said it again. "Your mom was right."

Danny looked up at him, so small and so resilient.

"I love Callie, you know," said Adam. Saying it out loud made him feel lightheaded, but the words needed to be said. It was time for truth-telling. "But I've always believed that a family should be together. She needs to travel a lot for her work, and I didn't think that would make for a strong family."

"Well, that's dumb," said Danny.

Adam laughed. "Yeah, well, I'm a little slow sometimes."

"My Dad said that his parents—your parents—were around all the time, but that they did a really bad job of being parents."

Adam slumped back in his chair. "He talked to you about that?"

Danny nodded, oblivious to his uncle's surprise.

"What else did he say?" asked Adam, still reeling.

"Just that he learned a lot from them being bad parents. He learned to do the opposite." Danny shrugged. "I guess it worked, because we had a good family." He gave Adam a hard look. "You love Callie, right?"

"I just said so," replied Adam cautiously.

"Well, me too," said Danny.

"I figured."

"Well, then, I think she should marry us. I think we should be a family."

"I agree," said Adam, matching Danny's serious tone.

"You do?" Danny had been gearing up for a fight.

"I do."

"Then let's go ask her," said Danny, standing up. "What are we waiting for?"

Adam fought a smile.

"Don't you have school or something?"

"It's Memorial Day, remember?"

"Right."

"Come on," repeated Danny, tugging on Adam's arm to get him to stand up. "What if she decides to marry somebody else while we're sitting here?"

"I don't think it works that way," said Adam, laughing as he let Danny pull him out of his chair.

"Fine, I'll go ask her myself." Danny marched right out the back door.

"Wait for me," called Adam, still laughing.

Thanks, man, he thought. *And you can stop laughing your ass off now.*

Callie continued to work her way through the old songs until she heard the slap of sandals on the flagstone path. She turned to see Danny racing toward the screen door, with Adam not far behind.

"Danny, wait for me," called Adam, but Danny either didn't hear him or chose not to listen. He burst into the summer house and skidded to a stop.

"We have something important to ask you," he announced.

Adam jogged the last few yards and followed Danny inside. Callie pulled the guitar strap over her head and laid aside the instrument, very curious to find out what was going on.

"Danny, I'd like to—" began Adam.

Danny plunked himself down on one knee. Callie's eyes widened, but she didn't interrupt.

"—speak to Callie alone for a moment."

Danny crossed his arms, which looked ridiculous when combined with his one-kneed stance.

"I'm a part of this family, too, and I'm not going anywhere."

Adam sighed and rubbed his forehead. Callie suppressed a smile. If they were butting heads now, she could only imagine what things would be like in five years.

"Fine, but I get to do the talking."

"Unless you say it wrong. Then I get to talk."

"Deal."

Adam cleared his throat. Danny uncrossed his arms. When Adam didn't start talking immediately, Danny gave him a threatening look.

"Okay, okay. I'm trying to think of the right words."

Danny sighed dramatically. Callie bit the inside of her cheek to keep from laughing.

"Danny and I were talking this morning about families."

"And love," added Danny.

This time it was Adam giving the threatening look.

"And love," he agreed. "Danny pointed out that love makes a family. Nothing else."

"Nothing else," echoed Danny.

Callie's eyes swam with tears, but she blinked them back.

"You're supposed to get down on your knee," whispered Danny to Adam. Adam closed his eyes briefly, then got down on one knee, reaching out to clasp Callie's hand.

"We were talking about love," said Adam.

"And families," said Danny.

"Love and families. And we realized that we want you to be a part of our family."

"Because we love you." Danny proclaimed the logical conclusion, but Adam was still stumbling through the words.

"We love you." He cleared his throat. "I love you," he said, his gaze strong and clear. "You complete us. You make us a family, even if you can't be here every day."

Callie lost the battle with the tears, which spilled over and rolled down her cheeks. She swiped them away, but Danny had already seen them. He jumped up.

"We did it wrong. She's not supposed to cry. You forgot to say the married part."

Adam laughed, and Callie laughed, cried, and hiccupped all at the same time. Danny grabbed her other hand.

"Will you marry us?" he asked, scared and serious.

She tugged her hands free and wrapped her arms around him.

"Of course I will," she whispered.

When she let go, he stood back, beaming with pride, as Adam pulled Callie to her feet and into his arms. He leaned his forehead against hers, looking into her eyes.

"Will you really take us on?" he asked, his voice gruff.

"In a heartbeat."

EPILOGUE

Kat wasn't sure why she had accepted Callie's invitation to the Memorial Day barbecue and bonfire. She hadn't realized it would be a neighborhood event, filled with people she had never met who shared a history that she would never know. But Callie had caught her indulging in a moment of weakness yesterday as the crowd at Lucy's dispersed. She didn't want to spend another holiday alone.

The barbecue was, apparently, the big kick-off to summer at the lake, and the event was full of quirky traditions dating back a century or more, or so Dora had told her. That woman could talk. Kat had chatted with her for half an hour and probably spoken no more than two sentences. Now Kat stood off to one side, enjoying the sunset and observing the chaos as the children played some kind of screaming and chasing game, the adults caught up with old friends, and the teenagers huddled in a pack under the big tree at the center of the commons. She might not be a part of the group, but at least she wasn't home alone.

She wondered briefly what it would have been like to grow up here, with only a handful of neighbors in the winter and then an influx of friends in the summer. Maybe things would have been better. Maybe her mother would have been stronger. And maybe she should stop dwelling on the past and worry more about the present.

"Make a wish?" asked Mel, appearing beside Kat and holding out a flat package wrapped in plastic.

Startled, Kat accepted the package before she even knew what it was.

"The directions are inside," added Mel, "and here's a pencil so you can write a wish on the side before you put it together."

"But . . ." Kat left the question hanging in the air because Mel was already gone.

Curious, Kat opened the package and pulled out the instruction sheet. It was a sky lantern. She had seen them on TV, but never in person. She glanced around at the crowd of people, many of whom now held packages of their own and were, like her, trying to figure out what to do with them.

She shrugged. Might as well give it a try. Even the best-laid plans could use a lucky break from time to time. She knew exactly what she would wish for.

Callie had been watching Mel make the rounds, wondering what in the world she was handing out. When Callie finally got hers, she opened it and an instruction sheet fluttered to the ground. She bent to pick it up, then her eyes flew to meet Mel's.

"Seriously?" she asked. "Where did you find them?"

"Ever heard of the Internet? It's just not that hard."

Callie threw her arms around her sister.

"You are the best," she said. "This is the perfect way to end the weekend. How did you know?"

"It's the triplet thing," said Mel airily. "Some things I just know."

Callie snorted in disbelief. "So what are you wishing for?" she asked.

Mel's eyebrows shot up. "Are you trying to jinx me?"

Callie laughed. "Of course not. I'm just curious, but if you're superstitious, I won't ask again."

"Don't," said Mel. Then she cocked her head to one side. "What are you wishing for?"

"Oh, so now you're trying to jinx me back?"

Mel shrugged. "I figure if you asked, then you might be willing to answer."

"To be honest, I don't know," answered Callie. "But while I'm thinking about it, I'm going to help Danny with his lantern."

"And I'm going to give Officer Jack a hard time. He has an unacceptable air of authority for a guy who used to wear Superman underpants."

Callie laughed as Mel headed over toward Jack, and then she began hunting for Adam and Danny. She found them down by the beach. They quickly shuffled their lanterns so she couldn't see what they had written on the side.

"Do we have a problem here, gentlemen?" she asked.

They looked up at her, wearing matching expressions of innocence.

"No, ma'am," said Adam. "No problem here."

"We're good," said Danny.

"Did you think of good wishes?" she asked.

The two looked at each other, then back up at Callie.

"Actually, it took us a while to think of a good wish," said Adam.

"We couldn't think of any," explained Danny. "All the old ones came true, and we didn't have any new ones yet."

Callie grinned at the pair of them, then sat down cross-legged beside them.

"I had exactly the same problem," she said.

"But then we thought of one," said Danny. "A good one."

"Really?" she asked, intrigued. She shot a glance at Adam, but he didn't offer any further details.

At that moment, Mel clanked a grill fork against a beer bottle to get everyone's attention.

"It's time, people. Let's launch these wishes."

Mel had armed several of the adults with grill lighters, and one by one they helped light all the lanterns. Then she gave the countdown to launch. As the lanterns began to float up into the sky, the kids were the first to react, their voices hushed, furiously whispering back and forth about their wishes and which ones were definitely going to come true.

Callie waited until both Mel and Tessa had released theirs before she let go of her own. She wanted to give her sisters' wishes a head start. It was their turn to find a happy ending.

The sight of all those lanterns floating up into the night sky left Callie breathless. This time around there was no full moon, but there were also no mishaps. All the lanterns floated up, up, and away, down the length of the lake, higher and higher, until they disappeared among the stars.

Everyone had fallen silent as they watched the lanterns fly, and they stayed quiet as they wandered back toward the bonfire. Callie fell in step with her sisters.

"That was beautiful," she said. "Nobody went down in flames."

"Hmmmm," said Tessa, retreating into therapist mode.

"Does that mean, 'I think my wish will work this time,' or 'I didn't actually write anything on my lantern'?" asked Mel.

Tessa laughed. "Oh, I wrote on it," she said.

"And?" asked Callie.

"I'm almost afraid to see what happens," answered Tessa.

Danny caught up with Callie and grabbed her hand. They walked together for the last few yards. Then Danny pulled her aside.

"Want to know what I wished for?" he asked.

She nodded.

"I wished for us to have a happy ending," he said.

She squeezed him in a giant hug.

"Me too," she whispered back.

When she released him, Danny ran to get a stick and a marshmallow and joined the other kids around the fire. She turned to find Adam standing beside her. He put an arm around her shoulder and together they watched Danny as he jostled for position. He didn't say much, but at least he was talking now, and the other kids accepted him without question.

Adam pulled her outside the circle of the firelight and wrapped both arms around her.

"So what did you wish for?" he murmured in her ear.

She laughed softly.

"You first," she said.

"Danny and I wished for the same thing," he said. "We wished for our happy ending."

"You've already got that," she said, and kissed him.

"What about your wish?"

She kissed him again.

"As someone very wise once told me, a happy ending is more of a journey than a destination," Callie said. "I wished for help along the way."

COMING SOON: TESSA'S STORY

Tessa caught the package just before it hit her in the nose.

"Make a wish!" Mel said, laughing.

Tessa shot her sister a dirty look and turned the package over in the fading light, trying to figure out what it was. Tall shade trees blocked the last of the sun's rays, casting long shadows across the lakeside commons and painting the water in shades of fire. The nearby bonfire warmed her back, but it didn't make reading the label any easier.

When Tessa finally figured it out, she couldn't help smiling.

"Where did you find this?" she asked. It was a wish lantern, almost identical to the ones from Annabelle's birthday party ages ago.

"Ah, the miracle of the Internet," said Mel drily. "You should try it sometime."

Tessa's smile faded as Mel handed her a tiny pencil and said, "For writing your wish."

Tessa could hear the subtle challenge in Mel's voice, but her sister should know better. She didn't throw coins in fountains anymore, or look for four-leaf clovers, or search the sky for shooting stars. She lived in the real world and made her own dreams come true. Recently she had begun to wonder how long that might take, but she had never—not even for a second—considered giving up.

"I'll just fly my lantern," said Tessa. "No need for wishing."

Mel refused to take the pencil back.

"Chicken?" she asked slyly.

"Of course not," said Tessa. "I just think wishing is a waste of time." She gave Mel a hard look. "You know that."

"Yeah, and I also know that you're late. Where the hell have you been?"

"At the house. Work stuff," said Tessa.

She lifted one shoulder in a half shrug, hoping to sidetrack Mel with the work-life debate. It was usually an effective distraction.

Mel didn't take the bait.

"So this should be no big deal, right?" she asked, gesturing to the paper lantern in Tessa's hand. "If you don't believe in wishes, who cares what you write? You could write anything."

"I don't need to prove anything," answered Tessa. She made a conscious effort not to clench her teeth.

"I see," said Mel, doing her best imitation of Tessa's therapist voice.

"What do you see?" asked Tessa. She knew she was letting Mel get to her, but she couldn't help it. Her sister had been perfecting this technique for twenty-seven years and she was really, really good at it.

"Your words are saying that you don't believe in wishing," said Mel, still doing her therapist impression, "but your behavior tells me that you do."

Tessa growled under her breath. She hated it when Mel was right. Mel raised an eyebrow, challenging her to deny it.

"Fine," said Tessa. "Let me demonstrate how much I don't care."

She ripped open the plastic sleeve and yanked out the folded lantern. She grabbed Mel by the shoulders, spun her around, and put the lantern on her back.

"Hold still," she said.

Using Mel as her writing desk, Tessa scribbled on the side of the lantern. She didn't think about it too much, writing the first thing that came into her head. Then she turned Mel back around, put the pencil in her hand, and said, "Happy now?"

"Sure am," said Mel. She threw an arm around Tessa's tense shoulders and began walking her down to the tiny strip of beach. "Let's go fire these things up."

Tessa fought the urge to dig in her heels. All she really wanted to do was cross her arms, plant her feet, and throw her lantern into the bonfire, but her inner therapist echoed Mel's words: *What is your behavior telling Mel? What does it tell you?*

That decided it. She would prove to both Mel and herself that she truly didn't care about wishing. She allowed Mel to lead her to the water's edge, where a small crowd had already gathered. Friends, neighbors, her parents, Callie—all of them stood around with their lanterns in various stages of assembly. Tessa put hers together without speaking, ignoring the lighthearted chatter that swirled around her. For most people, this was an amusing exercise, not unlike buying a lottery ticket or throwing a coin into a fountain. For her, it was incredibly depressing, dredging up memories of The Year of Failed Wishes. It wasn't so much that she mourned the wishes. She mourned the girl who had done the wishing.

The nearly full moon had risen above the tree line on the far shore as twilight faded into evening, providing the perfect back-drop for the lanterns as they rose into the air one by one. Some-one passed her a lighter. She used it to kindle her tiny flame and then handed it on to Mel. While she waited for the air inside her lantern to warm, she watched the early fliers rise higher and higher, wondering if any of them would tumble as hers had, or go down in flames. She hoped not. She wouldn't wish that disap-pointment on anyone. She would give anything to feel that sense of limitless possibility again.

At last her lantern was ready. Defiant, she lifted it to the moon and watched it rise. Mel followed suit and the two lanterns climbed side by side. A soft breeze caught them, carrying them farther and higher than the rest. It looked like their two lanterns might make it to the far end of the lake. When they were so far away that Tessa couldn't distinguish between their lanterns and the stars, she took a deep breath and turned to face her sister, steeling herself for an I-told-you-so, but Mel surprised her, staying quiet for at least a minute before saying anything.

"So," asked Mel, her voice thick, "what did you wish for?"

Tessa wasn't sure how to answer.

"Don't want to jinx it?" asked Mel. Her voice sounded stronger and Tessa could see a half-smile on her moonlit profile.

"It wasn't a wish," she admitted. "I'm done with those."

"So what was it?" asked Mel, finally turning to face her sister.

"A question," answered Tessa grimly. *"Where the hell is my Prince Charming?"*

RJ nursed his beer while he watched his friends and neighbors fuss over their sky lanterns. Thankfully, Mel had run out before she'd been able to saddle him with one. Craft projects weren't his thing, although he did enjoy watching everyone try to read and follow the directions in the dark. It looked like more fun than assembling IKEA furniture.

As he surveyed the crowd, he realized that all three of the James sisters were up for the weekend. He had seen Mel, obviously, as she distributed the lanterns. She stood just a few steps away from him now with Tessa. Their other sister Callie, stood at the far end of the beach, but he couldn't identify the man she was with, or the boy. Holy crap, did she have a kid? Now he really felt old.

He watched as Mel and Tessa released their lanterns into the sky. All three James sisters in one place. Damn. He hadn't seen that trifecta in action since his final summer at the lake. Had it really been ten years? That had been his last summer of freedom between junior and senior years of college. For the triplets and their posse of girlfriends, however, it had been the summer after high school graduation—their first taste of freedom, and all the wildness that went along with turning eighteen.

There had been a lot of skinny dipping that summer.

He had managed to stay out of trouble by focusing his attention on the older girls, the ones who were closer to the end of college than the beginning. Oddly, though, his clearest memories were of Tessa. She had offered unsolicited critiques of his early attempts at flirtation. To this day, whenever he approached an attractive woman, he tested his opening lines against his memory of Tessa.

WWTS: What would Tessa say?

As he approached her to say hello, he couldn't help overhearing the end of Tessa's exchange with Mel.

"Where the hell is my Prince Charming?"

How ironic that practical Tessa dreamed of fairy tales.

"Looking for me?" he drawled, smugly pleased with his 'charming' response to her question.

Tessa and Mel got one good look at him, long enough to realize who he was, and then the two of them dissolved into helpless laughter. He frowned, but it only made them laugh harder. Of all their possible reactions, he had not anticipated laughter. Charm was his specialty.

"RJ," gasped Tessa after several minutes of uncontrolled mirth, "what are you doing here?" She wiped tears from the corners of her eyes and struggled to get herself under control, only to lose it again when she met Mel's eyes.

"What, I'm not allowed to come home?" he asked. His knew his voice sounded grumpy, but he didn't bother to turn the charm back on. That had clearly backfired.

"No, it's not—" She stopped, took a breath, regrouped. "I thought you lived in California."

"I did," he answered simply, "and now I live here."

Tessa and Mel were avoiding each other's eyes and doing a crappy job of keeping straight faces.

"Really?" she asked, seeming genuinely surprised.

He could imagine all the questions that must be racing around in her head. *Why move back to the Midwest? Why come back to the lake? Have you lost your mind?* He didn't really feel like explaining.

"So what's so funny?" he asked.

He had learned a few tricks in his years of lawyering. Take control of the conversation. Answer a question with a question. By far his favorite was to ask the obvious question.

Tessa and Mel exchanged glances, then burst into giggles again, so he used another lawyer trick: patience. He crossed his arms and drummed his fingers on his bicep, waiting for an answer. Mel gave his bicep an appreciative glance, but Tessa kept her eyes on his face.

"Sorry," she hiccuped. She shot a questioning glance at Mel, then took the lead in answering the question. "It's just that . . . well, you're sort of the opposite of Prince Charming."

"What are you talking about?" he objected, on the grounds that her answer was both insulting and flat-out wrong. "I've been told by *many* women that I'm both charming and easy on the eyes. What's not to like?"

"That's exactly the point," answered Tessa. "You've enjoyed the company of many—"

"Many!" echoed Mel.

"—women."

RJ couldn't follow her logic. He was well and truly baffled.

"And the problem is . . . ?" He spread his arms wide in question. Tessa sighed.

"Prince Charming is kind of a one-woman man, if you know what I mean," she explained.

"He makes one woman happy in many ways, rather than many women happy in one way," clarified Mel. Before he could protest, she added, "Yes, I'm suggesting you're a player."

He opened his mouth to speak, but no words came out. Tessa choked back a laugh.

"Mel means that in the nicest possible way," she said, giving Mel a reproving look. "You're not exactly known as the happily-ever-after type. Not that there's anything wrong with that," she added hastily, throwing up a hand to forestall any arguments.

He still had no words. Would the insults never end?

"It's just that, well, I'm a happily-ever-after kind of girl, and Prince Charmings can be hard to find."

Finally he found his voice.

"So if I'm not Prince Charming, then who am I?" he asked, wanting to know exactly where he fit into the fairy-tale scene.

Tessa and Mel looked at each other, considering their options.

"Jack and the Beanstalk?" proposed Tessa.

Mel immediately shook her head. "Grumpy the Dwarf!" she said.

RJ frowned as they snickered together.

Then Tessa sucked in a breath. "Peter Pan," she said. Mel cocked her head, considering, then nodded her agreement. The two sisters turned to face him, their faces wearing identical expressions of smug triumph.

"Peter Pan," they announced.

"No way." He completely rejected their premise. He was not a boy playing at life. He was a man. A strong man. A hunter, even. "I think I merit at least the Huntsman from Snow White. Or what about the Wolf?" He liked that image, especially if Little Red Riding Hood was naked under the red satin cloak. He grinned at them. "I'm the Big Bad Wolf."

Mel shook her head. "Nope," she said.

Tessa pursed her lips. "Sorry, but no."

He must have looked sad, or disappointed, or something, because all of a sudden they were trying to make him feel better.

"Don't worry," said Tessa, putting her hand on his forearm. He realized that his arms were still crossed, and his shoulders were actually a little tense. "Just because you're not Prince Charming doesn't mean you're not sexy. You are. Totally sexy, I mean."

"Super hot," agreed Mel, only she didn't look quite as earnest or, frankly, as honest as Tessa did.

"Super hot?" he asked, giving Mel his best cross-examination stare. She didn't even blink, just grinned at him.

"The hottest," she said, patting him on the shoulder. "I have to leave now or I might jump you, and that would be embarrassing. Wine?" she called to Tessa as she walked away.

"Yes please," said Tessa. Her hand was still on RJ's arm, and she was standing close enough that he could smell her shampoo, something with flowers or berries.

"You smell good," he said.

She was the one who had trained him all those years ago to give authentic compliments. From the way her smile widened, she remembered.

"You're sweet," she answered, "but your superpowers won't work on me. I'm immune, remember?"

She looked up to meet his eyes, which must have thrown off her balance, because she swayed and held on tight to his arm.

"Too much wine?" he asked.

She shook her head.

"I'm out of practice," she answered.

Or at least that's what it sounded like. He was about to ask her what she meant when his phone rang.

*Visit www.lisamcluckie.com to sign up for news alerts.
You'll be the first to know when Tessa's story is available.*

ABOUT HIDDEN SPRINGS

Growing up, I spent a lot of time in the lake country of south-eastern Wisconsin. This area may not be quite as famous as the Finger Lakes region in upstate New York, or Lake Tahoe out west, but for me that makes it better. A little more down-to-earth. A little less crowded. The fictional town of Hidden Springs is a wonderful mash-up of all the different lake towns I love, past and present, large (relatively speaking) and small, fancy or not.

If you want to know more about the real-world lakes of south-eastern Wisconsin, these websites provide a great starting point.

http://www.travelwisconsin.com/southeast/walworth-county
http://www.visitwalworthcounty.com/
http://www.lakegenevawi.com/
http://www.discoverwhitewater.org/
http://www.cruiselakegeneva.com/
http://www.atthelakemagazine.com/

I'll see you at the lake!
   Lisa

ACKNOWLEDGEMENTS

Writing the acknowledgements for a first book is a daunting task. You want to thank not only the people who helped with this particular book, but also every single person who encouraged, inspired, nagged, and prodded you along the way to publication. This is clearly an impossible task, but one that must be attempted regardless. For those of you who I will inevitably miss on this round, I look forward to writing many more books and thanking you repeatedly in those.

First and foremost, I need to thank my husband for his unflagging support and love over the years. We're stronger together than apart, and I thank my lucky stars every day that we found each other. I also need to thank my children for their very low expectations come dinnertime, and for their patience (and quiet!) when mom is working. You are each a miracle, and I love watching you grow up.

Thank you to Charley and Angela, for showing me how to be brave, and to Chunka, for showing me how to think big. Thank you to Mom and Dad, for being living proof of happily-ever-after. Thank you, Kristin Nelson, for being the first person to consider my work bankable.

I'd like to honor the people who taught me to appreciate good books and strong writing: Mrs. Addie, Mr. Brauer, and Paul Carroll. Thank you as well to the Fontana Public Library, for providing a peaceful haven and an endless supply of books to the shy, skinny kid who needed some time away from all her siblings. A special shout-out here to Dan Handler and the entire poetry-writing class in college. Who knew, right?

Writing is a lonely profession, so we band together for moral support. Thank you to my family writing workshop: Dad, Kelly, Sarah, and Joe, for keeping me on track. Without your prodding, this project would still be a work in progress. Thank you to my magnificent writing crew: Marilyn, Karen, Simone, Erika, Sara, and Amey. If only we all lived on the same block. Particular thanks to Marilyn & Sara & Karen for reading the manuscript and to Simone for introducing me to Kristin.

Thank you to the Chicago-North Chapter of RWA® and all the good friends I made there, particularly Jennifer Stevenson, Ruth Kaufman, and Blythe Gifford.

Thank you to all the friends and family who have read drafts along the way and helped me to make this story stronger, including Charley Zeches, Pete Wilson, Carrie Turner, Ann Laing, Monica Goebel, Christine Fitzgerald, Julia Brannon, and Sylvia Mugglin. A special thanks to Pegeen Hopkins, for listening so gently to my first-ever cold reading of that first chapter many years ago.

I want to particularly thank the original Lucy for giving me permission to imagine a world where Lucy's doughnuts are once again available after church on a Sunday morning, and to name a character in her honor.

Many people helped me with research during the writing of this story. Special thanks to Shannon Wynn and Pete Wilson, for giving me insight into the legal world and helping me understand the role of a guardian *ad litem*. Thanks to Rachel Efron for talking with me about life in the music business. You can hear her amazing music at www.rachelefron.com. If, despite their best efforts, I've still managed to get something wrong, the fault is completely my own.

My heartfelt appreciation goes out to all the people who share their knowledge freely on YouTube about topics like boat restoration and how to tune a guitar. I can only imagine how difficult and time-consuming it must have been to do this kind of research in the pre-Internet era.

This first book has been so many years in the making that I am surely forgetting people who need thanking. I'll keep a running list of "Oh my gosh I can't believe I forgot . . ." and thank you all in the next book.

With love and gratitude,
    Lisa

ABOUT THE AUTHOR

Lisa McLuckie was born a wanderer. She has lived in four states and two foreign countries, had twenty-four different addresses, and explored five of the seven continents. She currently lives on the fringes of Chicagoland with her husband, three sons (sizes large, medium, and small), and a ridiculously adorable dog named Daisy. Learn more at **www.lisamcluckie.com**.